Far Above Rubies

Far Above Rubies

Elizabeth Jeffrey

PIATKUS

Author's note:
There was a silk mill in Colchester in the
nineteenth century and there was a stroke by
the girls working there. This much is fact. The
story and characters into which I have woven
these facts are all pure fiction.

204586

First published in Great Britain in 1996 by
Judy Piatkus (Publishers) Ltd of
5 Windmill Street, London W1P 1HF

**The moral right of the author
has been asserted**

*A catalogue record for this book is available
from the British Library*

ISBN 0-7499-0347-3

Phototypeset in 11/12pt Times by
Computerset, Harmondsworth, Middlesex
Printed and bound in Great Britain by
Bookcraft (Bath) Ltd

'Who can find a virtuous woman?
for her price is far above rubies.'
(Proverbs 31: 10–11)

Chapter One

Through the fog of agonising pain that had wracked her for hours without respite, Laura heard a woman's voice.

'Won't be long now. God knows she's suffered enough, poor crittur.' A cool, faintly sour-smelling cloth wiped the perspiration from her face.

'D'you think she'll live?' Another voice, the words spoken with complete indifference.

'Nah, she'll be gone by morning.'

She heard nothing more as the pain tore her in half. She was dying and she was glad. She couldn't stand it any longer. With one last agonised scream she arched her back and then sank back, utterly exhausted. The baby was born and she knew, without being told, that it was dead. Now she could die, too. A blessed blackness engulfed her.

A long time later she came to, shivering with cold under the thin blanket that covered her. It was a cold that she could smell as well as feel; damp, dank and thick with the stench of boiled cabbage, excrement and unwashed bodies. She opened her eyes.

'Oh, look, she ain't dead, after all,' she heard a voice say without enthusiasm. 'Better git 'er a basin o' gruel, I 'spect.'

'Nah. If we don't feed 'er she soon will be dead, then there'll be more for us,' another voice said, hopefully.

'No, we can't do that. 'T'ain't Christian.' She felt an arm round her, lifting her till she was able to prop herself on to one elbow. When everything stopped spinning round she saw that she was in a long, lofty room, with three rows of rough cots down its length. The room was lit by small windows set too high in the wall to give more than a hint that a bright autumn sun was shining outside. She saw that most of the cots were occupied by women who were either too old or too weak to get up and other women, filthy and ill-clad, seemed to be administering to them as best they could. The smell was appalling.

'Oh, God, what have I come to? What is this place?' she said, as much to herself as to anyone else. 'What's happened to me?'

'Gawd, she's a toff!' someone said.

'I told you she was. You could tell by 'er clo'se – what we saw of 'em afore *she* took 'em.'

'Shut up, you two,' a woman of indeterminate age said over her shoulder as she bent towards her, pushing back lank and greasy once-fair hair. 'You're in the work'us, dear,' she said, not unkindly, and Laura recognised her as the one who had helped her to sit up. 'They brung you 'ere when you c'lapsed at the railway station.'

Laura digested this with difficulty. She moved on the cot and felt her stomach. It was blessedly flat. 'The baby? Where's the baby? I did have a baby, didn't I? Did it die?' She frowned as she spoke. She was feeling dizzy now and weak, too weak to be sure she hadn't been dreaming.

'Yes. An' a good thing, too, if you ask me, poor little bastard.' The woman, whose name was Elsie, sat down on the side of the cot and took a basin of almost transparent gruel from the hand of a woman standing beside her. ''Ere, take some o' this. 'T'aintt all that special but it's all there is.'

Laura took a spoonful of the unappetising mess. It tasted like thick water that had gone bad, and at first it made her gag, but she forced it down. The fact that there wasn't to be a baby after all was nearly as difficult to digest as the gruel she was being fed. But not nearly as unpleasant. It was as if a great weight had been lifted from her, leaving her almost light-headed. She realised, with a pang of guilt, just how much she had hated the thing that had been growing inside her for the past eight months and she felt no pity for the poor innocent little wretch who had never even lived to draw breath. Because she knew she could never have loved a child that was a constant reminder of that dreadful man.

2

She forced down a little more gruel. Somehow she had to find out why she had been brought to this place and then take steps to get out of it and she wouldn't be able to do that if she starved herself. 'Why did they bring me here?' she asked. 'Why wasn't I taken to a proper hospital?'

''Cause you was destitute, o' course,' the woman called Martha said bluntly.

'But that's ridiculous. I haven't much money, but I'm not destitute.' She looked down at the ragged shift she was wearing. 'Where are my clothes? And my trunk . . ? And I have jewellery. My mother's jewellery. It was in a leather bag. I kept it safe on my wrist . . .' Laura held up her wrist. There was nothing but a red weal where the bag had been wrenched from it. Fear rose in her throat and threatened to choke her as she looked round for her possessions.

Martha and Elsie regarded her with pity in their eyes. It was always a matter of amazement to them just how naive the 'quality' could be. And this one didn't look much more than a child, although she must be going on for twenty.

'Don't you remember anything?' Elsie asked.

Laura frowned. 'I remember being at a railway station. . . I had just come from the boat. . .'

'What boat?'

'The boat from India.'

'She's ravin',' somebody said scathingly.

'No, I'm not.' Laura was indignant. 'I tell you I'd come from India; from the garrison at Mudkipur, near Lucknow.'

This meant nothing to the women clustered round the bed. 'Is that where your 'usband is? This muddy paw place?' Elsie nodded towards the wedding ring on Laura's finger.

'What?' Laura looked at her hand. 'Oh, er-yes, that's right.'

'Well, all I can say is, 'e should never 'ave let you travel on yer own. When you fainted at the railway station your trunk would be gone afore anybody could say knife, whipped away by some light-fingered Johnny,' Martha said. 'And as for waluables, well, I wonder they 'adn't bin cut orf your wrist long enough afore you dropped.'

Laura's eyes widened. 'Do you mean stolen? Everything I possess, stolen? But what about my clothes?'

3

'Oh, you won't see them no more. The matron'll see to that.'

'So everything I had is gone?'

'That's about the size of it,' Elsie nodded. 'This is the on'y thing we found belongin' to you. It was tucked in your glove.' She held up a train ticket. 'If it's any good to you you'd better keep it safe.'

Laura took it gratefully and looked at it. It was to Colchester in Essex, the home of grandparents she had never met. Her mouth twisted wryly at the irony of a Fate that had allowed her to make a journey of some five thousand miles across the world safely and then to strike when she was within fifty miles of her destination. But when it struck it did so with a vengeance, she thought bitterly, leaving her with nothing in the world but this train ticket and her dead mother's wedding ring, which she had worn to give herself an air of respectability for the journey. She lay back on the grimy pillow, trying to come to terms with her desperate situation and cursing the man who had been responsible for driving her to such depths.

Gradually, through youthful resilience rather than good food and care she regained her strength. Even so, she was forced to stay at the workhouse for nearly a fortnight, during which time her one thought was how to get out of the place. The two women who had befriended her and who, she learned later, had delivered her of the stillborn child, continued to care for her and shield her as best they could from the worst horrors of Victorian workhouse life, tending and feeding her until she was strong enough to leave the uncomfortable pallet that was her bed and could take her turn in helping the other sick women.

'If anybody come in, you git yerself back into bed,' Elsie warned, the first day she managed to stay on her feet. 'They'll on'y 'ave to see you up and about and you'll be down in the cellar pickin' oakum with the rest. And you don't want that! Not with 'ands like you've got.' She compared Laura's soft, white hands with her own cracked and chapped paws.

'An' 'ang on to your belongin's,' Martha said. 'People 'ere'd pinch the milk outa your tea – if there was any in it to

4

pinch,' she added grimly.

But Laura had no belongings except her train ticket, which she kept firmly tucked into her bodice and her mother's wedding ring, which she still wore, relieved to find that her fingers had swelled enough to make it a snug fit.

'Why are you here?' she asked Elsie one day.

''Cause I ain't go nowhere else to go,' Elsie said. 'My ole man died and there was me and five kids. I struggled on as best I could but I had to give up in the end. I reckoned it was better to come here than see me littl'uns starve.' She gave a grim laugh. 'I wouldn't have come if I'd knowed, though.'

'Why not? Where are your children?'

'Thass just it. They're somewhere here, in the children's ward, but I dunno whether they're alive or dead, 'cause I never get to see the poor little beggars.' She sighed. 'I might as well have kept 'em with me and we'd all 'ave starved together, instead of them starvin' where they are and me starvin' 'ere. Anyways. . .'

'Git back into bed. Here's the matron,' a voice from near the door warned.

Laura sank down on to her pallet and pulled the filthy blanket up round her chin, just as the matron came in with a short, thick-set man with a bull neck and dundreary whiskers. He had a florid face and little pig eyes that seemed to miss nothing. 'He's the overseer,' Elsie whispered, bending over in pretence of tucking her in. 'He's a reg'lar tartar.'

Matron fussed down the ward behind the strutting overseer, Jack Plant. He stopped beside Laura's bed. 'You're new,' he said. 'What brought you here?'

'She's just been brought to bed with a stillborn babe,' Elsie answered for her. 'She was picked up at the railway station.'

'What's your name? And where've you come from?' he asked, with a view to sending her back there at the earliest possible moment. Vagrants were an expense to the parish and the usual practice was to send them back from whence they had come at the first opportunity.

Laura looked up at him, her big violet-blue eyes wary. 'My name is. . . Mrs Bruce. And I've just come back from India,' she said.

Jack Plant raised his eyebrows. In those few words he

recognised that this was not one of the usual class of vagrant. He didn't believe her story but he was too interested in the slim, long-legged form he could detect under the grimy blanket to care whether what she said was true or not. 'This woman shouldn't be here. This is no place for the likes of her,' he said to the matron. 'Anybody can see she's a cut above this lot.' He waved his arm at the other patients in the infirmary.

'Well, Mr Plant, we had to put 'er hin with the rest. We reely 'aven't got, I mean, we've honly got the one 'ospital ward for women,' the matron said, wringing her hands.

'Then let her have a room to herself. There's a little room at the top of the stairs. It's only got boxes and things in it. Have it cleared and she can go there. I shall be back next week. See it's done by then.'

'Cor, ain't you the lucky one,' Elsie said enviously when the overseer had left with the matron. 'A room all to yerself. I wish I 'ad your luck.'

But Laura didn't see it like that. She had seen the look Jack Plant had given her, lingering and lecherous, and she was afraid.

Nevertheless, when the room was made ready for her she had no choice but to move to it, entreating both Elsie and Martha not to leave her alone there and begging them to help her to escape.

'But you ain't fit. Thass ain't two weeks since you was brung here and brought to bed,' Martha said.

'I can't help that. Don't you understand what that man has got in his mind?'

Understanding dawned on Elsie's face. 'Ah, yes. O' course. We shoulda realised. Well, don't you worry. We'll do what we can, dear. But thass a sure thing you can't leave till you've got suthin' different to wear. You can't walk the streets in your shift.'

So Laura had no choice but to wait, and while she waited Jack Plant came to see that his orders had been carried out. He came into the room, leaving the matron to go about her other business and stood looking down at her, his eyes feasting greedily on her form beneath the thin blanket. Then he sat down on the bed and gave her what passed as a smile,

6

showing a full set of bad teeth.

'Now, my dear, if you play your cards right you'll never want for another thing,' he said, and his hand crept under the blanket to caress her leg.

She sat up quickly in the corner of the bed and hugged her knees, as far out of his reach as she could get. 'Get out,' she spat.

He shook his head and his little pig eyes narrowed. 'Nobody speaks to Jack Plant like that, my girl,' he said. 'Don't forget I'm overseer here. You'll do as I say.' Then his tone became conciliatory, 'But I shan't have to order you, shall I? You'll be sensible when I tell you I've got a nice little room lined up for you a few streets away. You'll have your own front door, plenty to eat, all the clothes you want. And all you have to do,' he leaned over and she could smell his fetid breath, 'is be nice to me.' Unable to reach a more interesting part of her he began to stroke her arm.

She brushed him off as if he was a fly. 'Leave me alone,' she said through gritted teeth. 'I'd rather pick oakum than let you lay a finger on me.'

He laughed. 'You'll soon change your tune, madam, when you've seen what I got to offer you,' and he stood up and began to unbutton his trousers.

Quick as a flash she leapt out of bed and gave him a push, catching him off-balance so that he fell on to the bed. She rushed out of the door, nearly knocking over the matron, who had been busy at the keyhole and ran down the stairs and into the ward.

'Quick, where can I hide, away from that man?' she cried, trying to crawl under Elsie's bed. 'He wants to set me up in a house. I'll die first. He's nothing more than an animal.'

'Here, git in this cupboard,' Martha held open the door. She turned to Elsie. 'Can't unnerstand it, meself. If Jack Plant offered to set me up in a little room an' see me all warm an' comfortable, I'd put up wiv all the poker 'e give me. God, when all's said an' done, there ain't much else to look forward to in this life, is there! An' you hev to get it where you can. Thass right, dear, you'll be safe enough there.' She shut the door and Laura heard the lock turn.

She sat for what seemed like hours in the dark cupboard

hugging her knees and shivering. She couldn't believe that she had escaped from the clutches of Randolph Grey in Mudkipur only to fall into the hands of this horrible little pig-eyed man. She listened as Jack Plant and the matron came through the ward, ostensibly inspecting it, but in reality searching for her, and she held her breath when they demanded to look in the cupboard.

'Cupboard? Wot cupboard? Oh, that one! Ain't never looked in it, 'ave you, Elsie?' She heard Martha lie.

'No. There ain't no key, far as I know. Leastways, I never seen one.'

The voices moved on down the ward, Elsie and Martha protesting that they hadn't see the jumped-up little madam but they'd be only too jolly glad to hand her over to the matron if they did. At last the footsteps receded and Elsie came and let her out.

'That was a near one,' she said with a grin.

'Yes, it was. Too near.' Laura walked up and down the ward, willing strength back into her cramped legs. 'I must get away,' she kept saying. 'I must get away from this place. I refuse to stay here for the amusement of that dreadful man.'

'All right, dear. But you'll hev to wait till we can find you suthin' to wear. Like we said, you can't tramp the streets in your shift, now, can you?' Elsie said.

So she had to wait, hiding in the cupboard and sharing their meagre food, for a full twenty-four hours, while on Jack Plant's orders the workhouse was searched from top to bottom. Fortunately for Laura it was a half-hearted search, because the matron was not anxious to be supplanted in the overseer's affections by a younger and much prettier woman.

Ignorant of this, Elsie and Martha planned her escape carefully. Elsie had daringly stolen some clothes out of a cupboard in the matron's room, where garments that had been given by benefactors were stored. There was quite a smart dark blue dress that was only just beginning to go under the arms and a crinoline to go with it, a pair of shoes that almost fitted and a jaunty green hat. There was also a slightly moth-eaten green pelise.

By the time she had cleaned herself up, using precious water and carbolic soap to bathe and wash her hair in, and brushing it with the scrubbing brush because nobody possessed a hair brush – Laura looked quite respectable.

'Now, what you've gotta do is this,' Elsie said. 'Today's the day the nobs come to look over the poor house. They bring cake an' stuff and their cast-off clothes, like what you've got on. It don't do us no good but it make them feel better. The matron eats the cake 'erself an' keeps the clothes in the cupboard an' sells 'em off, a few at a time. Keeps 'er in brandy, anyway.'

'Never mind that,' Martha said impatiently. 'Tell 'er what we've planned.' She looked round at the women lying in their beds. Most of them were past caring what was going on but one or two were showing a beady-eyed interest in this smartly dressed stranger. 'An' you lot, keep your mouths shut, or you get no stew tonight. Not that you'll miss much,' she added under her breath.

Elsie caught her arm. 'Listen. When the nobs come round you tag on behind 'em. This is always the last place they visit, so all you've gotta do is walk along wiv 'em and out through the gate. You can get a 'Ansome there to take you to the station.'

'But I've got no money.'

Martha thrust a purse into her hand. 'There's a few coppers in there. Should be enough. It's all there was in Matron's drawer.'

Laura took it doubtfully. 'Won't you get into awful trouble?'

They laughed. 'Nah, why should we? We ollus knew that posh bitch was a thief.' Elsie planted a kiss on Laura's cheek. 'Now git back in the cupboard. We'll let you out when the time's right.'

Laura waited in the cupboard, trembling and clutching the little umbrella that Martha had discovered and which matched her hat. She hoped she wouldn't collapse with fright.

Before long there was the murmur of voices and soon after that the cupboard was unlocked. 'Quick, they've just gone,' Elsie whispered. 'Goodbye, Laura. And good luck!'

Laura took a deep breath and hurried after the group of about a dozen women. 'Terrible conditions. Something really should be done,' a grey-haired woman remarked, holding her handkerchief to her nose.

'Yes, I've never seen the like in all my life,' Laura answered, restraining herself with difficulty from breaking into a run as they walked along what seemed like miles of corridor before reaching the main door.

'Good afternoon, ladies,' the matron stood in the doorway, smiling obsequiously, and Laura walked out with the crowd, inclining her head in gracious acknowledgement as the doorkeeper touched his cap to them. The others dispersed in twos and threes to their own carriages or to one of the Hansom cabs waiting hopefully at the gate and Laura had no trouble in hailing one for herself. She was still trembling when she gave the cabbie every last penny from the purse and hurried on to the station. She kept looking behind, terrified that someone might have recognised and followed her and she didn't feel safe until she was on the train and rattling her way to her destination.

Then she relaxed, the first hurdle over. But as the train rattled along towards Colchester she realised her troubles were not yet quite at an end, since with all her possessions gone it might be difficult to convince her mother's parents that she was indeed their granddaughter. And even if they believed her would they welcome the child of the daughter they had disowned when she ran away with a penniless army surgeon? There had been no contact with them over the years, and whilst she was at boarding school all Laura's holidays had been spent either under sufferance with her father's sister, Aunt Miriam, or alone at school. There had never been any suggestion that she might write to her grandparents in the hope that they would offer her shelter. But now she had no choice, her parents were dead and buried in a grave for cholera victims in far-off India, Aunt Miriam was also dead and she was alone in the world. She couldn't believe her grandparents would turn her away.

The railway station at Colchester was a ramshackle affair of wooden sheds that looked more and more likely to fall apart with every train that shook and rattled its way into it. The ticket collector directed Laura to North Hill.

10

'Jes' keep right on up the road, over the river, an' you'll come to it. Thass a tidy step, mind yew.' He looked doubtfully at the ashen-faced girl in front of him. 'Are yew sure yew can manage it, dearie? Hev yew got. . .?'

'Oh, yes,' Laura said through bloodless lips, anxious to be on her way, 'I'm going to visit my grandparents.'

'Well, at least you ain't burdened with luggage, dearie.' The ticket collector watched her walk slowly away, shaking his head anxiously.

It was, as he had said, a tidy step. The railway station had been placed on the outskirts of the town because it was both noisy and dirty and local hotels did a nice trade in providing carriages for their clients. But there was no carriage to take Laura and she was forced to walk the long, unmade road, muddy from recent rains. She plodded on, in shoes that didn't quite fit, past fields and cottages till she reached the bridge over the river. She stopped and looked down into the shallow muddy water. It was hardly more than a stream compared with the great rivers she had travelled on in India. She eased her feet in the ill-fitting shoes and carried on.

The road began to slope upwards now and she was very tired because she was still weak from the difficult birth of the child. She leaned for a moment against a post by the side of the road and watched the carts and wagons trundling by. People, too, hurried about their business, taking no notice of her. Some of them were unkempt and shabbily dressed but nowhere did she see the abject squalor she had witnessed in the city of Lucknow. There were no beggars with festering sores, no heaps of rags by the side of the road, the only sign of life the brown clutching claw outstretched for alms. And the houses all had neat, iron-railed steps leading up to brightly painted front doors that weren't peeling and blistered from the heat. She dragged herself on. This, at last, was North Hill. Soon she would reach the haven of her grandparents' house. She sent up a swift prayer that they would welcome their only daughter's child.

Number seventeen had five steps leading up to a dark blue front door with a pretty fanlight. She banged on the door hopefully, nearly at the end of her strength.

A young maidservant opened the door. 'I've come to see Mr and Mrs Farthing,' Laura said, her hand on the door post for support.

The girl frowned. 'Albert,' she called over her shoulder, 'there's a strange woman 'ere. Say she want Mr and Mrs Farthing. Don't know nobody by that name, do you?'

Albert, an elderly retainer came shuffling along the hall. 'Mr and Mrs Farthing. Yes, thass the old couple who lived here afore Doctor an' the missus come. One died and the other worn't long after.'

Laura looked from one to the other, stunned. 'You mean my grandparents are dead? Both of them?'

'If their name was Farthing, yes, thass egsackly what I do mean. I mind it well,' Albert said. 'The ole lady died first an' he followed in a matter o' weeks. Doctor Shaw and 'is good lady live here now, and hev done for the past two years.'

'I see. Thank you very much.' Laura turned away, all her hopes and aspirations smashed by those few words.

Chapter Two

Utterly devastated, Laura dragged herself to the top of the hill and sat down by the well, taking a drink of cool, clear water from the cup that hung on a chain nearby. It was not very pure but it tasted like nectar after the filth she had been given to drink in the workhouse. She put her head in her hands. She couldn't believe that this was happening to her. All her hopes, all her faith had been pinned on finding her grandparents. She had been so sure she could win them round to give her a home. It had never once occurred to her that they might no longer be alive.

What was she to do now? She was in a strange town, with no money at all, and nowhere to go, except another workhouse. And she wouldn't go there. She would die, fling herself into the river she had crossed on her way from the railway station rather than suffer the humiliation of another of those dreadful places.

She sat in the late afternoon sunshine of early October, shivering, partly from the cool breeze of a climate that froze her after the heat of India, and partly from fear. It was unbelievable that not much more than six months ago she had been living a life of ease and luxury with Annabel, the girl who had befriended her in India. Filling the days with nothing more taxing than teaching Annabel's little son Peregrine his letters, an early morning ride across the plain or a trip to the bazaar, where they would idly spend a few rupees on trinkets they could have done without. And now she was destitute. She hadn't a penny. She sat twisting her mother's wedding ring round and round on her finger. Then, slowly, she turned her hand and looked at it. She had this left. She pulled it off her finger and laid it in the palm of her hand. It was all she had in the world.

She felt a light touch on her shoulder and cringed away, closing her hand protectively over the ring. Then she looked up, into the face of a man of about forty, shabbily dressed but clean and with a kind face. 'Are you in any trouble, dearie?' he asked.

She drew herself up, her innate pride coming to her rescue. 'No, thank you, I was just resting for a few minutes.' She got to her feet, giving him what she hoped was a bright smile, and tottered a few steps before utter hopelessness forced her to collapse back on to the bench, sobbing as if her heart would break.

Fred Taylor stood beside her, patting her shoulder and saying, 'There, there, dear, whatever it is there's surely no need to take on so,' over and over again, embarrassed by the stares of passers by, but reluctant to leave her, until her tears began to subside.

'I'm sorry,' she hiccuped, after a while. 'I didn't mean to cry like that. But I'm so alone. And so frightened. So dreadfully frightened.' And she began to cry again.

'Thass all right, dearie. Now, what you got to be frightened of? Do you want to tell me what's wrong?' Fred looked at her and saw a girl who was, as he put it himself, a cut above the ordinary, although she was none too tidily dressed and her thick, dark hair was screwed up any old how under that funny little green hat. But her face was fine-featured, with a wide, generous mouth and the most beautiful violet-blue eyes Fred had ever seen, red-rimmed though they were. He watched her for a few more minutes, not quite sure what to do about her, then he said, 'Tell you what. You come home with me and I'll get my missus to give you a cuppa tea. You'll feel better then, and you can tell us all your troubles. If you want to, that is,' he added awkwardly. He took her arm and helped her to her feet.

He seemed a nice, kind man so Laura was grateful to accept his offer and together they went along the High Street and turned into Stockwell Street and a little house in Ball Alley.

14

Fred's cottage was one of half a dozen, but unlike the others it was neat and clean, the step scrubbed and a geranium at the door. He took her inside and five pairs of almost identical grey eyes turned to look at her.

'Don't all stand there gawpin',' Fred said affectionately. 'Jest because we don't often hev a visitor. Kate, get the young lady a chair. Dot, pull the kettle forward for a cuppa tea.' He rubbed his hands together and turned to his wife. 'I dessay we can manage enough supper for an extra mouth, Muther, can't we?'

Laura had sat down on the chair provided, but now she struggled to her feet. 'Oh, no, I couldn't possibly. . .'

'Of course you could, my dear.' Nellie Taylor was a small stern-looking woman, without an ounce of spare flesh on her, and her hair was scragged back into her cap, giving her face, with its sharp nose, a pointed, bird-like look. Yet when she smiled she was transformed and her voice was full of kindness. 'Now, sit ye down, there's broth and to spare for you if you're willing to accept our humble hospitality.'

Nellie ladled broth into eight dishes and the oldest girl, Dot, cut a chunk of thick bread to go with each. 'Here, Kate,' she said to her sister of about twelve, 'take this upstairs to Ebbie, an' if he says he can't eat it you're to stay until he does.' Dot turned to Laura. 'Ebbie's our brother Ebenezer, he's a bit poorly. He's got a bad cough. But he'll be better soon, won't he, Dad?'

'Oh, yes.' Fred nodded firmly. 'I can see a difference in 'im every day.'

Kate went carefully up the narrow stairs and Laura could hear the sound of a dry, rasping cough coming from a room above.

The rest of them drew round the scrubbed table and Laura noticed that she was the only one with a chair, the others sat on stools or upturned boxes.

'Now,' Fred said, beaming, 'we'll say Grace and then we can begin.'

They all bowed their heads dutifully and Fred thanked his Maker for all the good things in their lives, for their food, for the fact that they were all in work and that Ebbie was getting better every day. They all said a fervent Amen and began to

15

tuck into the broth. It was very tasty, although Laura could detect no morsel of meat anywhere and she watched as the Taylor family ate their share, hungrily but not greedily, and in silence. It was clearly a rule that there was to be no talking at the meal table.

When the bowls were all empty and wiped clean with the last of the bread Dot got up and made the tea. Then, each with a mug in front of them, the conversation began. 'Dot's our eldest, she's eighteen,' Fred said, proudly, 'then there's Ebbie,' he pointed upstairs, 'he's fifteen. Kate there, she's twelve, Arthur's nine and this little madam here,' he picked up a dumpling of a baby, 'she's our Jinny, and she's jest two.'

'Me an' Mum an' Kate work at the silk mill down the road,' Dot said. 'Thass nice an' 'andy.'

'An' I help Dad an' look after Jinny,' Arthur said. He was a little lad, undersized for his nine years. They all looked expectantly at Laura.

'My name's Laura,' she said. She hesitated. There was no longer any need for pretence. 'Laura Chapman. I went out to India to be with my parents when I left–' she was going to say Finishing School, but realised this would mean nothing to this little family '–school. My father, Henry Chapman is – was – an army surgeon at the garrison at Mudkipur, near Lucknow. When I got there I discovered that they had both died in a cholera epidemic, so. . .' she hesitated, '. . .I came back to England.' What had happened in India during the intervening months she could still hardly bear to think about much less tell these kind people. She went on, 'I came to Colchester hoping to stay with my grandparents. But now I find they're dead, too, so I have nobody left.' Her voice was not quite steady as she finished.

They all greeted this news in sympathetic silence.

'So what you gonna do?' Kate asked, after a few minutes, her eyes round and wide.

'What's it like in India?' Arthur said at the same time.

'One at a time,' Fred warned. 'You know what I say about all talkin' together. We want no Tower of Babel here.'

'I'm not sure what I'm going to do,' Laura admitted. 'But first of all I must find work and somewhere to live.'

'You could stay here, with us,' Kate said eagerly.

16

'Oh, no, I couldn't possibly. . .'

'No, o' course she couldn't,' Nellie said, giving Kate a stern look. 'You couldn't expect a lady to wanta live with the likes of us.'

'Oh, it isn't that. I promise you it isn't that,' Laura said. She felt in her pocket. 'I'd be very grateful to stay here with you. But you see, I've got no money. I couldn't pay you. At least, not until I've sold this. It's my mother's wedding ring. Everything else I had was stolen when I. . . when I came through London.'

There were gasps of sympathy and Fred got to his feet. 'You're more than welcome to stay here tonight, Miss, that is, if you don't mind sharin' a room with Dot an' Kate. An' after that, well, if you wanta find somewhere a bit more posh we shall understand, shan't we, Nellie?'

Nellie nodded. 'You'll hev to be a bit careful in the girls' room because Fred's had to cut a hole in the floor to 'commodate the loom. You see, thass too tall for the room below, where he work. Thass a Jacquard loom you understand.' She said this with obvious pride, but the significance was lost on Laura, who knew nothing at all about such things.

'Thank you,' she said gratefully. 'You're most kind.'

At nine o'clock Fred got to his feet and went to the cupboard by the side of the fire to fetch the family Bible. He laid it on the table and the girls and Nellie quickly put away their mending and sat with the hands in their laps. Arthur had already gone to bed in the little truckle bed that had been pulled out from under the table and pushed back again when he was safely tucked in. Laura had been amazed that he should be expected to sleep under there with a room full of people, even though they were not noisy. 'Thass better for 'im to sleep under there than in with Ebbie,' Nellie explained. 'The coughin' might keep 'im awake. Although Ebbie hevn't coughed quite so much of late, I don't think,' she added hopefully.

When everyone was quiet Fred cleared his throat and began, pointing laboriously to every syllable as he read. 'And. . . the. . . Lord. . . said. . .' he paused and looked round the table to make sure he had everybody's attention, 'unto A. . . bra. . . ham. . .,' He stopped and looked up again. 'I dessay you can read better'n what I can, Miss Chapman,' he said. 'We'd take it as powerful good of ye if ye'd read the passage for us tonight.'

Laura smiled. It was little enough to do in return for their hospitality. 'Of course. I'll be glad to.' She took the Bible and began to read in a low voice, the beautiful old words flowing fluently and easily as the Taylor family sat round the table and listened, spellbound. When she had finished Fred took the Bible and reverently laid it back in the cupboard. 'That was beautiful, Miss Chapman, real beautiful. I ain't never heard the Good Book read in sech a way. Thank ye.'

After that the table was set ready for breakfast the next morning, and the girls kissed their parents good night and led Laura up the winding stairs, holding the candle high to guide her. They reached the first floor and Laura could see the shadowy outline of a large hand loom that filled almost an entire room and reached up into the ceiling. In the far corner the small double bed that Fred and Nellie shared was wedged between the loom and the wall. Beside this room, at the head of the stairs was an open door and in a tiny cupboard-like room she could see a little bed and hear the ragged breathing from Ebenezer. They went on, up little more than a ladder, to a single small room with a bed placed either side of projection from the room below.

'Careful not to touch the loom,' Dot whispered, edging round to the bed on the far side. 'Dad's got all 'is patterns on the cards there. If they get moved the pattern on the cloth won't be right an' 'e gets fined if thass flawed.'

Laura could see that the complicated system of laced-together cards Dot indicated were perforated by a varying series of holes that somehow governed the pattern of the cloth being woven. It all looked very complicated and she was careful to obey Dot.

'You can hev my bed, Miss Chapman. I'll get in with Dot,' Kate said happily. 'Then we needn't disturb you when we get up in the mornin'. We hev to be at the factory by ha' past seven an' we get stopped a quarter if we're more'n a minute late.'

'A quarter of what?' Laura asked.

'A quarter of an hour's pay,' Dot said, laying her clothes

18

carefully on the floor at the end of the bed.

'Oh, I see.' Laura undressed down to her shift and got into the bed with its lumpy flock mattress. Fred and his family, with their simple faith, accepting what life brought them and finding somewhere, somehow, something good in it, had restored her shattered faith in humanity. Not that she shared that faith. She couldn't believe in a God that allowed, indeed that willed, such suffering as she had seen over the past weeks. Yet she was forced to acknowledge an inner strength within herself that had, in spite of everything, kept her from total despair. Total despair, that was, until today at the well, when she had felt she could go on no more. And then Fred had come – been sent? – to her rescue. She didn't understand, but she was grateful and insofar as she knew the meaning of prayer she thanked God for her deliverance today. Then she fell asleep and slept soundly, safe in the knowledge that she was with real friends.

Parting with her mother's wedding ring the next morning was one of the hardest things Laura had to do. The pawn broker, a hook-nosed man with wispy ginger hair who looked as if he dressed himself from unredeemed goods, regarded it without sentimentality.

'Sixpence,' he sniffed, polishing it on his sleeve.

'Sixpence! It's worth far more than that,' she said, outraged.

'Not to me, it ain't. I got a box full of 'em.' He shrugged his shoulders. 'Take it or leave it. Don't make no odds to me.'

I'll take it.' She had no choice. She took the coin he pushed over to her and fled from the dim, smelly shop. At least it would buy her a few days' lodging with the Taylors while she looked for work. But what kind of work she had no idea because all she felt even remotely competent to attempt was the work of a governess and she realised that no one was likely to offer her such a position dressed as she still was in discarded clothes from the workhouse, especially without recommendation and with no money.

She walked for a long time, looking at the people she passed in the hope of seeing some glimmer of opportunity, but they were all intent on their own business and took no

19

notice of the slim, pale-faced girl in her battered blue crinoline and jaunty green hat. At last, tired and defeated, she went back to Ball Alley and the Taylor's house.

As she went in the whole house seemed to be vibrating with the noise from the clacking loom upstairs. She went up and found Fred sitting hunched over his work, throwing the shuttle rhythmically back and forth, a complicated pattern just beginning to appear on the cloth he was weaving. Little Jinny, tied by a long rag to the leg of the loom, was asleep on the floor.

If Fred saw her, which she doubted, he took no notice so she left the room and stood by the stairs, hesitating, not knowing quite what she should do.

'Is that you back, Arthur?' Ebenezer's voice came from the little room to one side.

Laura went in to him. He was lying propped with pillows, his face white under thick black hair and his eyes, very like his sisters', ringed with purple smudges. As he coughed Laura realised that the family were over-optimistic in thinking that he was recovering. Then he smiled, and she was struck by the thought that had he been healthy he would have grown into a very handsome young man.

'No, it's not Arthur, it's me. Laura.' She went and stood beside the bed where he could see her without turning his head.

'Don't disturb Dad,' he said. 'If he loses his concentration. . . the pattern slips. . . and he'll be fined for spoiling the cloth.'

'Oh, I see.' Laura nodded and sat down on the stool beside the bed. 'Then I'll be careful not to disturb him.'

He looked at her for some time. Then he said, 'You've come to live with us, haven't you? Arthur told me. He's gone on an errand for Dad. To fetch some more silk.' Ebenezer talked in short bursts, which even so left him gasping for breath. Laura had to strain to hear him over the clack of the loom.

'Only for a few days,' she told him. 'I must find work.'

'And you've come all the way from India?'

'Yes.'

'Tell me about it. I'd like to go there. One day. But I don't

20

think I ever shall. I wanted to be a soldier. . .' his voice faded and he closed his eyes. 'Tell me about India.'

As she talked about India Laura could again feel the heat of the plains, see the lush green banks of the Gumti River, and the beautiful palaces and tombs, rose-coloured or pale yellow according to how the light fell on them. She skirted over the squalor of the city and told him only of the beautiful or quaint things she had seen; the multi-coloured birds, the parrots, the chattering monkeys, the Commissioner's elephant decked with its ornate howdah, swaying round the grounds of the Residency, the strutting peacocks with their shrill, raucous voices.

When she had finished he said, 'Why did you come back? It sounds so beautiful. I would never have left.' Then, without waiting for a reply. 'Can you read, Laura?'

'Yes, I can read,' she said quickly, anxious that he shouldn't repeat his first question. 'Would you like me to read to you?' As she spoke she wondered where she would get a book from. She was certain the only book in the house was the Bible.

'No.' He shook his head slowly. 'I'd like you to teach me to read. But not now. I'm too tired. I always get tired if I talk too much.'

'Then perhaps you should go to sleep.' She got up from the stool. 'But I will teach you to read, Ebbie.'

'Promise?' he asked drowsily, his eyes already half closed.
'I promise.'

Laura left him and looked in to where Fred was still working. Jinny was awake now and trying to reach the little doll one of the girls had made her from an old bobbin, but her harness was too short and she was beginning to cry. Laura gave her the doll and Jinny looked up. 'I hungry,' she said.

Laura picked her up and unfastened the harness, holding her up so that Fred could see what she had done from the corner of his eye, and took her downstairs. There was a little milk and some bread so she warmed the milk and crumbled the bread into it. Jinny was just finishing it when Dot and Kate came in, followed closely behind by Nellie. They all looked tired and grubby as they took it in turns to wash in the scullery, after which they sat round the table and prepared the vegetables for the evening meal, Nellie with Jinny on her lap.

'Sech a to do there was,' Dot said, her eyes shining as she recounted the day's exciting news. 'We all knew Mr Charles fancied Rosie Goodwin, he was always going up behind her and putting his arm round her, you know the sort of thing.'

'I don't,' Kate said, reaching for another potato. 'I don't know what you mean.'

'Well, never you mind about it, then,' Dot said impatiently, anxious to get on with her tale. 'Anyway, where was I? Oh, yes. Mr Charles. Well, he told her to fetch something from the store room and we all knew what *that* meant!'

'Oh, dear,' Nellie sighed, pausing to give Jinny a cuddle before peeling another carrot, 'I hope he never turns his eye in your direction, Dot.'

'You don't need to worry about that, Mum, I'm not pretty enough,' Dot laughed. 'But what do you think Rosie said when he told her to go and fetch whatever it was?'

'I hope she said no,' Nellie said.

'Yes, that's exactly what she did say!' Dot's eyes widened. 'The rest of us girls couldn't believe our ears. I mean, nobody says no to Mr Charles, any more than they'd say no to the Master or Mr Jay or Mr Alex. She'd have done better to have made some excuse, that's what the rest of us. . . 'em, do.' Dot coloured a little under her slip of the tongue. 'But she didn't, she jest said, "No, Mr Charles. I'm here to work, not to run about at your beck and call."'

'What did 'e say?' Kate was all agog. She had seen Mr Charles from a distance and thought he was the handsomest and smartest man she had ever seen in her life.

'He didn't say anything,' Dot said. 'He just looked at her work and said, "You're very slovenly and very slow," which wasn't true at all, but none of us dared to stick up for her or we'd have been out on our ear as well.'

'Oh, dear,' Nellie said again. 'Got the sack, did she?'

'Yes. About half an hour later Mr Jay came along and stood behind her. He stood there for several minutes. Never said nothing, jest stood behind her. Well, you know how it is, if you're being watched you're all fingers and thumbs, ain't you? An' Rosie's a bit clumsy, anyway. Poor gal, she got into a rare muddle, you never saw sech a to do. Got her reels all of a tangle, then the thread broke, an' the faster she tried to put things to rights the worse they got.' Dot got up and put the saucepan over the fire. 'After about five minutes watchin' her Mr Jay said,' and she gave a fair imitation of his voice, '"Yes, I can see my brother is quite right. You are indeed very slow. We can't afford to employ slackers. Incompetent slackers, at that. Collect your money as you go out. You will not be required tomorrow."' Her voice dropped: 'I don't care for Mr Jay. He may be the eldest son but his father is still boss although you'd never think it, the way he throw his weight around.'

'Poor Rosie. What ever will she do? An' her with that widowed mother and poorly sister, too,' Nellie said. 'They depend on the few coppers she can earn.' She shook her head. 'Silly girl to answer back like that.'

Dot shrugged. 'She'd lose, either way. If she'd have gone with Mr Charles she'd have very likely ended up, well, you know,' she shrugged, '"like that".'

'Like what?' Kate asked innocently.

'Never you mind. You jest get an' lay the table,' Nellie said sharply. 'An' you watch your tongue, Dot, my girl. Remember, little pigs have big ears.'

'So she'd have been out on her ear, anyway. Only with another mouth to feed,' Dot muttered, determined to have her say. 'Seems to me a girl can't win.'

Laura said nothing but remembering her own experiences she felt sick at heart. Why was it that men were expected, encouraged even, to sow their wild oats, yet the women who were forced to reap the bitter harvest were treated like criminals? There was no justice.

'. . .an' they'll have to take on somebody in Rosie's place. So why shouldn't Laura. . .?' Kate's voice trailed off as she caught the look in her mother's eye.

'Miss Chapman to you, missie,' Nellie said sharply.

'No, please, I'd rather you all called me Laura,' Laura smiled uneasily. Kate had obviously said something out of place but she had been too preoccupied to notice what it was.

'I don't see why she shouldn't,' Kate muttered as she spread the cloth on the table.

'Ladies like Miss Chapman don't work in silk factories,'

Dot hissed in her sister's ear.

'They do if there's work to be had there and they can't find it anywhere else,' Laura said quickly, picking up the conversation. 'Why? Is there a position vacant?'

'Yes. A position next to me at the doubling machine,' Dot said. 'I'm quite sure it wouldn't suit a lady like you, Miss Chap. . . Laura.'

'Anything will suit me if I can earn my living by it,' Laura said simply. 'May I go with you tomorrow and see if they'll give me work?'

'All right,' Dot said reluctantly. 'But some of the girls I work with. . . well, they're a bit coarse. . . you may not like. . .'

Laura laid her hand on Dot's arm. 'I need the work, Dot. Don't worry about me. I'll manage.'

Chapter Three

But by six o'clock the next evening Laura was almost regretting her brave words. Although she didn't admit it she knew that Dot had been right and that she was totally unsuited to the work she had been put to. Her feet and legs ached, her back felt as if it was breaking and her fingers were sore and swollen. Added to that, she had developed a blinding headache caused by the continual noise from the machines that twisted the threads and then doubled four of them together on to reels to provide the warp in the weaving process. The stifling atmosphere in which they were forced to work because it was beneficial to the silk did not help either. If had not been for the fact that Dot had kept an eye on her and helped her to keep up with the others Laura knew she would never have lasted the day out.

'I told you it was no job for a lady,' Dot said, folding her clothes neatly as Laura fell into bed, having fallen asleep over her meal.

'I know I didn't do very well today, Dot, and I'm grateful to you for helping me. But I shall learn. And I shall do better tomorrow, you'll see.' With that Laura fell into an exhausted sleep, to be woken what seemed like only five minutes later by Dot telling her it was time to get up and start another day.

By the end of the first week when Laura received her wages she knew that if it hadn't been for Dot she would never have been kept on at Beresford's Silk Mill. Because it was Dot's quick eye that watched Laura's reels as well as her own and Dot's dexterous fingers that repaired the breaks in the thread as they occurred before Laura had even noticed them. But as the weeks passed she became used to the rhythm of the machine and learned how to cast her eye quickly over her reels to detect the broken threads and to tie them in the way she had been shown. Once she had learned the work, although she knew she would never be as adept as Dot, she found it boring in the extreme, because even if they could have heard themselves speak the girls were not supposed to waste time talking to each other. They worked standing side by side at the rows of machinery in the hot, noisy doubling room, with the overlooker, Mrs Ripley, constantly prowling to make sure there was no infringement of the rules. One of which was that no hoops or crinolines were to be worn because of the danger of them catching in the machinery.

Hetty Garfield, further down the room, disobeyed this rule.

'You'll hev ole Ma Ripley after you,' one of the other girls said during their ten minute break as they stood or sat by the yard wall in the winter sunshine, shivering in the cold air after the humidity of the doubling room and swigging their bottles of cold tea.

'She'll never notice,' Hetty said. 'Thass on'y a little hoop. Anyway, I'm fed up hevin' me skirts clingin' round me legs. T'ain't decent.' She took another swig of tea and wiped her mouth with the back of her hand. 'Damn fool rules. They on'y make 'em up to keep us under there.' She pressed her thumb on the wall beside her.

Mrs Ripley came to the door and rang the brass hand bell kept for the purpose. The girls scrambled to their feet and went back into the factory to begin work again.

They had been working steadily for about half an hour when suddenly, above the noisy clatter of the machines, there was a scream from Hetty. She had leaned too far forward to tie a thread and her skirt had become tangled in the whirring cogs of the machinery. The other girls began to scream too, as they stood and watched, frozen with terror. Mrs Ripley came hurrying from the other end of the factory floor to see what the commotion was all about, but before she could reach the scene Laura had got hold of Hetty round the waist and was trying to drag her clear, calling to the other girls to help. There was the sound of tearing cloth as the skirt was ripped from its bodice and Hetty was dragged to safety, leaving the skirt to mangle and shred before the machine ground to a halt. The whole incident was over in a matter of seconds and Laura had flung the window wide to revive the half-fainting Hetty before Mrs Ripley could get there.

'Close that window!' she barked. 'Who opened it? Don't you know it's bad for the silk? Whoever opened it will have a shilling stopped out of their wages this week.' She went over and banged in shut. 'Was it you?' she turned an accusing glare on Laura. 'I might have guessed it.'

'But this girl was fainting,' Laura protested, trying to fan Hetty's face now that the cold winter air had been denied her. 'Didn't you see what happened? Her dress got caught and she was nearly dragged into the machine.'

'And serve her right, too. She'd been warned about wearing that hoop. Look at that, now. The whole of that machine clogged up. Jessie, go and ask Mr Alex to send one of the men. Tell him one of the machines is out of action so it's urgent.' She made an impatient gesture. 'The rest of you, on the other machines, get back to work. As it is you'll get ten minutes pay stopped for time wasting.' She glared at Hetty. 'As for you, I shall make it my business to see that you lose a whole day's pay because it's all your fault. None of the others on your machine can work till it's put right.' She turned as a young man in overalls appeared. 'Oh, Mr Alex,' she simpered. 'I didn't mean for you to come yourself. One of the men would have done. But I'm afraid we've got a bit of trouble. This stupid girl got her dress caught in the machinery and it's clogged it up. I'm ever so sorry to have to trouble you, sir.'

'That's all right, Mrs Ripley,' Alex Beresford said with a hint of impatience. 'I'm sure we'll soon have it put right. But what about the girl? Is she hurt?'

'Girl? Hurt?' Mrs Ripley looked surprised. 'No, I don't think so. You're all right, aren't you, girl?' Her tone was grudging in the extreme.

Hetty nodded, her ashen face belying the gesture, as the other girls tried to group round her to hide the fact that she was stripped down to her drawers.

'I think she'd better be taken home,' Alex said. 'One of

27

you others go with her, I'll see that you don't lose your pay over it. I'm sure she's in no fit state to do any more work today.' He went over to the machine and with the help of the boy he had brought with him he extricated what remained of Hetty's dress. 'She was very lucky,' he said, collecting up the pieces of dress that were now nothing more than rag. 'Another few seconds and she would have been in the machine with the dress.' He shuddered at the thought. 'It's fortunate you took such quick action, Mrs Ripley.'

Mrs Ripley smiled and gave a deprecating shrug but said nothing.

'Mrs Ripley didn't drag Hetty outa the machine. Laura, here, was the one that saved her,' Dot stepped forward, so furious that Mrs Ripley was prepared to take the credit for something she hadn't had any part in that she took no notice of the overlooker's warning glare. 'Laura was the one that held on to her while the skirt was ripped off of her. Then the rest of us went to help. Thass Laura that saved Hetty's life, Mr Alex, sir, not Mrs Ripley.'

'Oh,' Alex Beresford paused in wiping the grease from his hands and looked up. 'And which of you is Laura?'

The girls parted and pushed Laura to the front. 'It was nothing,' Laura said, shaking her head. 'It was no more than anyone would have done. It was just lucky that I was quite near.' She lifted her head and found herself looking into a pair of unusual, hazel-flecked eyes, set in a long, square-jawed face that was liberally streaked with grease. Alex raised his eyebrows, which were thick and black, obviously surprised to hear such a fluent, well-modulated voice from the factory floor. Factory girls were normally tongue-tied when confronted by a superior, but there was no sense in which this girl was intimidated.

He regarded her thoughtfully for a few moments, his jaw set and unsmiling. She returned his gaze coolly; they were almost of a height. 'Well, Laura,' he said at last, 'your quick thinking saved the girl's life, there's no doubt about that. You're to be congratulated.' He turned away, collected up his tools and left, the boy running behind to keep up with him.

'Who was that?' Laura half whispered, half mouthed at Dot after he had gone and the machines were running again.

It was a method of communication that the machine girls had perfected over the years and as long as the overlooker was not near they could carry on quite a conversation. 'He seemed to set Mrs Ripley by the ears, whoever he was.'

'That was Mr Alex himself,' Dot said with something akin to awe. 'He's the Master's middle son. He's ever so clever with engines. Funny really. I mean, you wouldn't expect one of the Master's sons to be doing dirty work like looking after machinery and engines, would you?'

'He's a Beresford?' Laura said in surprise.

'Yes. That's what I'm saying. You'd expect him to be like the Master and Mr Charles and work in the office. Like Mr Jay. 'Course, Mr Jay's the eldest son. He's the one who really runs things. He's a reg'lar tartar. Hev you seen him yet?'

Laura shook her head. 'Not really. I've caught sight of him as he comes in in the morning sometimes. That's all. I haven't really seen his face.'

'Well, you're about to, now. He's just come in at the door.' Dot put her head down and concentrated on her work and Laura did the same.

After a few minutes Mr Jay came along with Mrs Ripley and the woman pointed to Laura. Laura pretended not to notice and after a minute she felt a tap on her shoulder. She looked round and saw a very tall man in his middle twenties, with auburn hair and side whiskers and grey eyes that held no vestige of warmth. He held her gaze for what seemed like an age, and she returned his look calmly, determined not to be intimidated by him. Then, without a word, he nodded curtly and gestured to her to get on with her work.

She inclined her head politely and turned back to the machine, giving no sign of the fury his haughty arrogance had roused in her. So that was Mr Jay. Laura had a feeling she had made an enemy.

Eleanor Beresford sat in the drawing room waiting for her husband and three sons to put in an appearance. It was six thirty, the time of day when she liked them to relax before the evening meal. She was even prepared to let Turpin, the butler, lay out a tray of drinks in order to secure their presence, although she herself never touched alcohol. She

29

waited, her hands in her lap, a small, neat woman, dressed in black, with pale lavender lace at her throat and wrists and a lavender lace cap perched on her greying hair. She knew they would come, even if one or all of them had to return to the factory after they had eaten, and she sat patiently in the large, pleasant room that overlooked the immaculately kept lawns and gardens. This was one of her favourite rooms, although in truth she was fond of the whole house. Bought by her husband, Javis, some ten years ago when the factory really began to prosper, it was one of the larger houses in Head Street, and it had been redecorated and furnished to her own taste. Now, whilst she waited for her family to arrive she looked round the room, savouring the pale green of the walls and the high moulded ceiling. She prided herself on her good taste as she had been careful not to overfurnish in the fashion of the day; and although there were several armchairs and sofas, small tables, even a small walnut grand piano, the room had an uncluttered look. Sitting in it, gazing at the portraits that hung on the walls, gave her great pleasure.

Charles was the first to appear. He was very like his oldest brother, although not so tall, and with a warmth in his grey eyes that Jay lacked. He went over and kissed his mother and she smiled affectionately at him. He was her last born and her favourite. 'And what have you been doing with yourself, my boy? Yes, that's right, fetch your drink. I know you can't sit and talk without it. Turpin has left the decanter. Well?'

Charles poured himself a whisky and swallowed it at a gulp. Then he poured himself another and came and stood with his back to the marble fireplace, where a huge coal fire burned.

'Well?' Eleanor repeated, smiling up at him. 'What's wrong, Charles? Sit down, boy, do. You're behaving like a cat on an onion bed. You might as well tell me, you know. I can always tell when there's something worrying you.' She reached for her reticule. 'And I daresay I know what it is. You've overspent your allowance. How much?'

'Twenty pounds. My tailor, you know. The new suit I ordered was more expensive than I'd anticipated. If you can help me out this month I'm sure I'll manage better in future.'

Charles spoke quickly, looking at the glass he was twirling in his hand to avoid facing his mother.

'Twenty pounds! That's rather a lot of money, Charles. I let you have ten only last month. You really will have to be more careful, dear. Are you really sure you need quite so many new clothes?' Nevertheless, Eleanor handed over the notes.

Charles stuffed them into his pocket and bent and kissed her. The old girl was really quite gullible. 'Thanks, Mater, you're a brick.'

'Well, see it doesn't happen again. I'm not made of money, you know. And I'm quite sure your father wouldn't approve. He thinks your allowance is too generous as it is.' But she smiled as she spoke.

'I work for my allowance. I'm at the factory every day,' Charles said defensively. 'I work quite hard.'

'Yes, dear, I know.' Eleanor sighed and looked at the clock. This was an old argument. Although it was beyond dispute that Charles put in an appearance at the factory every day, the amount of work he did was very much open to question. 'The others are late, aren't they?' she remarked, changing the subject.

'No, not really. I came early because I wanted to speak to you before they arrived. Ah, here they are now. At least, here are Pater and Jay.'

Jay stood aside for his father to enter the room. Javis Beresford was a short, thick-set man, coarse-featured, with a large nose and thick, fleshy lips. His hair lay close to his head in thin grey stripes through which the pink flesh was fast gaining the upper hand. He went over to his wife and kissed her dutifully, the firelight glinting on the gold chain stretched across his ample paunch. 'You're looking very well, my dear,' he said, absently.

'Thank you, Javis, I *am* very well,' she answered formally.

'Get me a whisky, Jay. I've had a hard day,' he growled, sitting in the armchair on the opposite side of the fire to his wife. 'Where's Alex?'

'Still at the factory,' Jay told him. 'There's trouble with one of the shafts and he won't leave till it's put right because the night shift can't begin work.'

'If trade doesn't pick up there won't be any night work,'

31

Javis said tetchily. 'We'll have to lay off some of the workers.'

'Be better to put them all on short time, then when things pick up we'll still have the work-force to cope,' Jay said thoughtfully. 'It's not economical to close the boilers down every night. Alex'll tell you, once the engines are running it's cheaper to keep them going.'

'Are you visiting Charlotte tonight, Jay?' Eleanor asked. She wasn't interested in talk about the factory.

'No. She's got some musical affair going on. I told her it didn't interest me,' Jay replied.

'But you are engaged to be married to her, dear. Don't you think it would have been polite to be there?' Eleanor looked anxiously at her eldest son.

'I've got better things to do than make myself pleasant to a bevy of women chattering over nothing,' Jay said testily. 'I've told her I'll take her to the Botanical Gardens at the weekend if I'm not too busy.'

Eleanor raised her eyebrows but said nothing. She was fond of Charlotte Rankin, her son's fiancee although she found her irritating in her over-anxiety to please Jay. Jay was like his father, he needed quite a firm hand, albeit in the proverbial velvet glove, and Eleanor was afraid Charlotte hadn't yet understood this. When she did it might be too late.

A door banged at the other end of the house and after about five minutes the door burst open and Alex appeared. As is the way with middle children he was totally unlike his brothers, dark where they were auburn and with hazel-flecked eyes where theirs were grey. Not handsome in the accepted sense, his features were well defined and regular. He had obviously made a quick and not very successful attempt to clean himself up. 'I'm not late, am I?' he said, pouring himself a drink.

'No, Alex, you're not late, but I hope you don't imagine you're going to sit down to dine with us in that state,' his mother said coldly.

Alex looked down at himself. His clothes were crumpled from a day spent under overalls and there was still a stubborn streak of grease on his hand. He shrugged. 'I'm sorry, but it was a case of come clean or come late and I know what a

32

stickler you are for time, Mama. In any case, I've got to go back. I've left my men working flat out and I can't just leave them to get on with it.'

'Why not?' Eleanor asked. 'Surely that's what they're paid to do.'

'Ha!' Jay gave a mirthless laugh. 'It may be what they're paid to do but you can't trust them to get on with it unless someone's there to make sure they're not slacking.'

'It's not that,' Alex rounded on his brother. 'I trust my men to work even when I'm not there.'

'Then you're a fool,' Javis growled from the depths of his armchair.

'Well, you're not sitting down at my table looking like that,' Eleanor said firmly. 'Either go and make yourself respectable or have your meal sent up to your room.' She put her handkerchief delicately to her nose. 'You reek of engine oil.'

Alex drained his glass, still standing by the drinks table. 'All right, I really can't spare much time anyway. I'll eat in the kitchen.'

'You can't do that, Alex.' His mother was horrified. 'I won't have a son of mine eating with the servants.'

'Oh, I shan't eat *with* them, don't worry, Mama. I know what's expected of me,' he said with a trace of bitterness, his hand already on the door knob. 'Mrs Mott'll let me have a corner of the kitchen table to myself. She often does when I'm late back.' He looked at the marble clock on the mantelpiece. 'I must go. I told Humphries I'd only be an hour or so.'

'Is the problem anything to do with the business in the doubling room this morning?' Jay asked idly.

'No,' Alex replied briefly, 'this is to do with one of the shafts in the boiler house.' He paused, halfway out of the door. 'That accident in the doubling room could have been nasty, though. If it hadn't been for that other girl's quick thinking we could have had a rather messy death on our hands.'

'Alex!' his father said sternly, 'remember your mother's presence.'

'Sorry, Mama,' Alex nodded briefly in his mother's direction.

33

'Who was that girl?' Jay asked. 'The one who acted so quickly.'

'I don't know. I'd never seen her before. I believe the others called her Laura.' Alex frowned. 'I must say she's very well spoken. Not like the usual run-of-the-mill factory hand.'

'Is that so?' Jay said, raising his eyebrows. 'Then she'll have to be watched, because she'll be the type that could breed discontent, if I don't miss my mark.'

'That's your department,' Alex said with a shrug, adding thoughtfully, 'But she certainly stands out from the crowd, I'll say that for her.'

'Can't understand my brother Alex,' Charles remarked after Alex had left. 'He seems to positively enjoy getting his hands dirty.'

'It's a pity you don't share some of his enthusiasm for hard work,' Javis said testily.

'Oh, that's not fair, Pater. I've been at the rotten factory all day.'

'That fact is not in dispute,' his father said. 'It's what you do whilst you're there that's in question.'

Eleanor got to her feet. 'I think that's quite enough factory talk for tonight,' she said firmly. 'Turpin has just signalled that dinner is served. Charles, I think it's your turn to give me an arm into the dining room tonight.' She smiled indulgently at her youngest son. 'Yes, thank you, I will have my shawl. It's very cold, moving from room to room. I really think we might have snow for Christmas.'

The first months of the year 1857 were bitterly cold. The girls at the silk factory, going from the warm, oppressive atmosphere necessary to work the silk, to the freezing fog of the dank, grey streets, where their breath hung visibly on the air and their noses glowed blue in pinched white faces, suffered continuous colds, coughs and bronchial complaints. They also had chilblains that swelled and stiffened their fingers, making them slow and clumsy. When the weather became too bad to go out into the yard for their break the girls tended to congregate on the stairs where, although there was an icy draught blowing, at least it was dry.

34

Laura was appalled at the sight of the children, some of them as young as eight years old, who made their way down from the top floor where they spent their days at the winding machines. They were, for the most part, pale and undernourished, with rickety legs bowed from climbing the three flights of stairs and then standing all day at the winding frames, known as swifts, where their job was to join up broken threads and replace the skeins as they were wound on to the bobbins. Among them was Kate, Dot's young sister, and she would come and sit with Dot and Laura, huddling between them on the stairs to keep warm while they ate their bread and dripping. Kate was one of the lucky ones. With all the family working she never went hungry; some of the children had no more than a dry crust to see them through the long day, and one or two not even that. Laura found it impossible to eat her slice while there were white-faced children with big, hungry eyes watching every mouthful and she took to surreptitiously giving them most of what she had.

'You'll never be shot of 'em if you feed 'em,' Dot warned her as Laura passed the last of her share to a ragged young lad. 'Don't forget you need to eat to keep your own strength up.'

'I shall have a good meal when I get home tonight,' Laura said, 'which is more than some of these poor mites will.'

'Dot laughed. 'You're too tender-hearted, Laura, my girl. But you'll learn.'

Kate licked the last morsel of dripping from her fingers. 'Teddy Hughes got his finger stuck in the machine this morning. Did you hear 'im yell? He didn't half kick up a shine. Mind you, so would I, I 'spect, if I'd lost the top of my finger.'

'Lost the top of his finger!' Laura was appalled. 'Did they take him to the hospital?'

'What for? The top 'ud come off. The danter, Mrs Lott, picked it out of the machine an' threw it in the rubbish bin. Well, that wasn't any more good, was it? She bound his finger up tight, though, an' sent 'im home. She said that wasn't any good him stayin' on if he couldn't work. I'll bet 'is mum'll be suthin' angry to think he's lost a day's pay.' Kate wiped her fingers on her pinafore and prepared to return to work.

'You watch out what you're up to, my girl,' Dot warned, holding her skirts aside for her sister to climb back up the stairs. 'We don't want you losing fingers. And tie your hair back. It's all come out of its rag. Oh, come here.' Deftly, Dot dragged Kate's hair back and secured it with the piece of tie rag. 'Go on, off you go.' She gave her an affectionate pat on the behind as Kate went back to work.

'Don't the machines have guards on them?' Laura asked, after she had gone.

'No. They'd only get in the way. It's all right as long as the children are careful. It's when they don't watch what they're doing,' Dot said. 'And if they get tired. Poor mites, it's hard for them to stand all day, especially with no food inside 'em. But what can you do? They need the money.' She shrugged.

'I think something should be done about it,' Laura said firmly.

'I don't know what,' Dot said, with another shrug.

But it was not only the plight of the children that shocked Laura. She was amazed at the snatches of conversation she heard from some of the other girls.

'. . . earn more when the summer come 'cause you can ollwus go in a field. They ollwus knock the price down when they hev to pay for a room. . .'

'. . . soldiers ain't fussy. . . as long as they can git under yer skirt they're jest as happy in a ditch. . .'

'Do they mean what I think they mean?' Laura said in a horrified whisper to Dot when they were in bed in the attic, with Kate fast asleep in Dot's arms. 'About soldiers. . .and earning more in the summer?'

'Oh, yes,' Dot said matter-of-factly. 'Thass how some of 'em get enough to live on. You don't get fat on silk factory wages, you ought to know that, Laura. A girl can make more in one night on the game than she can in a week at the factory.'

'But that's *awful*,' Laura said. 'Have they no self-respect? And what about their families?'

'Oh, Laura, you've got a lot to learn,' Dot said with a sigh. 'Not all families are like ours. We're lucky. We're all in work and Dad has been able to take young Arthur as his apprentice so the boy won't have to go winding at the factory. But even

36

so, with Ebbie's medicine and the doctor's bills we don't have anything to spare. And Dad don't drink, either. Young Sally Brooks, who stand at the machine at the far end, her father's never sober. He spends every penny he can lay his hands on in the pub. And thass mostly what Sally and her mum earn. And if they spend it on grub before he can get to it he beats the living daylights out of 'em. And there's four little'uns in that house. Can you wonder Sally's out every night trying to earn an extra copper or two.'

'But doesn't she. . .? What if. . .?'

'You mean doesn't she ever fall for a kid? Yes, once or twice she has, but you can always get stuff to take to get rid of it if you're quick enough.'

'But that's dreadful.'

Dot yawned. 'Thass life, Laura. And it ain't all bad, you know. Some of 'em say they quite enjoy it.'

After Dot was asleep and snoring gently Laura lay awake looking at the hump in the floor that was the top of Fred's loom. She could hardly believe what Dot had been saying, yet she knew it must be true from the conversations she had heard in the factory, and she had seen with her own eyes the way the young soldiers hung around the gates of the factory at knocking off time, waiting for their girls.

She was shocked, but she realised she shouldn't have been, not after her own experiences. She closed her eyes against the memory. Those months were best forgotten and laid to rest in the deepest recesses of her mind. But one thing was certain, she would starve to death before she would ever sell herself and she would fight to the death before she would allow herself to be defiled again as Randolph Grey had defiled her.

Chapter Four

Jay was annoyed. He, who regarded people who suffered from nerves as weak and lacking in self control, was nervous. And neither his nervousness nor his annoyance were in any way appeased by Alex telling him that all bridegrooms were nervous on their wedding day. Jay did not wish to be like 'all bridegrooms'. He was Javis Beresford, son of the owner of the biggest silk factory in the town; he should be above feeling nervous at a religious ceremony, however lavish the occasion Sid Rankin had organised for his only daughter. Jay allowed the hard line of his jaw to soften briefly. Charlotte was a pretty woman, and to give Sid Rankin his due he had made sure that she had been taught good manners and etiquette, even though they were attributes that he himself, and his wife, lacked. Sid had risen from a rag and bone man to owning the biggest furniture emporium in the town and Jay respected him for his business acumen as well as for the fortune he had bestowed on his daughter. But he tried to avoid contact with him at official functions, when Sid was liable to call a spade a bloody shovel and not to gloss over what he considered to be home truths. Sid was neither a diplomat nor a social climber. He made no secret of his humble beginnings; in fact, at times he seemed positively proud of them. Jay could wish he was a little less honest about them at times and he hoped fervently that he wouldn't hear him say, today of all days, that he had begun his career with selling rabbit skins for a penny each, having already sold the rabbits to the butcher for twopence.

He loosened his collar. That was no doubt why he felt

nervous; not because today was his wedding day, but because he was afraid that his new father-in-law would disgrace him in front of two hundred guests.

'Are you ready, then, Jay?' Alex and Charles came into the room. They were both looking exceedingly smart in cut away coats and frilled cravats. 'You look a bit white round the gills,' Charles remarked. 'Tot of whisky before you go?'

'No. Unlike you, Charles, I have no need of Dutch courage.' Jay picked up his hat and brushed a speck of imaginary dust from its crown, hoping neither of his brothers noticed that his hand wasn't quite steady. He made his way to the door. 'I'm still not convinced that the factory should have been closed for the whole afternoon,' he said. He felt on safer ground talking about the factory. 'I shouldn't have let you and Father overrule me. An hour would have been quite sufficient, I would have thought. Give the girls an inch and they'll take an ell. . .'

'It was a good opportunity to overhaul the engines,' Alex said. 'Now, we've been over all this, Jay. It's your wedding day. The men aren't interested, they're quite happy to work on the engines, but the girls all love to see a wedding and especially the boss's wedding. It won't hurt. They'll work all the better tomorrow.' He patted his elder brother affectionately on the back.

'More likely they won't work at all. They'll be too busy discussing what they saw,' Jay said sourly.

The wedding was at St James' Church on East Hill and the streets were lined with people; from the house in Crouch Street where the Rankins' lived, past the Beresfords' house in Head Street, along the High Street and as far as the gates of the church. Dot and Kate had taken Laura with them and secured a good vantage point on the wall of the churchyard where they would be able to see everything without getting in anyone's way.

'Oh, isn't Mr Charles handsome?' Kate said, as the three brothers drew up in their carriage and went up the steps and into the church. 'Oh, I think he's the handsomest man I've ever seen in my life.' She closed her eyes in ecstasy as she spoke.

'And yours'll be a pretty short life if you don't look what you're doing. You nearly fell off the wall into the crowd just then,' Dot said severely. But her sharp words were based on anxiety. Kate was becoming quite a pretty girl and Dot feared the consequences if she should ever catch Mr Charles' attention.

Laura said nothing. She had watched the three men but neither Jay nor Charles had caught her attention. It was Alex, whom she had never seen out of greasy overalls before, that she noticed. He was smiling at the cheering factory girls, whilst Jay looked wooden and Charles looked embarrassed. Laura's heart gave a funny little leap as he seemed to smile straight at her.

The crowd cheered and oohed and aahed as the guests in their expensive finery appeared, and then the bride, in one of the largest crinolines they had ever seen, all frothy with cream lace, followed by six little bridesmaids all dressed in pink, their frilly pantalettes peeping from under tiny matching crinolines.

But Laura watched almost without seeing. If her grandparents had still lived it was quite possible that she would have been among the guests at this wedding, instead of watching with the ragged, shivering mass of cheering factory girls. She sighed. If. If her parents hadn't died. . . If Randolph Grey. . . she shied quickly away from that name. . . If she had not been robbed of all her possessions. . . If her grandparents had still been alive. . . But all these things had happened and now she was working with some of the lowliest people in the town, as destitute as they were. And she could see no way of escape; no way of improving her lot. She was paid so little that it had taken her three months before she could manage to reclothe herself from the second-hand shop. By careful selection she had managed to buy a respectable dress and crinoline and boots, but there was nothing left for a coat or pelisse so she had to make do with a warm shawl. Luckily she had found one that was a good match for the dress and by wearing the shawl over her head she didn't have to worry about affording a hat.

There was renewed cheering when the bride re-appeared on her new husband's arm. To Laura's surprise Jay looked

40

slightly self-conscious and nervous; she had always regarded him as totally self-possessed. His bride looked radiantly happy as she gazed adoringly up at him. They were to honeymoon in Great Yarmouth, Laura had heard – a rather chilly place to choose in March, situated as it was on the Norfolk coast, but at least they were unlikely to be troubled by other holiday makers.

With a flurry of rice and good wishes the wedding party drove off and the onlookers dispersed, so unused to having time to themselves that they were for the most part unsure what to do. 'Are you comin' home with us, Laura?' Kate said, tucking her arm into Laura's.

Laura shook her head and freed her arm. 'No. If you don't mind I think I'd rather go for a walk,' she said.

Dot and Kate both looked at her in surprise. It was a freezing cold day and they were chilled to the bone from standing in the wind. Added to that, they were on their feet for such a long time every day that it would be the height of luxury to them to simply go home and sit down. But although she lived with them and shared their day to day fight for survival both girls realised that Laura was not like them so they made no comment but left her to her own devices and went home.

Laura pulled her shawl more closely round her and went over to the Botanical Gardens and walked among the flower beds for some time. The primroses were just beginning to bud and the daffodils were pushing up brave green spikes through the frosty ground. Laura remembered days like this at school, where the girls complained when they had to don warm capes and thick shoes to take their daily walk, their hands encased in fur muffs, saying that they were cold. And she had complained as loudly as any of them. She gave a rueful smile. In those days she hadn't known what it meant to be cold, chilled to the very soul, like she was now. She sat down on a bench, hugging her shawl round her for comfort, feeling restless and unhappy. This was the first opportunity she had had to sit quietly and consider her life and the thoughts were unsettling. It occurred to her that her mood might also be tied up with her feelings towards Alex Beresford. Time and again the vision of him walking into the church with his two brothers rose before her eyes, try as she might to stifle it. And the knowledge that in normal circumstances she might easily have met him on equal terms did nothing to calm her feelings. A tear rolled down her cheek. She felt like Cinderella, only she knew there was no fairy godmother to rescue her.

She sat on the bench until the lamp lighter came round and she realised that she must have been sitting there for an hour or more because she was frozen stiff. She got up, chafing her frozen limbs, and wandered slowly out of the gardens; she didn't want to go home to the Taylors, she wasn't ready to join in the discussions on the colours and designs of all the dresses, of who wore what and who was or wasn't there. She thought of her months in India, of the heat, of Annabel. . . Dear Annabel. She had been such a good friend she must be wondering why there had been no word since Laura's return to England. But how could she write? How could she ever tell Annabel of the terrible life she had sunk to? Better to keep silent and let Annabel think she had forgotten her. Not that she ever would.

Almost without realising what she was doing Laura found herself walking up the steps of St James' Church, the few grains of rice from the wedding that hadn't already been gathered either by the poor or the sparrows crunching under her feet. It was cold inside the church but it felt warm after the chill wind outside. She slipped into a pew and sat for a long time, gazing at the big gold cross and the stained glass windows above it. Suddenly the thought came to her that everything in life had a purpose and she had come to Colchester for a reason. She sighed. She couldn't see what that reason could possibly be, nor what she could do about it under her present circumstances, yet the thought persisted. Puzzled, she shook her head. She was probably light-headed with hunger; she hadn't eaten since breakfast.

'Are you all right? You've been sitting very still for quite a long time.' At the sound of the man's voice Laura started and turned to see Alex Beresford standing looking down at her, an anxious expression on his face.

'What? Oh, yes, thank you, I'm perfectly well.' Embarrassed, she stood up and pulled her shawl more closely

42

round her. 'I was just going.'

'There's no need to. Please stay as long as you like. As long as you're not ill or anything. . .' He smiled at her. 'It's Laura, isn't it? – I'm sorry I can't be more formal but I don't know you by any other name – aren't you the young lady who rescued the girl whose crinoline got caught in the machinery at the factory?'

'That's right,' she nodded, surprised that he should have remembered her.

'Well, please sit down again if you wish, Miss. . .?'

'Chapman. Laura Chapman.'

'Miss Chapman.' He indicated a pew and she sat down. He sat in the pew in front and turned so that he could talk to her. 'I came back because one of my more forgetful maiden aunts has lost her reticule and she thought she might have left it here in church. She hadn't, of course. But no matter, it's provided a providential opportunity for me to get to know you a little. You're not like the other girls at the factory, Miss Chapman. You're not like them at all. You puzzle me.'

Laura was glad of the semi-darkness in the church to cover the blush that she felt rising. 'No, I realise I've got a lot to learn,' she said, deliberately misconstruing his words.

'I didn't mean that and you know it,' he said quietly. 'You don't speak like the other girls, you don't conduct yourself like the other girls, in fact, if I may say so, you're like a fish out of water in the doubling room. Why are you there, Miss Chapman?'

She looked up at him. His face was little more than a pale oval in the dusk. 'I'm there because I've nowhere else to go,' she said simply.

'But surely. . . I mean, you haven't always. . .'

She shook her head. 'No, Mr Beresford. I haven't always.' She stood up and he rose with her. 'I must go. The Taylors will wonder where I am. I said I was only going for a walk.'

He walked to the door with her. 'Will you let me take you for a drive on Sunday afternoon?' he asked suddenly.

'But you can't! I mean, it wouldn't be right.' She spoke in a rush as she realised that there was nothing she would like more.

'It wouldn't be right for me not to,' he replied. 'I want to

43

take you for a drive, Laura. . . I mean, Miss Chapman. I want to know more about you. You–' he hesitated, 'you intrigue me. And worry me a little,' he added more softly. 'Will you come?'

She took a deep breath. She knew it would be wrong, foolish and unconventional – dangerous, even – to accept his invitation. She smiled up at him. 'Yes,' she said, 'I'll come.'

He relaxed visibly and smiled back at her. 'Good. Then meet me outside the factory at three o'clock on Sunday afternoon.'

They walked out into the cold March evening together. Suddenly, her black mood had gone and she walked on air.

Charlotte was very quiet on the journey to Great Yarmouth. She had never been this far from home and, more worrying, she was totally ignorant of what might be expected of a new wife. Her mother had said nothing beyond the fact that she must be obedient of her husband's every wish, which remark Charlotte thought was quite unnecessary, since she wanted nothing more than to please Jay, yet she sensed an underlying meaning in her mother's words that led her to think that there was some hidden message that she couldn't understand. She had no sisters to discuss such matters with so she was left to wonder what it was about marriage that she didn't know.

For his part, Jay kept up a stentorious commentary on everything they passed, which was of little interest to her and which she didn't understand was his way of hiding his own apprehension.

They reached the hotel and dined well, although Charlotte's appetite was small. 'They say there are pierrots on the beach, Jay,' she ventured, between courses.

'Only in summer, my dear. It's too early in the year to expect that sort of thing, even if one cared for it,' he added a trifle loftily.

Duly snubbed, Charlotte retired behind her fruit salad. 'The music here is very pleasant, though,' she tried again after a little while, indicating the three piece orchestra sawing away behind a potted palm.

'Mm. At least it masks the sounds of people eating.' He dabbed his mouth with his napkin. 'Have you finished your coffee, my dear?'

'Yes, thank you, Jay.'

'Then would you like to take a turn along the front, or would you rather go to your. . . our room?'

Charlotte hesitated. She was very tired and she didn't fancy going for a walk along the front, where it was dark and there was a strong wind blowing. At the same time she was reluctant to say she wanted to go to their room in case it was not the right thing to say. She had a feeling that there might be some etiquette attached to the situation but she didn't know what it might be. She smiled at him. 'I really don't mind, dear,' she said weakly.

'Then I suggest you go upstairs while I take a stroll and smoke a cigar,' he said, obviously relieved.

'Yes, that's a very good idea.'

Charlotte went up to the room they had been allotted. Her case had already been unpacked and the long frilly nightgown lay on the bed. She undressed and brushed her hair, coiling it into a long plait that lay over one shoulder. Then she climbed between the crisp, white sheets and waited for her new husband, with a mixture of apprehension and excitement. She had never shared her bed with anyone before and she wondered if she would be able to sleep with anyone lying beside her. That Jay might want to do anything more than lie beside her had never entered her head.

It was half an hour before he came into the room and she could hear him quietly going about his toilet in the darkness – he made no attempt to re-light the lamp – before climbing into bed.

She felt for his hand and squeezed it. 'Goodnight, dear,' she whispered, and turned her face for his kiss.

She was quite unprepared for what followed. This was not the Jay she knew, this panting, frenzied creature, rolling on her, squashing her, invading her most secret parts and making her cry out in pain. She was frightened, horrified and humiliated and when he had done and rolled away she lay staring up into the darkness, too frightened to move in case the whole terrifying business should begin again. She could only think he must have taken leave of his senses. He wasn't drunk, she would have smelled it as he breathed all over her.

At last she could tell by his regular breathing that he had fallen asleep and she crawled carefully out of bed to wash her bruised flesh and change the pretty nightgown that was now ruined. Then she climbed gingerly back beside him and eventually fell asleep.

When she woke he had gone, so she dressed and went down to breakfast. He was there, waiting for her. 'Ah, my dear,' he said with a smile as he got up and held back her chair for her, 'I trust you slept well.'

'Yes, thank you, Jay.' She kept her eyes down, waiting for him to apologise for his behaviour, but he talked easily about the weather, the impending General Election and the trouble that seemed to be brewing in India, if the scaremongers were to be believed, and never even mentioned it.

They had a very pleasant day, taking a blustery walk along the sea front and laughing as she nearly lost her hat; visiting the docks to watch the fishing boats return with their catch of silvery fish and taking tea in a quaint little tea shop that overlooked the sea. Jay was amusing and thoughtful and Charlotte felt she was more in love with him than ever. What had come over him the previous night she couldn't imagine, but she forgave him in her heart and prayed that it would never happen again.

But it did. Every night in the darkness, with never a word spoken between them. And never once did Jay refer to it in the morning as he gave her a chaste kiss and asked her if she had slept well. It was as if it had never happened, was something he was quite unaware of. Charlotte was puzzled and hurt, but she became used to it and once she knew what to expect it was no longer so painful. She wondered if other wives were ever subjected to this treatment and even whether this was what her mother had meant by her instruction to be obedient to her husband. But she dismissed this, she was sure her father would never treat her mother in such a cruel way. There was nobody she could ask, so she enjoyed the days and endured the nights of her honeymoon and returned to her new home outwardly as radiant as a new bride should be.

Laura told no one except Dot about her impending drive with Alex. She had grown to love the Taylor family and she was afraid that if they knew she was being taken out by the son of their employer it would ruin the good relationship she had with them. Because in spite of her obvious superior breeding Laura had learned to fit in very well with the way they lived. Indeed, as far as behaviour was concerned there was little adjustment needed because Fred saw to it that his children's manners were impeccable. The only thing Laura found difficult was the lack of space and privacy in the little cottage, and this she learned to adjust to, grateful to have found such a good family to shelter her. But the Taylors were very conscious that they were working class and poor; inferior to their 'betters'. Laura could easily have disillusioned them on that score, but she held her tongue. The past was over and done with.

As Sunday drew near she realised that she had been foolish to agree to meet Alex. For one thing, she had no clothes but the dress she wore every day – her wages hadn't yet run to a warm cloak, let alone a second dress – and this was already showing signs of wear. And nothing but trouble could come of it if the meeting was discovered. It was unheard of for a factory girl to consort with an employer, unless it was for the employer's pleasure. Laura was certain that this was not behind Alex's invitation although Dot had immediately jumped to that conclusion and warned her accordingly.

Laura was right. Alex behaved in a perfectly gentlemanly manner. It had been a stroke of genius on his part to suggest meeting outside the factory, because on a Sunday, their only respite from work, not one of the work force would be seen near the place so it was quite deserted. She climbed up into the chaise beside him and they drove out into the country towards Mile End. It was a cold, bright afternoon and Laura tried not to shiver under her thin shawl. Alex said nothing, but offered her a warm rug when they were out of the town.

They talked of general things and Alex pointed out landmarks and places of interest as they trotted along. They passed one or two people out for a stroll and Alex tipped his hat and smiled as they went by. But he began to look increasingly worried.

'I suppose I should really have suggested that you brought

a friend with you,' he said with a frown as he drew the horse to a halt and they sat looking back towards the town. 'To tell you the truth I didn't give it a thought. But I wouldn't like to ruin your reputation.'

Laura laughed, a low, musical chuckle. 'What about your own? What are people going to think, seeing you out with one of your own factory girls?'

'You don't look in the least like a factory girl,' he said shortly. He was quiet for a few minutes, then he said, 'How did you come to be working there, Miss Chapman? It's quite obvious it's not the kind of life you're used to.'

She looked down at her hands, clasped together on the rug over her knees, and shook her head. 'No, you're quite right, it isn't.' And she told him of her parents' death in India and her subsequent return to England – carefully omitting any mention of Randolph Grey or the stillborn child – only to discover that her grandparents had died. 'But I was lucky enough to be found by Fred Taylor,' she concluded. 'He and his family are good people and they are happy for me to live with them. And when they knew I needed work Dot suggested I come to the silk factory.' She sighed. 'Now you know my story, Mr Beresford.'

'But surely. . . you don't intend to stay there, do you?' he asked.

'No, of course not.' She gave a tired shrug. 'But it's not easy, you know. I work long hours and when I've finished I'm too tired to do anything except eat my portion and go to bed. I've thought of looking to see if I have other relatives in Colchester but even if I had the energy I wouldn't know where to begin. I know there are no close relatives, my mother had no brothers or sisters. Anyway,' she added, 'what would be the use? Who would welcome a practically destitute long lost relative turning up on their doorstep?' she gave a wry smile as she spoke.

'Thank you for telling me your story, Miss Chapman,' Alex said quietly. 'I knew you were not like the other girls in the factory. I wish I could do something to help you, but I'm not sure what. . .'

'Oh, please don't worry about me,' Laura said. 'To tell you the truth I'm getting quite used to the work, although I hate the factory, I think it's a dreadful place, and I can't bear to see the children working such long hours. . .' she bit her lip. 'I'm sorry. I shouldn't say such things to you about your silk factory. . .'

'It's not my factory,' Alex said quickly. 'I don't own it. It belongs to my father and when he dies Jay will own it. I'm glad,' he added quietly. 'I wouldn't want it on my conscience.'

'But you look after the machinery,' Laura insisted.

'Yes, but only until I can start my own engineering business.' He gave a brief laugh. 'But goodness knows when that will be. I shan't get any help from my father, he thinks I should put all my efforts into the family business. He only had me trained at Mumford's Engineering Company so that the silk factory could benefit.'

'But is it what you wanted to do, yourself?'

'What? Train to be an engineer? Oh, yes. I've always been interested in working with my hands. I'm essentially a practical man, unlike Jay and Charles.' His mouth twisted. 'I am what you might call the black sheep of the family. In more ways than one,' he added, almost to himself.

'I see.' Laura gave an involuntary shiver as a gust of wind chilled through her shawl.

'You're cold. We must go back.' Alex turned the chaise and headed back towards the town. They travelled in silence for some way before he said, carefully not looking at her. 'I'd like to see you again, Miss Chapman. Would you risk your reputation by coming out for a drive with me on another occasion?'

'You know as well as I do that it would be madness,' she answered, her voice low. 'What would your family say if they knew?'

'They'd be horrified. . . but not surprised. Nothing that I do would surprise them.' There was a note in his voice that Laura couldn't quite fathom.

She gazed at the hedgerows as they passed. 'I think you ought to know that I intend to fight for better conditions in the factory,' she said. She spoke slowly, as if the idea had only just occurred to her, as indeed it had.

'I'll back you,' he said. 'I think it's high time something

49

was done to improve conditions there.'

She stared at him. 'Do you mean that?'

He nodded. 'I'll do what I can – which may not be much,' he admitted.

'Then I should enjoy coming for another drive with you very much,' she said quietly.

Chapter Five

It was Friday. Laura looked at the big clock on the wall at the end of the doubling room. She had been at work since half past six with only half an hour for breakfast and another half hour for dinner and her back felt as if it would break in two, her legs ached and her feet were swollen in their boots from the length of time she had been standing. She could see the other women and girls rubbing their backs and glancing at the clock, too, but there was still another hour to go before knocking off time. She should be used to working these long hours, she told herself ruefully, she had been at Beresford's Silk Mill for over eight months now.

Suddenly, there was a shuffling on the iron staircase outside the doubling room as the children were released from the winding rooms on the top floor. They didn't work as long as the rest of the work force, but the hours were still too long for eight and nine year olds. Laura understood Nellie Taylor's relief that young Arthur worked with his father. Fred would see to it that his son wasn't overworked. The fifty or so children left quietly, too tired even for chatter and dispersed across the yard. Laura could see them from where she stood. They were a pathetic bunch; a few of the older ones, relieved to be out in the open air, played a brief game of tag as they went but the younger ones were too grey with tiredness to play and a few had difficulty in walking at all.

'Get back to your work. You're not paid to stand and gaze out of the window.' The overlooker jabbed Laura in the back as she passed. Laura turned back to the ever spinning and whirring reels. She was reasonably competent at the work

51

now, although she would never be as quick and dexterous as Dot. But Dot didn't mind the work. Laura hated it. She hated being penned up in the noisy, stuffy atmosphere, standing for long hours with hardly a shift in her position. And as her fingers worked her mind often wandered . . .

Three times now she had been out in Mr Alex's chaise. They were shafts of light in her dull life, but she was fearful of what the other women in the factory would say if they knew. Some of them were decent, like Dot, others were too cowed and poverty-stricken to do more than work their shift and drag themselves home, but others were coarse and foul-mouthed and she could imagine their reaction if they were to find out that one of their number had been consorting with one of the bosses.

In saner moments she hoped Alex would never ask her out again and steeled herself to refuse him if he did, because the whole situation was fraught with danger on both sides. For if Alex's family were to find out what he was doing not only would he get into serious trouble but she would be dismissed immediately. Then what would she do? She had no other means of supporting herself. Yet, though she realised all this, in her heart she knew that if he were to ask her again she would go. It was such a relief to talk to someone other than factory workers, whose preoccupation with staying alive naturally dominated their thoughts, although it had to be said that to his credit Fred Taylor had somehow managed to learn a good deal of the affairs of the country in the brief time he spent away from his loom. But he was unusual.

She sighed, knowing full well that it was not only that. She liked being with Alex; he made her feel she was somebody special, somebody he was fond of. . . A thread broke and she made an effort to thrust such foolish thoughts away and give all her attention to repairing it.

The next morning being a Saturday work was not started until after breakfast. As the women came in there was an obvious air of unrest and a good deal of unusual movement between the rooms where they worked. Several knots of girls congregated together and Mrs Ripley, the overlooker, marched about, ineffectually telling them to get on with their work.

'What's all the fuss about?' Laura asked Dot, in the mixture of mime and mouthing language that they used to speak above the noise of the machinery.

Dot lifted her shoulders and her eyebrows at the same time to indicate her ignorance.

Laura craned her neck to see what was going on and received a sharp crack on the arm with the back of Mrs Ripley's hand. 'Get on with your work,' she said, giving her a push.

But nobody else was working. They were all standing about in groups, with their arms folded, some looking truculent, some twitching with anxiety. Laura left her work and went over to the nearest group, a little away from the whirl of the machinery. 'What's the matter?' she asked. 'Is there some kind of trouble?'

The women eyed her up and down. They didn't altogether trust her because she was 'different' and 'spoke funny'. And there was even a rumour that she had been seen out in Mr Alex's chaise, although this was so unlikely that nobody really believed it and anyway there was no one who knew exactly who it was who had seen her. One of the women shrugged. 'Don't you know?' she asked truculently. 'Can't you count?' She turned her back on Laura.

'I don't know what you're talking about, but I would if you were to tell me,' Laura's voice was sharp.

Dot came up and tugged her sleeve. 'I shouldn't bother yerself too much,' she said, trying to draw Laura away. 'There's always somethin' wrong with this lot.'

'But if they've got a grievance...' Laura protested, shaking off Dot's hand.

'Oh, we got a grievance, all right,' a small, black-eyed woman muttered. 'How long is it since we bin promised a extra sixpence a week because o' the way prices've gone up? A month? Six weeks? An' hev we got it?'

'No, we bloody well hevn't, a tall woman with straggly grey hair came up beside Laura, arms akimbo, and looked over at her. 'Didn't you count your own money? Or hev you got so much you don't need to?'

'I got the same as I always do. The same as you.' Laura realised that with four shillings a week to spend largely on

53

her own needs she was well off compared with most of these women, although by the time she had paid her rent and helped with the food bill she needed every other penny she earned to keep herself clean and decently clothed.

Laura frowned and pinched her lip. She remembered a rumour circulating some weeks ago that there was to be an increase in wages but as she recalled no date had been agreed. 'When was this increase supposed to be paid?' she asked.

'Oh, they never said! They never do, do they!' a young, coarse-featured, heavily pregnant girl said, her voice heavy with sarcasm. 'They make promises to keep us quiet, then they forget about 'em. Thass always the same.'

'Then perhaps we should ask them,' Laura said reasonably.

There was silence as the rest of the women stared at her. Then the grey-haired woman stepped forward and jabbed her in the chest. 'Goo on then. You goo an' ask 'em. Ask the bosses where our extra sixpence a week is what they promised us. Ha!' she turned away. 'You 'on't do that, will you? Wiv all your fancy talk you ain't no different to the rest of us.'

Laura took a deep breath. 'All right. I will. I will go and speak to the bosses,' she said. 'Would any of you like to come with me?' She looked round at the group of women, which had grown as she had been speaking. They were all muttering that it would be a good thing to do but none of them would meet her eye and offer to go with her. She nodded. 'Very well, I'll go alone.' She turned round and left the group.

'Am I respectable?' she whispered to Dot. 'Is my hair tidy?'

Dot patted her hair to neaten it and twitched her skirt straight. 'I don't know what good you think you'll do,' she said as she surveyed Laura's appearance. 'Nobody's ever done anything like this afore.' She stood back. 'There. You'll do. And good luck. I reckon you'll need it.'

'Thanks, Dot.' Looking far more confident than she felt, Laura marched out of the room, down the stairs, and across the yard to the low building that housed the warehouse where the raw silk was kept, with the office at the far end. She was

54

aware of all the eyes watching her from the windows above and she kept her back straight although her knees felt almost too weak to support her. This was the first time she had been through the iron door that led to the warehouse and she found herself now in a long corridor with a door at the end. The door was large and had OFFICE painted on it in large gold letters. Taking her courage in both hands, she knocked.

Old Javis didn't usually come into the office on a Saturday; it was his day for playing golf, but he had called in to collect some papers that he wanted to study at home, where he could look at them quietly, without Jay constantly explaining everything to him as if he were an imbecile. Jay, of course, was at his desk as usual. Old Javis couldn't understand it; with a pretty little wife like Charlotte he had expected his eldest son to be late on many a morning since his marriage – and secretly would have applauded him for it, being a red-blooded man himself. But if anything Jay arrived at work even earlier these days.

'Where are those specifications for power looms? I want to have another look at them,' he said, sitting down and rifling through the papers on his desk. 'Not that I think we should have anything to do with them. It would mean extra buildings to house them, for a start, and we do well enough with the home workers.'

'I don't agree,' Jay said. 'I think it would be better to have the weavers working here, where we can keep an eye on them. And we've got plenty of space for extra buildings. Not that we would need to build. We could always convert. . .' At the knock on the door he stopped speaking and turned.

Old Javis looked up. 'Come in,' he called.

The woman who entered was tall and slim, with dark hair and eyes that were such a deep blue that they were almost violet. She held herself with a bearing that was almost regal, in spite of her shabby clothes. Jay frowned. He'd seen her before somewhere but he couldn't remember where. Old Javis looked equally puzzled but for a different reason. He was not used to women invading his domain.

'Good morning,' he said briskly. 'And what can I do for you, madam?'

55

Laura inclined her head graciously. 'Good morning,' she said. 'I would like to speak to you on behalf of the girls in the doubling and throwing rooms.'

'Oh, would you, indeed.' Old Javis frowned. 'I beg your pardon, madam, but I can't see what it's got to do with you. What goes on in my factory is my business and nobody elses.'

'What goes on in the doubling room has everything to do with me. I work with those girls,' Laura said quietly.

'Work with them!' The words came almost involuntarily from Old Javis, who could not hide his surprise.

Laura nodded. 'Yes. And I have come to represent them. They are dissatisfied because we were promised sixpence a week extra some five weeks ago and nobody has received so much as a farthing up to now. Can you tell me when the money is to be forthcoming, please?' Laura looked from Old Javis to Jay as she spoke. Her calm composure gave no hint of the turmoil of fear and apprehension going on inside her.

Jay scowled. He remembered now where he had seen her before. She had been the girl who had snatched that stupid woman from the machinery when her skirt got caught. It had taken a full hour to get the machine going again afterwards. Jay didn't like her, she was too intelligent by half. The sooner she was got rid of the better. He drew himself up to his full height. 'The women will get the extra money when they earn it. And standing about complaining instead of getting on with the work is no way to merit it. They were told that they would be paid extra if production was speeded up. So far I have seen no evidence of any attempt in this direction.' He stared down his nose at Laura, knowing that this was usually sufficient to cow even the bravest spirit.

She stared back at him. 'The money was promised because the price of food has risen, nothing was said about speeding up production,' she said levelly. 'Women can't work if they are hungry. And there is no woman there who will starve her children to feed herself. If you don't pay them they can't work, let alone produce more. That is a totally unreasonable argument.'

'Madam! You forget yourself!' Jay snapped. 'Remember who you are talking to.'

She inclined her head politely. 'I didn't mean to give offence, merely to explain matters as they stand,' she said quietly.

'And I will explain matters to you as they stand,' Jay's voice was cold. 'When production goes up the extra sixpence a week will be paid. Money doesn't grow on trees, you know. This factory isn't a benevolent society.'

'Indeed it isn't.' Laura lifted her chin. 'But no doubt you appreciate that if food prices rise your workers can buy even less to eat, and if they eat less they cannot possibly work harder and produce more. Some of them are already living at starvation level.'

'Then they should spend less at the gin shop,' Jay said unsympathetically.

Laura turned a look on him that was pure contempt. Then she inclined her head once more. 'Thank you both for giving me your time,' she said, her voice expressionless. 'I will go and tell my fellow workers what you have said.' She went out and closed the door quietly behind her.

'Hmph. She's got a bit o' spirit, that one. Don't you think you were a bit hard on her, my boy?' Old Javis said, helping himself to tobacco from the jar.

'No, I don't. I think she's a trouble-maker and the sooner we get rid of her the better,' Jay replied, his voice like steel.

'Oh, I don't know. I like a woman who's got a bit o' spirit. She's a cut above the rest, there's no doubt about that. I'd be interested to know her background.'

'You're too easy going, sir. That woman's nothing but trouble in this place and the sooner she's gone the better I shall like it.' Jay had picked up a pen and as he spoke it snapped in two between his hands.

'And you meet trouble before there is any. Now, help me to find these specifications or I shan't get my game of golf in today.' Old Javis leaned back in his chair to get his pipe drawing nicely while Jay went through the papers on the desk.

'Here they are,' Jay thrust them bad-temperedly at his father as the door burst open and Charles came in.

'I say,' he said, his eyes bright with mischief, 'Who was that I just bumped into in the passage? She was stalking along as if all the devils in hell were after her. Had somebody upset her?'

'You could say that,' Jay said dryly.

'Who is she? Where does she come from?'

'I believe she works in the doubling room.'

'She works *here*!'

'So she says.'

'Rather a cut above the usual riff raff wouldn't you say?' Charles grinned and looked from his brother to his father and back.

Old Javis re-lit his pipe. 'She certainly has plenty of spirit,' he remarked.

'You keep saying that, Father,' Jay said impatiently. 'Is it all you can think of? Her spirit could cause us a great deal of aggravation, remember. I think we should get rid of her.'

Old Javis shook his head. 'Not without good reason. You'd only be storing up more trouble for yourself.'

'You still haven't told me who she is,' Charles reminded them.

Jay and Old Javis looked at each other. 'Hanged if I know,' Old Javis said. 'We didn't think to ask her what her name was.'

'She works in the doubling room. Do we need to know more than that?'Jay asked.

'Not necessarily,' Charles said with a grin. 'But take that supercilious expression off your face Jay. I'm not too proud to make it my business to find out, even if you are.' He stroked his chin thoughtfully. 'She works in the doubling room, did you say?'

The factory girls were remarkably phlegmatic over Laura's failure to obtain the promised extra sixpence a week. 'We knew that wouldn't do any good,' they said with a shrug. 'They 'on't pay it till they think they will.'

They all resumed work and Mrs Ripley walked among them, relieved to have regained control and determined not to let it slip from her grasp again.

Laura was furious. Furious with Jay Beresford for being so callous; furious with herself for her inability to do more; and furious with the girls for their apathy and resignation. The situation worried her but she realised there was nothing more she could do at present. Many times since she had come to work at the silk factory she had longed for escape and thought of trying to find work elsewhere, but two things had prevented her. One was the fact that employers were chary of taking on girls who had come from the silk factory. They had a bad name in the town. For a girl to admit having come from the silk factory was to have the door shut in her face. No shopkeeper would employ her for fear of being robbed and no self-respecting lady would employ her as a maid for fear of having her husband or sons corrupted. And the fact that a good many, like the Taylors, were decent, hard-working people, cut no ice. Any girl from Beresford's was deemed to be 'no better than she should be' and stood no chance of bettering herself.

The second reason Laura was reluctant to leave the factory was Alex, because there was always the chance that she might catch a glimpse of him as he crossed the yard or came to look at a faulty machine. Reason told her that there was no future in her infatuation – she tried desperately to convince herself that it was nothing more that this. Alex had taken her out in his chaise several times because he found her pleasant company. There was no more to it than that as far as he was concerned. How could there be, in all conscience?

So, although she loathed the work and the surroundings in which she worked, she realised that she was trapped, with nowhere else to go.

And now there was an added thought. She remembered the day of Jay's wedding and how, while she was sitting in St James' Church afterwards, the thought had come to her that she had been sent to Colchester for a purpose. It dawned on her now that perhaps that purpose was to improve conditions at the factory. It was obvious that if she didn't do something nobody else would. The thought gave her no pleasure.

Fred and his brood had returned from church. Laura never accompanied them, Fred had never invited her to and she wasn't sure that she would have gone if he had. As it was, every Sunday she stayed behind and washed her clothes and helped Nellie to clean the house. But this particular Sunday there had been no house cleaning because Fred had an expensive piece of patterned silk nearly ready to come off the loom and the slightest hint of dust or dirt could spoil it.

'He hope he'll get it off the loom this afternoon,' Nellie said. 'As you know he don't usually work of a Sunday but this is special.' She sighed. 'An' once he get it off he'll hev to start puttin' the new pattern on for the next job. That can take a time, too. Once that took him three weeks, an' the Beresfords don't take that into consideration when they pay 'im. He on'y get paid for the material he produce – never mind how long that take 'im to set the job up. That don't seem right to me,' she shrugged. 'But there it is, nothin' much we can do about it, is there?' and she smiled at Laura, the smile transforming her pinched, bird-like face.

Laura wrung out the last of her washing and removed the bucket from the table. She had watched the material grow on the loom; it was an intricate pattern of reds, pinks and mauves on a blue background, and she knew how many weeks Fred had spent hunched over his loom to produce it. Once it was off there would be a furious spring cleaning of the little cottage as he prepared the loom for the next piece of work. Upstairs Ebbie coughed and grew thinner and paler, despite the expensive medicine that the family deprived themselves to buy. Laura had taught him to read – he was a quick and apt pupil – and had bought him a book of stories about far-off lands. This had opened up worlds to him that were beyond his wildest imagining. She consoled herself that if her coming to Colchester had done nothing else it had brightened fifteen-year-old Ebbie's poor life.

After they had eaten their midday meal, the main meal of the day on Sunday, Laura put on the flowered muslin she had recently bought from the pawn shop and which had needed very little darning and went out. She had bought a Dolly Varden hat to go with it and a pair of lace mittens. She knew the Taylor girls were envious, they sometimes bought clothes from the pawn shop, too, but they hadn't the eye for colour that Laura had and she didn't like to hurt their feelings by offering them advice. Nobody asked where she was going; the Taylors didn't consider it to be any business of theirs. They never forgot the fact that Laura was a 'lady' despite her present situation.

But Dot knew she was going to met Alex again and she had warned her to be careful. 'People are startin' to talk,' she whispered as Laura came down the stairs. 'You'd get set upon if the girls in the doublin' room was to find out what you was doin'.'

'I know, Dot,' Laura whispered back. 'I'm going to tell him this afternoon that I won't see him again.'

'It wouldn't be so bad if you met 'im after dark,' Dot said anxiously.

'That might be even worse,' Laura said with an impish smile.

She was excited. Alex had managed to have a word with her when she was taking a message to the room where the drawing frames were. 'It's been such a long time, Laura,' he'd said, as he pretended to read the note that wasn't even meant for him. 'I've missed talking to you. Meet me on Sunday and we'll go for a picnic.'

'People are beginning to talk,' Laura said quickly. 'I'll lose my job and you'll. . .'

'We'll meet down by the river, then. Do you mind walking that far? To the other side of East Mill?'

'No, I don't mind.'

'Three o'clock, then.' He handed her the note back. 'This is nothing to do with me, girl,' he said in a louder voice. 'It's for Mr Bannister, not Mr Beresford. Can't you read? No, I suppose not.' He winked and went on his way.

He was waiting for her and the hood of the chaise was up although it was a beautiful July afternoon. She got up beside him and they drove quite a long way out into the country until they reached a thickly wooded area with a cart track running through it. After a bumpy ride they came to a clearing, dappled with sunlight and hidden by a thicket. He helped her to alight, leaving the horse to graze gently.

He spread a rug and they sat down together. 'You know, this can't go on, Laura,' he said, as he opened the picnic basket. 'I can't keep meeting you in this hole-in-the-corner way.'

'No, of course not.' She felt as if there was a lump of lead in her throat. She had known that their meetings couldn't continue but now that it had come to it she couldn't bear to think of them ending. 'I realise that. I quite understand. I shouldn't have come today. It was stupid of me. A man in your position can't afford to be seen with a factory girl, I know that.' She spoke quickly, without looking up, her fingers busily pleating and unpleating her skirt. Suddenly, she felt very foolish, dressed in her flowered muslin and Dolly Varden hat. Trying in her second-hand finery to make herself into something that she used to be but wasn't any longer. She turned away, to hide the tears of humiliation.

He put his hand gently under her chin and turned her face to his. 'I don't think you quite understand what I'm saying, Laura,' he said. 'I'm not telling you I don't want to see you again, I'm saying we should come out into the open. I want you to come to my house and meet my mother and father. I want to be able to tell the world that you are the woman I'm going to marry.'

Her eyes met his and she noticed that they were a deep brown, flecked with gold and a hint of green. Although her heart leapt at the look in his eyes she managed to turn away.

'But you hardly know me. How can you say that?'

'Oh, Laura,' there was a hint of impatience in his voice, 'don't tell me you don't know. Don't tell me you haven't felt the same as I have. If I had known you all my life I couldn't be more sure that it's you I want to marry.' He gave her a tiny shake and said roughly, 'Don't play games with me, Laura. Answer my question.'

She still wouldn't look at him. 'You know it's not possible, Alex,' she said in a low voice, using his name for the first time. 'We're poles apart. I could bring nothing but unhappiness to both you and your family if you were to marry me. Not that they would agree, I'm sure.'

'My family!' he said, with what almost amounted to disgust. 'They'd probably be only too glad to be rid of me.' He turned her face to his again. 'But what about you? Would it bring unhappiness to you?'

She couldn't lie to him. She hesitated for a moment before saying, 'Yes, but only because I would know that I was the cause of your unhappiness.' She couldn't look away, he still held her face between his hands, and she knew that he was going to kiss her. Every bone in her body felt as if it was melting so she had no power to stop him. His kiss was very gentle at first, but as her lips parted under his he became more demanding and when at last he drew away he said, his voice deep, 'I love you, Laura, and I think you love me.'

The look in his eyes forbade any pretence. 'Yes,' she said quietly, 'I do.'

'Then will you marry me?'

She shook her head. 'How can I? It's impossible, Alex. You must know that as well as I.' She smiled at him, her eyes brimming with tears. 'For the moment it's enough for me to know that you love me.'

He caught her to him fiercely. 'Well, it isn't enough for me, Laura. I shan't rest until I've made you my wife.' He began to kiss her again.

She clung to him. 'Oh, Alex, if only you could.'

'I've got a little money,' he said, 'and I've always planned to have my own business one day.' His jaw set in a hard line. 'And it will be a success. If I have to work all day and all night it will be successful. I'm determined to show them. . .'

'Alex?' Laura drew a little away from him. She had never seen him like this before.

'What?' He looked down at her, almost without seeing her, then he laughed and gathered her to him again. 'I'm sorry. Sometimes I get a little carried away. But don't worry, Laura, somehow I shall find a way, so let's drink to that.'

She looked on doubtfully as he poured the wine he had brought into cups, but his enthusiasm was infectious and soon they were drinking to each other and giggling like children as they ate chicken legs with their fingers. They were happy but it was a happiness born of desperation because they both knew in their hearts that nothing but heartbreak could come of their love. Tomorrow they would see things differently; they would be sensible, but today in their new found happiness everything was possible. And as they delighted in each other's company they never even noticed the hoof beats as a lone rider passed by.

Chapter Six

Charles had made several excuses to visit the doubling room of late. This was nothing unusual, Mrs Ripley was used to seeing him around, and anyway he knew how to handle her. He only had to tell her that, By Jove, she was looking younger every time he saw her, and she would raise her eyebrows archly and say, 'Oh, reely, Mr Charles, you are a one,' with a silly little giggle. After that he could do as he liked and she would obligingly turn a blind eye.

He'd got it all worked out very well. He knew he only had to snap his fingers and most of the girls, the younger ones in particular, would be only too willing to jump to his bidding. He was careful, though, he made it his business to know which of them were little better than prostitutes and he avoided them. He wasn't anxious to find himself with a dose of the clap.

He soon picked out the dark-eyed beauty he had met in the corridor a couple of Saturdays ago. Although she did the same work and dressed in a grubby blue dress that was full of darns, she stood out from the rest like a poppy in a field of corn. And not simply because she was cleaner.

On closer inspection he saw that she wasn't exactly beautiful at all, especially with her black hair escaping and wisping all over the place. Her mouth, set in a thin, straight line as she worked was too wide for beauty and her nose, as she looked down it when he spoke to her, too long. But her slim, willowy figure and dark, almost violet eyes set his senses aflame and he knew he wouldn't be content until he had conquered her just as he conquered any other of the factory girls he fancied.

But Miss Laura Chapman, as he had discovered she was called, was not such easy meat. She responded to his overtures with cool politeness, wilfully misconstruing his invitations and misunderstanding his more blatant advances. He was not used to being frustrated and thwarted in this manner and he began to suspect that the other girls knew what was going on and were quietly laughing at him behind his back. He didn't like that and he spent an entire weekend working out how he could lure Miss Laura Chapman into one of the storerooms and what he would do with her when he got her there. He became so obsessed with the idea that he lost heavily at cards on Saturday night and had to go to his mother for another loan, which they both knew would never be repaid. All in all Miss Laura Chapman was occupying more of his thoughts than was good for either her or himself.

Nevertheless Charles was in a cheerful frame of mind when he wandered into the factory – late, as usual – on Monday morning. He had evolved a plan which was virtually foolproof. All he had to do was put it into action. And in this, for once, luck was on his side.

He met Laura on her way to the storeroom to fetch more reels. She kept her eyes down and tried to walk past him without speaking but he put out his hand and caught her arm. 'You're in a mighty hurry for a Monday morning, Miss Chapman,' he said, bringing her to a halt. 'Can't you even bid a fellow a civil good morning?'

Laura gave a slight bob. 'Good morning, Mr Beresford,' she said politely, still not looking at him, and would have continued on her way if he hadn't still held her arm. As it was she waited patiently for him to release her. When he made no attempt to do so she said, 'Please let me go. I have to fetch more reels. Mrs Ripley is waiting.'

'Let the Old Bat wait,' Charles said roughly. He had dreamed of what he would do to this girl so many times that now she was here, in front of him, and he could feast his eyes on her trim figure it was as much as he could do to keep his hands off her, here in the passage, even with the risk of people passing back and forth. 'No,' suddenly he changed his mind. 'Go and fetch your reels.' He dropped his hand from her arm.

Surprised at his sudden change of mood, she darted into the storeroom nearby to grab the reels from the bin just inside the door before he could change his mind and follow her.

But she was hardly inside the room when she realised he was right behind her. 'That's better,' he said, closing the door and leaning on it. 'Now we shan't be disturbed.'

Laura froze in the act of gathering up the reels. What a fool she'd been! She might have known he wouldn't give up so easily. She took a deep breath and turned to face him, her face white and set. 'Let me out,' she said quietly. 'Let me out or I shall scream the place down.'

He smiled. 'Much good that will do you. Didn't you know that when this factory was built the walls of the storerooms were made three bricks thick, with steel doors, because of the fire risk? You can scream as much as you like, no one will hear you.' He took a step towards her. 'Come now, Miss Chapman. All I'm asking is that you should be friendly. You know, I could pleasure you as much as I'm asking you to pleasure me.' He put his head on one side, his eyes narrowing. 'Perhaps even as much as you and my brother pleasured each other in Ratchet's Wood yesterday afternoon.' He smiled again at her horrified expression. 'Were you so wrapped up in each other that you thought no one saw you? Well, I did, Miss Chapman. And if you don't do as I ask I'll tell my father. And my brother. And my mother. They won't be pleased, you know.'

Laura stared at him. 'Alex and I... we did nothing... nothing that we should be ashamed of,' she said.

'That's what *you* say, Miss Chapman. What *I* say is, if you are nice to my brother, I feel entitled to expect you to be nice to me.' His voice became hard and he said through his teeth, 'You are a very desirable young woman.' In one movement he pulled her to him and thrust his hand down her bodice.

She twisted her head and bit his wrist hard, drawing blood, and as he yelped and tried to withdraw his hand in pain she twisted away from him, tearing the thin stuff of her blouse.

'You little...' he dived after her and managed to catch

66

hold of her skirt but she had already reached the door and she pulled it open, falling out into the passage, straight into the path of Alex himself.

Alex took one look at Laura, ashen and trembling, with her bloodstained skirt and the front of her blouse ripped out, and at Charles, dishevelled, with blood on his clothing, standing guiltily in the doorway.

'You filthy young swine,' he said through gritted teeth. 'You disgusting, despicable, filthy young swine.' And he brought his fist up and caught his young brother a stinging blow to the side of the jaw. Charles went down like a stone.

Laura watched, too shocked to move. She tried ineffectually to pull her tattered blouse into some semblance of decency and found that she was saying through teeth that chattered, 'It wasn't. . . I didn't. . . I couldn't help it. . .' and much else that didn't seem to make any sense.

Alex stepped over Charles and put his arm round her. 'It's all right, my darling. It's all over. There's nothing more to fear. I'll get one of the girls to take you home so that you can make yourself decent. Then I should stay there for the rest of the morning, if I were you. You've had a nasty–' he hesitated– 'experience.'

'I didn't. . . it wasn't my fault. . . I didn't want. . .' Laura began again, trying to explain what had happened, groping for words that wouldn't come. But Alex hardly listened, but stroked her hair and soothed her and told her not to talk about it any more. Before long Dot came and took her home. Laura was glad. She felt sick. Charles hadn't really harmed her but she felt defiled. For the second time in her life.

'I think you owe your brother an apology, Alex,' Old Javis was standing with his back to the empty fireplace in his study, facing Alex and Charles before they joined Eleanor that evening. This was a man's room, with dark leather armchairs and hunting prints round the walls. There was a rack of pipes by the marble fireplace, a box of cigars on the desk and a permanent faint odour of tobacco smoke overall. 'I suggest you get it over so that your mother knows nothing about it. From what I can understand it's not a fit subject for her ears.'

Alex lifted his chin. 'I knocked him down because of what

he did to one of the girls,' he said. 'I'm quite unrepentant. I'd have no hesitation in doing the same thing if I caught him again.'

Charles rubbed his chin, which was blue and still very sore. 'I can't see what all the fuss is about,' he said with an injured air. 'After all, I was only having a bit of sport, Father.'

'Well, it's not the kind of sport I find amusing. Shall we join Mama?' Alex turned to go.

'Not the kind of sport you find amusing?' Charles said with a sneer. 'You were finding it amusing enough in Ratchet's Wood on Sunday afternoon, weren't you?' And with the same young woman, too.'

Alex went white. 'Where were you?'

'Near enough to see what was going on, I can assure you,' Charles smirked.

'Then you must have seen that I was not behaving improperly in Ratchet's Wood,' Alex said. 'In fact, if you were that close you may have heard that I was asking the young lady to marry me.'

'Marry you!' Charles's jaw dropped. 'A girl from the factory! You must be stark, staring mad. But there,' he shrugged eloquently, 'I suppose it's no more than might be expected from. . .'

'Quiet, both of you.' Old Javis banged his fist down on the desk and looked from one to the other. Then he turned to Alex. 'Now, my boy, of course you can't be serious about wanting to marry a factory girl. I never heard such nonsense in all my life. Surely you can find yourself a decent girl to court.'

'It isn't nonsense. I fully intend to marry Miss Chapman,' Alex said firmly. 'And as for being what you call "a decent girl", she's more than that, she's every inch a lady. Oh, it's true that at the moment she works at the factory, but only because she has had a great deal of misfortune in her life. In fact, I had hoped to ask your permission to bring her home so that you could meet her and talk to her. I'm sure you would find her acceptable in every way if you knew her.'

'A factory girl! Here in my house! Never!' Eleanor's voice came from the doorway. 'I never heard such a preposterous idea.'

68

Old Javis spun round. 'My dear, this conversation was not for your ears,' he said reprovingly. 'You should have waited in the drawing room until we joined you.'

'If you didn't wish anyone to hear, Javis, you should have kept your voices down. Goodness knows what the servants must think. I could hear every word you were saying as I went past and I consider I have every right to speak my mind over who should enter my house. And I say again, *never* will I allow one of those. . . those *females* under my roof.'

'He not only wants to bring one under your roof, Mama, he wants to marry one,' Charles said laconically, examining his fingernails.

'Is this true, Alex?' Eleanor asked, turning a beady eye on her second son.

Alex bowed his head. 'Quite true, Mama, and as I was saying, if only you were to meet Miss Chapman. . .'

'Enough!' Eleanor raised her hand imperiously. 'You must be out of your senses to even suggest such a thing. We've lived down one scandal in the family, I will not tolerate the risk of another. You, above all people, should appreciate that, Alex.' She stared at him for a moment, then said, 'Now, we'll speak no more of the matter. Come, give me your arm in to dinner. I find this hot weather very tiring and bothersome, don't you? I think we'll take coffee on the terrace this evening.'

Old Javis followed with Charles. He hadn't wanted to involve Eleanor in this little hiccup yet he'd been glad when she intervened. The boys always took notice of their mother, she'd always had a firm hand with them. And she never minded grasping the nettle. He nodded to himself. A wonderful woman, Eleanor. He'd got a lot to thank her for.

Laura hadn't seen Alex for nearly a week. This was unusual because he often managed to make an excuse to come to the doubling room if he hadn't seen her in the passage or the yard for a day or two and she had a feeling that he was avoiding her. She couldn't blame him. It was her fault he had knocked his brother down and she had been too distraught to make him understand that Charles hadn't actually harmed her. Of course, it was the end of their friendship. She could imagine the scene with his father, with Charles the injured party and Alex being forbidden to ever see her again. She permitted herself a wry smile as she walked down the hill with Dot and Kate. It had been wonderful to be proposed to by Alex, something she would always remember and treasure, but she had known in her heart that nothing could ever come of it.

'What are you grinnin' to yourself for?' Dot asked, as they reached the factory gates at twenty-nine minutes past seven after their breakfast break.

Laura sighed. 'I was just thinking.'

'What about?' Kate asked.

'You mind your own business, Miss Nosey,' Dot gave her sister a playful cuff.

They went upstairs to the doubling room and Kate continued to the next floor, where she had been promoted to working on the drawing machines. The doubling room was seething with people and Mrs Ripley was trying ineffectually to get the girls back to work. 'What's all this?' Laura whispered to Dot.

Dot shook her head quickly and went over to a big woman with dirty blonde hair hanging in rat's tails round her face. 'What's up?' she asked.

The woman put her hands on her hips, her mouth set in a straight line. 'Aggie Cox from next door say Mrs Ripley's already started puttin' 'em on four reels instead o' three,' she said grimly.

'Well, we didn't complain about that when we did it before,' Dot said. 'Most people are glad of an extra shillin' in their wages.'

'Thass jest it. We ain't gonna be paid no extra for the extra reel,' the big blonde said. 'An' we ain't never had that extra sixpence a week what we was promised, neither.' She waited to see the impact of her words before adding, 'That ain't bloody right that we should be treated like bloody dirt.'

'No. We want our rights. We was promised a extra sixpence a week, not extra work wiv no pay,' a wiry little woman with a wizened face said.

'We're fed up bein' treated like bloody dirt,' another put in, parrot-fashion.

'Thass right. They put on us all ways round an' thass time

70

we put a stop to it.'

There was a general hubbub as the group grew bigger and the complaints grew louder. Mrs Ripley went from room to room trying to get the women back to work, but a few of the more vociferous ones were shouting to the others not to put up with being given the extra work with no extra pay. In the end the noise grew so loud that she rang the big hand bell. 'If you are not going to do any work, then you might as well go home,' she shouted. 'You won't get paid at all for standing about idle.'

For a moment nobody moved. Nobody had ever said anything like that to them before. They all looked at Laura to see if she was going to say anything to Mrs Ripley, remembering how she had stood up for them over the extra sixpence a week.

Laura took a deep breath; she hardly needed to raise her voice in the stunned silence that followed Mrs Ripley's words, 'I think we should do exactly that,' she said recklessly. 'There's a limit to how far we will allow ourselves to be exploited.' And with her head held high, she swept past Mrs Ripley and out of the room. It was a foolish thing to do, she realised that the minute she'd done it. To walk out of the factory was an unheard of thing. But there was no going back. As she went down the iron staircase and out into the yard she didn't dare to look behind to see if anyone else was following. Not that she expected them to. They wouldn't be so impetuous and foolish. But to her amazement, before she could reach the gates there was a clattering on the stairs and a great surge as the women all followed her example and walked out of the factory. By the time they were all out, there were about three hundred women in the yard and in the street beyond. Laura, crushed against the iron railings by the crowd, was almost fainting in the hot July sun, partly from the stench of unwashed bodies, but more from the fear of what she had begun.

Not all the women had wanted to come out on strike and this was plain from the fighting that was going on at the foot of the stairs as some tried to get back to work. But the more militant prevented them and looked to Laura to see what they should do next.

71

A barrel was pushed over and Laura was hauled up on to it. Three hundred pairs of eyes, some hostile, some expectant, some fearful, watched her. She swallowed and nervously pushed her hair back from her face.

'It's time we made a stand,' she said, raising her voice so that she could be heard all over the yard. 'While we allow ourselves to be expl. . .' she searched for a word that they would understand more readily, '. . .put upon by our masters, things will never get any better. If we are required to work an extra reel then we must be paid for it. We've never received the extra sixpence a week we were promised so it's quite unreasonable to expect us to do even more work for no extra money. A labourer is worthy of his – or her – hire. Don't you all agree?' She looked round at the upturned faces and hoped they could not see her knees shaking under her skirt.

There was a roar of agreement. 'But who's gonna tell Ole Ma Ripley that?' a voice shouted from the back.

'An' who's gonna wring the money outa Ole Skinflint Beresford? Thass like gittin' blood outa a stone, gittin' a farthin' outa him, let alone a shillun',' another yelled.

''Ere 'e is. 'Ere's the Ole Man,' someone cried. ''E's jest comin' down the road.'

As Mr Beresford's trap appeared there was a roar from the crowd and the women nearest to it shouted and waved their fists. 'We want our rights,' they roared. 'We 'on't be put on any longer.'

Old Javis stared in horror at the crowd of yelling women. 'What's going on? What's all this?' he shouted in bewilderment, trying to control his horse as it shied away from the commotion.

'Tell 'im. Tell 'im what you told us,' the women shouted to Laura and tried to push her forward. But the crush was too great for her to get through and before long someone began to throw stones at the bewildered man's trap. 'Send for the police!' he shouted, waving his arms. 'Send for the police to quell this rabble.'

Some of the men from the blacksmith's forge and from the engine room had come to see what all the fuss was about, although a good many kept their backs turned. They didn't want to be seen to be in any way involved with this unprecedented event. But one man ran to hold Old Javis's horse and guide it to stables at the rear of the building while another ran for the police. The women had by this time made a path for Laura to reach Old Javis but he waved her aside. 'I'll hear nothing till my son is present and these women are back at work,' he shouted. 'How can I listen to what anybody has to say with all this shouting and screaming going on? Behaving like a lot of fish wives, the lot of them. Go on, get back to work!' And he lashed out with his whip, holding the crowd at bay, while his trap was led away.

'Now what's going to happen?' Dot whispered to Laura. 'They're all looking to you to see what they should do. Some of 'em want to go back to work. Look, the others are havin' a job to hold them.'

'I'm going to the Moot Hall to see the magistrate,' Laura said in a clear voice. 'I shall put our case to him. Who's coming with me? You will, won't you, Dot?'

'Yes, I 'spec' so. I wouldn't like you to go alone,' Dot said reluctantly.

'An' I'll come,' a voice from the back said.

'So will I,' another called.

'You ain't goin' wivout me,' someone else tried to push her way to the front.

By the time Laura and Dot reached the Moot Hall, hurrying through the back streets to reach it, the crowd straggling behind them totalled some hundred angry and anxious women.

Only Laura and Dot were allowed in, the rest had to wait outside. The two girls were taken up the stairs to a large room furnished in heavy, dark mahogany and lined with books. It reminded Laura nostalgically of her old headmistress's study at school, but Dot was completely overawed, she had never seen a room like it in her whole life. They were left there to wait for nearly two hours before the magistrate put in an appearance and they could hear the crowd outside growing restive and then quietening again as they were threatened with police action if they didn't behave.

The magistrate was a large, florid man with grey dundreary whiskers which he constantly pulled when he was worried or perplexed. He bustled in with his best officious air and settled himself in the chair behind the big desk. He looked the girls up and down. He couldn't imagine what they'd come for but whatever it was he'd soon settle their hash with a few well-chosen words. It wouldn't take much to intimidate them; no doubt they were already frightened half to death. 'Well,' he said gruffly, pulling his whiskers. 'What do you want?'

'We have come to see you because the conditions at the silk factory where we are employed have become intolerable, sir,' Laura said in her usual well-modulated voice. 'Not only is the machinery unfenced – even on the top floor where the children work – but we are forced to work long hours in order to earn enough to live on. We were promised an extra sixpence a week, but we have never received it. And now, we have been put on to working four reels instead of three – and for no extra money.'

'Usually, if we hev to work four reels we're paid an extra shillin' a week,' Dot said, then blushed scarlet at her own temerity.

The magistrate closed his jaw, which had dropped in amazement at the sound of Laura's voice. He had never expected such a reasoned, clear complaint from a factory girl and he wasn't quite sure how to deal with it. He tugged at his whiskers, saying nothing for a few minutes. Then he got up from his chair and went to the door. 'Send to the silk mill for Mr Beresford,' he said. 'I need to hear both sides of this argument before I can make a judgement.' He turned back to Laura and Dot. 'I'll speak to you again when your employer arrives,' he said, and left them.

Laura closed her eyes. 'Just pray that it's Old Mr Javis and not Mr Jay who comes, Dot,' she said fervently as they settled to wait.

Chapter Seven

They waited a full half hour and when the magistrate returned Laura realised that their prayers had not been answered because by his side was the tall, aristocratic-looking figure of Mr Jay. Laura's heart sank. If only Old Javis had come he might have shown at least a modicum of humanity. Jay, she was convinced, was made entirely of flint.

'Well?' Jay said as he entered, turning cold eyes on both girls. Then he recognised Laura. 'Oh, I might have realised it would be you,' he said rudely. He turned to the magistrate. 'This girl is nothing but a trouble-maker, I've had dealings with her before,' he said, with more than a hint of impatience. He gave a long-suffering sigh and sat down. 'But now I'm here I suppose I might as well hear what she's got to say. No one can say I'm not a reasonable man.' He crossed his legs and flicked an imaginary speck of dirt from his trouser-leg.

Laura felt Dot grope for her hand and she squeezed it reassuringly even though her own confidence was at a low ebb.

'These er. . . girls say they've come to represent the women at your silk mill, Mr Beresford,' the magistrate said. 'It appears they consider that they are not being treated fairly.'

'Indeed? In what way?' Jay asked coolly.

'In the manner of not being paid the extra sixpence they were promised, for one thing,' the magistrate said, pulling his whiskers as he consulted his notes, 'and in the manner of being put on four reels, whatever that might mean, instead of three, for no extra money.'

'We're usually paid an extra shillin' a week if we work four reels,' Dot blurted out, again blushing scarlet at the sound of her own voice.

Laura nodded. 'And that's as it should be,' she said, 'because the extra reel increases each girl's work-load by almost a quarter. It means twenty-four per cent more threads to watch and manage. . .'

'What these girls don't seem to appreciate is that the silk trade is in a depressed state at the moment,' Jay interrupted tetchily. He shrugged. 'Anyway, it's no hardship to them to work four reels. It will at least give them something to do and prevent them from falling asleep at their work.'

'If they fall asleep – and it's only ever happened once since I've been there – it's because they are wearied by working such long hours,' Laura pointed out.

'They don't have to work overtime if they don't want to,' Jay replied. 'They are given the option.'

'It's scant option when they don't get enough to live on if they don't work overtime,' Laura said hotly. 'Remember, we've never even been paid the extra sixpence a week we were promised months ago.'

Jay stood up. 'I am not here to justify the way my factory is run,' he said. 'If a deputation had come to me in the first place the matter could have been sorted out satisfactorily without all this fuss and pother.' He stared coldly at the two girls. 'You realise, I hope, that if I were to press matters you could both end up in prison for creating such a disturbance. . .'

At these words Dot sank to the floor in a dead faint and it took several minutes to revive her with burnt feathers, but Laura stood her ground and met Jay's cold gaze without flinching as he went on, 'My inclination is to pay you for the work you have done this week and discharge you for creating a nuisance. As for the rest of them, I don't care if they don't return to work at all; I kept them on throughout the winter more from a sense of duty than of profit to myself. If it were not for my father I would be inclined to close the factory down; it's more of a liability than an asset at the moment. And if we are going to be subjected to such upset and hooliganism as we've seen today I should think the sooner this happens the better. I bid you all good day.' He turned towards the door.

'Just one moment, Mr Beresford,' the magistrate laid a hand on his arm. 'I don't think we should be quite so hasty.' He turned to Laura and Dot, who had now been brought a stool and was sitting, ashen-faced, on it. 'Now, you girls must realise that you acted very foolishly in creating a disturbance before you ever went to Mr Beresford...'

'I did try to speak to Mr Javis,' Laura insisted.

'Nevertheless, you should never have left your work and incited the other girls to do the same. You do understand that, don't you?' He was looking at Laura and she realised that he was not totally unsympathetic to their cause.

She nodded. 'Yes, I do, but there was no other way to bring the plight of the girls to anybody's attention,' she said. 'Mrs Ripley, the overseer, wasn't interested. She simply said if we weren't going to get on with our work we'd better go home.' She bit her lip. 'I realised as soon as I'd done it that it wasn't very sensible to walk out like that, and in truth I never expected them all to follow me. But when they did – well,' she spread her hands, 'what could I do but come to you... sir?' she added, almost too late.

He cleared his throat and tugged at his whiskers, unnerved by the clear gaze of those violet eyes. 'Yes, well, you did the right thing. Acted very responsibly, in the event,' he conceded gruffly. He shuffled his papers. 'Now,' he said more briskly, 'I recommend that you should all return to work on three reels for the rest of this week and see if you can come to some understanding with your employers, without resorting to such drastic measures again. Are you willing to do this?'

Dot nodded eagerly, anxious to get out; Laura with less certainty.

'I'm sure you will have no trouble in finding a spokes-woman to put your case,' he added dryly. 'Are you amenable to that, Mr Beresford?'

Jay sniffed. 'I shall have to consult my father before I can come to any definite decision. But providing the girls all return to work and make no further trouble...'

'I'm sure they'll do that,' the magistrate said smoothly. He turned to Laura. 'I think you should make it clear to your fellow workers that this kind of behaviour will not be tolerated. Next time anything like this happens there could be serious consequences. But I'm sure your employers will be receptive to any suggestions for improvements that you may make.'

'Ha! That's what he thinks,' Dot said under her breath as she and Laura emerged once more into the sunshine. 'I can't see Ole Skinflint bein' receptive to anything except more work for less money.'

'We'd better tell the others,' Laura said unhappily.

The girls, waiting eagerly for the outcome of the discussion, were disappointed but resigned when told they were to go back to work.

'We din't think it'd work,' one said.

'Naw! What more could you expect,' said another, shrugging her thin shoulders. 'The bosses 've got us under their thumb.'

'All is not lost,' Laura said, trying to offer a crumb of encouragement. 'At least we only have to go back to work three reels, not four. And somebody has to go and talk to Mr Beresford and Mr Jay. . .'

'That'll be you,' somebody from the back of the crowd said. 'You got us into this, you'll hev to get us out of it.'

Laura nodded. 'I was afraid they'd say that,' she said quietly to Dot. 'And I suppose it's only fair.' She raised her voice. 'Come on, then. We'd better get back to work. One of you go and find the others and tell them what's happened.'

The dejected little crowd made their way back to the silk mill and half an hour later Laura found herself once again outside the door marked OFFICE.

Old Javis and his son were sitting at opposite ends of the big partners desk that Jay had recently acquired. Old Javis didn't much care for the new desk, in a subtle, yet definite way it undermined his authority. While he had sat behind his old flat-topped desk and Jay made do with a large table in the corner he had felt that he was still in control; the master; the man without whom no decisions could be taken. Now, with the acquisition from his father-in-law of this great cumbersome article that was not quite old enough to have any value as an antique, Jay had managed to somehow put himself on an equal footing. Yet there was no reasonable argument against the new desk. It made more room in the office, gave more drawer space and was altogether an improvement. But Old Javis felt, and not without some justification, that in putting himself on an equal footing Jay was one step nearer to taking over completely. And Old Javis was not yet ready for that.

He looked up. 'And is that all that happened at the Moot Hall?' he asked, having listened to Jay's account of his summons there. Old Javis knew he should have gone himself, but in truth he had still been shaken from the incident outside the factory, when all those women had surged round him, frightening the horse – and him, too. He hadn't realised there were so many women employed at the mill, although heaven knew, the wage bill was high enough every week. In any event, he had been greatly relieved when Jay offered to go and see the magistrate in his stead.

'Yes, except that the women will be sending someone to us to plead their case.' Jay shrugged and began to leaf through some papers in front of him. 'I had to agree to that, but it's merely a formality. I don't foresee any problem.'

Old Javis steepled his fingers. 'I wonder who they'll send.'

'We shall know directly,' Jay said, as there was a knock at the door.

They both looked expectantly as it opened in answer to Jay's terse, 'Enter.'

Old Javis recognised the woman as soon as she walked in. It was the one who had come to do battle over the extra sixpence a week that had never been paid. He hadn't agreed with Jay over that, but Jay had insisted that they couldn't afford to pay it. He wondered how his son would handle this dispute.

'Your name?' Jay asked, looking down his nose at her.

'Chapman. Laura Chapman.' She held her head high and didn't seem in the least intimidated. Old Javis remembered thinking the last time that she had spirit. He liked a woman with spirit. Good-looking, too, in striking sort of way. Not beautiful, not pretty-pretty, like young Charlotte, but definitely good-looking.

'Well, Miss Chapman. . .' Old Javis heard the sneer in Jay's voice as he said the words and suddenly it came to him that Alex had talked about a Miss Chapman. . . had wanted to bring her to the house. . . had even spoken about marrying her. Good heavens, this must be the gel! He puffed his cheeks. Well, of course, he could see what the attraction was, but it was out of the question. Quite out of the question. He'd be the laughing stock of the Conservative Club if he were to allow the boy to marry a factory girl. Heaven knew he'd caused enough trouble in his time as it was. He dragged his mind back to the matter in hand – in Jay's hand, as it were.

'. . . nothing but trouble and discontent among the women ever since you came here to work.' There was a tell-tale white line each side of Jay's nose which indicated that his temper was becoming short. 'You seem to have lost sight of the fact that this silk factory is lit by gas. Nobody has to work by candle-light here, like they do in other factories, with each girl issued with her own candle which she has to hold into the machine in order to see to join the broken threads. In fact, I'll have you know that this was the first factory in the town to have gas lighting.' Jay could never resist that boast. 'It was very expensive.' he added loftily.

The girl inclined her head. 'That is all very commendable and not in dispute,' she said evenly. 'But it hardly makes up for the fact that the women who work for you are not treated fairly. They should be paid a fair day's wage for a fair day's work. You know very well that in putting them on four reels instead of three you are increasing their work load by a quarter. You cannot expect them to do that if you don't pay them for it.' She paused. Old Javis looked from her to Jay and back again. The boy had met his match here, and no mistake. He admired her for standing her ground. 'And the children,' she went on, 'they are being exploited. . .'

'Enough, woman,' Jay rose to his feet. Since his marriage he had put on weight, which with his height made him an imposing figure and a less courageous girl would have been immediately cowed. But not this one, Old Javis noted with satisfaction only slightly tinged with guilt at his disloyalty.

She drew herself up to her full height and repeated, '. . .they are being exploited, too. They are made to work for too long and for too little money. And there is no provision for schooling, either. Their parents are too poor to complain and you, sir, are too mercenary to do anything about it. I think it is quite disgraceful.'

'Get out!' Jay spoke through gritted teeth, banging his fist on the desk, his knuckles white. 'Get out before I throw you out. I have never been spoken to like this in my whole life. How dare you come here and criticise the manner in which I conduct my affairs! You can collect whatever money is due to you and leave, madam. You have made trouble here once too often. I don't wish to see you at this factory ever again.' He left his desk and strode to the door, flinging it open.

She lifted her chin and looked him straight in the eye. 'Believe me, sir, I never wish to enter this factory ever again. I shall be glad to leave it.' She swept past him with a dignity far beyond the ken of a normal factory girl.

Jay came back into the room and resumed his seat. 'Such insolence!' he said, mopping his brow in the heat.

'Such courage,' Old Javis said under his breath, shaking his head admiringly. But he had to concede that Jay was right, if for no other reason than that the fiery Miss Chapman must be put right outside Alex's reach.

As for Laura, the courage Old Javis had so much admired sustained her until she was out of the office, then she leaned against the wall, drooping with defeat. She had handled everything badly. She had lost her temper when she needed to be calm; she had dragged the plight of the children in when that was not the issue. And now it was too late. She had lost her job and soon she would lose the roof over her head, because with no money she wouldn't be able to stay with the Taylors. She had lost everything and she had achieved nothing. What was she to do now?

'Charlotte, my dear, how nice to see you. And just in time for tea.' Eleanor greeted her daughter-in-law over the silver tray that Lydia the housemaid had just brought in. 'Bring another cup, Lydia.' Eleanor waited until the second cup had been brought, then said, 'And how are you, my dear? Is everything

81

well with you? I must say you look blooming.'

Charlotte smiled wanly. 'Yes, thank you, Mama-in-law. I'm very well.'

'One sugar, or two?'

'I – I won't have any tea, thank you. If you don't mind.'

Eleanor frowned. 'Not have any tea? But, my dear. . .' She looked searchingly at her daughter-in-law. Then, suddenly her face cleared and she smiled. 'I see, my dear. And when do you expect to be confined?'

Charlotte frowned. 'I don't. . . I'm not sure. . .'

'I'm sorry, my dear. I thought you were trying to tell me you were *enceinte*.' Embarrassed, Eleanor busied herself with the teapot. 'I do apologise. But you must understand that it is every mother's wish to become a grandmother when her son – or daughter – marries. I can see I was a little too hasty in jumping to conclusions.' She smiled across at Charlotte.

Charlotte bit her lip. She really didn't understand what her mother-in-law was talking about but she felt she owed her an explanation. 'I don't like tea any more,' she said firmly. 'I don't know why, Mama-in-law, but I just don't. It's probably because I'm all upset inside. I keep being sick. Every morning, I'm sick. I can't think what I've eaten. If it goes on I shall have to go and see Dr May, I'm afraid. But I don't like making a fuss.' She stared down at her hands, fidgeting in her lap.

Eleanor digested this outburst. There was no doubt that the child was pregnant. She looked across at her daughter-in-law. She looked very innocent sitting there, with her golden ringlets framing her face and dressed in a very fetching dress of apple green, with matching strings to her bonnet. Was it possible that she didn't know? Eleanor put her head on one side. 'How long have you been married, my dear?'

'Nearly five months.'

'And are you happy? You and Jay, I mean?'

'Oh, yes.' Charlotte blushed. She couldn't tell anyone, not *anyone* about what Jay did to her in the privacy of their bedroom.

'Charlotte,' Eleanor looked at her intently, 'Tell me. You do know where babies come from, don't you?'

Charlotte gazed guiltily at her distorted reflection in the silver teapot on the tray. She had never really believed her mother when she had said they came from under the gooseberry bush so she felt it better to shake her head. 'No,' she whispered. She had bitten her lip so hard that she could taste the blood.

'You mean, your mother let you go off on your honeymoon without. . .' Eleanor stared at her in utter disbelief. 'She didn't talk to you? Tell you *anything*?' Eleanor didn't like the Rankins, she considered that they were common and vulgar. How they had ever bred such a sweet girl as Charlotte was beyond belief. If it hadn't been for that and the fact that Sid Rankin's money might be useful one day she would never have approved the marriage. She had an idea that Jay had similar thoughts. But she had credited the Rankin woman with more sense than to allow her only daughter to go to her marriage bed in complete ignorance.

'About what?' Charlotte looked up wretchedly. 'She told me to be obedient to my husband.'

'Is that all?'

Charlotte nodded. She had no idea of the heart-searching that had gone on in her mother's mind before she and Jay were married. Lottie Rankin was a big, blowzy woman, very conscious of the fact that now her husband was rich she must mind her manners and try and hide the fact that for years she had served behind the bar at the Weaver's Arms. She tried hard and over the years had managed most of the time to suppress her loud voice and coarse laugh and she rarely dropped her aitches these days. Sometimes she went a little too far in her efforts to be genteel. As with Charlotte. If it had been left to Lottie's good sense she would have enlightened Charlotte not only on what to expect from her husband but how to increase his, and her own enjoyment. But she understood that this was 'not the done thing' in the circles in which they now moved and rather than make a social gaffe by over-informing Charlotte she had erred on the side of too much discretion and left her in total ignorance. Charlotte had no sisters or brothers and, because the Rankins were not quite accepted socially, no close friends, so there had been no one else to enlighten her either.

Eleanor sighed. 'Well, my dear, I think it's time that somebody had a little talk with you, and seeing that your own mother didn't see fit to speak of these things, then I must. Although I must confess I feel ill-prepared. With three sons and no daughters I never expected it to fall to my lot to discuss such intimate matters.' She took a deep breath. 'First of all, Charlotte, my dear, there is no need for you to worry about your health. You are *enceinte*; pregnant. You have Jay's baby growing inside you. . .'

Eleanor talked for nearly half an hour. When she had finished, Charlotte, whose expression had gone from horror to incredulity and had finished up with tears of relief rolling down her cheeks, got up and kissed her. 'Oh, thank you, Mama-in-law. I can't tell you what a load you've taken off my mind. I thought Jay. . . I thought I. . .' she stopped, lost for words.

Eleanor patted her arm. 'It's all perfectly normal, perfectly right. And in, oh, about six or seven months you will hold your own baby in your arms.' She smiled at Charlotte. It had never occured to her that in this day and age a girl could go so innocent to her marriage bed. She felt a stab of disgust to think that her mother could have allowed such a thing to happen. It was a mother's duty to prepare her daughter. 'You must go and see Dr May. He will look after you till the baby is born.' She patted the sofa beside her and when Charlotte sat down she leaned over and kissed her. 'I'm very happy for you, my dear. I'm sure you'll make a splendid mother.' She thought for a few minutes. 'I should wait until you've seen Dr May before you tell Jay, my dear. Husbands tend to take more notice if there's medical backing.' She put a finger to her lips. 'I won't breathe a word until you've told him.'

Three days later, at breakfast, Jay frowned at Charlotte, nibbling a piece of dry toast. 'No kidneys, my dear? The bacon's very good this morning, too. Won't you have some?'

'No, thank you, Jay. I don't feel very well in the mornings, these days.'

'Don't feel well? Then you should see Dr May.'

'I have, Jay. He says I'm to have a child.' Charlotte smiled shyly at her husband.

Jay flushed to the roots of his hair. 'Well,' he cleared his throat. 'Well, I never. That's capital news, my dear.' He folded his newspaper carefully and got up from his chair to go round the table and kiss her on the cheek. 'Capital news, indeed. And is everything. . . are you. . .?'

'Dr May says I'm perfectly well and healthy. He doesn't foresee any problems of any kind.'

'And is there anything you shouldn't do? I mean. . . anything?'

'No, Jay, he didn't say there was anything I shouldn't do.' Bewildered, Charlotte shook her head.

Jay cleared his throat again and resumed his seat at the breakfast table. 'Nevertheless, it might be best if I were to move into my dressing room for the time being,' he said. 'I'm sure it will be better for you. We – er – we don't want to take any chances, do we?'

'No, Jay, of course not.' But Charlotte experienced a stab of disappointment. Just recently, and especially since Eleanor's frank conversation with her, she had begun to quite enjoy Jay's attentions in bed. In fact, she wondered if there might be something wrong with her in that sometimes she looked forward to them so much that she had difficulty in restraining herself. But this was something she couldn't confess to anyone. Not even to Eleanor. And certainly not to Jay.

Chapter Eight

It was over a fortnight since Laura had been dismissed from the silk factory. Each day she had gone out into the town to look for work although she knew it was a hopeless venture. Nevertheless, she had tried shops of all kinds, from high-class milliners to grubby little corner shops; she had spent precious pence on putting an advertisement in the Essex Standard, offering her services as a private governess; she had even gone so far as to knock on the basement doors of some of the bigger houses, asking if they needed servants.

The results had been humiliating. Her shabby clothes, which she daren't spend her meagre savings to replace, told against her in the higher-class establishments and her precise, well-modulated speech aroused suspicion in the rest. When asked about her history, nobody believed her when she told them the truth and she wasn't a very convincing liar. One old man presiding in a dimly-lit corner shop stacked with goods that were turning brown with age gave her a lascivious, yellow-toothed smile and offered her a shilling a week to work for him. But the way he said, 'And yer keep, m'dear,' laying a grimy, proprietorial claw on her arm, made her flesh creep and she couldn't escape from the place fast enough.

She walked dejectedly back to the Taylor's cottage, her feet sore and unprotected in the wafer-thin soles of her boots. She had three shillings left in the world, enough to pay her rent for another two weeks at one and sixpence a week if she bought nothing and was careful not to eat very much. She wouldn't even be able to get a book for Ebbie from the penny library. After that, even if she hadn't found work she knew she must leave; she would have to pretend to have found a position because she knew that the kind-hearted Taylors would never turn her out on to the street even if she couldn't pay them for her keep.

Everything had gone wrong and it was all her fault. She had let the girls in the doubling room down. Their conditions were no better now than they had been before and by letting her hot temper get the better of her she had put herself where she could no longer fight for them. Not that the girls blamed her. In fact, Dot had brought home a shilling, all in ha'pennies and farthings, that the girls had collected for her because she'd been sacked. Laura had made Dot take the money back, she knew what sacrifices had been made to collect it, but it had touched her to know that the girls had appreciated what she had tried to do, even though she hadn't been successful.

She wondered if Alex Beresford was aware of what had happened. No doubt he was. His father and elder brother would have lost no time in letting him know that Laura Chapman the trouble-maker had been dismissed.

But whatever they said, however they blackened her character, they couldn't take away her memory of that last afternoon spent with Alex. She would always cherish the thought that he had told her he loved her and was prepared to take her home and introduce her to his mother. He had even spoken of marriage. There was no possible chance of that happening now, of course, but her common sense told her that in truth there never had been. Nevertheless, she would cherish the memory of his words to the end of her days.

Suddenly, she realised that she would have to leave Colchester, because one day Alex would marry and she couldn't bear the thought of seeing him married to someone else. It might not be a bad thing. It might be easier to find some kind of employment in Ipswich or Sudbury.

She dashed a tear from her cheek and let herself into the Taylor's house. She often wondered how the little cottage stood up to the noise of Fred's loom. The rhythmic clack, clack, clack, shook the house, hour after hour. It was hard, grinding work that the little silk weaver did, standing at his loom, with his right leg constantly pushing up and down, working the treadle that controlled the jacquard patterns, while his left hand operated the beam and his right hand threw the shuttle back and forth, back and forth, as the complicated pattern appeared. Fred had once told her that years ago the warp threads were raised by a boy – known as a draw-boy – sitting on top of the loom. Sometimes the draw-boy would have to hold up as much as twenty-five or thirty pounds in weight if it was a complicated pattern. This was now all done by the Jacquard machine, which used cards with a series of perforations, stitched together in a continuous band. The perforations allowed some needles to pass to raise the warp threads and not others, and thus the pattern was created. The cards were clearly visible on the machine where the loom reached up through the ceiling into the bedroom above, and a rough fencing had been put round the hole in the floor as much to protect the cards on the loom as to prevent the girls who slept in the room from falling through. Fred had once told Laura he had counted how many times he treadled in a minute and how surprised he had been to find that it was a hundred times. She didn't wonder he was exhausted at the end of the day.

Laura hung up her bonnet and pulled the pan of stew forward so that it would be ready when Nellie and the girls came home. Then she turned to go up the stairs to see Ebbie. He loved to be read to, even though he was quite capable of reading for himself, and if she closed the door and spoke clearly he was able to hear most of her words over the noise of the loom.

She was halfway up the stairs when there was a knock at the door.

Puzzled, she smoothed her hair and straightened her skirt as she turned back to answer it. The Taylors didn't often have callers.

It was Alex. For a moment she couldn't believe her eyes. Then the thought flashed through her mind that he had come to tell them there had been some kind of accident involving Nellie or one of the girls, but chasing this came the realisation that he was not dressed in his working overalls but in a grey suit, and there was no sign of grease on his hands.

'I. . . Good afternoon,' was all she could manage to say,

her hand on the door jamb for support.

He smiled at her. 'Aren't you going to ask me in, Laura?'

She stepped aside hurriedly. 'Yes, of course. I'm sorry. . . please, come in.'

'You know why I've come, don't you?' He held a chair for her to sit down at the table and then sat himself opposite to her.

She shook her head. 'No, but I suppose it's got something to do with the business at the mill,' she said wearily. 'I tried so hard to help the girls but I got it all wrong.' She looked across at him, her eyes dull. 'If you've been sent by your brother. . .'

'The reason I'm here has nothing whatever to do with my brother and nothing at all to do with the mill,' he said sharply. He reached over and took her hand. 'Laura, I've come to ask you once again. Will you be my wife?'

Her eyes widened and she withdrew her hand. 'You can't be serious, Alex. After all that has happened. . . Do you mean you don't *know* all the trouble I caused?'

'Of course I know,' he said, reaching for her hand again and giving it an impatient shake. 'I also know that I can't possibly let you disappear from my life.' He covered the hand he held with his other one. 'Nothing has changed as far as I'm concerned, Laura. I still want to marry you, if you'll have me.' He looked at her intently. 'Dear Laura. Will you do me the honour of becoming my wife?'

She passed her free hand over her eyes. 'How can we be married, Alex? It was difficult enough before – you knew your family would oppose your marrying a factory girl. But now I'm not even that! I've put myself quite beyond the pale by standing up to your father and brother Jay over conditions at the mill. Now your family would never, ever accept me as your wife, you must realise that.'

'I'm not asking them to,' he said quietly.

She looked up quickly. 'What do you mean?'

'Do you really need to know?' he asked with a sigh.

'Of course I need to know.' She withdrew her hand from his and sat bolt upright in her chair. Then she relaxed. 'I could never even contemplate marrying you if I didn't know where you stood with your own family,' she said. 'But of course I know very well where you stand. They are totally against your marrying me and it would break your mother's heart.' Her voice was flat and unemotional. 'Oh, Alex, how could I marry you, knowing that?'

He leaned back in his chair, locking his hands behind his head, his jaw set. She was right, of course, and she'd made a pretty shrewd guess at his family's reaction. But she didn't know the whole story and he didn't want to tell her; he didn't even want to remember the scene there had been when he announced his intentions. He hadn't expected the family to care what he did. But they'd cared all right. By heaven they had!

'If you marry that girl you realise that you won't be able to stay at the mill,' his father said, and Alex had the feeling that in a funny sort of way the old man almost admired him, might even have sided with him if it hadn't been for Jay. 'Your brother would never countenance it, you understand.'

'Neither will I ever allow you to set foot inside this house again,' his mother put in. She was white with fury; Alex had never seen her so angry. 'I simply can't imagine what's come over you, Alex. And after all we've done for you. . .' She turned her head away. 'I think the best thing for you to do is to go to your room and stay there until you've come to your senses.'

'I assure you that I am in full possession of my senses, Mama,' he said levelly, 'and I wouldn't want you to think for one moment that I'm not grateful to you for all you've done for me.' He turned to Old Javis. 'Neither would I ever dream of embarrassing you, Papa—.' It was funny, even at a time like this Alex still thought of him as 'Papa'. '—Or Jay, by remaining at the mill. I have other plans.'

'You'll be the laughing stock,' Charles remarked, pouring a generous measure of whisky and handing it to Alex. 'Here, have a drink, drown your sorrows and forget that tr. . .' he stopped in deference to his mother, '. . .woman.'

Furiously, Alex dashed the glass from Charles's hand and it rolled, unbroken, across the thick pile carpet, leaving a trail of amber liquid. 'Dare to speak like that again about Laura and I'll knock you down. I've done it once, remember. Next time I could easily kill you.' He spoke in a venomous whisper so that only his brother could hear.

'Oh, Al, no woman's worth breaking up the family for,' Charles said easily, picking up the glass, re-filling it and draining it before Alex had a chance to waste it. 'Especially one like that.' He grinned. 'Heaven sake, man, I should know.' Charles's exploits were common knowledge.

Eleanor rose to her feet. 'I don't wish to discuss the matter any further. I'm deeply upset, Alex. But I suppose blood will out and it's no more than we might have expected under the circumstances. But God knows, we've done our best to make amends for the past and to bring you up decently.' She dabbed her eyes with her handkerchief. 'I shall go to my room and leave your father to talk some sense into you. When you have thought better of this ridiculous idea you may come and apologise to me. Until then I bid you good afternoon.'

'Goodbye, Mama,' Alex said sadly.

After his mother had left the room Old Javis said, 'And what are these plans that you have, my boy?'

'I plan to start my own engineering works. In a small way, of course. But it's what I've always wanted to do.' Alex's eyes began to sparkle. 'I'm quite sure engineering is the thing of the future. Look at the number of machines there are on the farms – and the farm workers are always having problems because they don't understand how the things work and don't know how to look after them properly.' Alex began to pace up and down the room. 'I know there must be an opening there for men like me. Oh, you don't need to fear, I shan't lack work, Papa.'

'You will if you haven't got any capital to begin with,' Old Javis said bluntly.

'I've the legacy Grandmama left me. I'll use that. If I'm careful it will last me long enough to get started.'

'Where will you live?'

'There's a small house in East Street, with a shed at the back where I can work. The rent's quite reasonable. I've already enquired.'

'You seem to have it all worked out.' Old Javis stroked his whiskers thoughtfully.

91

'I think you're mad,' Charles said. 'I think you're quite out of your mind.'

'I don't give a damn what you think,' Alex said, without looking at him.

Old Javis sighed. 'I can accept that you want to leave the business, Alex,' he said slowly, 'and I'm sure your mother would accept this, too, in time. But must you insist on marrying this woman?' He held up his hand as Alex opened his mouth to protest. 'No, let me speak. I know she's a pleasant enough gel, and she's got spirit, I'll say that for her. . .'

'And so will I, by Jove!' Charles agreed with a grin.

'Leave us, Charles,' Old Javis barked. He waited until Charles had slammed out of the room, then he continued, 'But she's not the kind of woman for a man in your position to marry. Surely you must realise that.' He stroked his whiskers and gave a slightly embarrassed sniff. 'There are other ways, you know, my boy. You don't have to *marry* the gel. You could keep. . . ' He stopped and cleared his throat.

Alex stopped pacing and grasped the back of the chair, holding his temper with difficulty. His father's last remark was not even worth a reply. 'You simply don't understand, sir,' he said, trying to keep his voice even. 'Miss Chapman is *exactly* the kind of woman a man in my position should marry. If you were to talk to her and listen to her story you would known what she's really like. Her father was a doctor in the Indian Army. . .'

'A likely story, my boy. You mustn't be taken in by such tales. Don't you know what accomplished liars these gels can be to get what they want?' Old Javis got up from his chair and went over and patted Alex on the shoulder. 'You think about it, my boy. I'll tell you what,' he said on a sudden burst of inspiration, 'forget this young filly and I'll set you up in your own engineering business wherever and whenever you like. There now, what about that for an offer?'

Alex turned away. 'No, Papa. You can't bribe me,' he said firmly, 'I love Laura and I think – no, I *know* – she is the woman for me. I'm sorry, but if you refuse to give us your blessing then we must marry without it. Because marry her I shall, make no mistake about that.'

Old Javis shook his head and went back to his chair. He sat down heavily. 'I can't say I'm not deeply upset about this, Alex, my boy. It'll break your mother's heart, and for that I can't forgive you. On the other hand, I admire you for sticking to your guns. I must admit that from what I've seen of her the young woman doesn't appear to be like the usual run-of-the-mill factory girl, but be that as it may, you must understand that it simply will not do for a man in your position to run off and marry the first pretty face that tickles your fancy.'

'It's not like that, Papa, I assure you. Anyway,' his lip twisted bitterly, 'I'm surprised you don't find it appropriate. . .'

'Enough!' Old Javis held up his hand. 'I'm not prepared to discuss the matter any further. I think you're making a grave mistake, but you're of age, and if you won't listen to reason then you must abide by the results. We shall miss you at the mill, there's no doubt about that. Nobody else understands that confounded machinery like you do.'

'Humphries is very good, sir. And of course, if at any time you need me. . .'

His father gave a wry smile. 'I fancy Jay would see the place burn down before he'd call you in, after the showdown he had with the gel you intend to marry.' He was quiet for several minutes. Then he tried one last time. 'Are you sure you won't change your mind, Alex?'

'Quite sure, Papa.'

'Very well, then. So be it.' Old Javis got up and went to the door, his shoulders stooped in defeat. When he reached it he stopped with his hand on the knob and without looking round said, his voice not quite steady, 'Should you ever need to go to the bank for assistance you are at liberty to mention my name. My personal credit is good. I'm deeply upset, nevertheless I wish you well, my boy.'

'Thank you, Papa.' Alex found he could hardly speak.

Alex told Laura as much of the story as he felt necessary, leaving out the unpleasant things that had been said about her, especially by his brother Charles. He had never been sure just how far Charles had got with his attack on Laura

93

before she escaped, although he had no doubt Charles would have told him if he'd asked, sparing no lurid detail. But, although half of him longed to know the truth, the other half shied away from what he might hear. He knew he could never bring himself to ask Laura.

'But doesn't it worry you, that you will be cut off from your family?' Laura asked anxiously when he had finished speaking.

'I can face anything as long as I have you, Laura.' he said simply.

She shook her head unhappily. 'No, I can't let you do this, Alex. What if. . .?'

He pushed back his chair and went round the table and laid his finger on her lips. 'What if I were to walk out of the door and you were never to see me again?' He smiled with satisfaction at the bleak expression that crossed her face. Yet she still persisted. 'It can't be right for me to allow you to sacrifice your whole family's happiness for mine.'

'And mine.' He bent and kissed her gently on the lips. 'My mind is made up, Laura. I intend to marry you. I've fought my family, surely I won't have to fight you as well.' He looked down into her eyes and she smiled up at him. 'That's better.' He straightened up. 'Now, be a good girl and collect your things together. I shall be bringing a trap round to the stables of the George Hotel in an hour. Meet me there.' He bent and kissed her again. 'I believe I've thought of everything, Laura. I've made all the arrangements and I have the licence in my pocket. By tomorrow you will be my wife.'

Alex Beresford and Laura Chapman were married at eight o'clock the following morning, the first day of August 1857, at St James' Church on East Hill. It was the same church at which Alex's brother Jay had been married less than six months before, but there the similarity ended. Laura was married in the only decent dress she possessed, a blue gingham that was decidedly grubby round the hem and darned under the armpits and there were no bridesmaids. Fred Taylor was there to give her away and Dot had been prepared to lose three hours pay to act as a witness. Young Arthur and Jinny had come with her, as a special treat but it had been decided that Nellie and Kate should go to work as usual, much to Kate's disappointment. This was partly because they couldn't afford to lose too many pennies but even more because it wouldn't do for it to be known too widely around the factory that the Taylors supported the rift in the Beresford family.

It was inevitable that the news quickly leaked out. The girls in the doubling room were quietly exultant. They had all grown to like Laura and to understand that she had done her best to improve conditions for them and they gloried in her marriage to Mr Alex, whom they all respected, and chortled that it was 'One in the eye for Ole Beak-nose', as they disrespectfully dubbed Jay. They waited impatiently for Dot to come in, avid for every last detail of the wedding. It wasn't every day that one of their work-mates married an ostracised son of the factory owner.

As for Laura, she had spent a sleepless night in the lodgings Alex had obtained for her. There was one episode in her past that she had never spoken of to anybody. She knew it wasn't right to marry Alex without telling him, yet she was terrified that if he knew he would reject her. At the same time she was fearful that he would somehow discover the fact for himself. Would he know on their wedding night that there had once been another man? Would he discover that she had borne a child? She tossed and turned on the unfamiliar, comfortable feather bed, going through the whole of her life. Her childhood, spent moving from place to place wherever her father's profession as an army surgeon took the family; boarding school, where she learned to be self-reliant and self-disciplined; holidays spent under sufferance with an elderly aunt; then Finishing School, where she learned skills that she had barely had any opportunity to make use of and which, in the light of her later experiences seemed unnecessary and irrelevant. Her voyage to India only to find her parents already dead seemed almost like a bad dream now: she simply couldn't imagine what life might have been like for her if they had lived. She thought about Annabel and her little son Peregrine. Although their friendship had only lasted a few months Laura had grown very fond of the pretty, vivacious girl with her terrible, blinding headaches and of the

95

little boy, too. Perhaps before long she would be able to write to Annabel; up to now there had been little enough that she would have been willing to relate, but it would be so nice to renew their friendship now that she was herself married. But thoughts of Annabel inevitably led to memories of Randolph Grey and the worry and fear over her past began to haunt Laura again.

In the end she did nothing. Said nothing. And if she was pale and nervous at the wedding ceremony nobody thought it amiss under the circumstances.

After the wedding Fred and Dot took the children home and the vicar went back to the vicarage to have his breakfast.

Alex took Laura's arm as they stood together at the church gate in the morning sunshine. 'Now I'll take you to your new home. Our home,' he said smiling at her. 'It's not far. Just down the hill and over the bridge. I do hope you'll like it,' he added, a trace of anxiety in his voice. 'It's not very grand. . .'

'Oh, Alex, as if that was important.' She gave his arm a little squeeze. 'All that matters to me is that you'll be there.'

Nevertheless, she was quiet as they walked down the hill and when they reached the bridge over the river by the mill she stopped and stood looking down into the water, sparkling in the sunlight as the tide reached full flood.

'Alex,' she said, not looking at him, 'whatever happens always remember that I love you. I love you more than life itself and I would never willingly do anything to harm you. All that I am is yours and if you find, as you surely must, that I am less than perfect. . .'

He didn't let her finish what she was about to say, but caught her round the waist and danced her to the other side of the bridge, much to the amusement of passers by. 'Laura, my love, my life, I couldn't live up to a perfect wife. Let's hear no more talk of perfection. We'll take each other as we are; me, the impecunious son of a silk manufacturer and you the most wonderful and courageous woman in the world.' He kissed her roundly as he released her and she laughed with him, the tension dropping away as she became infected by his high spirits.

Chapter Nine

The little house in East Street to which Alex took his bride was old and full of character. It had begun life as a one up and one down and been added to over the years, ending up as a veritable hotch-potch of rooms and passages with uneven floors and low, beamed ceilings. Alex had already furnished most of the rooms and the whole place had a cosy, comfortable atmosphere. Laura loved it on sight.

'But, Alex,' she said anxiously, 'are you sure we can really afford all this?' They were standing in the parlour, which had two stuffed armchairs, a round walnut dining table with four chairs round it, and a what-not in the corner.

He kissed her on the nose, delighting in her pleasure, which even her anxiety couldn't dampen. 'I told you, my love, I had a legacy from my grandmother which has paid for everything. The furniture's not new, you understand,' he added quickly. 'I bought it from Sid Rankin, from the second-hand store at the back of his shop. He let me have most of it quite cheaply. He's a regular fellow, old Sid, although I know my brother Jay doesn't think much of him as a father-in-law.' He gave her a hug and then held her away from him so that he could look down into her face. 'You're sure you like it, Laura? I know it's not very grand. . .'

'I love it.' She nodded, her eyes bright with tears. 'Everything's exactly what I would have chosen myself.' She laid her head on his shoulder. 'Oh, Alex, I'm so happy I'm almost frightened. I didn't know it was possible to feel so much happiness and still live.'

'Nor did I, my dearest love.' He held her close for several

minutes. Then, suddenly, he put her from him, a wide grin on his face. 'Oh, I nearly forgot. I haven't finished showing you quite everything yet, my dear. I've another surprise for you. I haven't given you a wedding present yet, have I?'

She looked up at him in amazement. 'But you've done all this, Alex. What more could I possibly want?'

'Close your eyes and stand right there, in the middle of the room,' he commanded, his face alight with excitement.

She did as he told her and heard him move across to the door and clap his hands loudly. Soon after there was a scuffle, then silence. 'All right, you can look now,' he said.

She opened her eyes and saw a diminutive little creature standing before her, with thin, scrawny features and wild ginger hair escaping from under a cap that was several sizes too big. But she was spotlessly clean and wearing a blue striped dress and voluminous white pinafore which were also several sizes too big. She was smiling eagerly up at Laura.

'This is Maudie,' Alex said proudly. 'She's your own servant and she assures me she can sweep and clean and cook plain fare.'

Laura's eyes widened. 'A little maid! For me! Oh, Alex, I don't need a maid. I can look after the house, myself. In any case, I'm sure we can't afford. . .' Her voice died away at Alex's warning glance, and she saw Maudie's smile fade as she hung her head in disappointment.

She laid her hand on the girl's thin shoulder. 'How old are you, Maudie?' she asked gently.

'Twelve, m'm. Well, nearly twelve,' Maudie replied with a little bob, her blues eyes wary as she sensed the precariousness of her position.

'And where have you come from?'

'Back Lane, m'm. I live wiv me mum 'n' dad 'n' six bruvvers 'n' sisters.'

'Not any more, Maudie. You live with Mrs Beresford and me, now,' Alex said firmly and Laura's throat constricted, partly at the expression of sheer delight and relief that crossed the girl's pinched face and partly at the pride with which Alex had called her 'Mrs Beresford'.

'The little room up under the eaves where you were hiding till I called you is your room,' he went on. 'That's where you'll sleep, and that's where you'll keep all your personal possessions.'

'Oh, sir!' was all Maudie could say, and a large tear ran down one cheek. 'What's personal possessions, sir?' she asked, saying the unfamiliar words with great care when, after a great sniff and dragging her sleeve across her nose, she had pulled herself together.

'Things that you own. Things that belong to you,' Alex explained.

'Oh, I ain't got none o' them,' she said with a shrug, losing interest.

Laura and Alex exchanged amused glances, then Alex said, 'You'll have to train her, my love. I'm afraid she's got a lot to learn.' He leaned over and kissed his wife's cheek. 'It's all right, Laura, my darling,' he whispered. 'We can afford to employ her, although, in truth, I believe she'd have been happy to work for nothing more than her keep, she was so delighted to come.'

Laura's face cleared at Alex's words and she smiled at the undersized little scrap. 'We'll learn together. I'm quite sure we'll manage. Can you make tea, Maudie?'

'Oh, yes, m'm. I'll go an' make some now.' Maudie scuttled off importantly to the kitchen. Ten minutes later she came back with a tray that was nearly as big as she was, laden not only with teapot and cups but also a plate of bread and butter, the bread cut in thick doorsteps and the butter scraped on so thinly that it was barely visible. 'There!' she said, beaming with pride. 'I thought you might be hungry.'

'That was very thoughtful of you, Maudie,' Laura said with a smile. 'You may go back to the kitchen now.' She picked up a little brass bell that was on the table. 'I'll ring this little bell if I want anything.'

'Yes, m'm.' With another little bob Maudie disappeared back down the passage to the kitchen to enjoy the crust she had spread for herself with a scraping of real butter, the first time she had ever tasted it.

'I told you she'd got a lot to learn,' Alex said with a grin as he helped himself to a doorstep of bread.

'Indeed she has.' Laura burst out laughing as she picked up the teapot and poured a stream of barely coloured liquid into

99

the teacups. 'But at least we shan't be able to accuse her of extravagance!' She sipped the insipid brew and made a face. 'Ugh. No, it's no use, Alex, I really can't drink this. I think I shall have to give her a lesson in making tea right now.'

Another ten minutes and they were drinking properly-made tea and eating toast and marmalade. 'After all, it's barely ten o'clock, so we can still call it breakfast,' Laura laughed.

They ate their first meal together sitting at the table in the little parlour with the sounds from the street wafting in through the open window. They spoke little but they were both completely happy in each other's company. At eleven o'clock Alex took out his pocket watch.

'Will you think I'm most terribly rude if I go to work on our wedding day, my love?' he asked anxiously. 'I don't want to, I'd far rather stay here with you, but I did promise Joe Cross at Tye Farm in Wyford that I'd go and look at his threshing machine. It's a new model out and it's giving him trouble. I'm sure it's only because he doesn't know how to look after it.'

'Of course I don't mind, Alex. I understand. I know you must work.' Laura looked at him in surprise. 'But you've very quickly found work, haven't you?'

His face hardened. 'Contrary to what my brother Jay might like to think, there's no shortage of work for men with my skills. I was often called out to the farms, even when I was working at the factory, so a lot of people know me. Anyway, engineering is the coming thing. And with all the farms around going over, however reluctantly, to what they call "these new-fangled ideas", they need people like me to keep the machines running.' He got to his feet and went over and kissed her. 'We shan't starve, my love, never fear. I'll see to that. I've already got several jobs in my order book. And I'm prepared to work all the hours God sends to get myself established. I'm determined to succeed, Laura.' He turned briefly away. 'In a few years' time people will look up to Alex Beresford, not down on him.' There was a trace of bitterness in his tone.

A little alarmed Laura stretched out her hand to him. 'I'm sorry, Alex.'

'Sorry? For what?' He looked as if he had almost forgotten

she was there.

She shook head. 'Nothing.' She held his hand briefly to her cheek. 'I promise you I shan't complain, Alex. And I'll do everything in my power to help you.'

'Just be here. That's all I ask.' He pulled her to her feet and held her close. Then he went upstairs and changed into his greasy working clothes. When he came down he put some money on the table.

'I want you to go and buy yourself a new dress and. . .' he hesitated, '. . .whatever else it is that women wear. I would have bought them for you so that you could wear them for your wedding but I wanted you to have what you like and not what I chose.' He grinned and kissed her, 'In any case, I could hardly go shopping for ladies' things, could I? It wouldn't be seemly.'

'But won't we need the money for food?' Laura asked anxiously. 'This dress, it's a bit darned, but it's quite respectable. I don't need. . .'

'I had to get Maudie new clothes because she hardly had a rag to her back. Now, I can't have my wife's maid dressed better than my wife, can I?' He kissed her again. 'That money is the last of Grandmama's legacy, and what better way to spend it?' He gave her a hug. 'Don't worry, Laura. You're not working at the silk factory now, we shall have enough to live on, I promise you. Trust me.'

'But if you don't get work. . .?'

'I've got work.' He pulled away from her with some reluctance. 'And I've also got a boy to help me and if I don't go now I'll be late. I told Joe Cross we'd be there at noon. Young Jake's already started to walk and I must get my horse saddled up or he'll be there before me.' He came back for another kiss, 'But if a chap can't be a little late on his wedding day it's pretty hard luck, wouldn't you say?' He went to the door. 'You'll find there's plenty of food in the larder,' he said over his shoulder. 'I asked Lottie Rankin what I should buy – I knew it was no good asking Charlotte – and she gave me a grocery list. I've quite enjoyed myself, you know.' He grinned and blew her a kiss and went to saddle his horse, waiting in the stable next to his workshop at the back of the house.

101

After he had gone Laura took her time and explored the whole house, every nook and cranny from the attic to the cellar. It was not very big; a tiny attic bedroom for Maudie, then two bedrooms on the floor below, one three steps down from the other, both with gently sloping floors and ceilings. A third tiny room at the end of a passage Laura mentally earmarked as a nursery and then blushed at the thought although there was no one to see. At the foot of the little winding staircase was the door to the parlour. This room faced the road and the front door opened straight into it. Behind the parlour was a passage with an oddly-shaped room to one side, empty except for Alex's desk, and at the end of the passage, three steps led down into the kitchen, a stone-flagged room with a kitchen range at one end and a scrubbed table in the middle. It was the biggest room in the house. Beyond the kitchen, across a sizable yard, was a tiny washhouse and a stable for Alex's horse, Hector, next to the workshop. Laura peeped through the window of the workshop and saw the work bench neatly laid out with an array of strange-looking implements, then she went thoughtfully back into the house. Alex really had thought of everything, down to the last scrubbing brush and duster; there was even a cookery book on the shelf in the kitchen. And he had done everything, even planned their wedding, without a word to her, and in not much over a fortnight. She smiled to herself. She had learned a great deal about her new husband during her tour of inspection; not least his thoroughness when he decided on a course of action. It had clearly never occurred to him that she would refuse to marry him, or if it had he must have been quite confident that he would succeed in changing her mind. She realised that Alex Beresford was a strong, determined character and something of a perfectionist. A force to be reckoned with.

It was nearly seven o'clock by the time Alex returned home from Wyford. He was tired and grimy but Laura had had the forethought to put a pan of water to boil on the kitchen range which he took over to the washhouse in order to clean himself up.

When he came back, smelling of shaving soap and with his hair still damp Laura rang the little bell for Maudie to bring in the stew that they had made between them, with the aid of the cookery book.

'I'm afraid the dumplings may be a little heavy, Alex. I'm afraid neither Maudie nor I have had much experience of cooking,' Laura apologised as they sat down at the table, set with a snowy cloth and the pretty rose-patterned china Alex had chosen. 'Stew was almost the only thing the Taylor's ate, and it had very little meat in it, most of the time. But I shall learn.' She handed him his plate. 'I intend to make a meat pie tomorrow, I'm warning you.'

He nodded gravely as he cut into a slightly chewy dumpling. 'Thank you, my dear. I shall remember to bring a hammer and chisel in with me to cut the pastry.' His eyes danced as he spoke and she noticed that their hazel lights had deepened to a warm brown.

After they had eaten and Maudie had cleared the table Alex sat down in the big armchair and she sat in the matching lady's chair opposite to him. 'Why aren't you wearing your new dress?' he asked, eyeing the blue gingham she was still wearing.

'I haven't been out to buy it yet,' she admitted. 'I've been far too busy exploring the house and everything.' She got up and went over to sit at his feet. 'Oh, it's all so. . . so perfect, Alex,' she said, looking up at him, her eyes full of happiness. 'I don't know how you could have known, but everything is exactly what I would have chosen myself. I can't believe it. And Maudie is such a dear, so willing and eager.'

'I'm glad you like it, my love.' He stroked her hair. 'But you really must go and buy yourself some new clothes tomorrow. I can't have my wife going round. . .' he hesitated.

'Looking like a factory girl,' she finished for him wickedly. She was so happy she could even laugh about that.

He shook his head, his face serious. 'No, Laura, you don't look like a factory girl. You never did. You always looked out of place in the doubling room. Nevertheless, I would like to see my wife dressed a little more suitably, if you don't mind.' He yawned. 'But now I rather think it's time for bed. It's been quite a day.' He looked down at her. 'Shall we go up, my love?'

Laura froze. It had been such a perfect day and the little house was everything she could have wished for. Was it all going to be ruined now? Could she bear it if Alex discovered her secret and rejected her? She loved him so much.

She allowed him to help her up from the floor. 'Alex, I. . .' she began.

He smiled and nodded. 'It's all right, my love. I understand. You go up. I'll follow in a few minutes.'

Saying no more she went upstairs and prepared for bed, undressing down to her shift. It was no use, she couldn't carry this dreadful burden without telling Alex. Whatever the consequences he would have to know. She brushed her hair and then got into bed and waited for him, biting her lip till it bled in her anxiety.

'Alex,' she said, as soon as he climbed in beside her and made to take her in his arms. 'I have to tell you. . .' But before she could continue he had begun to kiss her and her senses began to swim, 'there's something. . .' her voice sounded as if it was coming from a long way off because she seemed to be drowning as he began to caress her.

'It's all right, my love,' he whispered against her ear. 'I understand. It's all right.'

'No, I have to. . .' She never finished what she was about to say.

Afterwards he held her close and she clung to him, her face wet with tears of relief. It was all right. He had said nothing. He hadn't realised. She breathed a fervent prayer of thankfulness that the past was over and done with. She need never worry about it, never need even to think about it again. She fell asleep with her head on her husband's shoulder, completely happy.

But Alex lay staring up into the darkness, his mouth a thin, hard line. So that bastard Charles had deflowered her. That was what she had been trying to confess but he hadn't let her because he hadn't wanted his suspicions confirmed. But now they were. And there could be no mistake, he knew enough about women to know that Laura hadn't come to the marriage bed a virgin. God, but he was glad he'd knocked the bastard down in the corridor that day, even though Charles was his own brother. He was only sorry he hadn't killed him, the swine. He would never forgive him for what he had done to Laura. Never.

It was a long time before Alex slept.

The days passed in a haze of pure happiness for Laura. She taught Maudie how to keep herself, as well as the house, clean and neat and helped her to memorise a few simple recipes because as yet she couldn't read – a deficiency Laura intended to rectify as time went on.

She went shopping for the clothes Alex was so anxious to buy her and he particularly liked the dress of green sprigged muslin, with a wide dark green sash that emphasised her tiny waist, although privately she had been reluctant to spend the money on it, since they were not likely to be invited anywhere for her to be seen in it. But it pleased Alex and that was all that was important to her, so she wore it every afternoon as she waited for him to return from his work.

One day, less than a month after the marriage, she was sitting and looking through the newspaper he had left behind when a small item caught her eye.

'The siege of Lucknow is now entering its third month with no sign of being broken. It is estimated that nearly three thousand souls are trapped in the British Residency there, under the leadership of Sir Henry Lawrence.'

She sat staring into space. She had been to Lucknow when she was in India. It was only a few miles from the garrison at Mudkipur, a lovely city, she recalled. But why should it be under siege? She scanned the newspaper to see if she could discover anything further, but there was nothing. She realised then that she was sadly lacking in knowledge of what had gone on in the outside world during the past year. Fred Taylor couldn't afford the luxury of a newspaper and she had been so preoccupied with the new, hard life she had been plunged into that she had never given much thought to what might be going on beyond her own tight little horizon. True, she had occasionally thought briefly of Annabel and her little son, Peregrine, but not often, because most of her memories of

India were best buried in the recesses of her mind.

She stared unseeingly out of the window on to the street beyond, remembering the ordered life of the garrison at Mudkipur, where, it had always seemed to her, the residents had tried to ignore the fact that they were in India, in spite of the heat, and to treat it as a corner of England, at the same time taking full advantage of their Indian servants. It had seemed a very unnatural way of life to Laura but even if the same conditions prevailed at Lucknow she could see no reason why it should be besieged. Nor by whom. She waited with some impatience for Alex to return home.

She managed to contain herself until they were sitting down to the meal Maudie proudly brought in, having cooked it entirely by herself, before asking him. 'I feel so woefully ignorant of what's been going on in the world, Alex,' she finished apologetically, 'but Lucknow is not far from where I stayed in India.'

'It's to do with the native troops, I believe. Sepoys, are they called?'

She nodded. 'That's right.'

'Well, they've mutinied and turned on the English.' He dabbed his mouth with his napkin. 'It's hardly dinner table talk, my love. I believe it has been quite a blood bath.'

'Oh, dear. This is dreadful. But why?'

'It's all to do with their religion, as I understand it.'

'Ah, yes,' Laura nodded. 'Some of them are Hindus and some are Muslims. But I still don't see... There was no trouble whilst I was there, at least, not that I knew of.'

'Well, there is big trouble now, it seems, although I don't know the ins and outs of it. I believe it's partly to do with the new rifles the Sepoys have been issued. Apparently, the bullets are greased with some kind of fat which the Hindus think is from cows, which are sacred to them, and the Muslims think comes from pigs, which is equally abhorrent to them. My feeling is that there is good deal more to it than that but I haven't been following it very closely.' He smiled across at her. 'I'm afraid my mind has been fully occupied with other things.' He became serious again. 'All I can tell you is that the Sepoys have surrounded the Governor's Residence at Lucknow and the English, including all those who had come in from the surrounding districts for refuge are besieged there. God knows how long they'll be able to hold out.'

Laura looked across at him, her expression sombre. 'Mudkipur is not far from Lucknow, Alex. If I hadn't left India when I did. . .' she didn't finish the sentence. 'Oh, God,' she whispered, 'I wonder if Annabel and Peregrine are safe.'

He reached over and covered her hand with his. 'There's nothing you can do, dearest.' He didn't like to see her so anxious.

She gave him a wintery smile. 'No, you're quite right, Alex. But I can't help wondering. . .'

After that, every night, before she slept, she offered up a prayer for the safety of the girl who had been her friend for such a short time, yet who she still remembered with affection, and she scanned the newspaper every day for the news, which didn't come until late in November, that the siege of Lucknow was over.

Chapter Ten

Jay was annoyed, but he contained his annoyance as he knew he must in his mother's presence. He went over and gave her a perfunctory peck on the cheek.

'You're looking very well, Mama,' he managed to greet her, wishing she didn't keep the confounded room so hot. Surely it wasn't necessary to have the fire halfway up the chimney, even in the middle of winter.

Eleanor inclined her head. 'Thank you, Jay. I can't complain. At my age I daresay I'm lucky if a few twinges of rheumatism are all I'm prone to.' She rubbed her hands in their black lace half-mittens as she spoke. 'Sit down by the fire, dear, and I'll ring for Lydia to bring some tea. It's not often I have the pleasure of your company in the middle of the afternoon.' She smiled at him as she pulled her cashmere shawl more closely round her shoulders.

Jay sat down on the edge of the overstuffed sofa opposite to his mother, but quickly got up again and went over to the window. 'I really came to see Papa,' he admitted, flapping his coat tails impatiently.

'Yes, dear, I quite believe that. I never for a moment thought you might have come expressly to see me. Not at this time of day.' Eleanor spoke drily. She rang the bell by her side and ordered tea when Lydia appeared. 'But now that you're here – and your father isn't – you may as well stay and have tea with me.' She gazed thoughtfully at her firstborn son, so very like his father in appearance. 'Is there something wrong at the factory, dear?'

Jay sat down again, shaking his head. 'Nothing that needs

to concern you, Mama.' He stroked his new mutton chop whiskers; he still wasn't sure whether he liked them. Charlotte said they gave him a look of maturity, but in truth they made him feel rather elderly although he was barely twenty-eight. 'Where is Papa?'

'Why, he's playing golf with Dr Franklyn. Didn't he tell you he'd arranged it for today?'

'No. Yes. He might have done. I forget.' Jay shook his head irritably.

Eleanor tried another approach. 'How is Charlotte dear? Is she well?'

'I think so, thank you, Mama. She doesn't complain. Of course she has to rest a good deal of the time now.'

'Yes, of course.' Eleanor was silent for a moment, trying to remember exactly when her daughter-in-law was due to be confined. It was not something she felt she could discuss with Jay. She began again. 'Are you sure I can't be of any help, dear? Thank you, Lydia. Yes, put it down there. Ah, muffins, too. That's nice.' She looked up and smiled. 'Your favourite, Jay. You've always been partial to muffins, haven't you.' She poured the tea and handed the delicate china cup to her son. 'You know very well Dr Franklyn told your father that he must take things more easily, Jay,' she reminded him as she passed him a muffin. 'Not that I think those chest pains were anything other than indigestion, myself. But it won't hurt him to take life a little more gently, that is if you call walking miles round a golf course taking life gently.' She put her head on one side. 'Are you finding it difficult to manage without him? It's only the odd day that he takes off and I'm sure you and Charles. . .?'

'Charles!' He bit savagely into his muffin. 'A fat lot of help Charles is! He's never there. Not that I'd consult him if he was. He's worse than useless.'

'I'm sure that's not true, Jay. Charles often tells me what he's been doing. And I'm sure he'd take more interest if you gave him more responsibility,' she said sharply.

Jay gazed at his mother, his face set. She didn't know what she was talking about. Charles was the apple of her eye and always had been; she had simply no idea what he was really like. The scoundrel could twist her round his little finger.

'You don't understand, Mama,' he said. He finished his muffin and licked his fingers before wiping them carefully on his napkin. 'Charles is nothing more than a lazy spendthrift. He's never done a real day's work in his life.'

'Jay! I won't have you speak like that of your own brother!' Eleanor said sharply. 'I always knew you were jealous of him, but I never thought you would stoop to be so spiteful and unkind.'

He shrugged. 'I'm only telling the truth as I see it. You've spoiled him Mama. You always indulged his every whim and he still thinks he's entitled to everything he wants without lifting a finger.'

Eleanor put her cup down on to its saucer with a clatter. 'At least Charles hasn't brought disgrace on the family,' she said through gritted teeth.

'I know, Mama.' Jay passed his hand across his brow. 'And that's really what I came to see Papa about. Alex. It pains me to say this but it has to be admitted that Alex knows the running of the machines at the factory better than anyone. He could always tell just by listening what was wrong – in fact, what was likely to be going wrong. Humphries is a good chap, but he's been used to taking his orders from Alex and he simply doesn't have his experience.'

'You're not suggesting reinstating Alex, I hope,' Eleanor said coldly. 'I'm sure your father would never agree to that.'

'No, Mama, of course I'm not,' Jay said quickly. 'But I'm beginning to think we shall have to call him back to take a look. The new machine in the cleaning sheds is giving no end of trouble and it's hardly run in yet. We can't keep calling the manufacturers back, it's embarrassing as well as expensive. Especially as I'm sure Alex would know exactly what to do.' He hung his hands between his knees and sat looking down at them. 'The problem is, I don't quite know how to approach Alex without giving the impression that all is forgiven.'

Eleanor stared at him. 'I'm amazed that you should consider approaching Alex at all, Jay. After all, you would have had to get round these problems if he had died; there would have been no calling him back from the grave to look at a troublesome engine.' Her expression hardened even further. 'And as far as I am concerned, in marrying that *factory girl* he *is* dead. As dead as if he was lying in his coffin six feet under the ground. I never wish to hear him spoken of again.' She gave a shrug, her back as stiff as a ram rod. 'His action brought disgrace on the family. And after all that had been done for him, too. If we had not been so well thought of in the town it could have been our ruin as well as his own.' Her voice dropped to an angry whisper. 'For that I can never forgive him. Never.'

Jay got to his feet and began pacing up and down the room. 'Don't imagine for a moment that I want to ask Alex for help, Mama,' he snapped. 'I feel just as strongly as you do about him. But on the other hand I can't afford to hold up production at the factory. It could take Humphries a week to discover what's wrong, whereas Alex would only have to listen to the machine and he would know.'

'I won't have you reinstating Alex!' Eleanor was white with fury.

'I've no intention of reinstating Alex!' Jay, too, had tell-tale white lines running from his nose to the edges of his mouth. He spun round. 'Are you running Beresford's Silk Factory, or am I, Mama?'

She glared at him. 'You may be running it but I'll have you know that I'm quite entitled to have my say because it was *my* money that financed it. Your father could never have hoped to built it without my backing and because of that he has always listened to my opinion.' Eleanor's shoulders sagged. Suddenly she looked old. 'I should never have told you that, Jay. It's all in the past. There was no need. . .'

Jay sat down again. 'I have no intention of reinstating Alex, Mama,' he repeated more gently. 'But I must reserve the right to call him in – as hired labour – to look at the machines from time to time.'

'You must do as you think best.' Eleanor waved her hand wearily. 'But I would ask you to make it clear to him that whatever happens he will never worm his way back into the family. Make sure he understands that he will never be accepted in this house again.'

'Indeed, Mama. I can assure you there is no question of that,' Jay said firmly and with more than a hint of satisfaction.

After Jay had gone Eleanor picked up her embroidery, but she had no heart for it and put it down again almost immediately. She had to admit that Jay was the son with whom she had always felt least comfortable. There was something about him that she could never understand; a coldness, a cruel streak even, that was completely lacking in Charles. And Alex, too. Although heaven knew Alex could be obstinate. She sighed. Perhaps it was just something she imagined, because she knew that Jay was his father's favourite. Like father, like son. Yet Javis was neither cold nor cruel; he was a shrewd man who drove a hard bargain. Even though it had been her money that had financed the factory – why had she felt impelled to drag that up? It was all in the past, Jay hadn't needed to know, it had been Javis's business acumen that had made it prosper and his sound common sense that had dictated the right time to expand. Not that he had ever done anything without consulting her. She had made it quite plain right from the beginning that it was what she expected although as the years went on she had learned not to remind him quite so often that it was *her* money he was using. She sighed again. Perhaps that was what she saw in Jay; not coldness, not cruelty, but the tough, entrepreneurial streak he inherited from his father. That and jealousy of his two brothers, especially Charles. He had always been jealous of Charles, her baby. And of Alex. . . She pursed her lips into a thin line. She refused to even think about Alex.

Two days later, Laura, clad in a voluminous apron, and with a cookery book in one hand, was in the kitchen teaching Maudie to make a fruit cake when there was a knock at the front door.

'Go and answer it, Maudie, and don't forget to say "Good afternoon" when you open the door,' Laura said. She smiled at the girl. 'And wipe that smudge of flour off your nose before you go.'

Full of importance, Maudie went to answer the door. A moment later she came back. 'Thass a man. He say 'is name is 'Umphries or some sech. I left 'im in the parlour, m'm.'

'Humphries?' Laura frowned. She only knew one man named Humphries and that was the foreman engineer at the silk factory. It was hardly likely to be him. 'Thank you, Maudie. Good.' She nodded and smiled at the girl. Her manner wasn't perfect but it was improving. She glanced in the little mirror that hung over the kitchen mantelpiece and patted her hair into place. Then she took off the vast apron and went along to the parlour.

To her surprise it was Humphries from the silk factory. He smirked as she entered the room and she saw him glance at her waistline. She flushed with annoyance. 'Yes?' she asked coolly.

He grinned conspiratorially. 'Done all right for yerself, ain't yer? Marryin' the boss's son. Trapped 'im good an' proper, din't ye?'

Laura went to the door and held it open. 'If that's all you've come to say, then please go.'

'All right. Don't get yer dander up, puttin' on yer airs and graces. Don't fergit I know who you are.' He sat down in Alex's chair and crossed one leg over the other. 'Anyway, thass not all I've come to say, as it happens.'

'Well then, please state your business and go.' Laura remained at the door. She hoped she looked calmer than she felt. If Humphries refused to go she didn't see how she could force him.

'You needn't be so uppity. Thass by way of work for Mr Alex that I've come,' he said huffily. 'Mr Jay say Mr Alex had better come an' give the new machine in the cleanin' shed a look. Thass a real cow of a engine. Can't do nothin' with it. We've had the manufacturers down to look at it twice but thass still not right.'

Laura raised her eyebrows, the only sign of her surprise. 'I'll give my husband your message,' she said, then on a burst of inspiration, 'I'm expecting him back before long.'

To her relief her words brought Humphries to his feet. 'Tell 'im 'is bruvver say 'e better come tonight,' he said, ramming his hat back on his head and moving towards the door. 'Thass holdin' up production.'

'I'll give him your message. When he comes will be entirely up to him. No doubt it will be when he can fit it in with his other work. Good afternoon.'

'Arternoon.'

'And next time please don't come to the front door.' Laura said smoothly. 'The tradesman's entrance is at the back.'

'Good for you,' Alex said admiringly when she repeated her conversation with Humphries. 'Insolent beggar.'

'He made me feel dreadfully nervous. I was afraid I wouldn't be able to get rid of him.' Laura gave a little shudder at the memory.

'He could do with taking down a peg or two. He's always been above himself.'

'But what does it mean, Alex? Do you really think your brother wants you to go back to work at the factory?'

He gave a shrug. 'Whether he does or not, my love, I'm not going. These last three months I've done better than I could ever have dreamed.' He reached across the table and took her hand. 'You're my lucky charm, Laura. I know I can achieve anything as long as you're by my side.'

'I hope you'll always think like that, Alex,' she said quietly. 'But I know your success has little to do with me. It's because you drive yourself to work every hour that God sends, not because I'm here that you're so successful. You never stop working, Alex. And now you've been called back to the silk factory and your brother says you must go tonight.' She gave a deep sigh. 'And I suppose you will.'

Alex leaned back in his chair and yawned. Then he grinned at her. 'All right, my dear, after your little homily I won't go till tomorrow. I think I can fit it in some time tomorrow afternoon.' He yawned again. 'I'm quite tired and I guess we shan't starve if I don't work half the night tonight, which is what it would mean, I've no doubt.' He rubbed his chin thoughtfully. 'I wonder if my father knows I've been sent for.'

Dot was amazed to see Mr Alex tie up his horse and cross the yard to the cleaning shed the following afternoon and she craned her neck to watch until he disappeared.

'What are you finding so interesting down there, may I ask?' Mrs Ripley's voice was like a whiplash behind her. 'You come here to work, not to stand gawping out of the window.'

114

'It's Mr Alex. I've just seen Mr Alex,' Dot said eagerly. 'Do you think he's come back? Do you think he's been forgiven?'

Mrs Ripley gave a prim shrug. 'I shouldn't think so, for a moment. Not after the way he disgraced the family. But I know there's some problem in the cleaning sheds that George Humphries can't seem to get to the bottom of.' She pinched her lip thoughtfully, watching for Alex to re-emerge. When he didn't she rounded on Dot and the other girls who had crowded round the window. 'But whatever it is, it has nothing whatever to do with you. Now get back to work, all of you, or I'll see to it that you lose ten minutes pay apiece.'

The girls all returned to their reels, but Dot, who was lucky enough to work near the window, kept a covert watch on the yard, waiting for him to emerge. He was still there at seven o'clock when knocking off time came.

Dot clattered down the iron stairs with the other girls and then stood aside to wait for her mother and Kate. As she stood there Alex came out of the cleaning shed, covered in grease and wiping his hands on a dirty rag. 'It should be perfectly all right now, Humphries. But it was a sticky one, I'll grant you that,' he said.

'You took your time getting here,' Jay said, emerging from the direction of the office. 'It's been another full day wasted. It's lucky for you it's repaired before the night shift starts.'

'It's lucky for you I came at all,' Alex replied. 'I have my own work to do, remember.'

'Pah! It's your duty to come here if you're called. Blood's thicker than water.'

Alex went white. 'Only when it suits your convenience, it would seem, brother,' he said bitterly. He turned away. 'I shall send you my bill. See that it's paid promptly.' He walked a few steps then came back. 'Every day you make me wait for my money will be a day extra you will wait if you need to call me in again. And I've no doubt you will need my services from time to time. I bid you good day.'

'I was so near I could have touched him,' Dot said, repeating the conversation she had heard as she hurried up the hill with her mother and sister.

'I don't suppose he even noticed you was there,' Nellie

115

said sensibly.

'No, I don't suppose he did. But I would have liked to ask him about Laura. It's near on four months since we last seen her.'

'Well, you couldn't expect her to visit us. Not now. It wouldn't be right and proper, would it, now?'

'No, I s'pose not.' Dot sounded doubtful.

'Well, she's gentry now, ain't she? She couldn't 'sociate with the likes of us. Anyway, I wouldn't want her to. I wouldn't know what to say to her.' Nellie knew her place.

'I wonder if they're happy, Ma.' Dot didn't quite share her mother's resignation. 'We were all so fond of Laura and Mr Alex is such a nice man; thass a shame things couldn't hev bin a bit different – with the family an' that.'

'I think Mr Charles is nicer than Mr Alex,' Kate said dreamily. 'He's so *handsome*. . .'

'Handsome is as handsome does, my girl,' Nellie said sharply. 'Mr Charles has got a reputation.'

'What's a reputation?'

'It means he's a sight too fond of the ladies.' Nellie pursed her lips. 'So you mind and keep out of his way. Come on, now, together, don't drag your feet. You know Ebbie was feverish when we left this morning. I didn't like leavin' him but your dad said he'd be all right with him and the Lord knows we need the money.'

They made the rest of the journey up the hill without speaking. When they arrived home and Nellie pushed open the door they all looked at one another. The loom was ominously silent.

'It must be Ebbie. I knew I should never have left him this morning.' Nellie threw off her shawl and hurried up the stairs, followed by the two girls. Fred came out of Ebbie's room before she was halfway up. 'He's bad,' he said, his face working. 'I've sent Arthur for the doctor, but. . .' he shook his head and stood aside for Nellie and the girls to enter the cramped and stuffy sick room.

Jinny was there, standing by Ebbie's bed, holding his hand and frowning because he was taking no notice of her. His other hand was resting on the book he had been reading. Gently, Nellie drew the little girl away and took her place.

116

Dot automatically picked Jinny up in her arms.

'Thass too late for the doctor,' Nellie said softly. She bent over and kissed the boy's forehead. 'My pore boy. But at least he went peaceful.' She stood aside as each of the girls kissed their brother, then she gave a sniff and pulled the sheet gently over his head. 'You an' me'll see to him when the doctor's bin, Dot,' she said. 'Can't do no more now. We'd better go downstairs.'

'I'll be down in a minute,' Fred said and went and knelt beside the bed.

'We should've taken in another lodger after Laura left,' Dot said later, when, the first flush of grief over, they all sat round drinking tea and dabbing red-rimmed eyes. 'At least her money helped to pay for his medicine.'

Nellie shook her head. 'That medicine wouldn't never have made him well. The Quack knew that, but he was happy to pretend it did as long as we coughed up the money for it.' She shook her head again and her voice broke. 'We knew it, too. But while he had it we felt we was doing *something* to help him.'

'What did him more good than anything was Laura teachin' him to read,' Fred said. 'That book she bought him gave him more pleasure than anything. I should like him to be buried with his book.'

'But Laura might want it back!' Dot said, horrified.

Fred gave a little smile. 'No. She gave it to him. It was his book. Anyway, I'm sure she'd understand.'

Chapter Eleven

News of what had been going on in India reached English newspapers late and the enormity of the uprising and the accompanying atrocities only gradually emerged. Laura followed the news reports with mounting horror. She could hardly believe that the beautiful country that she had lived in for such a short time could have become such a blood bath. She remembered vividly the Residency at Lucknow; the extensive grounds, colourful with exotic flowers and the white houses of Company officials dotted around among the trees. And the tall, square imposing building of the Residency itself, with the banqueting hall across the lawn. In her memory it was all so elegant, so peaceful. It was beyond her imagination to visualise the scenes, the atrocities described so graphically by the newspapers, and she prayed every night that Annabel had somehow avoided being caught up in the terrible events. She wished now that she had written to her friend, but she could never have told Annabel the hardships she had suffered on her return to England and so it had seemed better to remain silent altogether. It saddened her to think that she would never see her friend again, and her little son, of whom she had grown so fond.

It must have been the memory of the ball she had attended at the Lucknow Residency that prompted Laura to dwell yet again on these things as she dressed for the Mayor's New Year Ball at the Moot Hall in Colchester. As she slipped into the sumptuous blue satin gown that had been Alex's Christmas present to her she studied her reflection in the long cheval mirror.

It could have been a trick of the light, but for a moment she saw not Alex Beresford's wife but the woeful, homeless orphan who had arrived in Colchester a little over a year ago, clad in somebody's cast-off gown, ill-fitting shoes and without a penny to her name. A girl who had been only too thankful to find employment at Beresford's Silk Factory – a place where few respectable girls worked. With such a history how could she dare to even think she might be accepted into the cream of Colchester society?

She sat down on the bed and covered her face with her hands.

Alex came into the room struggling with his cravat. 'I can't fix this wretched thing. Give me a. . .' He stared at her. 'Laura? What is it? What's wrong? Are you ill?'

She shook her head. 'No. But it's no good, Alex. I can't do it. I can't come with you tonight,' she sobbed.

'Why ever not?'

'I don't think I can face it, Alex. I'm sorry.' She looked up at him, her face tear-stained and anxious. 'How can I walk into the place where all those people are? The Mayor and all the dignitaries. And your parents. . . they'll be there. . . And your brothers. . . They all know who I am and where I came from.'

Alex left his cravat hanging and went over to the bed and sat down beside her, taking her hands in their silly little blue lace mittens in his. 'Now, Laura, we've had this argument before and I've told you there's nothing whatever for you to worry about.' He gave her hands a little shake. 'Of course you must come with me. There's no question of you staying behind. You know I can't possibly go without you, dear. Anyway, I've already accepted for you, so the matter is closed.' He got up and went to struggle again with his cravat at the dressing table mirror. He glanced at her reflection as she perched on the edge of the bed, the dress spread around her. It was a deep, midnight-blue that matched her eyes, flounced and ruched and trimmed with matching lace. He turned and smiled encouragingly at her. 'You look absolutely beautiful, my darling. And I'm sure you know how to behave at these functions far better than most of the people who'll be there. Anyway,' he laughed, 'that dress cost me half a week's

119

wages. You must wear it now you've got it.'

'Yes, it was rather expensive,' she agreed, smoothing her hands across the shining fabric. 'Perhaps I shouldn't have. . .'

'Perhaps nothing,' he silenced her. 'You look ravishing in it and with your black hair the colour is perfect. You'll be the belle of the ball.' He went over and kissed the tip of her nose. 'Now, listen, Laura. You know how important this is to me. My business is going well; my name is becoming known in my own right; not as part of Beresford's Silk Factory, but as Alex Beresford the engineer. And it's in that capacity that we've been invited to the Mayor's Ball tonight. *We've* been invited, Mr and *Mrs* Alex Beresford, not just me on my own. You can't let me down, Laura.' He drew her to him and kissed her again. 'It'll be all right, my love. You'll see. It's not as if you've never been to a ball before, is it?'

She shook her head, still full of doubt. 'No. But your family. Supposing they make a scene, Alex. . .'

'Then they'd be damned bad-mannered.' He pulled her to her feet. 'Don't worry, my darling. Everything will be all right. I promise you. But you must come,' a stern note crept into his voice. 'You're my wife. You can't hide yourself away.' His face broke into a smile. 'If nothing else, let people see how wrong they were in thinking I've married a common or garden factory girl. You've a damn sight more breeding than most of the people who'll be there, so why not let them see it?' He pulled her to her feet and held her close to him. 'Anyway, what's more important is that I need you by my side. I'm proud of you and I want everybody to see what a wonderful wife I've got.' He took a step back and looked her up and down. 'There's just one more thing,' he said mysteriously and went over to the military chest where he kept his shirts and underclothes. After a moment's rummaging he came back hold a rather battered leather jewel case. 'I think it's time I gave you these, my love. I've been looking for the right opportunity and now it's arrived.' He clicked open the box to reveal a triple string of perfectly graded pearls.

She put out a finger and touched them. 'Alex, they're beautiful,' she breathed. 'But where did they come from?'

'They were my grandfather's wedding present to his bride.' He took them carefully from the case and laid them round her neck. 'And now I'm giving them to you, Laura, my dearest love.' He stood back with his head on one side and studied the effect of the pearls against her creamy neck and the dark ringlet of hair that fell over one bare shoulder. 'They're exactly right for you.' He took her hand and kissed it. 'Now, Mrs Beresford, will you do me the honour of accompanying me to the ball?'

The Moot Hall glittered with the light from twenty crystal chandeliers on the dazzling array of dresses. Laura caught her breath. For a moment she was reminded once again of the ball she had attended in Lucknow although the dark evening dress of the men tonight bore no comparison to the dress uniforms of the officers at the garrison that night. If the newspapers were to be believed there had been little cause for celebration there these past months. A little shiver went down her spine at the thought.

'Are you all right?' Alex had noticed her hesitate and he took her arm protectively.

She nodded and determinedly put thoughts of India from her. 'Yes, I'm perfectly all right,' she said steadily and smiled at him.

Reassured, he led her in and gave their names to be announced. At the name 'Mr and Mrs Alex Beresford' the hum of conversation ceased and all eyes were turned to catch a glimpse of the upstart of a common factory worker that had riven the Beresford family apart. They were quite unprepared for the striking, black-haired woman in the blue satin gown who stood, outwardly poised and serene by her husband's side. Of course, what had happened to the Beresford family was common knowledge in the town and surrounding countryside and many a farmer had been torn between calling in Alex, the best man for the job, and listening to his wife's condemnation of his reputedly irresponsible behaviour. Fortunately for Alex, business sense had usually won.

The Mayor and local dignitaries made their formal greeting with wooden faces, each one trying to suppress his secret amazement at the cultured tone of this woman and the grace with which she moved. This was not the common harlot they had expected and most were hard pressed to conceal their admiration for easily the most attractive woman in the hall.

As for Laura, it took all the courage she possessed to follow her husband down the unwelcoming line and she was quite unaware of the figure she presented as Alex swept her into the first dance.

'They can't believe their eyes,' he whispered gleefully into her ear. 'I don't know what they expected, but they're all talking about you.'

'I'm certain they are,' Laura said, her mouth dry with nervousness. 'I just wonder what they're saying.'

'They're saying that I'm the luckiest man in Colchester. There's not a man here that doesn't envy me my stunning wife,' he smiled down at her with a wealth of love in his eyes.

'Is that the woman Alex has married, Javis?' Eleanor tapped her fan on her husband's arm as Laura danced by with Alex.

'What?' Javis adjusted his pince nez. 'Yes, my dear, I believe it is.' He followed them with his gaze. She was a damned fine-looking filly and no mistake. And the way she was conducting herself tonight did her credit, because it couldn't be easy for the gel.

'I thought it must be because she's wearing your mother's pearls, Javis. Do you see that? The hussy is wearing your mother's pearls.' She gave her husband another sharp rap with her fan. 'Where did she get them from?'

'From Alex, I suppose, my dear. After all, they were left to him as part of his legacy.'

'Hmph. They should have gone to Jay. He was the eldest. But Alex was always your mother's favourite. I suppose she felt sorry for him. Little did she know how he would disgrace the family name. She would turn in her grave if she could see her pearls now.' Eleanor said no more but sat with her lips set in a thin line.

Javis pursed his lips. Whatever Eleanor might say the pearls looked damned fine on the gel's long white neck. Although he could never say so aloud he was beginning to have more and more sympathy for young Alex and more and more respect for the gel he'd married. Alex might have picked her up off the factory floor but she had breeding, anyone could see that with half an eye.

As the evening progressed Laura found to her surprise that she was beginning to enjoy herself. She had no shortage of partners when Alex went off for what he called his 'duty' dances with the wives of potential clients and business associates, because a good many of the men there were frankly curious about her. They were even more baffled after partnering her, amazed to have been in the company of such a cultured, well-informed and well-mannered woman. They discovered that she had a sight more knowledge of current affairs than most women and spoke with real feeling about the dreadful business in India, where all those ungrateful Indian chappies had turned on their English masters. It was almost as if she'd been there. They didn't understand her, but they did begin to understand Alex's attraction towards her.

But the evening was not without its awkward moments. During the Lancers Laura found herself face to face with Jay Beresford. He was forced to partner her briefly but his face was thunderous. 'How dare you, madam!' he hissed into her ear. 'How dare you come here tonight and humiliate my family in this manner!'

She was completely taken aback by the venom in his voice and his cruel remarks made her feel sick, nevertheless she managed to smile politely at him. 'Thank you, sir,' she said as she curtseyed and moved on to her next partner.

Charles was hardly less insulting, but in a different way. 'You've got a nerve coming here tonight, haven't you?' he said with a grin, trying to hold her close enough to get his hand on to her breast. 'Quite set the family by its ears, you have. Mater is furious and so is Jay. Don't know so much about Pa, he's got an eye for a pretty girl himself, on the quiet. And so have I, by Jove. Damn me if I wouldn't have had you myself if old Alex hadn't forestalled me. You're quite a filly, aren't you?'

Laura didn't reply. She found Charles's approach even more insulting than Jay's. Sometimes it was hard to decide which of Alex's brothers she disliked the most.

'She's wearing your grandmother's pearls. That woman is wearing your grandmother Beresford's pearls,' Eleanor hissed to Jay as he escorted her into the supper room.

'I can see that. I think it's outrageous,' Jay agreed. It had always been a sore point with him that his paternal grandmother had overlooked him in her will, favouring Alex instead. 'I'm amazed he had the effrontery to bring her here in the first place and I told her as much when I was forced to partner her briefly. Shall you sit with the Rankins Mama? I believe Father is escorting Mrs Rankin.'

'Yes, dear.' Eleanor sighed. 'I suppose it will only be polite to sit with your parents-in-law.' She sat down, a small, neat, elegant woman, and smoothed her black silk gown. It was trimmed with cerise ribbons as befitted the occasion, but the ribbons were very tastefully placed and not too profuse. Eleanor Beresford knew exactly how to obtain the best effect.

'I declare I'm all of a lather.' Lottie Rankin flopped down beside Eleanor, her emerald green taffeta rustling round her. 'Get me a drink, Jay, do. I'm as dry as chaff after all that hoppin' around.' She fanned herself with a fan of floppy feathers dyed the same colour as her dress. 'I don't believe I've danced so much since our dear Queen's Coronation – and that must be over twenty years ago. Whew! Thass hot in here and no mistake.' She looked it, too, with dark sweat stains under her armpits and her coarse, ruddy features shining with perspiration.

'Here y'are, gal, I've brought you a pint o' porter. That'll tickle your ribs an' put hair on your chest.' Sid Rankin sat down beside his wife. 'Evenin', Mrs Beresford,' he leaned across Lottie to greet Eleanor.

Eleanor inclined her head graciously. 'Good evening, Mr Rankin.' She could never bring herself to address him as Sid and nobody ever called him Sidney.

'Well, thass a real good do, here tonight. Cost a pretty penny, too. An' the money we paid for our tickets 'on't cover the cost so that'll hev to come outa the rates.' He took out his snuff box, put a pinch on the back of his hand and took a long sniff. Then he sneezed. 'Well, as I was sayin', we might as well eat our fill, cause you might as well say we've paid twice.' He got up and went to the long buffet tables, laden with food.

'Can I get you something, Mama? Mama-in-law?' Jay asked, glad that his father-in-law was out of the way.

'Just a small bite, Jay, please. I'm not hungry,' Eleanor said.

'I am,' Lottie laughed. 'Yes, Jay, I'll hev one of whatever's goin'. An' two if that look extra special. Them oyster patties look very nice. I wouldn't mind a couple o' them. But you tell my Sid to lay off 'em, 'cause he know what they do to 'im an' I shall be too tired for that sorta thing when we get back tonight.' She winked at Eleanor, who was carefully looking the other way, and took another long draught of her porter. Lottie was enjoying herself tonight and although she had been very carefully on her best behaviour at the beginning of the evening, by now her resolve had slipped and she had relaxed into a manner that would have mortified Charlotte, had she been there, and would give Lottie herself waves of hot, embarrassed blushes in the morning.

'Is Charlotte keeping reasonably well?' Eleanor asked politely. She had seen the girl herself only three days ago but it provided a talking point.

'Yes, I don't reckon she's got much more'n a month to go now before she make us both grandmothers,' Lottie nodded happily. I reckon that'll be a boy, meself. She seem to be carryin' all at the front an' they say boys are carried at the front and girls all round. I remember I carried Charlotte all round. Were you all front with your boys, Mrs Beresford?'

Eleanor took out her handkerchief and held it to her nose to cover her discomfort. 'I really don't know. I really can't remember,' she said quickly.

'Can't you?' Lottie looked surprised. 'Oh, I can. I remember. . .' Suddenly, she realised where she was and who she was talking to and she gave a little laugh. 'Oh, well, never mind. Thass all over now.'

Javis sat opposite the two women, sipping a whisky and soda and taking no interest in their conversation. Nevertheless, he watched his wife making forced conversation with Lottie Rankin and it occurred to him that Alex's wife, the girl Eleanor so despised, had more breeding in her little finger than the whole of the Rankin family – including Charlotte, the daughter-in-law Eleanor had been happy to welcome into the family. He took another draught of whisky and savoured it. Sid Rankin's money made up for a great deal, he decided with more than a degree of cynicism. He glanced down to the other end of the room, where Alex and his wife were sitting. Sometimes he felt he would like to get to know his second daughter-in-law, even though she was so unacceptable to the family. But of course he never could.

Alex had been careful to make sure that he and Laura were as far as possible from the rest of his family in the supper room. He had positioned Laura so that she had her back to them but from his position he had watched, with a certain amusement, as Eleanor did her best to hide her feelings for the Rankins and Jay tried to cover his embarrassment at their coarse behaviour, and he was struck by the irony of it all. At least Laura knew how to conduct herself. He smiled at her.

'Shall we go back, dearest?'

'Yes, I can hear they're playing a schottishe. My feet are tapping already.' Laura picked up her evening bag.

He squeezed her arm. 'See? It's not so bad, is it? In fact, I do believe you're glad you came.'

But he spoke too soon. As he led her out of the supper room by one door to return to the ballroom, by an odd quirk of fate, Eleanor left at the same time with Javis and Jay by another. Unavoidably, they met face to face in the corridor.

Alex felt Laura's hand tighten on his arm and he put his other hand protectively over it. 'Mama, Papa, Jay.' he inclined his head to each in turn. 'May I introduce you to my wife, Laura?'

'No, sir, you may not.' Eleanor said, through gritted teeth before either Javis or Jay could speak. 'And I would have thought you might have had more respect for our family than to allow her to accompany you here tonight, knowing that we should be attending. I, myself, would never have come, had I known the disgrace you would bring upon us.'

Old Javis cleared his throat. 'Now, now, my dear.' He laid his hand on his wife's arm. 'It's not like you to make a scene.'

'I am not making a scene, Javis.' It was true, her voice was

126

deadly quiet with fury. 'But I mean every word that I say. And I'll thank you to remove your grandmother's pearls from that woman's neck.'

'I bid you good night,' Alex said, putting his arm round Laura and holding her close to his side, his face white and set. 'I refuse to stand here and listen to my wife being insulted.' He tried to guide Laura past but the three of them were barring his way.

'Those are family pearls,' Eleanor went on as if he hadn't spoken. 'And if you had an ounce of respect for your mother, Javis,' she said to her husband, 'you would demand that they be returned to you instead of draping the neck of a. . . a. . .'

Laura didn't hear what Eleanor called her. As she stood beside Alex, trying to remain calm whilst his mother vented her bitter hatred on her, she felt the whole world turning black around her and with a gasp as she realised what was happening she crumpled to the floor in a dead faint.

When she came to she was lying on a sofa in an ante room with feathers being burnt under her nose. 'Oh!' She began to cough.

'Ah, that's better.' Alex slipped his arm under her head. 'Now, just drink this and then I'll take you home. 'I'm so sorry, my darling. I knew you were reluctant to come here tonight but I honestly didn't think anything like this would happen. It was unforgivable of my mother to behave like that. I'm not surprised it made you ill. But just lie still. I've already asked someone to call a cab, it should be here in a few minutes.' His face was a mask of anxiety.

Laura smiled up at him. 'I'm all right, Alex. Really I am. It was stupid of me to faint like that and I'm sure it had nothing to do with what happened. . .'

'I still say it was unforgivable of my mother. I don't know what came over her,' Alex said savagely. 'And when you fainted she just looked down at you and then walked away. I wouldn't have thought anyone could be so heartless.' He bit his lip, too upset to say more.

Laura sat up. 'It doesn't matter, Alex,' she said sadly. 'Really, it doesn't matter.' She gave a rueful smile. 'But after what's happened here tonight I know that there's nothing I can't cope with. I was worried and afraid, but not any more because I know I've done nothing to be ashamed of tonight. I just feel sorry for your mother. I think she may very well regret behaving in such a manner when she thinks about it tomorrow.'

'I'm sure you're right about that. But it doesn't alter the fact that the strain of it all made you faint.'

She put out her hand and touched his face. 'It wasn't that, Alex, I'm sure of it. It was. . . it was . . Oh, Alex, I'm to have a child!'

He stared at her for a moment. 'Why didn't you tell me, Laura? I would never have . . . Are you quite sure? Have you seen Dr Franklyn? Oh, my dear.' He gathered her to him and kissed her, hardly knowing what he was saying in his excitement. He held her away from him for a moment. 'Are you quite sure, Laura?'

She smiled at him. 'Yes, Alex, I'm quite sure. And yes, I've already seen Dr Franklyn.' But although she could never tell Alex this, she had known, even before she visited Dr Franklyn, that she was pregnant. Because hadn't she been through it all before?

Chapter Twelve

Charlotte's baby was born on a cold, wet day in February. It was a girl.

Of course he never actually said so, but Charlotte knew she had displeased Jay by giving him a daughter rather than the son he had assumed she would produce. At first she consoled herself that a man could hardly be expected to show any interest in a tiny baby, but as time went on and he never asked to see his daughter, never even enquired after the child's health, Charlotte realised how bitter his disappointment was.

Nevertheless, she did her best to ignore the way he slighted the child.

'What shall we call baby, Jay?' she asked one day, when he was sitting by the fire with his pipe after their evening meal. 'She's two months old now, we can't just keep calling her "baby", can we?'

'Call her what you will, my dear,' he said with a shrug. 'It's all one to me.'

'I had thought perhaps Eleanor – after your mother, dearest.' She thought that would please him.

'As you like. It's as good a name as any other, I daresay.' He picked up the newspaper.

She lifted the baby from her cradle. 'Look, Jay. I believe she's smiling. Smile at your papa, Ellie.' She held the baby for him to see. 'She's very like you, Jay. Already she has auburn tints in her hair and her features. . .'

'Oh, for goodness sake, Charlotte, stop behaving like a fool.' He threw down the newspaper and stood up, giving his daughter what might have passed for a glare had it not been so brief. 'It doesn't look like anybody except itself. And I thought babies were supposed to be pretty little things.'

Charlotte pouted. 'Oh, Jay. Don't tease me so. She is pretty. She's quite beautiful, aren't you, my pet?' She smiled adoringly at her little daughter.

He shrugged again. 'Very well, if you say so, my dear.' He went over to the bell pull and rang for his hat and gloves to be brought. While he was waiting Charlotte looked up at him shyly. 'I know you're disappointed that Ellie's a girl, Jay, but next year's baby will be a boy, I'm sure of it. A baby brother for Ellie's first birthday, wouldn't that be nice?'

Jay permitted a smile to flit across his face. 'Yes, my dear, it would be very nice. In fact there's nothing I'd like better.' He brushed an imaginary speck of dust from his lapel. 'A man needs a son to carry on the family name.'

'Of course he does.' Charlotte smiled happily. 'And you shall have your son Jay. Next year.'

He bent and kissed her on the cheek. 'Don't be too hasty, my dear. You must recover fully from this confinement before you begin to think of another. . .'

She clasped his hand. 'Oh, but, Jay, I feel so well. I've never felt better in my life. And Dr May said that by the time Ellie is three months old it will be quite in order. . .'

Jay freed himself and straightened up, clearing his throat loudly. 'I must be going, Charlotte. I've already stayed too long talking to you. I shall be late for my appointment.'

'Oh, Jay, you surely haven't got to go back to the factory tonight, have you? It's past eight o'clock.'

'I'm afraid so, my dear.' He went to the door. 'And then I shall call in at the Conservative Club for an hour. Don't wait up for me, I may be late.'

'Very well, dear.' There was a hint of a sigh in her voice.

After he had gone Charlotte laid little Eleanor back in her cradle and sat down at the window overlooking the street. The lamp lighter had already been round and by the light from the street lamps she watched her husband's tall figure striding away until it was lost in the distance. Then she drew the curtains and turned back into the room.

'Oh, ma'am, you didn't need to draw them curtains. I could hev done that,' Lucy, the maid had just bustled in to light the lamps and she went over and gave the curtains an extra flick, as if to show that they hadn't been done quite to her satisfaction.

'It's all right, Lucy, I'm not entirely helpless,' Charlotte said with another sigh.

She didn't know why she was so full of sighs. She was very lucky. The house on North Hill where Jay had brought her after their marriage was spacious and furnished with the best furniture her father's shop could provide, most of which had been of her own choosing. And she enjoyed being mistress of her own house, with three maids and a cook to do her bidding. And now there was a nursemaid for Ellie, although she had assured Jay that she was quite capable of looking after the baby herself. But he had insisted.

She sighed yet again. Jay was very good to her but sometimes she felt he had provided so many people to look after her welfare that there was nothing much left for her to do except call on people and receive them in return. Now that she was fully recovered from her confinement she would soon have to begin that dreary round once more. She gave a slight shiver in the cool, April evening and went to pick up the fire tongs, then changing her mind rang the bell instead for Lucy to come and put coal on the fire. It wouldn't do to offend the servants.

Idly, she picked up her embroidery. At least it wouldn't be long before she could resume her wifely duties to Jay. She coloured faintly at the thought, because there was no denying she was looking forward to that.

Alex made his way home from the ironmongers at the end of the High Street near the castle. He was tired; he'd had a busy day and he looked forward to a quiet meal with Laura before he told her the good news. At the thought of this his step became lighter and he began to whistle as he walked along.

'Feelin' good-natured, Charlie?' A wheedling, whining voice came from a shadowy doorway.

Alex stopped. 'Who are you? What do you want?'

A girl, she could have been anything from sixteen to twenty-six, stepped out of the shadows. She had on a ragged yellow crinoline and had tied a yellow rag of ribbon round her lank hair. She was incredibly dirty.

'Feelin' good-natured, Charlie?' she repeated. 'I know where we could go. I can give yer a good time. . .' She laid her hand, with its black, broken fingernails, on his sleeve.

He shook it off and looked at her in disgust. 'Get away, girl. I want none of your vile favours,' he said and hurried on.

'Well, there's plenty o' your sort that do,' she snarled after him. 'I could tell yer a tale or two, I could, about the toffs. All so respeckable, butter wouldn't melt in their mouths. Oh, yes, I could tell yer. . . You'd be surprised if you knew some o' them that ain't so fussy. . . Some o' yer own fam'ly, too. . .' But he wasn't listening so she went back to the shadowy doorway, muttering and hugging herself in her thin dress against the chill night air.

He didn't mention his encounter with the street girl to Laura. In fact, as soon as he entered the comfort of his own house he forgot her existence.

Laura was sitting by the window, knitting a shawl for the coming baby. There was a delicious smell of cooking coming from the direction of the kitchen and the table was laid ready. Alex looked at the peaceful, domestic scene and thought that he must be the luckiest man on God's earth.

Laura lifted her face to his kiss. 'Hurry and clean yourself up, Alex, dear. Maudie has made her first unaided meat pie and she's desperately anxious to serve it before it spoils.'

'I'll be two minutes, that's all.' He kissed her again and hurried out to the back kitchen.

Ten minutes later a beaming Maudie brought in a succulent steak and kidney pie with a crisp golden crust that smelled delicious and tasted even better. And Maudie herself had undergone quite a transformation in the months she had been with the Beresfords. Gone was the undersized little scrap in a uniform two sizes too big, with carroty hair spiking out from under her cap and a pale, pinched face. Maudie would always be pale and freckled, but her skin was clear now and her face had filled out. Her hair had grown thicker, though it still defied taming, so her cap sat precariously on the wild, frizzy ginger mass, anchored with hairpins that constantly fell out. She had put on weight with regular meals and Laura declared she had grown at least an inch in her service.

'That was excellent, Maudie,' Alex said, when she came in to clear and bring in a bowl of stewed fruit.

'An' I did it all meself, sir,' Maudie said with her habitual smile. 'The missus never 'ad to 'elp me at all.'

'That's quite true,' Laura said. 'You've learned so much so quickly that now I really don't know what I'd do without you, Maudie.'

Maudie straightened her shoulders and smoothed her apron, preening herself at Laura's words.

'She's very happy here, isn't she?' Alex said thoughtfully, as Maudie returned to her own meal in the kitchen.

'Oh, yes. She often tells me she thinks she's the luckiest girl in the world,' Laura smiled. 'And she's been very quick to learn. She's quite sharp, you know.'

He nodded and pinched his lip. I'm afraid she can't stay here, though, my dear.'

'Not stay here! Oh, Alex, what do you mean? I thought the business was doing well. You didn't tell me.' Laura stretched out her hand to him, her face creased with anxiety.

He put his hand over hers. 'She can't stay here because we shall be moving,' he said soberly. Then, unable to keep up the pretence any longer his face broke into a grin. 'Oh, Laura, my love, we'll be moving into one of the new houses in Lexden Road in the autumn. I've been and signed on the dotted line this afternoon.'

'Alex! Oh, how wonderful! But isn't it a bit soon?' She was torn between excitement and anxiety. 'I mean, it's under twelve months since you left the silk factory. Can we. . . you afford to move to Lexden Road?'

'Yes, my dear, we can. And not only that, I've taken a lease on a workshop in Stanwell Street so we shan't be forced to "live over the shop" so to speak.'

'Oh, you know I've never minded that, dear. It's been nice to know you were working so near.'

'All the same, I felt it was time I provided my wife and family with something a thought more roomy than this little rabbit warren.' He pulled her to her feet and hugged her.

'I won't have a word said against this little house, Alex,' she said reprovingly, 'I loved it the minute I came into it and I've never for one second changed my mind.'

133

'I'm sure you'll feel exactly the same about the new one,' he assured her.

She laid her head on his shoulder. 'As long as I'm with you, Alex, I think I'd be happy to live in an old barn.'

'I don't think that will be necessary, dear,' he grinned. 'I'm expecting us to be comfortably settled in the new house by the time the baby is born.'

'But that's less than two months!'

'That's right. Shall we go and choose curtain material tomorrow?' It was only her advancing pregnancy that prevented him from dancing her round the room. 'And I'll take you to look at our new home at the same time.'

'Oh, Alex,' her eyes filled with tears. 'I'm so happy.' But even as she spoke the words a sudden feeling – it was not strong enough to be called a premonition – flitted through her mind like a shadow crossing a brilliant sun, gone almost before it had formed. She gave an almost imperceptible shiver and repeated, 'so *very* happy.'

Laura stood beside Alex on the pavement outside the house and looked up at it. Two large bay windows flanked an impressive front door with an elaborate brass door knocker and an ornate Georgian fanlight; there were three long windows on the floor above and four small ones up under the eaves.

'Isn't it rather large for the two of us, Alex?' she whispered, tugging at his arm.

'We shall soon be three,' he reminded her with a smile, 'and eventually four or five, I hope.'

She blushed. 'It's very grand,' she said. 'Are you sure. . .?'

'Quite sure,' he said firmly. He put his hand under her elbow and guided her up the four steps to the front door and made a great play of finding the right key to open it. 'There, now,' he flung it open, 'your new home, Mrs Beresford.'

It was everything she could have wished. She went from room to room, upstairs and down, exclaiming and delighting in everything she saw. There was a spacious hall, tiled in black and white, from which the staircase curved elegantly to the floor above. On the right a long drawing room ran from the front of the house to the back, where a large window overlooked the secluded garden and on the left there was a study and a small sitting room, and behind them was a good sized dining room. Upstairs were five bedrooms and above that the nursery and servants quarters. The kitchens were in the basement.

'I'm afraid Maudie will be a bit overwhelmed with all this,' Laura said as she looked round the spacious kitchen, with its long table and large kitchen range. 'I don't quite know how she'll manage.'

'She won't have to manage, my love. Not on her own, at any rate. We shall be entertaining so we shall need a proper cook. And a housemaid and a kitchenmaid at the very least.'

Laura bit her lip. She could see trouble ahead if Maudie found her position usurped but for the moment she said nothing and allowed Alex to make extravagant and wonderful plans which she couldn't believe would ever come to fruition.

But to her amazement everything was done exactly as Alex had envisaged. He consulted her at every turn as she lay resting on her bed, fuming at her inability to do more than choose materials and carpets because Dr Franklyn had warned her against any undue exertion.

She hated the inactivity, not least because it gave her time to compare this pregnancy with the last one. Things couldn't have been more different. Lying in the pretty little room she shared with Alex, surrounded by books, fruit and everything she could possibly want, it was difficult to recall that she was the same girl who had struggled back to England, pregnant and alone, and had ended up giving birth in a London workhouse. She closed her eyes against the memory. But she wasn't the same girl. All that had happened in another life. A life that was buried in the past, never to be resurrected.

Unless Dr Franklyn knew. But could a doctor tell? She was woefully ignorant about such things and there was not a soul in the world that she could ask. All she could do was to pray fervently that Dr Franklyn hadn't discovered her terrible secret.

The Beresfords moved into the new house in Lexden Road on the first day of August, a year after their marriage, and a fortnight later Laura's baby was born. It was a difficult birth and she hovered between life and death for three days before the doctor pronounced her out of danger. Alex, his elation at the birth of his son totally overshadowed by frantic concern over his beloved wife, hardly left her side.

On the fourth day, she opened her eyes and saw Alex, unshaven, slumped in the chair at the foot of the bed. Dr Franklyn was standing beside him.

'There you are, my boy,' the doctor said, nudging Alex when he saw that she was awake, 'I told you the fever had gone and she was out of danger.' He came over and took her hand, an unfathomable expression on his face. 'First babies are notoriously difficult to birth,' he said, not taking his eyes from her face. He put his hand on her brow and smiled. 'You'll do, my dear. You've got a bonny son. Make the most of him, it's unlikely that there'll be any more.'

So Dr Franklyn knew. And that was his way of telling her that her secret was safe with him. She smiled gratefully at him as he stood back to make way for Alex.

'I've sent messages three times, telling him we've got problems with that new doubling machine, but has he shown up? No. And not even a word to say when he'll be here. Alex is getting a sight too big for his boots now that he's moved into that new house in Lexden Road, if you ask me. Needs taking down a peg or two.' Jay drummed his fingers impatiently on the desk.

Old Javis looked over the top of his gold-rimmed glasses. 'I believe his wife has been very ill,' he remarked.

Jay stared at his father. 'What's that got to do with it? It shouldn't keep him from his work.'

'I'm told she almost died giving him a son.' Old Javis spoke casually, but he was watching Jay like a hawk and was rewarded by seeing the jealous flush that suffused his eldest son's face.

'How do you know that?' Jay growled.

'I heard it at the Golf Club. Jack Marfleet is one of Alex's customers and he told me the boy was so worried he never left her side for three days. Alex is very well thought of in the town, you know.'

'He'd be a damn sight better thought of at Beresford's if he was to come when he was summoned,' Jay snapped. 'I never heard such nonsense. Men are best out of the way at times like that.'

'Would you have left Charlotte's side if she had been at death's door?'

'Hmph.' With an enigmatic grunt Jay pulled some papers towards him. The question hadn't arisen. Charlotte had given birth without fuss, although she had let him down badly by not giving him the son he craved. Again he felt a shaft of jealousy to think Alex had achieved what he had not. And on a factory girl, too, he thought with disgust.

There was a knock at the door and a small, grimy boy announced nervously that Mr Alex had arrived.

'And about time, too,' Jay got up from his chair so abruptly that it fell over. 'I'll come and have a word with him. It's time he was reminded that time is money. My money. And time wasted is my money wasted. And there's been far too much of that, these past few days.'

He strode out of the room, nearly knocking the little messenger over as he went. Old Jarvis looked after him, shaking his head. There was something strange about Jay; in spite of having a devoted wife and family, in spite of having almost a free hand in the running of one of the most successful businesses in the town, he was a driven man. Why that should be so Old Javis was completely at a loss to explain. What more could the boy want, in heaven's name? He picked up the day's *Times* and turned to the crossword.

Chapter Thirteen

There was a knock at the bedroom door and Marcus came in. Laura, sitting at her dressing table, finished fixing the diamond earrings that had been Alex's birthday present to her the previous year and turned round, holding out her arms to her four-year-old son.

'I've come to say good night, Mama.' He trotted over to her, a small replica of Alex, dressed in a little red dressing gown over a striped nightshirt. 'Maudie said you'd be too busy to come up to the nursery to kiss me goodnight because you were going out.' He held up his little face for a kiss.

Laura took him on her lap, heedless of crushing the voluminous pink silk ball gown. 'I shall never be too busy to come to the nursery to kiss you, darling,' she said. 'And I shall come up and read you a story like I always do, as soon as I've finished here.' She kissed him and laid her cheek on his dark head, gazing at their reflection in the mirror in front of her. She was so happy that sometimes she thought her heart would burst. Alex was everything to her and their love for each other had increased, if that was possible, with each year they were together. And Marcus, darling Marcus, the treasure of her heart, was growing to be an affectionate, intelligent boy, idolised by Maudie, who loved being his nursemaid, but nevertheless ruled the nursery with a firm hand. Laura sighed. The only cloud on her happiness was her inability to give Alex more children because of something that had gone wrong at Marcus's protracted and painful birth. She gave a small secret smile. There was no doubt that she would have conceived again had the possibility been there;

she and Alex enjoyed each other with an uninhibited enthusiasm that had never diminished since the day they married.

'What are you smiling at, Mama?' Marcus turned his head
to look up at her.

'I'm smiling because I'm happy,' she said, giving him a
hug. 'Now, run along to bed. I'll be up to read to you in five
minutes.'

She put him gently down from her lap and he ran to the
connecting door of Alex's dressing room. 'I'll see if Papa
will carry me up on his shoulders,' he said eagerly.

A minute later, Alex, his tie still untied, came through,
with the little boy perched on his shoulders, making train
noises, stopping and starting, reversing and then going
forward again, while Marcus screamed with laughter and
waved his arms. 'I'm the guard, waving my green flag,' he
shouted.

'Oh, Alex, he'll never sleep if you make him so excited,'
Laura laughed with them. 'Maudie will have an awful time
with him.'

'Will you read me the story of Augustus when you come
upstairs, Mama?' Marcus called gaily as they reached the
door. 'I'll have it ready at the right page.'

'All right, dear.' Laura smiled again and turned back to her
reflection in the mirror. A calm, composed woman looked
back at her with clear, violet-blue eyes and her black hair was
piled thickly on top of her head, accentuating her long white
neck and shoulders. She put her head on one side. She had
come a long way since that fateful New Year's Ball when she
had been sick with nerves and fright because Alex's parents
were likely to be there. She was not nervous any longer. The
past four years had established Alex as one of the leading
engineers of the town; his business had grown and prospered
and he was respected and admired by his associates. And as
Alex's reputation had grown, so her early beginnings in the
town had been forgotten. People now accepted her for what
she was, a polite, perfectly-mannered, gracious woman,
attractive enough to turn the head of any man and sufficiently
intelligent to hold her own views on most things without
appearing to be a blue-stocking. The scandal of Alex's
marriage to one of his father's factory hands had been

conveniently forgotten by all of Colchester society except a few who were directly attached to the Beresford family.

Alex came back into the room and rested his hands lightly on her shoulders. 'Our son is sitting up in bed with his book,' he said with a smile. His hand moved to her neck and chin as he turned her face up to his. 'But he can wait a few more minutes, can't he?' he said, beginning to kiss her.

She twisted away from him, laughing a little breathlessly. 'Not now, Alex. We're all ready to go out. We can't arrive at the Midsummer Ball looking like a couple of haystacks.'

He straightened up. 'No, I suppose you're right.' He sighed. 'But you look so beautiful that I'm not sure I wouldn't rather stay at home and be a haystack.' He bent towards her again, laughing.

Again she evaded him and looked at the tiny gold watch she wore on a chain at her waist. 'I'm going up to read the story of Augustus who wouldn't eat his soup, to Marcus now. It's his favourite story at the moment. You can call the carriage for ten minutes. I shall be ready by then, so make sure you are.' She laid her cheek briefly against his before leaving the room.

On the landing she paused, looking down the wide, sweeping staircase with its thick red carpet to the black and white tiled hall below. She loved this house; it was roomy, light and elegant in a way that the funny little house in East Street where they had begun their married life had never pretended to be. She glanced briefly at herself in the full length gilt mirror at the top of the stairs. Yes, she'd do. She wouldn't disgrace Alex. She turned to go up the narrower stairs to the floor above that housed the nursery and Maudie's room next to it.

As she had predicted, Maudie had been a problem at first. She was jealous of her position as their only servant and had objected to the employment of a cook, housemaid and kitchenmaid when they moved to the new house. It was only Alex's brilliant suggestion that she should be Marcus's nursemaid that had saved the day. And Maudie was used to children, having so many brothers and sisters of her own, so the decision had been a happy one. Laura smiled to herself as she mounted the stairs, careful of her wide crinoline. She could hear Maudie's voice, instructing Marcus that he was to snuggle down and go to sleep the minute the story was finished. 'An' no half larks, Master Marcus,' she finished as Laura entered the room.

The ball took the usual course of such events. Laura had no shortage of dancing partners and the fact that the Beresford family were there in force no longer worried her unduly. There had never been another scene like the one five years ago when Eleanor had made such a fuss about the pearls. Nowadays, if confrontation was unavoidable Laura gave a smile and brief greeting and received a curt nod in response.

Charlotte, Jay's wife, was the only member of the Beresford family who ever showed any sign of a thaw. She always returned Laura's greeting with a friendly smile, provided Jay wasn't looking and Laura often had the feeling that she would like to have done more if she hadn't been so hidebound by the family.

Halfway through the evening Laura went up to the powder room for a short respite and to repair the ravages of the ballroom, which was stifling from the temperature of the hot, summer night and compounded by the heat from the chandeliers and the sweating, dancing bodies.

Charlotte was there, sitting on a small gilt chair and fanning herself. She was wearing cream satin, which with her pale complexion and fair hair gave her a faintly ethereal look. She smiled shyly at Laura. 'How do you manage to look so cool in this heat?' she asked.

Laura fanned herself. 'I can assure you I don't *feel* at all cool,' she smiled back. She noticed that Charlotte's skin looked almost transparent tonight and she remembered hearing that it was only a few months since the birth of her second stillborn son. She felt very sorry for the girl; it must have been a terrible disappointment to lose two male children. Especially for her husband. Men were always anxious for a son to continue the family name.

'You are quite recovered now?' Laura asked, smoothing a stray hair into place and turning from the mirror to Charlotte. 'I heard. . .'

141

'Oh, yes, I'm quite well now,' Charlotte said quickly. She hesitated. 'I should like. . .'

Laura raised her eyebrows attentively, but the other girl bit her lip and shook her head. 'Nothing. It doesn't matter.' She hurried out of the room.

A few minutes later Laura followed her, puzzled, because again she had had the feeling that the other girl would have liked to extend the hand of friendship if only she had been allowed to. She reached the ballroom and looked across to where Jay was sitting. He stood up as his wife rejoined him but no smile lit his face and Laura couldn't help wondering if Charlotte's life with the Beresford heir was entirely happy.

The supper break was always an opportunity for the dignitaries and businessmen of the town to meet and talk to each other. Laura was used to this and while Alex talked business with the men she usually talked to their wives, some of whom were as nervous as she herself had been at her first ball. Often, the younger wives thanked her for her words, saying they had helped to put them at their ease and she realised just how far she had come in those few short years. Tonight, as Alex escorted her in to the supper room he was stopped by the Town Clerk.

'Ah, Mr Beresford, I don't believe you and your good lady have met Mr Plant and his wife, have you? Mr Plant has just been appointed the new master of the workhouse on Balkerne Hill. This is his first opportunity to what you might call socialise.'

It took all Laura's self control not to run away, but somehow she managed to smile as the introductions were made. But she needed no introduction to Jack Plant. She remembered him only too well. How could she ever forget him? True, his face had grown a little more florid since she saw him last and his whiskers were now grey, but he had the same little pig eyes, the same bull neck, the same pot-belly and strutting walk that she remembered from those nightmare weeks in the workhouse near Spitalfields. She could only hope to God he hadn't recognised her. Her heart hammering as if it would choke her she made brief, polite conversation with the man's wife, a small, hatchet-faced woman who looked entirely lacking in human compassion.

142

She heaved a sigh of relief when the Town Clerk moved on with them.

'You look a little pale, my love. Are you feeling unwell?' Alex asked, as she passed her hand across her brow.

'Yes, I am feeling a little faint.'

He took her arm. 'Sit down here and I'll bring you a drink. You've gone white to the lips, my darling.'

'It is rather hot in here, Alex,' she murmured.

She waited where he had left her, fanning herself and looking round for some means of escape. If only she could slink away somewhere. . . Then sanity prevailed and she straightened her shoulders. Why should she run away like a frightened rabbit? It was unlikely that Jack Plant had recognised her, indeed, the chances were that he had forgotten her very existence. She caught sight of her reflection in the mirror. The well-dressed, self-assured figure she presented now was nothing like the dirty, ragged, half-starved creature Jack Plant had taken a fancy to in the workhouse.

Alex came back and she took a draught of the drink he had brought her. 'Oh, thank you, dear, I feel much better now.' She smiled up at him.

'Are you sure?' He looked anxiously at her. 'You're still a little pale.'

'I'm perfectly recovered, Alex, thank you. I'll just sit here quietly for a while. Oh, look, that man over there looks as if he's waiting to speak to you.'

'Yes, he is. He's just installed a new machine in his factory and wants me to take a look at it.' He smiled ruefully at Laura. 'Midsummer Balls are not simply for dancing, you know, my dear.'

She tapped his arm with her fan. 'I quite understand that, Alex. Go and talk to him, I shall be perfectly all right here.'

He picked up her card. 'You won't lack partners, at any rate, but at least I see you've saved the last dance for me.'

'But of course. Who else?'

In spite of her determination not to be intimidated by Jack Plant, Laura danced her way through the rest of the ball as if in some kind of nightmare. It seemed that everywhere she looked his beady eyes were looking back at her, following her, mocking her. She counteracted this by an attitude of almost reckless gaiety and thanked heaven that her card was full. At least there was no danger of having to dance with him. Or so she thought.

'May I have this dance, ma'am?' She looked up, fanning herself after a particularly strenuous set of Lancers, and found herself looking straight into the little pig eyes of the workhouse master.

She managed to remain calm, although her heart was thudding painfully. 'I don't believe you are on my card, Mr Plant. This dance is promised to Mr Reeves, the Town Clerk.' She drew out her card and pretended to consult it.

'His wife is ill. He has had to take her home. I offered to take his place.' Jack Plant smiled a smarmy grin that showed his bad teeth.

'Oh,' Laura looked round. There was no escape. 'Very well,' she said, feigning indifference and stood up, a full head taller than he was.

He made hardly any pretence at dancing but managed to guide her across to the long windows that led on to the terrace. 'It's a bit warm in here. Shall we step outside?' He gave her no chance to argue, but with amazing strength manoeuvred her out through the open window and into the sultry night air. 'Ah, that's better. We can breathe easier out here, can't we?' He leered up at her, his face shining with sweat.

'No, I would prefer to dance, if you don't mind,' she said, her voice cool although she was shaking inside. She turned to go back into the ballroom but his hand shot out and grasped her by the wrist. 'Not till I've said what I want to say, lady,' he said, his voice menacing in its quietness.

'I can't think that you and I can possibly have anything to say to each other, Mr Plant,' she said, putting on an air of superiority that she hoped would fool him. It didn't.

'An' I think we 'ave. I think you an' me've got an important little matter to sort out.' He grinned, his eyes narrowing. 'Because I don't reckon as how you'll want your husband to know you dropped a bastard in Spitalfield's work'us, now, will you?'

She tried to free herself from his grasp without attracting the attention of the other couples enjoying a breath of air in the garden. 'Let me go. I don't know what you're talking about.'

'Oh, yes you do, missy, and don't you try to pretend otherwise,' he said, his expression becoming ugly. 'Jack Plant don't forget a face and that don't matter whether thass covered in grime or powdered an' painted up to the nines, 'cause thass all the same underneath. You can't fool me.' He gave an unpleasant laugh. 'I reckon all your fancy friends 'ud be very int'rested to hear how you was brought to the work 'us with a bellyful an' 'ithout a penny to your name, wouldn't they? My word, that'd make 'em all sit up! Wouldn't do your 'usband much good in his business, neither, would it? What would people think of 'im, marryin' a whore?'

Laura rounded on him. 'I was *not*. . .' She bit her lip. She had as good as admitted that he was right about her past.

'Thass better.' He gave a satisfied grin. 'Now, my dear, you an' me's got to come to some arrangement if you want your little secret kept, haven't we?' He tapped the side of his nose. 'Well, that shouldn't be too hard. I'm a reasonable man. Tell you what. I fancied you when you was in Spitalfield's and I could fancy you even more now you're clean and dressed to kill. You're a comely wench and no mistake. Now, what about if you come an' pay me a visit on a Wednesday arternoon? I'll arrange a place an' time – reg'lar, mind – an' we'll say no more about. . . that other business.'

Laura shuddered. She had difficulty in not being sick. He took her silence for agreement. 'Shall we say next Wednesday for a start?' he asked, grinning lasciviously.

'No, we will not,' she got out between clenched teeth. 'Not then. Not ever.'

'Well, all I can say is you're being very silly, 'cause if you don't do as I say then I shall be forced to 'ave a word with your 'usband.' He picked his teeth. 'Pity, reely, an' 'im such a swell in the town. Make 'im look a right Charlie, won't it?'

'He'd never believe you.' The words came out as if she was being strangled.

'Mebbe not. At first. But 'e'd wonder, wouldn't 'e? An' the rest of the town wouldn't have no trouble believin' it, 'cause wasn't you one o' the silk factory girls afore you was wed? A lot o' them ain't no better than they should be, an' like'll find like. Ain't that true, now?' He leered and gave her a nudge that nearly knocked her off balance.

Hardly knowing what she was doing she dragged off the diamond earrings she was wearing. 'Here, take these for your silence,' she said, her voice verging on a sob. 'They're worth a lot of money. Now, get out of my sight and don't ever speak to me again.'

He looked down at them in his hand, his little black eyes alight with greed. 'All right, my dear. I'll take them in lieu...' he pronounced it leo. 'They'll do for a start, anyways,' he added softly.

He left her then and she made her way back to the ballroom. The rest of the evening passed in a haze and as the carriage took them home Alex took her hand.

'You're very quiet, my darling,' he said, 'are you still unwell?'

'I've got a headache. It was the heat, I think. It was very hot there tonight.' It was true. She had a blinding headache. But it had nothing to do with the heat and everything to do with Jack Plant. She had paid him off; paid him generously, at that; but she didn't trust him and she knew she would never know a minute's peace whilst that man lived in the town.

Over the next months Laura was not the only one with problems. In the house in Head Street one afternoon in March Eleanor's eyes flashed as she looked up from pouring herself and Charles a second cup of tea.

'Five hundred pounds! You must be out of your mind, Charles. Where in the world do you think I should find that amount of money?'

'I know, Mater, and it's deuced inconvenient that I need to go and order another suit when the last one's not yet paid for.'

Eleanor put the teapot down carefully. 'Charles, how is it that you owe so much money to your tailor? *I* have paid your bills to Mr Cranfield quite regularly for some years now, although goodness knows you get a large enough allowance from your father...'

146

'It's not an allowance, Mater. It's my salary. It's what I earn working at the factory.'

'If you got paid for the work you do at the factory you'd get very little, according to your brother Jay. But that's not the point in question at the moment.' She waved her hand in the air. 'Oh, let's have no more of these charades, Charles. It's not simply your tailor's bills I've been paying these past years, is it? I've been paying your gambling debts. You know it and I know it and it's got to stop. I didn't mind the odd twenty pounds here and there, although heaven knows that's a terrible lot of money to owe, but now it's gone beyond a joke. How on earth did you get yourself into such debt, Charles? Five hundred pounds! That's a fortune!'

He shrugged uncomfortably and looked at his feet in their expensive calfskin boots. 'Well, you know how it is, Mama. . .'

'I do *not* "know how it is", Charles, and kindly do me the courtesy of not assuming that I am conversant with the ways of gamblers.' Eleanor's voice was cold.

'I beg your pardon, Mama.' Charles bowed his head in what he hoped was a suitably abject manner. 'Well, it was like this. I'd been on a winning streak, so I upped the stakes. But then I began to lose. . . Oh, I was sure it was only a flash in the pan and I'd start winning again. When I got near the end of my money I played double or quits and I won. I won and kept winning. And I thought just one more time and I'll stop. . .'

'It's a pity you didn't,' Eleanor said acidly. She rummaged in her reticule for her cheque book. 'How much do you owe your tailor?'

'Ninety-four pounds.'

She scribbled for a few moments. 'There, I've made it out to Mr Cranfield, himself. Make sure he gets it. And don't order any more clothes for at least a year.'

'Thank you, Mama.' Charles looked down at the cheque in his hand. 'You're very generous, and don't think for one moment I'm not grateful. . . but as I told you, I'm in this fix. . .' He tapped the cheque nervously on the back of his other hand.

Eleanor lifted her chin. 'Then you'll have to get yourself

out of it,' she said, with uncharacteristic lack of sympathy towards her last born. 'I'm sorry, but I've turned a blind eye to your gambling for long enough, Charles. It's got quite beyond a joke.'

'Is that your final word?' Charles got to his feet.

'Yes. It's high time you mended your ways. And you won't if I keep paying your debts for you. I don't have a bottomless purse, you must understand.'

'No, of course not.' He went to the door, such a picture of dejection that Eleanor nearly relented and called him back. But she knew that if she did that the whole business would begin all over again. And five hundred pounds was an awful lot of money. He'd never asked her for even a quarter as much as that before.

'Tell them, whoever "they" are, that you'll pay it off month by month,' she said as he went out. 'And make sure you do,' was her parting shot.

Charles went back to the factory and sat down at his desk to do some careful calculations. When he had finished he threw the pen down. Whichever way he worked it he was in deep trouble. It was all very well for his mother to tell him to pay his gambling debts off month by month from his salary; she didn't know, and he could never tell her, that most of that was already going to pay Solly Cohen, the money-lender, who charged such extortionate rates of interest that he was never going to get out of his clutches. He put his head in his hands. He didn't know which way to turn. He couldn't ask his father, the old boy wasn't exactly in the pink of health although he insisted that it was only a touch of indigestion. Anyway, he suspected, quite rightly, that Old Javis left all the financial dealings either to his wife or to Jay – these days it would seem he left *most* things to either his wife or Jay, his main interest in life was golf although he spent just enough time at the factory to keep an eye on what Jay was doing. And it was no good going to Jay. After that business when he borrowed a hundred pounds from the safe – fully intending to put it back the following day, only the cards had run badly and he'd lost it – Jay had been absolutely livid and had told him he'd have been out on his ear if he hadn't been his own brother. He'd also said that if the gambling didn't stop he *would* be out on his ear. Oh, no, he couldn't go to Jay.

He tapped his pen on his teeth. There was always Alex, of course. He hadn't see him for ages, not since the family rift in fact, but he was doing all right for himself by all accounts. He nodded to himself. Ye-es, if he went about it the right way he was sure Alex would stump up and clear all the outstanding debts. Then he'd be able to start again with a clean slate. And once that weight was off his mind he vowed he'd never touch another playing card again as long as he lived. 'So help me,' he said aloud, and solemnly made the sign of the Cross over his heart. Then, with a light step he picked up a sheaf of papers and left his office.

In the passage he encountered a pretty little thing who worked in the doubling room if he wasn't much mistaken. He put his arm out and barred her way. 'And what's your name, my dear?' he asked, smiling at her.

She blushed. 'Kate, sir. Kate Taylor.'

It was an omen. Here was little Kate Taylor, looking so coyly up at him on the very day when his mother had given him a cheque to pay off his tailor's bill and he'd had the brilliant idea of tapping Alex for the rest of what he owed. She looked clean, too, cleaner than a good many of the girls who work at the factory. He put out a hand and lifted a lock of her hair and let it fall. 'And where do you think you're off to, Kate Taylor?'

'To fetch some more reels from the storeroom, sir. An' I mustn't be long or Ole Ma. . . Mrs Ripley'll be callin' out for me.'

'Then I'd better come and help you to find them, hadn't I?' He opened the door of the storeroom and held it for her to enter.

A little while later Kate, flushed and a little dishevelled, hurried back to the doubling room and Charles went on his way, a little smile playing about his lips. He hadn't deflowered her. He had been sorely tempted but for the moment he had resisted the temptation, for some reason reluctant to defile her pure innocence. That was something he still had to look forward to, for wasn't the chase almost as pleasurable as the capture. . .?

149

Chapter Fourteen

Alex was sitting by the fire with Laura while the wind howled and the rain lashed at the windows. He looked round the room, it was decorated in pale wedgwood blue with rich crimson hangings and a turkey carpet. The good, solid walnut furniture – the best Sid Rankin could provide – reflected his business success. Laura had chosen the Chelsea figurines that graced the mantelpiece on either side of the French ormolu clock and the expensive etched ruby glass epergne which had pride of place on the table beside the fireplace. He was a contented man. Laura was everything he could ever have desired in a wife, he had a beautiful home, a thriving business and a son he adored to hand it on to. What more could a man want from life, he often asked himself.

He put his head on one side and studied Laura, sitting with her sewing on the other side of the fireplace. He never tired of looking at her, she seemed to grow more beautiful every day.

'You never wear those little diamond earrings I bought you, dear,' he said suddenly. 'Don't you care for them? I always thought they suited you rather well.'

Laura looked up and put her hand nervously to her ear lobe, where a pearl drop dangled. 'I seem to have mislaid them, Alex. I can't think where I've put them,' she lied. 'I'll have to turn my jewel case out yet again. Although I'm very fond of these at the moment.' She touched the pearl drops again.

He gave a boyish grin. 'You've got so much jewellery now,

that you have trouble deciding which to wear, don't you, my love?'

'Yes, you're very generous to me, Alex.'

He got up and kissed her. 'I love you, Laura. And I love to buy you beautiful things.'

Agnes, the housemaid, knocked and came in at Alex's command. With a bob, she said, 'There's a gentleman to see you, sir. I've took the liberty of puttin' 'im in the study.'

'That's right, Agnes. Tell him I'll be there in a minute.' Alex stood in front of the fire, warming his coat tails. He took out his pocket watch and looked at it. 'Nine o'clock. I wonder who can be calling at this time on such a wild night,' he mused.

Laura bent over her sewing. 'You'd better go and see, dear.' Her heart was in her mouth. These days, whenever there was a visitor for Alex she was terrified it might be Jack Plant, although only last week she had given him a brooch to keep him quiet because he had begun to pester her again. She dared not think what might happen if Alex discovered that the brooch was gone. Nor if he missed the garnet ring she had been forced to part with just before Christmas. Alex liked her to wear the things he bought for her and he knew exactly what she had got. She was fast becoming a bundle of nerves. In the past eight months she had lost weight and jumped at every sound because of that dreadful man, Jack Plant. Oh, why didn't he go away? Or die? Why didn't somebody kill him? Hadn't she suffered enough in the past without him coming back into her life to ruin everything? A tear dropped on to her sewing. God, how she hated that man. Please God, he wasn't in the study telling Alex her dreadful secret at this very minute. She got up and began to pace up and down the room.

She needn't have worried. As Alex entered the study his brother Charles turned from looking at the expensive portrait of Laura that hung behind the desk. 'You're quite the successful businessman now, aren't you, brother mine?' he said admiringly. 'I didn't realise you were quite so prosperous, Alex, old boy.'

'What do you want, Charles?' Alex asked coolly, although his fingers were digging into the palms of his hands. He

151

hadn't spoken to Charles since his marriage but he still couldn't get out of his mind the sight of him coming out of the storeroom behind Laura, as she clutched the remnants of her tattered clothing and dignity round her, and even as Charles stood there smiling at him, Alex experienced an almost overwhelming urge to knock his brother's teeth down his throat for his attack on her even though it had been all those years ago.

'You could ask a fellow to sit down, Alex.' Charles sat down without waiting for an invitation. 'And to think I never realised. . .' he said admiringly, looking round the comfortable room with its tooled leather-topped desk, thick carpet and book-lined walls. He whistled. 'I never realised that you'd done quite so well for yourself, Alex, old boy. Leaving the factory was the best day's work you ever did, I'd say. You must be making money hand over fist.'

'Come to the point, Charles.' Alex went round the desk and sat down in the big comfortable chair behind it. He didn't know why he should need it, but it gave him an added sense of security to have the wide expanse of leather and mahogany between him and his brother. 'I'm sure you haven't decided to call on me simply to congratulate me on my business acumen. I'd be obliged if you'd say what you've come to say and then go.'

'Aren't you pleased to see me, Alex? After all these years without any contact with the family, aren't you pleased that I've come to offer an olive branch?'

'From whom?' Alex began ticking off his fingers. 'Mama? I don't think so, she's still too bitter. And anyway she was probably only too glad to see the back of me, having fulfilled her obligations towards me. Papa? He wouldn't dare, not against Mama's wishes. Jay? Oh, no, not Jay. Apart from the fact that he's never really liked me, now I'm out of the way he's got practically full control of the factory – not that I was ever a threat – which is what he's always wanted. So, Charles, if you've come to offer an olive branch it's on your own behalf.' He leaned forward and put his elbows on the desk. 'What do you want? No, don't tell me, let me guess. Money?'

Charles gave a little laugh and shifted uncomfortably in his chair. 'No need to be quite so blunt about it, old boy, is there?'

'Why not? If that's what you've come for, say so.'

'Yes, well, it is, as a matter of fact. I'm in a bit of a stew, to tell you the truth.' Charles leaned forward. 'My luck. . .'

'Oh, spare me the details,' Alex waved the words aside. 'Gambling debts mounted up and Mama won't bail her darling boy out any more? Is that it?'

Charles nodded. 'More or less.'

Alex looked at his young brother. Already he was showing signs of the dissipated life he led. His face was losing its handsome, boyish look and taking on a slightly bloated, coarsened appearance. It came to Alex with something of a shock to realise just how much he hated Charles for what he had done to Laura and he marvelled that the man could sit there in cold blood, asking for money, in full knowledge of what he had done, probably even gloating to himself over the fact that he had been first with his own brother's wife. Alex got slowly to his feet, rigidly holding on to his temper.

'Well, it's no use coming to me, Charles. As you say, I've done quite well for myself, but it's been by dint of bloody hard work and long hours and I'm damned if I'm going to see my hard earned cash frittered away on the gaming tables. Not for you nor anyone else.'

'It's not for gambling. I have to pay. . .'

'You have to pay off gambling debts. It amounts to the same thing. No, Charles. I won't help you out. Not by so much as a farthing. I bid you good night. Agnes will see you out.' He went over to the bell pull and gave it a sharp tug.

When Charles had gone Alex went back to Laura.

'Who was it, dear?' she asked and he thought for a moment that she looked anxious.

'My brother Charles paid me a visit after all these years,' he said grimly. 'He wanted money.'

'Oh.' He thought Laura flushed but he wasn't sure. 'Did you give him any?' she asked.

'No, I did not!'

'He must have been desperate to come to you, of all people.'

'Why do you say that?' Alex flashed a suspicious look at her.

She looked up from her sewing and gave a slightly twisted smile. 'I should have thought it was obvious, dear. Surely even Jay – never mind your mother – would have given him money rather than let him come begging to you, the black sheep who made good in spite of marrying a factory girl.'

Alex went over to the sideboard and poured himself a stiff whisky from the heavy cut glass decanter, replacing it carefully in the tantalus afterwards. He stared at the rich amber liquid and then tossed it down his throat. For some reason Charles' visit had left him edgy and uneasy, reminding him of a part of the past he would have preferred forgotten. He had no regrets about refusing to lend Charles the money; in a some strange way it was almost a retaliation; revenge for his violation of Laura. Looking back on the conversation he had had with his brother, Alex was surprised at just how much satisfaction he had derived from refusing to lend him the money.

Two days later Charles rode out to Ratchet's Wood and shot himself.

The whole town buzzed with the news. Charles had been well-liked by everyone as a cheerful, generous-hearted, open-handed man who had lived life to the full. Unlike his brother Jay he had had many friends – not all of them gambling partners – some of whom would have been only too willing to help him out of the financial difficulties he had been at pains to conceal, had they known about them. Little Mrs Denham, a pretty young widow living in a tiny cottage on the outskirts of Boxted was completely broken-hearted. And not merely because Mr Charles paid the rent.

Charles's body was brought home on a farm cart and, at the sight of it, Old Javis seemed to crumple into a very old man. He managed to retain enough dignity to attend the burial, in unconsecrated ground as befitted a man who had committed the sacrilege of taking his own life, along with Jay and a surprising number of men – some of whom neither Old Javis nor Jay knew – who had come to pay their last respects to a good friend. There were no women at the funeral, it had not been deemed appropriate, so Charlotte sat at home with Eleanor, both clad in unrelieved black, quietly reading the

154

burial service from the prayer book. There were no tears, to Eleanor it would have been unthinkable to shed tears in the presence of anyone else – even her own daughter-in-law – and Charlotte did not dare to cry in the face of such fortitude, even though she was almost sure she was pregnant again and pregnancy always made her emotional.

When the men returned Jay helped his father down from the carriage and straight upstairs to bed. His heart, never in recent years very strong, had been unable to stand the strain. In less than a week Old Javis followed his youngest son to the grave.

But not before he had set his house in order.

The day before he died he put out his hand. 'Eleanor?'

She took it. 'I'm here, Javis. I've never left your side.'

'I know it.' He squeezed her hand with what little strength he had left. 'I want you to do something for me,' he said, stopping frequently for breath. 'It will be the last thing I ever ask of you, Ellie, so don't refuse me.'

'What is it, Javis?' she leaned over him, tears suddenly springing to her eyes at the name he had not called her since the early days of their marriage.

'I want Alex and his wife to come to my funeral.' He opened his eyes and saw her mouth assume a straight, hard line.

'We'll talk about that when you're better. There's plenty of time,' she hedged.

'There's no time, Ellie, and you know it,' he said, his voice assuming a little of his old tetchiness. 'This is my dying wish. You can't refuse me.' His voice dropped again. 'We were wrong. Alex is a good boy, and his wife. . .' he closed his eyes and paused, '. . .a lively gel if ever I saw one. A damn sight more about her than Charlotte. . . she could be a good friend to you, Ellie. . . a good friend.' He looked up at her, his eyes bright and steely-grey as he imposed his will on her. 'You haven't got Charles now, Ellie, and soon you won't have me. You'll need Alex, if Jay isn't to run rough-shod over you. Anyway,' he repeated, his eyes closing wearily, 'Alex is a good boy. One of the best. Make it up with him, Ellie. For my sake.' His voice faded. 'Remember, it's the last thing I'll ever ask of you. . .' Old Javis never spoke again.

Alex turned the black-edged letter over in his hand, his face grim. He read it for the third time and then silently handed it across the breakfast table to Laura.

'It's from your mother!' she said, looking up in surprise before she had even read it.

'Very carefully worded, too.' Alex dabbed his mouth with his napkin. 'She obviously hasn't written from choice.'

Laura read the letter. It read: 'My dear Alex, Your father's dying wish was that you and your wife should attend his funeral and that thereafter there should be a reconciliation between us. For that reason and no other I invite you both to the funeral service at St Peter's Church next Thursday at 2.30pm and to a cold collation at my house after the burial. I hope that you will respect his wishes as I have been forced to do. Yours sincerely, Eleanor Beresford.'

'I've a mind not to go,' Alex said, when she had finished. 'It's a barely concealed insult to us both.'

Laura shook her head. 'You mustn't look at it like that, Alex.' She tapped the letter with her finger. 'Haven't you any idea what it must have cost your mother to write this?'

'She could hardly have made it plainer that it's not of her choosing.'

'Then it's up to us to make it as easy as we can for her when we meet.'

Alex studied her across the table for several minutes. 'If only you knew. . .' he began.

'If only I knew what?'

He shook his head. 'Nothing. It's all in the past. It doesn't matter. Of course you're right, we must go. Have you got a black dress or shall I give you some money. . .?' he reached for his notecase.

It was not until the party returned to the house after the funeral and Eleanor threw back her veil that Laura saw how grief had ravaged her once beautiful face. Even now, she held herself erect, making the most of her diminutive height and greeted her guests with dignity and calmness, although when Alex stooped to kiss her cheek Laura saw her eyes close briefly as she struggled to keep her composure.

'Thank you for inviting us, Mama,' he said quietly. 'May I

introduce you,' he hesitated, 'formally, to my wife, Laura.'

Laura sensed rather than saw the hesitation on Eleanor's part and leaned forward and kissed her lightly on the cheek. 'I appreciate what it must have cost you to write to us, Mrs Beresford,' she said, so that no one else could hear. 'And I'm sorry you've had to bear this extra burden when what you need most is support. But I hope, eventually, you will be glad and that we shall be friends.' She smiled gently at the older woman.

Eleanor instinctively recoiled and put a hand to her cheek. She looked at Laura in surprise; she had expected a look of triumph, of victory, but there was nothing but kindness and sympathy in the girl's face. She seemed to understand how hard it had been to agree to Javis's dying wish, to know how bitterly she had resented having to write to Alex. Yet she showed no sign of animosity or acrimony. Face to face like this it was difficult to continue hating her. . . blaming her. . . But blaming her for what? Alex was successful and showed every evidence of being happily married. What more could a man ask? She pulled herself together and managed a brief nod at Laura's words. 'Perhaps,' she murmured. But her voice held no warmth.

'I thought Mama conducted herself extremely well, under the circumstances,' Jay remarked to Charlotte as he warmed his coat tails in front of the fire on their return home after the funeral. 'It can't have been easy for her. I'm more than surprised at Papa, making her promise to invite Alex and that wife of his to the funeral. As if poor Mama hadn't enough to contend with. I can't think what made him impose such an unreasonable obligation on her.'

'He clearly thought it was time the family rift was healed,' Charlotte ventured, trying to push her feet in their swansdown slippers a little nearer to the blaze.

'Well, of course, it won't be.' Jay rocked back and forth on his heels. 'I, for one, shall avoid speaking to them both. I spoke to neither of them today,' he added smugly.

'Oh, didn't you, Jay? I did. In fact, I found Laura a very pleasant woman to talk to. She said how sorry she felt for Mama Eleanor, losing her son and her husband in such a

157

short time. She asked me to let her know at once if there was anything she could do to help.'

'I hope you put her in her place and told her that the family would look after Mama,' Jay said shortly.

'But Alex and Laura *are* family, dearest. Surely it's up to us. . .' Charlotte broke off and searched for her handkerchief in her reticule. She blew her nose and surreptitiously wiped her eyes, knowing how much Jay disliked shows of emotion.

He looked down at her. 'Not crying again, are you, my dear? I should have thought all your tears were spent by now. You seem to have spent the whole of the last week weeping into your handkerchief.' He sniffed. 'I feel bereft enough, goodness knows. My father and my young brother, both dead and gone in less than a fortnight, but one has to keep up appearances and one has to carry on. One can't weep for ever.' Jay didn't give the impression that he had wept at all.

'I'm sorry, dearest,' Charlotte began to cry even more, 'but I'm afraid I can't help it. I always become rather emotional when I am. . . when I am with child.'

He looked down at her, raising his eyebrows. 'Well, in that case,' he cleared his throat, 'in that case you may be forgiven, my dear. I'm sorry. I didn't realise. . .' He leaned down and kissed her cheek. 'Let's hope this one has a more successful conclusion, eh?' He smiled and patted her shoulder.

She gave him a watery smile. 'Yes, Jay. I do hope so. I do so want to give you a son.'

He fetched her a foot stool. 'Are you doing everything Dr Franklyn tells you?' he asked, immediately solicitous. After the last confinement Dr May had been given his marching orders in the hope that a change of doctor might effect a change of fortune.

'Oh, Jay, I *always* do whatever the doctor tells me. You know that. It just seems. . . well, it sometimes seems that I shall never manage to bear a son that isn't stillborn.'

'Maybe this one will be a girl, then. There was no problem with Ellie, was there?'

'No, it just seems to be with boys.' She began to cry again. 'I do so want to give you a son, Jay. I know that's what you want. Every man needs a son to carry on the family name.'

'There's still plenty of time, my dear.' Jay sat down on the arm of her chair and stroked her hair. He could afford to be affectionate now that she was again pregnant, for tonight he would move back into his dressing room, as he always did during her pregnancies. He was glad. He hated sleeping with her, defiling her with his carnal desires that afterwards left him full of self-loathing and disgust. Not that he didn't love her, he did, he loved and cherished her in the same way a collector would love and cherish a delicate piece of china and for that reason he tried to curb his passions. Not that Charlotte ever complained. She was always patient and submissive. Indeed, apart from her obvious pleasure in bearing another child he had no idea of her feelings on the subject. And he knew he could never bring himself to ask her.

Chapter Fifteen

Eleanor was lonely. The constant stream of sympathetic friends and well-wishers that had called on her, hardly leaving her a minute's peace in the weeks after the double tragedy, had now diminished, leaving her with time – far too much time – to think, to remember, to grieve for both her husband and her youngest and favourite child. If only I had given Charles the money he needed they would both be here now, she chided herself over and over again. Yet she knew in her heart that she had been weak with Charles for far too long; that she had blinded herself to his faults, accepting his glib lies because she couldn't bear to admit that her darling was capable of being less than truthful; shielding him from the wrath of his father and elder brother, who knew him for what he was, a charming, open-hearted, open-handed man whose downfall was his weak will.

She put down the lace she was crocheting for a new altar cloth at church and picked up her shawl. The weather was glorious; the early June sun bathing the garden in a golden light. It might help to lighten her spirits if she were to go and sit in her favourite corner of the garden. She rang the bell for Lydia and told her to bring tea outside.

'I was jest comin' to tell you, m'm. There's a lady come to see you.'

'Oh, who is it?'

'Mrs Beresford, m'm.'

'Oh. Well, tell her to come to the arbour. And bring another cup, Lydia. She'll stay for tea.' Eleanor made her way unhurriedly out into the garden. It would do Charlotte good to sit in the sunshine. These continual pregnancies couldn't be good for her health, poor child, but she seemed determined to give Jay the son he needed – the family needed, if the name was not to die out.

The garden was not big but, enclosed by a high brick wall, it trapped the sun and kept out the wind. Flowers bloomed abundantly and the bees kept up a lazy drone as they sauntered from blossom to blossom, spoilt for choice in the riot of colour.

Eleanor crossed the lawn to the arbour – it was hardly big enough to warrant the name of summer house – in the corner and sat down. A few minutes later Lydia appeared, bearing the tea tray, and behind her a tall woman in black, holding a child by the hand. It wasn't Charlotte, it was Alex's wife. Eleanor straightened her back and glared at her. She would never have agreed to receive this woman, had she realised, in spite of Javis's wishes.

Laura didn't appear to notice that she was unwelcome, but smiled and greeted Eleanor with a warmth that was in no way over-familiar. 'I haven't been to see you before because I knew you would have lots of visitors,' she said. 'I thought it best to wait . . . once the well-wishers stop coming it can be rather lonely.'

Eleanor looked at her sharply. How did this factory girl know exactly the right thing to say and do? She sniffed. 'I suppose Alex . . .' she began.

'Alex is sorry he couldn't come with us, but he's been called to the workhouse. Something's gone wrong with a boiler there, I believe.' Laura gave no hint of the panic she'd experienced when she knew he was going there. She had given Jack Plant a gold necklet only last week, but even so she didn't trust him not to betray her secret to Alex if the mood took him. Sometimes she wondered how much longer she could go on living this terrible double life. She put the agonising problem from her mind and managed to smile again. 'He was anxious that I should bring Marcus to see you.' She turned to her son, neat in a dark blue suit edged in black and with a black ribbon round his straw hat. 'Take your hat off, Marcus and say good afternoon to your Grandmama.'

Marcus took off his hat and stepped forward, uncertain

whether to kiss this stern-looking old lady or not. She gave him no encouragement so he held out his hand. 'Good afternoon, Grandmama,' he said solemnly.

She gave him the tips of her fingers. 'Good afternoon, child.' She studied him for several minutes, then she turned to Laura. 'He's very like his father. How old is he?'

'Nearly seven.'

'May I walk round the garden, Mama?' Marcus said, bored with being stared at.

Laura looked questioningly at Eleanor and received the barest of nods. She smiled at her son. 'Yes, dear, of course you may. But don't touch anything. See if you can count the number of different flowers.'

Marcus ran off. Eleanor said nothing, but poured two cups of tea and handed one to Laura. As they sipped their tea Eleanor's eyes never left the boy as he skipped and danced over the lawn, chasing butterflies both real and imaginary. 'He has something of his grandfather about him,' she mused eventually, unthinkingly voicing her thoughts.

'Do you really think so?' Laura said in surprise. Then she gave a little laugh. 'But of course, how could I know what your husband was like as a boy, or even a young man.'

'My husband . . .?' Eleanor said blankly, replacing her cup in its saucer with a clatter, and for a moment Laura thought she must be ill or deranged from the strain of the past months. 'Hasn't Alex . . .?' She pulled herself together with an obvious effort and took another sip of tea. 'No, of course not. I'm sorry, it was stupid of me. How could you know?' For the first time she gave Laura what passed as a smile. She shivered a little. 'It's becoming a little chilly. I think we should go indoors, don't you? Marcus, come inside, child. If you go down to the kitchen Lydia will give you a Bath Oliver. Would you like that?'

Marcus came running across the lawn. 'Oh, yes, Grandmama. I should like that very much.'

'Come along then, I'll tell you the way to the kitchen.'

Laura stayed a further twenty minutes with her mother-in-law. She expected some explanation of Eleanor's strange words in the garden but none was forthcoming. Eleanor was once again perfectly in command of herself and made no

162

reference to her strange lapse. She showed Laura the lace she was crocheting for the altar cloth. 'It gives me something to do to pass the time,' she said, folding it carefully away, and Laura felt suddenly very sorry for this lonely old lady.

She picked up her gloves, preparatory to leaving, then, on an impulse she couldn't explain, even to herself, she asked, 'I wonder . . . is it possible that you knew my grandparents? They lived in Colchester.'

Eleanor froze. 'I shouldn't think so, for one moment,' she said haughtily. 'I know very little about the lower classes, apart from my own servants.' She reached out her hand to ring the bell.

Laura bit back a sharp retort, regretting the impulse that had led her to ask the question. Eleanor was a born snob. With difficulty she ignored the jibe and continued, 'They used to live at number seventeen North Hill. Their name was Farthing. I don't know if that means anything to you.'

'I told you, I know nothing of other people's servants,' Eleanor said coldly. 'That kind of thing is of no possible interest to me.'

'My grandparents were not servants,' Laura said briefly. 'I believe my grandfather had some kind of business in the town, although I don't know what it was. However, it's of no importance. I simply asked because it was possible that you had known my mother in her youth. Her name was Vera.'

'Vera Farthing?' Eleanor raised her eyebrows. 'Yes, I knew a Vera Farthing in my younger days. Not well, but I was acquainted with her. As I recall, her parents were quite well-to-do and very well thought of in the town. But I hardly think . . .'

'My mother became Vera Chapman when she married my father. He was an army surgeon and my grandparents were so against the marriage that they disowned her. That's my background, Mrs Beresford, but as you say, it's of no interest to you and it was stupid of me to mention it.' Briskly, Laura pulled on her gloves, suddenly irritated by this arrogant old woman. 'Perhaps you would be good enough to ring for my son. I won't take up any more of your time.'

Eleanor reached out for the bell but didn't ring it. She

remembered the scandal when young Vera Farthing ran off with her army officer – handsome man he'd been too, if her memory served her aright. They'd made a charming couple. Could it possibly be that this girl – this creature that Alex had picked up out of the silk factory – was Vera Farthing's daughter? She certainly behaved very differently from the usual factory worker, yet if her story was true she would never, ever, have lowered herself to work in such a place. At the same time, if she was not Vera Farthing's daughter where did she get the story from? 'Your parents, where are they now?' Eleanor asked frostily.

Laura hesitated, unwilling to be cross-questioned. She wished now that she had never mentioned her family. 'They are both dead,' she said briefly. 'I went out to India to live with them when I left Finishing School, only to find they had both died in a cholera epidemic. So I came back to England in the hope of finding my grandparents – I thought that after all those years they might be pleased to see their daughter's only child.' Laura shook her head. 'But I was too late, because they, too, had died.' She nodded towards the bell. 'My son, please?'

'One moment.' Eleanor remembered hearing that Vera had ended up in India. The girl's story must be true. But it didn't explain . . . 'Why were you working in my husband's silk factory, if you are who you say you are,' she asked, her voice sharp because she found the question distasteful.

Laura gave an impatient sigh. 'Because I was robbed of what little money and valuables I possessed when I got back to England,' she said simply. 'All I had was my train ticket. I pinned all my hopes on my grandparents' charity. But they were dead. If it hadn't been for the Taylor family, who befriended me and took me to work with them at the silk factory, I don't know what I would have done.' Laura looked up, meeting Eleanor's eyes with a clear gaze. 'I didn't find it easy, working in such awful conditions, Mrs Beresford. I felt sorry for those girls and I was determined to do what I could for them, although, God knows, it wasn't much, as it turned out.'

Eleanor dropped her gaze. 'I know nothing of factory

conditions. They are not something ladies of my standing are concerned with. However, I'm inclined to believe your story . . .'

Laura stood up, tired of the subject. 'It's of no concern to me whether you believe my story or not, Mrs Beresford,' she said coolly, buttoning her glove. 'My only concern was to discover whether you might have known my grandparents. It would seem that you did, slightly. Perhaps one day you will remember something about them that you could tell me; it would be nice to know that I have some background to my life. The rest of my story really need be of no interest to you, indeed, is none of your business.' She lifted her head. 'If you would ring for Marcus, please?'

'No, sit down a moment longer.' Eleanor put out her hand. 'I apologise. It was unforgivably rude of me to doubt your word, Laura. The more I look at you, the more I can see a likeness to the Vera Farthing that I knew. But you must admit that your history is – somewhat unusual. One would hardly expect to find a woman of your breeding working in a silk factory.'

Laura sighed. 'That was seven years ago, Mrs Beresford. It was only a brief episode in my life. Can you not leave it where it belongs? In the past?'

Eleanor stood up. She reached barely to Laura's shoulder. Suddenly, she smiled. 'You're quite right, my dear. It's in the past.' She put her hand on Laura's arm. 'Please accept my apologies; I realise that I've been most impolite to you. Nevertheless, I hope you'll come and see me again, Laura. And bring Marcus with you. Thank you for visiting me, you've given me much to think about.'

After Laura and Marcus had gone Eleanor picked up the altar cloth but didn't resume her crocheting. Instead she sat gazing out through the open doors into the garden. Javis had been right to insist on a reconciliation with Alex and his wife. However reluctant she had been to recognise the fact, Laura was a perfect lady. What was it Javis had said about her? 'The gel has spirit, I'll say that for her.' His words came back as clearly as if he had just spoken them aloud. 'You always were right, Javis,' she whispered,and a tear fell on the lace on her lap.

'I don't care for that workhouse master – what's his name? Jack Plant. I don't care for him at all,' Alex remarked. Earlier, Marcus had sat on his father's lap and told him all about the visit to his grandmother that afternoon before being whisked off to bed by Maudie. Now he and Laura were sitting in the drawing room, Alex with a glass of whisky, Laura with a small sherry, waiting for dinner to be served in the dining room.

Laura felt her throat constrict and she put down her sherry glass carefully on its coaster. 'I seem to remember him as a rather course man,' she said, managing with difficulty to keep her voice level.

'Oh, have you met him, then?'

'Yes. Once. At the Moot Hall. Don't you remember? The Midsummer Ball, I believe it was. About this time last year.'

'Oh, yes. Fancy you remembering it.'

As if I could forget, she thought bitterly. The wretched man has been like a spectre in my life ever since, haunting me and hounding me. Oh, how I wish he was dead. She managed to smile. 'I'm good with faces.'

Alex drained his glass. 'Well, I don't care for him. And in my opinion he's up to something, although God knows what. He's far too prosperous-looking for the job he does and the orphans are all frightened out of their wits of him. I'm going to make it my business to keep an eye on him. He's making money somewhere, and it's not only through keeping the inmates short of food. That wouldn't account for the smart way he and his wife dress. For instance, his wife was wearing a brooch very like the one with the sapphires and diamonds that I bought you for your birthday a year or two ago. Come to think of it, you haven't worn it lately. Where is it? Go and get it, will you, dear? It can't have been the same, I'm sure, because yours were real stones, but I would have thought that even a paste replica would cost far more than he could ever afford. I've got an idea he must be fiddling the books at the ratepayers' expense.'

Laura put her hand to her throat. She felt sick, but she got up and hurried out of the room. What was she going to tell Alex? That she'd lost the brooch? She'd already confessed to losing earrings so she could hardly lose a brooch as well. She was rifling through her jewel box to give herself time to think of something when Alex came into the bedroom. 'Can't you find it? Surely you haven't lost that as well as those diamond earrings?' He sounded a little sharp.

'Oh, no, how stupid of me. I've just remembered. I took it into the jewellers to have the clasp mended. It was rather slack and I was afraid it might come undone while I was wearing it.' She turned to Alex with a bright smile. 'I can't think how I could have forgotten.'

He kissed her lightly on the forehead. 'Never mind, dear, it wasn't important. Let's go downstairs. The soup is served and we don't want it to get cold.'

Laura didn't sleep that night. She knew things couldn't go on as they were. Sooner or later it was inevitable that Alex would discover she had lied to him. And then what? She tossed and turned, thumping her pillow until she was afraid he would wake and ask her what was wrong. She almost wished he would. It would almost be a relief to tell him about Jack Plant's blackmailing. But that would mean telling him about the rest of her past and that she couldn't do. Not now. Not after all these years. Oh, why couldn't it all have remained buried? Why did Jack Plant have to come to Colchester of all places and ruin her life? What had she done to deserve such punishment? Dawn was breaking before she fell into an exhausted sleep.

'Aren't you well, dearest? You're looking very pale,' Alex said from the other side of the breakfast table the next morning.

'I have a headache. I didn't sleep well,' she replied, resting her head on her hand. It was true. Her head felt as if it was being pounded by heavy hammers.

'I should go back to bed then, dear. I'm sure your appointments, whatever they are, can wait a day.' He got up from the table and dropped a kiss on her head before leaving for work.

She sat at the table for a long time after he had gone, drinking coffee and going over and over the events in her life that had led up to this crisis. If only. . . if only Randolph Grey had been a decent, respectable man. . . if only Jack Plant hadn't come to Colchester and recognised her. In the end her head was spinning so much that she felt dizzy.

'Is it all right if I clear, madam?' Agnes came into the room. 'Or would you like me to make you some fresh coffee?' She looked at her mistress. 'Are you all right, madam? You look quite ill.'

Laura dragged herself to her feet as the clock struck ten. She hadn't realised how long she had been sitting there, gazing into space. 'No, thank you, Agnes, I don't want more coffee. And I'm perfectly all right, thank you. I shall go upstairs and get dressed now.' She gave Agnes what passed for a smile and went out of the room and up the wide, sweeping staircase to her bedroom.

Agnes watched her go. Something was up, that was a sure thing. She'd never seen the missus look so awful. She wondered if the missus and the master had had a row; some of her friends in service told the most dreadful tales of rows between their master and mistress, with things being thrown and voices raised so that you could hear what was going on right down in the kitchen. But there was never anything like that in the Beresford household. Agnes had never known such a happy couple as they were. If anything, the older they got the more in love they seemed to be. Jest like a couple of love birds, they were. She hoped the missus wasn't ill.

Laura got dressed and sat down at the dressing table. She put her hand to her face; there was not a vestige of colour in it. She laid her head in her arms and began to cry; huge sobs that wracked her body. Alex would never forgive her when he found out what she had done with the jewellery he had given her; he wouldn't understand that she had had to buy Jack Plant's silence. But he would find out soon. She realised that she couldn't keep it from him for much longer. He was becoming more and more suspicious, wanting to know where different items of jewellery were. And now the sapphire brooch. He would keep asking if it was back from the jewellers . . .

She lifted her head and looked at her ravaged face in the mirror. There were two courses open to her. She could confess to Alex or she must leave him. She knew it was too late to confess.

Having made up her mind she got to her feet and began to pull things out of drawers and cupboards. If she didn't think

168

about it, if she simply concentrated on thinking what she must take with her she could bear the pain. Mustn't take too much, but must take enough. No ball gowns, there would be no balls where she was going. Where was she going? Don't think about that. Pack the bags and take a cab to the railway station. Not to London. London was full of nightmare memories. Ipswich? No, that wasn't far enough from Colchester. Norwich? Yes, that was better. Take a train to Norwich. Take plenty of money, too. Alex wouldn't begrudge that. And make sure it couldn't be stolen. . . Take enough to pay for a respectable hotel room whilst advertising for a position as governess. Yes, that was it. Become a governess, like she had been to Peregrine. Only this time she was aware of the pitfalls . . .

All the time she was stuffing clothes into valises and bags, then pulling them out and choosing different things, but at last she stood surrounded by luggage, packed and ready to leave. She closed her eyes. Now she must go up to the nursery and say goodbye to Marcus. Every instinct told her to take him with her but she knew it would be a selfish thing to do. Marcus would be better cared for with his father than being taken to some unknown destination with her. She went up the stairs to the nursery, where Miss Procter, his governess was about to read him a story.

'May I read to him today, Miss Procter?' Laura asked.

Ada Procter looked up in surprise. She was a dried-up woman approaching forty, a spinster left without means, glad to eke out her life teaching the small children of Colchester gentry, visiting them in their homes and returning to her single room over a booksellers at the end of each day. 'Why, of course, Mrs Beresford. You will find that Marcus can read several of the words for himself.' She handed the book to Laura. 'I will prepare some sums for him while you read,' she said, her smile showing yellow, horsey teeth, as she made sure Mrs Beresford wouldn't be able to accuse her of wasting any time.

But Laura hardly heard what she was saying. She picked up the book and began to read, conscious only of her son curled up against her, and the warmth of his little body against her own. Her voice was unsteady as she read, holding back the tears, but she struggled on. This was a moment to savour, to remember, to last her for the rest of her life. . . 'and so they lived happily ever after.' She closed the book and smiled down at Marcus. 'Did you like that story?'

'Oh, yes, Mama. And I like it when you read to me. You make the voices all different. Will you read my bedtime story tonight?' His little face was eager as he grinned Alex's grin at her.

'We'll see.' She held him close for a moment, but he struggled free. 'Is it time for my milk and biscuit?'

'Yes, and then it's time for these sums,' Miss Procter said, brandishing his slate.

Laura went down the stairs not daring to risk a backward glance or she knew her resolve would weaken. When she reached the landing she saw Agnes just coming out of the bedroom. 'Oh, madam, I was jest lookin' for you,' the girl said, looking bewildered. 'I didn't know you was goin' away. You never said. . . But there's a woman downstairs wants to see you. Says it's urgent.'

Chapter Sixteen

Laura passed a hand over her face. 'Who is it, Agnes?'

Agnes shrugged primly. 'Well, to tell the truth, madam, she don't look much cop to me, but she said you'd be sure and see her if I said it was Dot Taylor. I can easy send her packin' though, if you're in a hurry.' She looked as if nothing would give her greater pleasure.

Wearily, Laura shook her head. 'No, no, Agnes, don't do that. I'll see her. Put her. . . let me see. . . yes, put her in the morning room. I'll see her there.'

'Not the mornin' room, madam, surely,' Agnes protested, bridling. 'She's common. Like I said, she ain't no cop. . .'

'I said put her in the morning room, Agnes.' Laura's voice was sharp. She didn't know how much more she could take today, but whatever her own troubles were she could never refuse to see Dot, her old friend. 'And bring us some coffee, please.'

Agnes opened her mouth to protest again, thought the better of it and whisked away, disapproval in every movement.

Laura took a deep breath and went slowly down the stairs to greet her visitor.

Dot was standing uncomfortably in the middle of the room, her shabby shoes nearly disappearing into the thick carpet. Laura went over to her and kissed her, to Dot's obvious surprise. 'Oh, Mrs Beresford. . . surely you shouldn't. . . thass not right. . .' She put her hand to her cheek, at the same time bobbing a curtsey.

'Oh, Dot, don't be ridiculous. I'm still the same Laura, and

171

always will be, as far as you're concerned,' Laura said, giving the girl's arm an impatient shake. 'Now sit down and make yourself comfortable. Agnes will be bringing some coffee in a minute. Ah, here it is. Yes, thank you, Agnes, put it down there.' Laura ignored Agnes's disgruntled sniff and the glare she gave Dot, perched on the edge of a deep settee.

'I hope as how you won't keep the mistress long. She's all packed up ready to go on 'oliday,' Agnes remarked as she flounced out of the room.

'That will be quite enough, thank you, Agnes,' Laura rapped. She managed to smile at Dot as she handed her the delicate china coffee cup. 'It's lovely to see you, Dot. I know our paths don't cross these days, but I often think about you. I was sorry when poor Ebbie died. . .'

'Yes, thank you for the letter you wrote. 'Course, we all knew it 'ad to come. 'E was mortal ill.' Dot looked sad, then she smiled. ''E was buried with the book you give 'im. Dad said that was what had given 'im the most pleasure in 'is last months an' 'e was sure you wouldn't mind.'

'No, of course not. It was a lovely thing to do.' Laura spoke over a lump in her throat. 'And how are the rest of your family? You must remember me to them. Are they all well?'

Dot put her cup down carefully. 'Most of us is very well,' she said slowly. 'But, an' this is what I've come to you about, because I'm worried sick and I don't know which way to turn. I know Mum and Dad'll die from the shame of it . . .' she broke off, biting her lip.

'Shame of what, Dot? What are you talking about? I don't understand.' Laura frowned.

Dot took a deep breath. 'Thass my young sister Kate, Mrs Beresford, I mean Laura. She's in pod. . . er, got 'erself into trouble.' She glanced at Laura. 'You know – a baby.'

'Oh, dear. Oh, the poor girl.' She looked at Dot. 'She's not married, I take it?'

Dot shook her head.

'Do you know who the father is?'

The girl nodded. 'Thass why I've come to you, Mrs – Laura. Kate say thass Mr Beresford. Mr Alex's brother.' She shrugged. 'Well, you know how she was always sweet on 'im.' She looked anxiously at Laura. 'I wondered if there was

172

anything you could do... anything you could suggest. I know me Dad'll turn her out of the house when he finds out. 'E's always said thass what 'e'd do if any of us girls ever brought trouble 'ome.' She sniffed and perched a little further back on the settee, her face working, 'Kate ain't a bad girl, Laura. She's silly, p'raps, but she ain't bad. But what'll become of 'er if Dad turn 'er out?'

'When's the baby due?' Laura asked.

'Oh, not for six months or so. She's tried drinkin' gin. . .' her voice tailed off.

Laura put her fingers to her temple, trying to arrange her jumbled thoughts. What could she do? She was going away, leaving, never to return. How could she be expected to help Kate Taylor? Yet how could she turn her back on the family that had taken her in and cared for her when she was most in need?

'You will help, won't you Laura?' Dot asked watching her anxiously.

Laura nodded. 'Yes, Dot, of course I will.' She frowned. 'But I must think... I must have time...' She stood up and began to pace up and down the room. After a few minutes she said, 'Come back next week, Dot – a week won't make that much difference, will it? I promise you I will have thought of a way... I'll think of something, don't worry.' She managed to smile at Dot.

'But what about your holiday? Your maid said you were all packed up . . .'

'I needn't go for a few days. It won't make that much difference,' Laura shook her head, suppressing a sigh.

After Dot had gone Laura sat down in an armchair and drank cup after cup of coffee. Oh, God, she prayed silently, what am I to do? Haven't I got enough to worry about without this? Yet she knew she could never simply abandon Kate to her fate, not after the way the Taylor family had cared for her when she was in distress.

When Alex came home after his day's work Laura was waiting in the little sitting room, a cosy room that was a favourite with them both. She had put on a dress of blue shot silk that she knew suited her, and outwardly she was perfectly composed – resigned might be a better word. After

173

a day of indecision and misery she knew exactly what she must do. Although it would mean putting off her departure and enduring more of Jack Plant's blackmailing and the deception that went with it, she knew she couldn't simply go off and leave Kate to her fate. Someone must take responsibility for Charles's despicable behaviour. Added to which her conscience would not allow her own personal misery to get in the way of helping any member of the Taylor family.

Alex dropped a kiss on her head. 'Are you feeling any better, my love? You still look rather pale,' he said, regarding her with his head on one side.

'Yes, thank you, dear.' She smiled up at him and patted his hand as it lay on her shoulder.

'Good.' He nodded and went over to the whisky decanter and poured himself a drink. 'Shall I pour you a sherry?'

'Yes, please.'

She waited until he had handed her her drink and settled himself in the chair opposite, then she said, 'Alex, I had a visitor today. Dot Taylor.'

He frowned as he sipped his whisky. 'Taylor? Weren't they the people you lived with when . . .?'

'Yes,' she interrupted, 'that's right. Dot was the daughter about my age, well, a little younger. I worked beside her at the silk factory.'

An expression of pain crossed his face at the mention of the silk factory. 'I remember. What did she want? I didn't realise she was in the habit of calling on you, my dear.'

'She isn't in the habit of calling on me. She came because she was worried about her young sister, Kate.'

He shook his head. 'I don't remember noticing a younger sister.'

'Don't you? She was the pretty one of the family. A fact that obviously didn't escape your brother Charles, Alex. Dot came to see me because she was at her wits' end to know what to do. Kate is expecting his child and Dot is terrified that her father will turn the girl out of the house when he finds out. She thought I – we might be able to help.'

Alex shrugged. 'Why come to us? Surely there are places . . .'

'I should have thought it was quite plain why she came to

us,' Laura cut across his words. 'If the child belongs to your brother . . .'

'*If* it belongs to Charles. We've only the girl's word for that.' He smiled at Laura. 'I don't know what you have in mind, my love, but we can't be expected to set ourselves up as some kind of sanctuary for girls who are foolish enough to get themselves into trouble, now, can we?'

Laura froze. 'It's our duty to help Kate, Alex,' she said, holding her temper with difficulty. 'I owe that family more than I could ever repay. They took me in when I hadn't a friend in the world. And if the child she carries belongs to Charles then you owe them something, too.'

'*If*. Those factory girls will say anything to get themselves out of a hole.'

'You're forgetting, Alex, I know the Taylor family. They may lack worldly goods but they have had a strict moral upbringing. I think Fred Taylor was the most morally upright man I have ever known and he passed his standards on to his children.'

'It looks like it, doesn't it, if one of them goes and gets herself pregnant!' Alex laughed indulgently at his wife's outburst.

'Girls don't *get themselves* pregnant, Alex. It takes two.' Laura lowered her voice, the only sign of her fury her white knuckles as she grasped the arms of the chair she sat in. 'I want to help Kate. I feel we have a responsibility towards her and towards the child.'

Alex finished his whisky and got up out of his chair, still smiling indulgently. Laura was a kind-hearted little goose and he was prepared to humour her. 'So how much do you want to give her, my love?' he asked.

Her lips drew into a tight line. 'I don't want to give her *money*,' she spat. 'I want to give her a home.'

'Oh, come, come, Laura, my dear. Surely that's going a bit far.' Alex's expression hardened as he heard the words. He turned back from pouring himself another whisky and refilling Laura's sherry glass to turn and look at her.

'I think we should give her a home,' Laura went on as if he hadn't spoken, 'we could do with another maid to help Cook and Agnes. And when the child is born I think we should adopt it as a brother or sister for Marcus, since he is otherwise destined to remain an only child. After all, the child will have Beresford blood in it,' she added, as Alex jaw dropped in amazement.

'The devil we'll adopt some factory girl's bastard!' he said, his eyes flashing with rage. 'What do you think I am, Laura? We'd be the laughing stock of the town. We'd have every pregnant trollop from miles around knocking on our door. You must be out of your mind.' He swallowed his whisky at a gulp and put the glass down. 'I'll agree to give the girl some money, but let that be an end of it.'

'No.' Laura stood up. 'I will not let that be an end of it. Kate is pregnant by your brother. I think we should adopt the child. The Taylor family befriended me. I can repay them by befriending Kate. She's a good, decent girl . . .'

'She can't be that good or decent if she goes round getting herself pregnant. Oh, grow up, Laura. You know what these girls are like.' He held up his hand as she opened her mouth to speak. 'Oh, I know young Charles was no plaster saint. For all I know the town is littered with his bastards. But that's the way of the world. All young men sow their wild oats – well, a good many of them, anyway – it was never anything that appealed greatly to me . . .'

'And what about the girls who reap the harvest of those same wild oats?' Laura flashed. 'Have you ever considered them?'

'Well, for the most part they get paid for their trouble.' He stepped forward to take her into his arms. 'They know what they're doing, dearest. They're no better than they should be. If they go round asking for trouble they shouldn't be surprised when they get it,' he said, as if explaining to a child.

She stepped back out of his reach. 'How dare you say such things!' she said, her voice full of barely controlled fury.

'I dare because they're true, my love,' he said with a shrug.

'And what about all those girls for whom it is not true? Those whose only other alternative is to starve? Those who are victims of people like your brother and are forced to give in or lose their jobs? Those whose lives are ruined by rape? It's a downwards spiral for them, till they end up in the gutter.'

176

'Oh, come now, Laura. Men are men and know what they want and there will always be women ready to sell it to them, to be quite disgustingly frank. But take my word for it . . .'

'I don't need to take your word for it,' Laura said through clenched teeth. 'I know exactly how Kate Taylor will end up if somebody doesn't help her. What your brother took as five minutes self-gratification she will be reduced to selling – until she's too old to be desirable – in order to keep the bastard he carelessly foisted on her.'

Alex was beginning to lose patience. 'Now, Laura, listen to me. You've no idea what you're talking about. You can't begin to imagine . . .'

'I don't have to imagine, Alex. Believe me, I know exactly what I'm talking about.' Laura turned away, her eyes blazing, and went over and stood looking down into the fire, trying to control her temper.

'Don't be so melodramatic. Of course you don't. How can you?' Alex sat down in his chair. Then he remembered the scene between Laura and Charles he'd witnessed outside the storeroom, and his shoulders sagged. 'All right . . .' he began, but she wasn't listening.

'How can I know?' She had spun round and was looking down at him, her face twisted with fury. 'I'll tell you how I know. I know because it happened to me. I was raped . . .'

He held up his hand. 'I know, Laura. I'm sorry. Charles . . .'

She tossed her head impatiently. 'It had nothing to do with your brother. Charles didn't get near me. I saw to that. What happened to me was in India and it was brutal.' Tears were streaming down her face but she ignored them as she forced herself to relate what she had never hoped to think, let alone speak of again.

'As you already know, I went out to India to be with my parents when I left Finishing School, not knowing they had been killed in a cholera epidemic,' she began, her voice flat and unemotional. 'As you can imagine I was devastated, but a young subaltern's wife offered me a home if I would act as governess to her son. I was only too pleased to accept her offer, remember I was barely nineteen at the time. Annabel's husband was very handsome and renowned for his bravery

177

and I could see that they were very much in love. It seemed that the only cloud on their horizon was the blinding headaches that Annabel suffered.

'For about a month things went very smoothly. Peregrine, Annabel's little boy, was very amenable and easy to teach and sometimes Annabel and I would go out into the country or to the bazaar together. We became great friends.

'One night there was a ball. It was quite a glittering and colourful occasion, with the officers' dress uniforms and the ladies' beautiful ball gowns.' Her mouth twisted wryly. 'I remember being envious of the brilliant colours because etiquette demanded that I should still wear black mourning for my parents.' She took up the story again. 'Unfortunately, Annabel was forced to leave early because of a bad headache. Naturally, I accompanied her home and put her to bed. Since it was already quite late, I went to bed, too.

'Several hours later I heard Randolph, Annabel's husband return. He was drunk. He was often drunk so this was nothing new and I could hear him swearing at his servant and crashing about. I remember worrying that he would disturb Annabel, although with the drug she took for her headache I knew this was unlikely. After a while all was quiet and I assumed his servant had put him to bed. But suddenly the door of my room opened and he stood there, saying something to the effect that he'd had his eye on me ever since I'd arrived – a cherry ripe for the picking, I believe was the phrase he used – and hadn't it been clever of me to wear black tonight when all the other women were decked out like rainbows. Now Annabel was ill his chance had come and by God he was going to take it.'

She closed her eyes on the memory but forced herself to go on. 'I tried to talk to him. I appealed to him, I even pretended not to take him seriously because I thought I stood a better chance if I could talk him out of it, but it was no use. When he tried to get hold of me I screamed, but that did no good. Nobody came and it obviously gave him a sense of power. I twisted out of his grasp and made for the window but he caught me and dragged me back; the more I fought the more he enjoyed it.' She shuddered. 'He was an *animal*.' For a moment she couldn't go on, then she continued, her voice barely above a whisper, 'When he'd finished with me he warned me that if I breathed a word to Annabel he would tell her I had lured him to my room and that I was nothing more than a slut. He would see to it that I was turned out and that nobody else on the garrison would give me a home.

'So, because I had nowhere else to go, I kept quiet. In any case, Annabel was so sweet, so trusting, I couldn't bear to shatter her illusions over her brute of a husband. He knew that. He knew his power over me . . .'

Her voice began to rise as the terrible confession poured out. 'You simply can't imagine how filthy and degraded it made me feel. And then, when I discovered I was pregnant . . . I didn't know what to do, where to turn. I was absolutely terrified and tried to commit suicide. Annabel thought I'd done it because I was homesick and insisted in giving me the fare home. I took it, thankfully, clinging to the hope that if only I could get to Colchester my grandparents would take me in if I told them I'd been widowed.' She swallowed painfully and went on, 'I got as far as London and there I collapsed. When I came round I found myself in a workhouse, robbed of my clothes, my mother's jewellery, in fact everything I possessed except my train ticket to Colchester. The child was born, prematurely. Thank God it didn't live to haunt me with memories of the man who fathered it.' She turned now to look at Alex, her face ravaged with the painful memory of it all. 'So don't ever say to me that I don't know what I'm talking about when I speak about girls like Kate Taylor. Because the life she's doomed to live if we do nothing to help her is the life, but for the Grace of God and the help of Fred Taylor and his family, I might well have been reduced to living myself.' Her story finished, she turned and left the room, closing the door quietly behind her.

Alex remained where he was, staring into the fire. The quietness with which she had left the room gave it even more of a sense of finality than if she had slammed the door. He couldn't believe it. He couldn't believe any of it. But in his heart he knew Laura hadn't lied. Rather it was that he couldn't bear to face the truth; the knowledge that she had already borne a child before their marriage. His mind dwelt on this for a long time trying to come to terms with the fact that she had been violated, that it had happened against her will, that it was not her fault, if what she said was true. And he knew it was true. Laura wouldn't lie.

But she had deceived him . . . and he, in his ignorance had blamed his brother Charles . . . He put his head in his hands. 'Oh, what have I done?' he moaned to himself. 'All these years I've been blaming Charles – hating him for something he didn't do. What was it she said, "Charles didn't get near me . . ." Oh, God, if only I'd known. But it is too late. Charles is dead, dead because he couldn't face his debtors. Dead because I refused to lend him the money he needed. It was my revenge for what I thought he had done to Laura.' Alex was tortured by the thought. The agony of it all was too new, to raw for him to be rational and to face the fact that he would never have lent Charles his hard-earned money to pay off gambling debts whatever the circumstances.

After a long time, it could have been one hour, it could have been two, Alex had no idea, he got up out of his chair and made his way upstairs. Laura was lying on their bed, her face swollen and streaked with tears, a handkerchief crumpled into a wet, soggy ball lying beside her. Exhausted with crying, she was fast asleep. Alex looked round the room. Over the chair a cloak was flung carelessly and there was a half empty valise beside it. A hat waited on the dressing table and a pair of boots stood beside the valise.

He sat down heavily on the end of the bed. This was a nightmare. It couldn't be happening. His world seemed to be cracking apart and there was nothing to clutch at to hold it together.

Laura, wakened by his weight on the bed, sat up and passed her hand over her face.

'You're going away?' he asked dully.

'I was. I was all packed and ready. Then Dot came to see me and I decided that I couldn't leave Kate to her fate . . . I would have to face it out until she was taken care of . . .'

'Face it out? Face what out?' They were both speaking in flat, emotionless tones.

'I told you that I had a child in a London workhouse.' Laura didn't look at him as she spoke. 'What I didn't tell you was that Jack Plant was the overseer of that workhouse. He recognised me as soon as he saw me at the Midsummer Ball and he's been blackmailing me ever since. That's where all my missing jewellery is. It was that or . . .' she shuddered, '. . . agree to a Wednesday afternoon assignation.' She shuddered again. Suddenly, she looked up. 'I couldn't bear the deception any longer, Alex. I was going to leave you a note, explaining . . . I couldn't go on . . .' She covered her face with her hands.

'Why didn't you tell me all this before?'

'I tried. When we were first married. I tried to tell you. But you wouldn't listen. And then, when it seemed that you hadn't realised you were not . . . the first . . . I thought you need never know and I could forget the past. God knows, I didn't want to remember. It was a part of my life that I wanted to bury for ever. And I had. Almost. It was as if it had all happened to someone else. Not me at all. At least, not the me that is now, if you can understand. And then Jack Plant came to Colchester and ruined everything.'

'And I thought it was Charles,' Alex said, half to himself. 'All these years I've blamed Charles.'

Dusk had fallen and the room was dim and shadowy. He got up and lit the gas and closed the heavy gold brocade curtains. Then he stood with his back to them and regarded her as she sat on the edge of the bed, wringing her hands together.

She lifted her head. 'I'll go away, Alex,' she said, lifting her head. She was quite calm now, her tears were spent and she knew that she would never cry again. It was as if all feeling, all emotion had been washed out of her heart, leaving nothing. 'I realise that you won't want me to stay. I should have been gone already, had it not been for Kate. I hope you will find it in your heart to do something for her. She deserves a better future than the one she faces at the moment. As for Marcus . . .'

He held up his hand. 'I don't think you should go, Laura. Marcus needs you. And I think you're right. We should take Kate as you suggested, give her a home and adopt the child when it is born.' He bowed his head. 'I owe my brother that much, since it was I that sent him to his death.' He looked up. 'But I can't . . . things can't be the same between us, Laura.

I can forgive . . . I could have forgiven . . .' his face crumpled in pain. 'In God's name why didn't you *tell* me your story before we were married, Laura? Why did you have to deceive me? I've been deceived once in my life. Why did *you* have to do it a second time? I can't bear being deceived!' He thumped his closed fist into the palm of his other hand to emphasise each phrase.

She looked down at her hands for a long minute and then met his gaze. 'Tell me honestly, Alex. Would you have married me if you'd known the full story?' she asked quietly.

He stared at her in amazement for a moment, then he turned away. 'I don't know,' he admitted. 'I honestly don't know.'

She got up off the bed and went over to the dressing table and absently began to move jars and bottles. 'I couldn't bear to risk losing you, Alex. That's why I didn't tell you before we were married. But afterwards I realised it wasn't fair, that you had to know. I didn't want anything – not anything at all – to come between us and spoil the precious thing that we had. But when I'd plucked up the courage to tell you, you refused to listen. So I decided that perhaps it was unimportant anyway. It was all in the past and didn't in any way affect us.' Her mouth twisted wryly. 'I couldn't have been more wrong, could I?' She looked at his reflection in the mirror.

He hung his head and turned away. 'I'm sorry, Laura. Perhaps in time I shall be able to. . . but for the present I think it will be best if I sleep in my dressing room. I'm sorry. But I just can't accept . . .'

'I understand, Alex,' she nodded wearily. 'Really. I do understand.'

'Otherwise things will go on as before. You can tell your Taylor friends that we will take Kate in. I owe that much to my brother . . .'

'Very well, Alex.' She picked up a pair of jet earrings and looked at them before fastening them into her ears. 'At least I shall no longer need to buy Jack Plant's silence. I can't tell you how relieved I am over that,' she said.

Alex's mouth assumed a thin, straight line. 'I've been making enquiries about that man,' he said in a more normal voice. 'I've discovered quite a lot about the way he treats the young girls in the workhouse. There are even rumours of babies being born and never seen again. There's no doubt he's not a fit person to be in charge of a place like that. I just need a little more hard evidence and then it shouldn't be difficult to have him removed.'

'Thank God for that.' She turned on the stool where she sat. 'One last thing, Alex. I do understand how you feel about what I've told you and I don't blame you, really I don't. But whatever you think about me, however you judge me, please never forget that I love you. You are, and always will be, the love of my life, and I would never willingly have caused you hurt.' She spread her hands. 'I couldn't help my past, Alex. I only wish to God I could.'

He looked at her, his face devoid of emotion. 'You'd better wash your face. Agnes will be serving dinner before long. We must keep up appearances.' He went through to his dressing room and closed the door.

Chapter Seventeen

Jay paced up and down the room, his hands behind his back, impatiently flicking his coat tails as he went. 'It's preposterous. God knows how the woman managed to worm her way into my mother's presence. And to think she had the effrontery to take the child with her, too . . .'

'A little boy, I believe.' Charlotte was resting on a chaise longue by the fire although the day was warm. This was not one of her good days, she felt tired and washed-out although she tried hard not to let Jay see how ill she felt. To this end she had coloured her cheeks and had sat uncomfortably but patiently while her maid brushed and curled her hair. She laid her hand on her gently swollen stomach. 'I'm sure we shall have a little boy – a healthy little boy – this time, Jay. Dr Franklyn is watching over me even more carefully than last time.'

'I hope so, my dear.' He spoke absently. Suddenly, he swung round. 'What does that woman think she's doing, trying to ingratiate herself into the family! And it very much looks as if Mama is likely to be taken in by her plausible lies, just as Alex allowed himself to be. I won't allow it.' He thumped his fist on the mantelpiece, 'I *will not* have it. I've told my mother she is not to let the woman inside the house again.'

'I don't think you have any right to dictate who your mother entertains in her own house, dearest,' Charlotte said mildly. 'And as for Alex's wife, I've met her, briefly, and found her the most charming of ladies. I think you would, too, if you were to meet her and talk to her.' She smiled up at her husband.

'I *have* spoken to her. From the other side of my desk, where she belongs. I found her insolent in the extreme.' He scowled down at Charlotte. 'I'm surprised at you, my dear,' he said in a slightly less belligerent tone. 'I would have thought you would have known better than to associate with such a woman. Where is your breeding, Charlotte? Have you forgotten *all* I've taught you?'

'No, indeed. But I think it's far more ill-mannered to cut people, don't you, dearest? In any case, from what you've told me Laura is far from ill-bred. Didn't you say your mother had known her mother and grandmother?'

'If the woman's story holds any credence, which I very much doubt. She probably made it all up.'

'I wouldn't have thought that very likely, dear. After all, it would be very easy to check. And don't keep calling her "the woman" in such a disparaging manner, Jay. She is, after all, your sister-in-law.'

'She is *not* my sister-in-law and I shall never accept her as such.' He gave the fire a vicious poke and then put the poker down with a clatter. 'And I'll thank you to remember that and act accordingly. You are my wife, Charlotte, we can't risk being made a laughing stock by the likes of that person.'

Charlotte sighed. 'I think you're making a mistake, dearest. . . ' But she was too tired to argue further and closed her eyes.

Jay looked down at her. He hoped to goodness this child would live. He knew she felt she'd failed him because in spite of a pregnancy every year she had so far been unable to give him the son he craved. She knew how important it was. He needed a son to hand the factory on to. With young Charles dead – a bad business, that, a very bad business, it did the family name no good at all – there would be no one except young Eleanor to inherit. Except Alex's son. He pursed his lips. Never. The factory must never be allowed to fall into the hands of anyone with such doubtful ancestry.

He dropped a kiss lightly on Charlotte's forehead. 'You must look after yourself, my dear. And if there is anything you would like you have only to ask for it.'

She opened her eyes and looked up at him in some

surprise. He was rarely demonstrative towards her in the daytime. He smiled, another rare event. 'I'm very fond of you, you know, Charlotte,' he said.

'Then... would you read to me for a little, Jay? Time sometimes hangs a bit heavy when my eyes don't focus well enough for me to read myself.'

'Not now, dear.' He patted her arm. 'But I'll try to get back early tonight. I'll read to you then.'

She sighed. 'Thank you, Jay.' But she knew that by that time she would be in bed and he would not disturb her even though she would be lying awake.

It took several visits to the little house in Ball Alley – which, when Laura re-visited, seemed even smaller than when she had lived there with the Taylor family – to convince Fred and Nellie that she really wanted to help Kate, whose fall from grace had shocked her parents into total bewilderment.

'There's never bin nothin' like this in our fam'ly before. Never,' Fred said, dolefully shaking his grey head. 'The shame of it! We shan't never live it down. I dunno what could've come over the gal, straight I don't. We thought we'd brought all our gals up to be decent and God-fearing, not to...' He shook his head again, words failing him. 'She oughta be horse-whipped, thass what she deserve.' But it was an empty threat. Fred wasn't, nor could ever bring himself to be, a violent man.

Nellie, surprisingly, was less compassionate. 'There's no need for you to take 'er in, Lau ... Mrs Beresford, ma'am,' she said firmly. 'She's no better than she should be and she deserve to be turned out on the street. She'd have bin gone before now if I'd had my way. I've always said I wouldn't hev shame brought upon my house. I've told all my girls time outa number, that if they bring trouble home here they'll be shown the door. An' that I'll stand by. We're respectable folk an' always hev bin.' She glared at the weeping Kate; her fury at her daughter's condition knew no bounds.

Laura was amazed at Nellie's lack of charity towards Kate. She would never have believed that the older woman could allow family pride to come before compassion for her daughter. 'I think Kate needs help,' she said gently. 'What happened may not have been entirely her fault, that we don't know, but surely she needs help now, not condemnation.' She laid her gloved hand on Fred's arm. 'You and your family took me in when I needed help, Fred. It's no exaggeration to say that you saved my life. Now I am in a position to repay your kindness in some small way by giving your daughter Kate a home and a position in my house.'

'What about the . . .' Nellie had nodded distastefully towards Kate's still flat stomach.

'When the time comes my husband and I have agreed that we shall adopt the child. After all, from what Kate has told us it has Beresford blood in it and there's no possibility that I shall have more children, dearly though I should like them. Marcus needs a companion.'

Fred and Nellie stared open-mouthed when they heard Laura's words but she took no notice. She stood up and said briskly, 'However, that's all in the future.' She turned to Kate. 'Go and put your things together, my dear. I have the carriage waiting so you can come back with me now. Agnes, my housemaid, will look after you. Are you happy to come with me?'

Tears streamed down Kate's face. 'Oh, Mrs Beresford, ma'am, I dunno what to say.' She scuttled off upstairs to collect her few belongings, unable to believe her luck.

It all worked very well. Kate was a likeable girl, and proved a willing and able worker. If there had been any resentment among the other servants when she arrived it was quickly dispelled by her adaptability and eagerness to be useful.

As for Kate, she couldn't believe her good fortune and it was weeks before she uncrossed her superstitious fingers and accepted that it was not all a dream. Working in the Beresford's house was a far cry from the silk factory; the surroundings were comfortable, warm and to her inexperienced eyes, opulent in the extreme. To show her gratitude there was nothing Kate wouldn't do for any of the other servants, let alone Alex and Laura. Her pregnancy was causing her very little inconvenience and for the most part she ignored it, glad to think she wouldn't have to be responsible for the child when it was born. The maternal instinct was entirely lacking in her and she had been more than happy to agree to give the child up to Mr and Mrs Beresford when it was born. To her way of thinking it was the least she could do after they had been kind enough to take her in and give her a home and employment, after her bringing such shame on her family.

Not that it had been her fault. Not really. And she hadn't enjoyed it; he had made her feel dirty, somehow. Afterwards he had given her some money and told her she wasn't to tell a soul, which made it all the more sordid. Not that she wanted to tell anyone; not about the things he'd done. She'd tried to avoid him afterwards but he'd kept seeking her out and threatening her with dismissal if she didn't do as he said.

So she'd kept it secret, like he said, till she found out about the baby. Then she knew she'd have to tell. But by that time Mr Charles had shot himself so she didn't think it would matter if she said she was having his baby.

On the last day of November Kate's daughter was born, without fuss, up in the servants' quarters. She looked down at the child at her breast and thought that she had something of the look of Mr Charles in her. Maybe, given time, she could learn to love her. At any rate, she didn't wish her any harm. But she felt no sorrow at giving her up; no regret that the child would never know that she was her real mother.

But if Kate was less than enthusiastic about her daughter, Maudie was delighted at the prospect of a baby in the house again. She was a pretty baby, tiny, delicate and perfect, with a fuzz of fair hair and grey-blue eyes. Maudie, a born nursemaid, took to her at once. Maudie herself would never be even halfway pretty, with her riotous carroty hair and freckled snub nose, but she had filled out into a plump, good-natured girl, blissfully happy with her lot, who said grateful prayers each night to a God who looked, Laura suspected with amusement, remarkably like Alex.

Laura chose the child's name, Victoria, and Alex agreed.

'If that's what you would like, my dear,' he said unenthusiastically, without raising his eyes from his book.

That was how he greeted most of Laura's suggestions nowadays. Either with polite agreement or by saying, 'No, I don't think so, my dear.' There were no arguments, no

188

discussions between them, just as there was no warmth, no sign of affection. No love? That was not true. She still loved him desperately and her heart often ached for some sign that his love for her had not completely died. But she never found one. He was unfailingly polite to her, and to all outward appearances they were still happily married, but he never made any attempt to touch her, let alone to kiss or embrace her. It was as if there was a wall of glass between them; invisible, yet so solid and complete that it was almost tangible. And there was nothing she could do except wait on her side for him to find a way through it, because it was of his building, not hers.

Night after night she would lie awake, alone in the bed where they had been so close, so often, staring dry-eyed up into the darkness. She realised now that she might have known that the happiness she had enjoyed with Alex was doomed to end. It had been too wonderful, too perfect to last.

She searched her mind and discovered that she didn't blame him for the way he felt; she understood that he couldn't help it if her confessions had so shocked him that he could no longer bear her near him. She realised that she was besmirched in his eyes; God knew she had felt the same about herself. And she had the added – totally unreasonable – burden of guilt, because what had happened to her had been none of her choosing. But it was cruelly ironic that having risen above the whole sordid business once, it had again surfaced to ruin her life. It was ironic, too, that now she was accepted in the higher echelons of Colchester society her own private world should be in tatters.

Just how completely she was accepted into the town's elite came home to her the following summer, when little Victoria was just over six months old. Mrs Johnson, the wife of one of the richest men in Colchester called, ostensibly to take tea but with an underlying motive.

She was an ample lady, tastefully dressed in purple-trimmed lavender, with purple feathers nodding in the lavender hat perched rakishly on her grey head. She put her cup down delicately on its saucer.

'Mrs Beresford,' she said, 'no doubt you've heard that

from time to time I like to give the gels from the silk factory a little treat – tea in my garden when the weather's nice, allow them to walk round the grounds – that kind of thing.' She looked over at Laura, who was presiding over the tea tray in the garden and smiled winningly. 'I wondered if you might like to come along this year? It's on the twenty-fifth of July. I do hope you're free on that day. I always make a point of having one or two other ladies there – it gives the gels even more of a sense of *occasion*, you understand.'

'Why me, Mrs Johnson?' Laura asked. She was immediately on the defensive, although she covered it by refilling the cups and offering her companion another teacake.

Muriel Johnson looked surprised. 'Why, because you're a lady of standing in the town, of course. And also because of what you've done for that poor unfortunate gel from the factory, my dear. It was such a *noble* thing to do.' She wiped her mouth delicately on her napkin and clasped her hands together. 'I do so *admire* you.' She leaned forward confidentially. 'I have to admit I could never do such a thing, myself. Oh, I'm very happy to organise the odd party or outing – really, it's the least one can do for the poor creatures. But to give one of them a home . . .' She shook her head, suppressing a shudder, her action saying very loudly that she felt Laura was totally misguided. Her voice dropped. 'I understand she still has the child. . .?'

'That's right, Mrs Johnson. Victoria will remain with us.' Laura smiled, knowing that although Mrs Johnson would be dying to question her further, good taste would prevent her. 'Now, when is this tea-party? The twenty-fifth of July did you say?' She took her silver-edged diary out of her reticule and consulted it. 'Yes, I'm quite free on that day. I'll be pleased to come.'

The Johnsons lived in a large mansion on the outskirts of Colchester. Hubert Johnson, apart from having quite a substantial family fortune, was something – something quite important, it was hinted – in the City. They enjoyed a lavish lifestyle and Mrs Johnson was generous with both her time and the substantial allowance her husband put at her disposal in her efforts to help those less fortunate than herself. She

190

didn't mean to be patronising and was quite unaware that her efforts were directed as much to self-gratification – she basked in the admiration and esteem in which she was held – as to helping the 'poor gels'.

She certainly spared no effort in organising the summer party. Over a hundred of the factory girls were brought to the Johnsons' estate on the outskirts of Colchester by a fleet of horse-drawn carriages decorated with coloured streamers and flags and they sang all the way from the town, modifying their songs as the convoy came in through the large wrought-iron gates and up the drive. As they tumbled from the carriages out on to the rolling lawns Laura could see that they had dressed themselves up for the occasion as best they could, in jaunty hats with cheap feathers, tattered boas and glass beads. Some were rowdy and it was plain that they would have to be carefully controlled, and some were quieter and more dignified. They were all excited at the prospect of an afternoon out and a 'posh tea'.

The tea was all laid out on long trestle tables under the trees at the edge of the lawn. They were covered with snowy tablecloths draped with swathes of brightly-coloured material and laden with mountains of dainty sandwiches, a riot of multi-coloured jellies and great slabs of fruit cake. The kitchens at Lexden Grange had been kept busy for several days preparing the feast and maids in stiffly starched aprons whisked haughtily about, the tails of their caps flying, smug in the knowledge that they were the elite of servants in one of the largest households in Colchester.

After Grace, said by the vicar of St Leonard's at Lexden, Mrs Johnson and two other ladies – the mayor's wife and somebody else Laura didn't know – moved among the tables. Holding parasols that exactly matched their expensive dresses to shade them from the sun, they smiled benignly and bestowed brief words of welcome on the awe-stricken factory girls.

'Are you sure you're having enough to eat? There's plenty, you know. And it will only go to waste if you don't eat it.'

'We want you to enjoy yourselves. That's what you're here for.'

'Yes, it really is a beautiful day. When you've eaten do

stroll round the garden. The roses are particularly lovely just now.'

Laura realised that she should never have come. She had worked side by side with some of these women, sharing their griefs and troubles, and now she was expected to move among them like some patronal Lady Bountiful. She couldn't do it. She couldn't parade to these unfortunate creatures how far she had come up in the world. And worse, how far behind she had left them.

Dot Taylor had come in a carriage that had held a group of less gaudily dressed, slightly older women, some clutching children by the hand and Laura went over to where some of them were sitting in the shade of the large old cedar tree. Somebody stood up to give her a chair but she waved it aside and sat down on a branch growing so low that it rested on the ground. 'Have you had all you want to eat?' she asked a little awkwardly. 'It's certainly a very lavish spread.'

'Yes, it's always like this,' Dot said, with a contented sigh. 'The food's ever so nice. But I like to come jest to sit in this beautiful garden. You don't see nuthin' like this in Ball Alley,' she added with a wry smile.

Laura looked at her. 'I'm surprised you've stayed at the Silk Factory all these years, Dot. I'm sure you could have done better for yourself.'

Dot shrugged. 'Thass handy.' She spread her hands. 'I don't hev far to go to get to work. Anyway, I don't know what else I could do . . .'

'You oughta married that fella you was keen on,' one of the others said.

'Well, Mum was ill at the time. I didn't feel I could leave home, not so soon after Ebbie bein' taken, as well.' Dot shrugged. 'I didn't blame George for marryin' someone else. I couldn't expect 'im to wait for ever.' She seemed quite resigned to her fate.

Laura got to her feet. 'I suppose I'd better go and talk to some of the others.' She sighed. 'I don't find this kind of thing very easy, I'm afraid.

'Go and hev a word with Molly Wilson over there,' Dot nodded towards a solitary figure sitting huddled on the grass. 'She'll be glad to talk, I reckon.'

Laura frowned. 'Yes, of course. But what's wrong with her? Is she ill?'

'No. She ain't ill. She's grieving for her little'un. He died last week. Fell outa the window while she was at work. Poor little beggar was only four.'

'Oh, how dreadful!' Laura closed her eyes and shuddered. 'But how did it happen? Wasn't anybody looking after him?'

'Her mum was s'posed to be. But the trouble is, Fanny Wilson's a sight too fond of the gin; half the time she can't see after herself, let alone look after the boy. And she was never that fond of him, seein' as how Molly shamed her by hevin' him in the first place. You know, not bein' married, an' that.'

'Oh, poor girl, that's awful. Of course I'll go and talk to her.'

Laura fetched a cup of tea and a plate of sandwiches and went quietly over and sat down on the grass beside Molly Wilson, who was sitting with her head bent, tears streaming down her cheeks.

'I've brought you some food,' she said gently. 'It might help if you have something to eat.'

Molly took the plate and munched in silence for several minutes. Suddenly, she said, ''E was a little bugger, but I loved 'im,' automatically assuming Laura knew her story. 'An' I don't blame Mum for what 'appened, not with her legs bein' bad, an' that.' She shook her head. 'No, I don't blame Mum,' she repeated, a shade too emphatically.

'What was his name?' Laura asked.

'Charlie. 'E was a Charlie, an' all,' she gave a ghost of a smile. Then she said dully, 'I s'pose it's for the best, reely. 'E hadn't got that much to look forward to, had 'e? But at least 'e was never left at home alone. I never had to leave him tied to the bed post like some do. And 'e was never left to roam the streets, nor never would hev been, while Mum lived. She wouldn't hev done that, even though she used to knock 'im about a bit. Well, she wasn't all that fond of 'im.' She wiped her sleeve across her mouth and watched the children running round the lawn for several minutes. 'Look at them. Most of 'em hev never seen so much grass and all them flowers.' She sighed. 'Them kids don't hev a very good time of it, do they? Left to fend for theirselves till they're old enough to work and then shut up in the winding rooms all day to earn a few coppers, poor little beggars. And it ain't much better when they get growed up, is it?' She looked up suddenly and smiled. 'But it ain't all bad, so I 'spect we shouldn't grumble. An' we've got a nice day out today. Can I hev a bit o' that fruit cake?'

Laura went to fetch her a generous slice of cake. When she returned a group of women had congregated round Molly and they were laughing and talking. Laura went off to talk to some of the children, who, from their shrieks of happy laughter, didn't realise how deprived their lives were.

At six o'clock a bell sounded for everyone to gather round. The vicar made a speech, impressing on the girls their debt to Mrs Johnson for the most excellent tea and reminding them what a privilege it was for them to walk freely in the beautiful garden. He then picked up his Bible. '"The kingdom of Heaven is like a net that was cast into the sea, and gathered in of every kind,' he read. 'Which, when it was full, they drew to shore, and sat down, and gathered the good into vessels, but cast the bad away. So shall it be at the end of the world: the angels shall come forth, and sever the wicked from among the just, and shall cast them into the furnace of fire: there shall be wailing and gnashing of teeth." Matthew, chapter thirteen, verses forty-seven to fifty.' He closed the Bible and looked round at the faces upturned towards him. 'Now, you all know what that means, don't you? There is no doubt that Mrs Johnson and her ladies here will be like the fish gathered into the vessels; they will not be cast away. These good ladies have earned their place in heaven over and over again, not least for their generosity this afternoon.' He gave a sycophantic glance in Mrs Johnson's direction and waited to see what impact his words had made on the girls. A cheer went up. He nodded and leaned down towards them.

'But what about all of you? Will you be gathered into the vessels? Or will you be cast into the furnace of fire? Look into your hearts, my children. What do you find there? Do you find purity of heart, generosity of spirit like that which radiates forth from your benefactors here? Or do you find greed, self-indulgence and worse? Think on these things, my children. It is only by self-denial, abstinence and clean living in this world that you will find reward in heaven . . .'

His voice droned on as Laura looked round at the assembled company. Mrs Johnson and her ladies beaming approvingly, basking in the sure knowledge that their place in heaven was secure. That their generosity was but a drop in the ocean of their wealth and that all the hard work had been done by others was, to them, an irrelevance. The women and girls on whom this self-indulgence had been lavished hung on the vicar's words and prayed to be less selfish and greedy in future. One or two even sidled up to the table and replaced the cake they had secreted to give to other members of their families when they returned home.

Laura watched all this and was uneasy but nobody else appeared to find anything amiss. The girls were effusive in their thanks as they presented Mrs Johnson with a Bible bought with their hard-earned money as a token of their gratitude, before climbing into the carriages that would take them back to their squalid homes.

'I do hope they enjoyed themselves,' Mrs Johnson said anxiously to Laura after the last carriage had rumbled away. 'They have such hard lives it seems the least we can do is to try to bring a little sunshine to them now and then.' She looked at the Bible in her hands. 'I shall treasure this. I didn't expect it and they could ill-afford to buy it, I know.' Her eyes filled with tears. 'I'm so grateful to them. I'm sure this afternoon has given me even more pleasure than they've had.' She smiled at Laura through her tears. 'I expect you think I'm silly, Laura. Anyway, thank you for coming. You were a great help.'

'Thank you for inviting me.' Laura picked up her bag and prepared to leave. Perhaps she had misjudged Muriel Johnson's motives after all. Perhaps it was the vicar who was misguided.

Chapter Eighteen

For several days Laura turned over in her mind the sort of thing she might do to give the children she had heard about at Mrs Johnson's garden party a better start in life – patronising them in the best sense of the word and not in the way she had seen their mothers treated there. In the end she went to see Dot Taylor and discussed it with her because Dot knew not only what the needs were but what help would be acceptable.

'You could make a collection, I s'pose,' Dot said doubtfully.

Laura shook her head. 'Money wouldn't necessarily benefit the children, would it?'

'No.' Dot laughed. 'That might do the publicans a bit o' good though.'

'Yes, that's what I think and I'm not interested in that. I want to do something for the *children*. To keep them off the streets. . .'

'Well, I dunno,' Dot gave a shrug. 'I s'pose you could do something like Parson Doubleday does. He rounds 'em up on Sunday afternoons for Sunday School and teaches 'em about the Bible an' that.'

'And do they go?'

'Oh, yes. They ain't interested in learnin' but he gives 'em toffees afterwards.'

'I see.' Laura went home mulling over what Dot had told her.

'I think it's a preposterous idea,' Alex said coolly when she spoke to him a couple of days later. 'In any case, I don't see how you can do it.' He was standing by the window, looking out on to the garden, drumming his fingers on the window sill with every appearance of impatience. It was only because Laura had insisted that she had something important to say to him that he was there at all. He spent a lot of time at his club when he was not working, these days.

'*I* can but try. All I'm asking is your permission to try.' Laura twisted her hands together. She hadn't realised how nervous she was.

'You must do whatever you wish, it makes no difference to me, although heaven knows where you got such a crack-brained idea from.' He took his watch from his pocket and looked at it.

'I first got the idea that something must be done when I went to the tea-party organised by Mrs Johnson last month for the girls from the silk factory.' She spoke to his back.

He swung round. 'The devil you did. Then you're on dangerous ground, interfering with the silk workers, aren't you?'

She lifted her head. 'No, I don't think so. What I am proposing to do has nothing to do with the women's work at the factory. As I've already explained, it's their children I am concerned with.'

He shrugged and went to the door. 'It makes no difference to me what you do with your time, provided you do nothing to upset the family.'

'The Beresford family? Do you still regard me as part of the Beresford family, then?' she asked bitterly. 'I wasn't aware that you did.'

He stopped short and for a moment his shoulders sagged. With his back to her Laura didn't see the look of pain that crossed his face. Then he straightened up. 'What happens within these four walls is one thing; what happens in the public eye is quite another matter. There is such a thing as family unity and I won't have you seen to be publicly opposing my brother Jay, either as owner of the biggest silk factory in the town, or in the position he has recently been given as a Justice of the Peace.'

Her mouth twisted. 'I'm sure he would be gratified to think that you were on his side over something,' she remarked dryly, '– particularly as it is in opposition to me.'

For a moment he closed his eyes. Then he half turned and held out a hand, looking at her with an expression that was almost suppliant. But her head was bowed and turned from him as she struggled to compose herself. His hand fell to his side. 'You do whatever you choose,' he said briefly and left the room.

In truth, although in talking to Dot she had conceived somewhat grandiose plans Laura was not at all confident that the venture would work. But after hearing the stories that Molly Wilson and some of the other girls had told her and then talking to the children themselves she knew that something had to be done. She didn't know which was worse, leaving little children alone in a cold room all day, paying some grasping old hag a penny to look after them with a dozen others, or letting them loose on the streets to fend for themselves all day and half the night. At best they were left to look after each other, putting responsibility on to shoulders far too young to bear it.

Taking her courage in both hands she hired a draughty, disused church hall and let it be known, through Dot, that a small school for the instruction and education of little children would be opening at ten o'clock on the following Monday. All would be welcome, regardless of age.

With her heart in her mouth she arrived on the day armed with slates and slate pencils and a map of the world to pin on the wall. She put two rows of chairs facing the rickety black-board that she found in a corner, chalked up the date and waited.

She waited until twelve o'clock then, disappointed, she locked up and went home. The same thing happened the next day and the day after. She looked round the empty hall and at the two neatly arranged rows of chairs, and the old proverb about leading a horse to water came into her mind. It was plain nobody was interested. More disappointed than she would admit, she gathered up her things and prepared to leave, thankful she had only hired the hall for a week so there were only two more days to go.

As she took a last look round to make sure she had left

198

nothing behind there was a rattle at the door and a ragged little figure poked its head round the door. When it saw she was alone it came right in and Laura could see that it was a little girl of about six. She marched up the hall in boots several sizes too big, looking to left and right as she came.

'Is this what a school is?' she asked curiously. 'All them chairs and things?'

Laura smiled. 'Not exactly. The chairs are for the children to sit on.'

'What children?'

'The children who come to the school.'

'I can't see no children.'

'No, there aren't any.'

'Why not?'

'Because they haven't come.'

'Why haven't they come?'

Laura spread her hands. 'Perhaps they don't want to learn anything.'

'What's learn?'

'Being taught how to read and write. Look,' Laura picked up a slate and wrote CAT on it. Then she drew a cat with a long tail. She pointed to the drawing. 'Do you know what that is?'

The child nodded. ''Course I do. Thass a cat.'

Laura pointed to the word she had written. 'If you didn't want to draw a cat you could write cat. CAT. Like that.'

'Thass words, ain't it?'

'That's right. Would you like to be able to read words?'

The child nodded.

'Then come along here tomorrow and I'll teach you to read some more words. I'll teach you to write words, too. And count numbers.'

'Will there be any grub?' the child asked eagerly.

Laura smiled at her. 'Yes, if you come tomorrow there'll be some soup and bread after lessons.'

'What's lessons?'

'Lessons are when you learn. Be here at ten o'clock tomorrow and you'll see. What's your name?'

'Roof.'

'Very well, Ruth, I'll see you tomorrow. And you can bring

your friends if you like.'

Laura went home in a happier frame of mind. The next day when she arrived at the hall Ruth was waiting and she had with her a four-year-old boy she said was her brother, Albert. He spent the morning making his slate pencil squeak on the slate but Ruth was keen to learn and by the end of the morning could manage to write CAT for herself in shaky capitals. Kate arrived with a can of soup at twelve which the two children polished off between them and at one Laura turned them out and locked up.

'Can we come termorrer?' Albert asked.

'Yes. And bring your friends.'

'Will there be soup?'

'Yes, there'll be soup.'

The next day there were five children.

'Will there be soup every day, missus?' a weedy boy with no shoes asked as he came up for a second helping.

'Yes, provided you come to lessons first,' Laura said, trying to look stern.

'Oh, I don't mind that. As long as we git the soup.' He slurped his soup and had a final scribble on his slate before he left.

Laura went home happy. Even if they only came for food initially she was confident that her little school was beginning to grow.

In fact, it grew faster than she had anticipated. The following Monday when she arrived, taking Kate with her to help with the little children, she found that there was already quite a crowd of ragged children standing by the door, pushing and squabbling to be first in. They were a motley crowd, Ruth was there, and Albert, trying proprietorially to marshal the newcomers into some kind of order, plus the three that had been on Friday and some twelve or fifteen newcomers. They all seemed to be dressed in rags or hand-me-downs that were none too clean and several were barefoot in spite of a chill autumn wind. Laura knew that the oldest of them couldn't have been more than eight years old or they would have been at work, but two of them carried babies that looked nearly as heavy as they were themselves and several more dragged toddlers.

200

She quickly sent Kate home with a message for Cook to make extra soup which Banks the gardener could bring along on the dog cart, and then set to work with the children.

It was difficult enough to get them to sit on chairs and almost impossible to keep them quiet. At last, in desperation she shouted, 'If you don't do as I say there will be no soup today.'

There was instant silence.

It was hard work. A few of the children, like Ruth, were eager to learn, but most had simply come to be fed and it was only the promise of soup each day that kept them manageable.

Nevertheless, Laura felt she was making some kind of progress when the older ones could all chant the alphabet without prompting from her and several of them could say their two-times tables. Kate was proving invaluable at keeping the smaller children amused in the corner, in spite of taking such little interest in her own child.

Each day, after they had finished their soup Laura began the practice of reading them a story, which they received with varying degrees of interest. Some listened intently, some fell asleep and some didn't wait to hear it at all.

'Ungrateful little beggars,' Kate said when they had finally gone, as she helped Laura finish clearing up. 'Several of 'em clear off when they've got all they can get.'

Laura nodded. 'I know, Kate, but at least they come. If I can only gain their confidence I shall be able to do more for them.'

'Hmph,' Kate said, then realised who she was talking to and added apologetically, 'beggin' your pardon, ma'am.'

Gradually, to Laura's delight, more and more children began coming, but that meant that Cook began to complain that all her time was taken up with making soup for paupers. Laura sympathised. It hadn't been her intention to set up a soup kitchen, it had only been a carrot to get the children to the school but as such it had worked beyond her wildest expectations and she was inclined to think that the children benefited as much from being fed as from being educated.

The trouble was, the bigger the numbers, the more they squabbled among themselves. Some were happy to chant the

201

simple words she put up on the blackboard and to listen to the story she read every day, but as the weather became colder they often fell asleep in the warmth from the tortoise stove. Eventually, there were too many to do much with at all. She realised that she simply couldn't manage to teach, let alone try to feed the growing numbers that were coming. She began to despair.

Help came from a totally unexpected quarter. One Friday afternoon, as Kate was clearing away the last of the soup bowls and Laura was cleaning off the blackboard, Muriel Johnson walked in with a rustle of silk and a waft of lavender perfume.

'Oh, Mrs Beresford, my dear, I've just heard what you're doing here. I do so admire your efforts and I would have come before but I've been away,' she said, looking round at the unpromising surroundings. 'Now, how can I help? I know I'm too late to do much today, but I'm willing to come next time. That is, if you'll have me.'

Laura sat down at one of the tables that was still wet from Kate's scrubbing brush – at least she had managed to get the children sitting at tables before they ate now – and leaned her head on her hand. 'I could certainly do with some help, Mrs Johnson, but are you sure you realise quite what I'm trying to do?'

Mrs Johnson sat down opposite to her. 'You're trying to give these unfortunate children the rudiments of an education,' she said, pulling off her gloves and laying them carefully on the table.

Laura made a face. 'That was my idea, to set up some kind of a school. But it hasn't quite worked out like that, I'm afraid. Most of them only come for the soup they get, they're not really interested in learning anything. Apart from a few girls, that is.' She sighed and spread her hands. 'The trouble is, now I've begun to feed them I can't find it in my heart to stop, even the ones that won't listen to me. I can't get some of them to even pick up a slate pencil.' She indicated a box with brand new slates and slate pencils on the end of the table. 'Poor little mites, I can't blame them, I suppose, they're all underfed, several of them have rickets and quite a few are already suffering from colds and coughs that will only get worse as the winter gets colder. I feel so sorry for them. But what more can I do?'

Muriel Johnson was silent. Laura stole a glance at her. She had obviously no idea of what she had walked into and was looking for an excuse to leave. Laura felt quite sorry for her. 'I fear there's very little you can do, either, Mrs Johnson. But thank you for coming, all the same.' She got to her feet as she spoke.

Mrs Johnson remained seated. 'Wait a minute. I was just thinking. You've already made a good start by getting the children to come here. At least it keeps them off the streets so we must build on it.'

'I'm not sure that I can. My cook is already complaining about the amount of soup she has to make,' Laura sighed.

'Ah, so that's the first thing. I'll get Effie, my cook, to take a turn. That will ease things a bit. And I'm sure I can get one or two of my other friends to do the same.' She smiled. 'They'll be quite happy to provide soup although they probably won't want to come and serve it.' She pinched her lip. 'And what about getting the mothers to come along, perhaps on a Saturday afternoon? Give them a cup of tea and show them what we . . . you are trying to do.' She warmed to her theme. 'We might even set up some kind of clothing stall for them.' She smiled at Laura. 'I've no doubt you have clothes that your son has outgrown and my two girls have wardrobes full of dresses they never wear.'

Laura sank down on her chair again. 'Oh, what a good idea! They say two heads are better than one. Yes, if we can get the mothers' support . . .'

'It would be even better if we could get official recognition,' Muriel Johnson said thoughtfully. She looked up. 'I am on the Hospital Board of Governors. We meet every Thursday at twelve. I wonder if there's anything they might be willing to do . . .' Her eyes twinkled. 'Perhaps the best thing would be if you came to plead your case, Mrs Beresford. Would you do that?'

'Of course. If you think it will help,' Laura said warmly.

'Very well, I'll see what I can arrange.' She picked up her gloves. 'Now I must go. Goodbye, Mrs Beresford. And remember, next Monday I shall provide the soup. *And* I shall come and help you with the little ruffians. If there are two of us they might take more notice.'

'Oh, thank you.' Laura watched her go. It was as if a great weight had been lifted off her shoulders and she realised that once again she had misjudged Muriel Johnson.

It was such a relief to have someone to share the joys and sorrows of the venture with, to know that someone else cared about what she was trying to do and didn't regard her as at best misguided and at worst simply foolish. Because although he never said as much – Alex rarely passed any comment on anything that she did these days – Laura knew that that was how he regarded her efforts. She sometimes wondered if he realised how much she needed her little school; if he knew that it was the only thing, apart from Marcus, that gave her life purpose now that their estrangement was so complete.

Muriel Johnson was as good as her word. Most days she came and helped Laura and she organised a rota among her friends to provide soup and bread for the children. When she couldn't come herself she arranged for someone to take her place. She was a tower of strength to Laura.

And she managed to arrange for Laura to attend the weekly governors' meeting at the hospital.

'I don't know whether it will do much good, but at least we can try,' Muriel said cheerfully as they went up the steps and into the hospital together.

The meeting was informal, held in the rather drab board room, at which the matron and house apothecary produced their account books and note was made of admissions and discharges, operations performed and the rate of success. Then there was a long and rather pointless discussion over the amount of coal used to heat the wards and whether patients' relatives should be allowed to bring food in to supplement their diet. Laura sat quietly at the back, watching everything with interest. She had been rather disconcerted to see that one of the other governors was Jay Beresford, her brother-in-law. Fortunately, he hadn't appeared to notice her presence in the background.

The proceedings were drawing to a close before Muriel found the opportunity to speak.

'Ladies and gentlemen, I would like to draw your attention to what I and my friend are trying to do in the town,' she said. 'As you know, there are a great many children left to their own devices whilst their mothers are at work.'

'I dispute that,' an elderly woman with a lorgnette said. 'There are always older brothers and sisters to look after the young ones. That's how it has always been in the working classes and always will be, I daresay. I don't feel it is anything that should concern us as hospital governors.'

Jay Beresford nodded. 'I agree with Mrs Roland. In any case, I already play my part in keeping the brats off the streets,' he said smugly. 'As soon as they are of an age I give them employment in my silk factory. Not that they earn their wages,' he added. 'Most of them are idle and irresponsible in the extreme.' He gave the impression that he was a public benefactor.

Laura couldn't contain herself. She jumped up and said, 'They are barely eight years old when you employ them. How can they be expected to work hard and behave responsibly?'

Jay looked round furiously at the sound of Laura's voice. 'What is that woman doing here?' he snapped. 'She has no business at this meeting.'

Muriel Johnson stood up. 'This is the lady who has started caring for these children. She is trying to give them the rudiments of an education. . .'

'That's no concern of ours,' Jay interrupted rudely. 'This is a meeting to discuss hospital matters and nothing else. She has no place here.'

'There's nothing to say that these meetings must be held in private, Mr Beresford,' Dr Armitage, a youngish man with a shock of prematurely grey hair and kind brown eyes who was presiding, said, 'although they usually are. However, to my mind this is an admirable cause and perhaps we can all give some thought as to how we can further it.' There were nods all round.

'Perhaps we can give financial support,' somebody suggested.

'What? Out of hospital funds? Impossible! We're hard put to it to keep the hospital financed let alone handing money out,' someone else was quick to point out.

'Then perhaps out of our own pockets,' the first speaker looked hopefully round at the assembled company.

'I have quite enough calls on my time and my money as I am sure do we all,' Jay said firmly. 'I refuse to lend my support to a scheme that has no official sanction.' He got up from his chair.

'Very well, I declare this meeting closed,' the chairman was forced to say quickly, in order to preserve the formalities, although his eyes rested on Laura with sympathy.

Jay strutted down the room towards the door. When he reached Laura he stopped. 'You!' he hissed, his face livid with fury. 'I might have guessed as much. You're a born trouble-maker and the sooner you are out of this town the better it will be for all concerned.' He looked her up and down. 'I blame Alex, of course. It's his fault, besmirching the family name by marrying beneath him. Although I suppose it's no more than was to be expected,' he added, half under his breath. 'Like father like son.' He stalked off.

She stared after him, speechless. Oh, what a dreadful, horrible man! Then his last words registered. What could he have meant, 'like father, like son'? What on earth could Old Javis have done in the past to provoke such a statement, from his eldest son, too? She shook her head. There was still a great deal that she didn't know about the Beresford family.

Curious as she was, she couldn't question Alex about the matter. They hardly spoke these days, and then only about mundane, household things. Since their estrangement he had immersed himself in his work, with the result that the business had expanded and succeeded far beyond his wildest hopes or expectations. But she suspected that it gave him little satisfaction or pleasure, and when she recalled the early days of their marriage, the little cottage Alex had taken so much pleasure in furnishing for her, and their happiness together, she felt her heart would break. How could it be that he, who had loved her so much that he had happily given up everything – including his family – to marry her, could allow that love to be killed by her past. A past over which she had had no control and to which she thought she had already paid her debt in suffering and misery before she even met him.

She searched her heart to discover whether anything Alex did, or might have done in the past, could kill her love for him but could find nothing. Even his rejection of her hadn't diminished her feelings – she felt nothing but sorrow to think that she had caused him so much suffering and anguish that it appeared to have hardened him into a man she hardly knew.

Chapter Nineteen

Unlike Muriel, Laura was not in the least surprised to receive no support for her school from the Hospital Board of Governors. Once she had discovered that Jay was a member she knew only too well that even if the rest of the Board had wanted to help her he would have found some way of preventing it.

Nevertheless, the school flourished and if it was hard going trying to instil even a modicum of knowledge into most of the children it was rewarding to see a real talent emerge here and there – a scribble on a slate that revealed a rearing horse, a whole page of a book read without fault, or an aptitude for numbers.

Laura's star pupil was little Ruth. She was tiny, wiry and full of zeal, absorbing knowledge like blotting paper and able to hand it on to the other children with an infectious enthusiasm. If ever there was a born teacher, thought Laura, Ruth was one. But for the daughter of a silk mill worker and a consumptive father what chance was there of that? Her fate was set. As soon as she was old enough Ruth would follow her big sister into the silk mill.

The Saturday afternoon club for mothers and children that Muriel had instigated also worked well. The mothers, some little more than children themselves, were only too pleased to pay a ha'penny or penny a week into a clothing club in return for better garments than they had ever seen, let alone worn before, both for their children and themselves.

'It's not much,' Muriel said as she handed the coppers over to Laura at the end of a busy Saturday afternoon, 'but it will buy a few books or slate pencils.'

'There's really no need,' Laura looked at the money doubtfully, 'I can afford. . .'

Muriel's hand closed over hers. 'I know you can, my dear, and so can I, several times over. But clothing that has to be paid for with hard-earned cash will be valued far more than free hand-outs.'

Laura smiled at her. 'I hadn't thought about it like that. You're probably right, Muriel.'

Even more children came to the little school when the winter weather was at its worst. They had heard about the warmth and the free soup and they gravitated to the church hall like moths to a lighted candle.

'It's a pity we can't set up medical checks for them,' Muriel said one day, looking round at the clusters of children, some of the older ones laboriously scratching away on slates, some chanting tables with Ruth, some playing in the corner under Kate's somewhat sketchy supervision and some sitting huddled apathetically round the fire. 'Most of them look peaky and undernourished. And they've all got coughs and colds.'

'We couldn't do that without the help of the Hospital Board though,' Laura pointed out, 'and as you will remember, I didn't have much success last time I approached them. Mind you, I did have the impression that the chairman – what was his name, Dr Armitage, wasn't it? – would have been sympathetic, given the chance. But of course he couldn't do anything on his own.'

'We've got a new doctor on the Board now,' Muriel said, pinching her lip. 'He's not long back from India, I believe. Maybe if I were to talk to him he'd back Chris Armitage and between them they could get something done.' She smiled at Laura. 'I'll see what I can do. But I don't think that it would be advisable for you to come back, my dear, I could see that your brother-in-law. . .'

Laura made a face. 'Oh, I quite agree. Jay and I have had several disagreements,' she said. 'He'll never back anything that I have dealings with, on principle. No, it's far better that I keep out of his way.'

'All the same, I'd like you to meet Dr Bristow. And you

will, of course, because I'm arranging an informal dinner party shortly and he'll be there. You and your husband will receive an invitation in a day or two. I do hope you'll both be able to come.'

'I'm sure we shall,' Laura said, with more conviction than she felt. 'Did you say Dr Bristow had just come back from India?'

'Yes. Oh, my dear, didn't I hear that you'd been out to India once upon a time?'

'Yes, my father was an army doctor there.'

Muriel clapped her hands. 'Then it's quite likely that you've already met him. Wouldn't that be strange?'

'Oh, Muriel, I hardly think so.' Laura said with a laugh. 'India is a very big place and it was a long time ago.'

'Yes, of course. How stupid of me.'

The invitation arrived and Alex passed it to her without a word.

'You will come, Alex, won't you?' she asked anxiously. 'The invitation is addressed to both of us.'

'Not if I can help it,' he replied without enthusiasm. 'Not if it's another of your do-gooding, fund-raising affairs.'

'It is nothing of the kind.' Her voice was sharp. 'It is a private dinner party, which you would have seen if you had read the invitation properly.' She handed it back to him.

'Hm.' He handed it back. 'Very well. You had better accept for us both.'

'Thank you, Alex.' She gave a sigh of relief. At least he hadn't refused to accompany her.

Although Muriel Johnson's dinner party was what she called 'quiet and informal' there were upwards of thirty guests seated round the dining table, which was so decorated with complicated flower arrangements, towers of fruit in silver bowls and epergnes laden with elaborate sweetmeats that it was impossible to see who was sitting opposite, let alone hold a conversation with them.

Laura, in a gown of midnight blue taffeta, with Alex's pearls at her throat, found herself strategically seated next to the new doctor. Dr Bristow was a tall, lean man with blue eyes, made even bluer by the remains of a deep tan and fair hair. On her other side was a rather deaf gentleman called Mr Graham who was plainly more interested in food than conversation.

She lost count of the number of courses that were served. There was a pale, clear soup, followed by fish in aspic, partridges in wine, a sharp lemon sorbet, roast beef, then a selection of desserts, before fruit and cheese. Peter Bristow divided his time equally between Laura and the lady on his right, Mrs Fairweather. Laura tried to converse with Mr Graham but found it next to impossible to overcome not only his deafness but his unwillingness to concentrate on anything but the food on his plate. He ate steadily and massively, to the exclusion of all else and his figure pointed to the fact that this was nothing unusual in his behaviour. If she craned her neck she could just see Alex, further down the table on the other side, half hidden by a large cluster of grapes. He had a rather pretty girl on his right, who seemed to be going out of her way to charm him. Laura couldn't see who was on his left but she felt a sharp stab of jealousy at the way he was smiling at his young companion. It was a very long time since he had smiled at Laura like that.

'Mrs Johnson tells me you spent some time in India, Mrs Beresford?' Dr Bristow was speaking to her.

'I beg your pardon? Oh, yes. But I wasn't there long and it was, oh, let me see, something like ten years ago now.' She smiled at him. 'I'm sure things have changed a lot since I was there. Especially after that dreadful mutiny.'

'Yes. It was a terrible time. But things have changed.'

'Have you just come back to England?'

'I've been back six months. I was in London, but I was anxious to come to Colchester so that I could be nearer to my ward. He boards at the Royal Grammar School here and I promised his mother I would keep an eye on him.' He smiled. 'Fourteen-year-old boys can be a bit rebellious and Perry's no exception.'

Laura's hand went to her throat. 'Perry? That's an unusual name. . .'

'Short for Peregrine, of course.'

Laura was silent and Dr Bristow turned to make polite

conversation with his other companion. She did rapid mental calculations. Ten years ago Annabel's son had been four years old. And his name was Peregrine. Perry. He would now be fourteen. But it was not possible. . . This man's ward couldn't be Annabel's son, it was too much of a coincidence.

Dr Bristow turned back to her. 'Can I pass you anything?'

'No, thank you. Your ward. . .'

'Perry?'

She nodded. 'Does he come from an army background?'

'Yes. His father is Captain Randolph Grey of the. . .'

'And his mother's name is Annabel?' Laura interrupted eagerly.

A faint flush coloured his face. 'That's right.'

'I can't believe it,' she said, shaking her head. 'Of all people, that you should know Annabel.' She looked at him. 'I'm sorry. I should explain. Annabel Grey befriended me when I arrived in India to be with my parents and found that they had both died in a cholera epidemic. I stayed with her for several months as governess to Perry. She was a lovely person.'

'She still is, Mrs Beresford,' he said, his voice low. 'A wonderful person. I met her at the Residency in Lucknow where we were besieged during the mutiny and we've remained friends ever since. I'll tell her when I write. . .'

'No.' Laura shook her head. 'She's probably forgotten I existed by now.'

'Forgive me. May I ask, is your name Laura?' he said.

She nodded. 'I was Laura Chapman when she knew me.'

'Then she has most certainly not forgotten you. I've heard her speak about you often. In fact, she has called her little daughter after you. She is Laura Jane, Lolly for short.'

'Really?' Laura bit her lip, touched beyond words. 'So Annabel has a little girl,' she said when she had composed herself again. 'Are they well?'

'They were when I left India.' He hesitated, playing with his fruit knife, then he looked up. 'The only thing is, Lolly was born blind.'

'Oh, how dreadful. Oh, the poor, poor child. How old is she now?'

'Eight.' He smiled. 'But there's really no need to pity her,

Mrs Beresford, because she copes amazingly well. I suppose it's a case of what you've never had you never miss and her other senses seem to be more finely tuned to compensate. But you will be able to meet her before long because Captain Grey is being posted back to the garrison here in Colchester and I've promised to look for a house for him and his family.' He smiled at her again.

Somehow she managed to smile back. But her thoughts were in a turmoil. However much she longed to renew her friendship with Annabel she knew she could never face that dreadful man again. How could she ever take tea and make polite conversation with the man who had raped and humiliated her as he had done? It would be an intolerable situation.

There was no time for further conversation because Mrs Johnson gave the signal for the ladies to leave the men to their port and retire into the drawing room. This was a large room decorated in blue and gold brocade with a grand piano on a raised platform at one end. Gilt chairs had been arranged to face the piano and for those not interested in the musical entertainment, there were several settees and armchairs set at the other end of the room, with jardinieres holding a veritable jungle of greenery between them, and several aspidistras on tall pedestals. There was even a palm tree in a pot growing near the piano; giving the whole room a very sophisticated, modern appearance. Laura was very impressed by it all as she sat with the other ladies, drinking coffee and waiting for the gentlemen to arrive so that the entertainment could begin.

It was not long before the men rejoined them. Alex's pretty companion from the dinner table was quick to commandeer him again and she bore him off to listen to the music. Laura got up to follow with some of the other ladies when she felt a light hand on her arm. It was Peter Bristow.

'Are you terribly interested in Handel arias and Mozart sonatas?' he whispered, 'or would you mind staying at the back here? I'd like to talk to you further.'

She hesitated for a moment. Then she saw Alex's companion tap him playfully on the hand with her fan and another stab of jealousy shot through her.

'Of course, Dr Bristow.' She gave him her most dazzling smile.

He led her to a settee half hidden by a potted plant and they sat down together.

He looked down at his hands. They were long and slim with sensitive, tapering fingers. 'Annabel will be so happy when I tell her I've met you, Mrs Beresford. I know she was very disappointed that you never wrote to her. Even during that terrible siege she still remembered and spoke of you.' He moved his shoulders slightly. 'You can say it's none of my business if you like but why didn't you write, Mrs Beresford? I am surprised that you didn't, since it is obvious that you held her in equally high regard.' He smiled. 'She would have been so pleased to hear of your good fortune. Your husband is very well thought of in the town, I know.'

Laura spread her hands. 'Oh, it wasn't always like this, Dr Bristow. I won't bore you with the details, but I arrived in Colchester quite destitute, having been robbed of all I had on my way through London. By the time my fortune had improved. . .' she shrugged, 'it was too late. I no longer knew where to write to. Anyway, I thought she would have forgotten. . . But I've thought about her so often.' She bit her lip. 'So often.'

'I'll make sure that you are the first person she meets when she arrives,' he promised. He was silent for several minutes, then he said, 'Perhaps I should warn you, Mrs Beresford, Annabel and her husband. . . they are not. . .' he paused and then began again, 'he is a difficult man to live with. Very brave. The bravest man I've ever known. But not a good husband.' He closed his eyes. 'How anyone could be married to that sweet girl and not worship the ground she walks on is a complete mystery to me.' He opened them again and smiled at her. 'Annabel is a brave woman, though. She never complains.'

'I understand, Dr Bristow.' Laura smiled back at him, wondering if he realised how clearly his words had revealed his own feelings towards Annabel.

'You made quite an exhibition of yourself this evening, didn't you, skulking behind the potted plants with your doctor friend,' Alex remarked with heavy sarcasm as they travelled home in the carriage.

'I wonder you noticed,' she replied coolly, 'since you were so engrossed with that young girl, nearly young enough to be your daughter.'

'She happens to be the daughter of a business acquaintance of mine. He asked me to look after her since he and his wife were unable to be there.'

'A duty you both enjoyed and exceeded,' she said, peering out into the gas lit street.

'There was nothing in the least improper between Miss Marchant and myself. Unlike you and your doctor friend, we were in full view of the whole company all the time.'

Laura didn't reply but her heart was heavy. This was the usual level of their conversation these days, they were perpetually sniping and bickering with each other. She turned her thoughts to Peter Bristow. It was incredible that he should not only know Annabel but that Peregrine should be his ward and actually here at school in Colchester. Perry must be very grown up now and she longed to see him. Annabel, too. It was so exciting to know that Annabel was on her way not only to England but actually to Colchester, surely there must be some way they could meet without Randolph's presence. She glanced across at Alex, eager to share the news with him, but then her spirits sank at the sight of him sitting stony-faced and silent in his corner. He wouldn't be interested.

Suddenly, as they approached the house, he leaned forward. 'What the devil. . . Why are all the lights on? I told Agnes and George they had no need to wait up for us.'

They both got down from the carriage and hurried into the house. George took their coats, saying. 'It's Master Marcus, sir. He's bin took bad. Agnes took the liberty of callin' Dr Franklyn. We're a-waitin' for 'im now.'

Alex took the stairs two at a time and Laura followed as fast as her voluminous skirts would allow. 'I wonder if it's anything to do with the sore throat he's complained of. He's been a bit off colour for the past couple of days, but we thought it was just a cold,' she said, half to herself as she hurried along behind him. 'I spoke to Maudie about it when I went up to kiss him good night. We were going to call Dr Franklyn tomorrow if he was no better.'

In the nursery, Maudie nursed Marcus, who was clinging

215

to her as he struggled for breath. A steaming kettle over the fire was helping to keep the air moist. 'He started to get worse soon after you left, m'm,' Maudie said, ''an' I could see he was hevin' trouble swallowin' anythin'. Poor mite's as hot as fire, too.'

Gently Alex took his son from Maudie, stroking his hair and easing his nightshirt away from his throat. 'There, there, laddie, Papa's here now. And Mama. And soon Dr Franklyn will come to make you better.'

Almost as if the sound of his name had summoned him Dr Franklyn walked into the room. He had obviously just got out of bed and dressed in a hurry and Laura realised for the first time that he was becoming an old man.

He took Marcus from Alex and laid him on the bed to examine him. Marcus lay very still, but there was an ominous rasping in his throat as he struggled to breathe. The doctor straightened up. 'He has diphtheria,' he said, his voice solemn.

An icy hand seemed to clutch Laura's heart. 'Are you sure? What can you do? Is there medicine?'

He shook his head. 'I'm afraid it's too late for that. Once the membrane covers the windpipe. . .'

'No. No. That's not true. There must be something. I've heard that people recover. I'm sure you can do something. You can't just let him die, Dr Franklyn. You can't.' Laura clutched his arm, her voice rising hysterically.

Dr Franklyn stroked his beard. 'Perhaps . . . I think I'd like a second opinion. I believe Dr Armitage at the hospital is very good. He's made a study. . .'

Before he could finish what he was saying Alex had rushed from the room and down the stairs to find George and send him hurrying for the hospital physician.

In less than five minutes Chris Armitage was there, still in evening dress as he too had been at the Johnsons' dinner party. He took one look at the child, then he turned to consult in quiet tones with Dr Franklyn. Laura couldn't hear what they were saying but she saw Dr Armitage point to a spot on the child's throat and heard the words, '. . . help with his breathing, temporarily. . .'

Dr Franklyn looked doubtful but nodded.

After a few more minutes discussion Dr Armitage came over to where Laura and Alex were standing. 'Wait in another room,' he said, guiding them to the door. 'I'll tell you when you can come back. 'You,' he turned to Maudie, 'you stay here in case we need anything.'

Laura and Alex went into the school room next door. It was cold; the fire had gone out hours before when the children went to bed and Laura sat on a low stool, huddled into her evening cloak, shivering as much with fear and anxiety as with cold. Alex stood motionless, his elbows on the mantelpiece, staring down into the cold embers. Neither of them spoke.

After what seemed like hours Dr Armitage came into the room. 'We've done what we can for him and he's comfortable.'

'Will he. . .?' Laura couldn't bring herself to say the word.

'Oh, yes, Mrs Beresford, he'll live. He is a healthy lad, with a strong constitution. He'll recover, there's not a doubt of it.' He smiled. 'I've left your little maid with instructions. She's a sensible girl, she'll do what's needed. The important thing is to keep the tube clear so that the air can get to the lungs.' He went to the door. 'Have you other children?'

'Yes, a little girl. She's just over a year old.'

'Well, keep her away from him, if it's not too late. I shall be in every day so I'll keep an eye on her, but call me immediately if she displays any symptoms.'

Alex and Laura exchanged anguished glances and a tear spilled over and ran down Laura's cheek.

'Don't cry. The doctor says he'll be all right,' Alex said, with a ghost of a smile, handing her a large white handkerchief.

She blew her nose. 'Alex. . .?' She longed for him to take her in his arms and comfort her. She longed to comfort him. Their worry over the two little people they both loved so much was a common bond. They should be such a happy family. 'Alex. . .?' she said again.

He helped her to her feet and for a moment she thought he was going to take her in his arms but he released her hand and let his own fall to his side. Together they went into the nursery, where Maudie was keeping vigil over Marcus.

'He's sleepin' quite peaceful now,' she whispered. 'Look, they've made a little hole in his throat for him to breathe through. The doctors say he'll be all right.' She looked up at them. 'Don't worry, sir, m'm, I can manage here. I'll be sure to call you if there's any need.'

'Yes, all right.' Laura turned away. She knew that if Marcus woke, his beloved Maudie would be the first person he called for.

'You're very tired,' Alex said as he followed her from the room. 'The best thing to do is to go to bed and get some sleep. Maudie has said she'll wake you if there's any need.'

'Yes.' She waited a moment, hoping for some sign, some gesture that he felt as she did, that he needed her as much as she needed him in this anxious time. But there was nothing; his face might have been that of a stranger. She turned away and went to her room, to lie awake aching for the signs of comfort that hadn't been forthcoming. She knew that if this didn't bring them together again, nothing would.

Thanks to Dr Armitage, Marcus made a good recovery from his illness. The doctor came in every day to check on the little boy's progress and to make sure Victoria showed no signs of contracting the illness. To Laura, who spent most of her time in the nursery, he was a tower of strength and she found herself turning to him for the comfort and reassurance that she so desperately needed. Because Alex blamed her.

'No doubt you brought the infection home with you from your precious school,' he said cruelly.

'I'm sure that's not so, Alex,' she protested. 'Surely, I would have been the one to catch it, if that had been the case. Anyway, none of my children have shown any symptoms.'

'Your children!' he mimicked. 'What about *my* children? Where else could he have picked it up from, then? Tell me that.'

She shook her head. 'I don't know. Maybe he didn't have to "pick it up", maybe it just happened.' She sat down at the school room table and rested her head on her hand. 'Oh, Alex, why must you be so unkind to me? I know you're worried about the children. But so am I, and Dr Armitage says Marcus is making a good recovery and Victoria is out of danger now, she's not likely to catch it. We've got such a lot to be thankful for.'

'Yes, you're quite right. We must thank God that the children are out of danger. Let's hope they don't become exposed to anything else.' His tone was clipped and he turned and left the room.

She sat there for some time after he had gone. She knew he was alluding to her work with her little school and it was yet another wedge driven between them. She gave a sigh that seemed to come from the depths of her being. They ought to be such a happy family. Marcus was a lovely child, and so like Alex, with his hazel-flecked eyes and straight nose. Even his hair grew the same way as his father's. And Victoria was a pretty baby, placid and good-natured, with more than a hint of Charles about her. Laura, loving both children with equal intensity, marvelled that Kate could be so indifferent to the child of her body, but she had given her over completely to her adoptive parents and showed no interest in her at all. All her affections were centred on Alex and Laura, who she served with an almost dog-like devotion, realising the life they had saved her from.

It was some three days later when she went in to kiss the children good night that Maudie said, 'Can I hev a word, m'm. There's suthin' I want to tell you.'

'Yes, of course, Maudie. What is it?' Laura looked at her expectantly.

The girl stood in front of her, twisting her pinafore round her fingers nervously.

'You'll make your pinnie all creased and limp,' Laura pointed out with a smile, 'I'm sure what you have to say can't be as bad as all that, Maudie.'

'Oh, it is, m'm,' Maudie nodded her carroty head vigorously. Laura had never seen her look so worried. 'But I gotta tell you. I can't hev it on me conscience no longer.'

Laura sat down, frowning. 'What in the world are you talking about, Maudie?'

'It's Master Marcus, m'm. The dipthery. I know how he caught it.' The words came out in a rush, then Maudie held her breath and looked at Laura.

'You do?' Laura looked doubtful.

Maudie nodded. 'I knowed I shouldn't have done it but I

took 'im 'ome with me to see me mum 'cos she wasn't well. My sister's little'un was there an' 'e was complainin' of a sore throat. 'Course, we didn't know then it was the dipthery an' we let 'em play together while we 'ad a cuppa tea.'

'How is he now?'

Maudie looked blank for a minute. 'Who? Alfie? Oh, 'e died, poor little beggar.' She clasped her hands to her heart. 'Oh, I was that worried about Master Marcus when that 'appened, m'm.'

'And where was Miss Victoria while all this was going on?' Laura asked, her voice stern with fear. 'Was she there, too?'

Again the carroty head shook. 'No, Kate said she'd keep a eye on the baby as long as she was asleep. I wanted to leave Master Marcus as well, but Kate said she wasn't hevin' him, 'e'd be too much trouble. She was busy doin' sutthin' else, I forget what.'

Laura digested Maudie's confession without speaking. Maudie was watching her all the time, her eyes wide and anxious. 'I'm sorry, m'm. You don't know what I went through when Master Marcus was so ill. I wished I coulda died meself. You won't . . . I shan't . . .'

'No, Maudie, you won't lose your place,' Laura said with a sigh. 'And I'm sure you've been punished quite enough never to do such a thing again. But you did the right thing in telling me.'

'You won't tell the master, m'm, will you? Promise you won't tell the master. He'd pitch me out on me ear . . .'

'No, Maudie, you're probably right. It's probably best that I don't tell the master,' Laura agreed. In his present frame of mind Alex was quite likely to dismiss her on the spot.

But as she left the room it came home to Laura that Maudie was asking more than she could ever know, because in agreeing to keep Maudie's secret Laura had lost her defence against Alex's accusations towards herself.

Chapter Twenty

Laura's promise to Maudie cost her dear. Alex accused her of insensitivity in continuing her school and carped about what else she might 'bring home', insisting that it was the school that had been to blame for their son's illness, and there was nothing she could do about it.

'It shows a total lack of consideration for your own children that you persist in coddling those back-street brats,' he said scathingly, one morning as they faced each other across the breakfast table.

'You're being totally unjust, Alex. There haven't been any cases of diphtheria at the school either before or since Marcus's illness so it couldn't have come from there. In any case, I'm quite sure that if there was ever any danger to our children Dr Armitage would be the first to advise me,' she replied, trying to keep her voice level.

'Oh, yes, Dr Armitage. You'll listen to him, won't you?' He slit open another envelope from his pile of post as he spoke.

'Of course I listen to him. He's a doctor. He visits the school nearly every day.' Her shoulders sagged as she picked up her coffee cup. Didn't Alex realise that it was only her little school that gave her a purpose in life now that their marriage was dead?

'No doubt that pleases you!'

She looked up, puzzled. 'What do you mean?'

'No doubt it pleases you that you've got Dr Armitage running around after you.'

'He doesn't run around after me, Alex, he comes to see the

children,' she explained patiently.

'That's what you say.' He continued dealing with his post in silence and Laura forced down a second piece of toast. In a way he was right, of course, she thought sadly. Chris Armitage was a widower and childless. She guessed he was a lonely man and although ostensibly he came to the school to keep an eye on the children, whom he loved and often treated with medicine paid for from his own pocket, she was aware in her heart that he would come less frequently if she were not there. Not that he ever, by even the flicker of an eyelid, gave any indication that his regard for her was anything other than professional. But somehow she knew.

Unwilling to pursue this train of thought she got up from the table and prepared to leave for the church hall in Maidenburgh Street where there would be the usual crowd of unruly children waiting for her. Alex probably wasn't aware that she kept special clothing, including a large overall, for her days at the school and when she returned home she always washed herself thoroughly and changed back again before coming into contact with her own children. She had been even more meticulously careful about this since Marcus's illness.

As she donned her blue merino 'work' dress with its white collar and cuffs she reflected that today was likely to be a long day, because on Saturday afternoons the childrens' mothers came to the hall when they had finished work for a free cup of tea at Muriel's ever-popular clothing club.

The morning went smoothly enough. Little Ruth had learned her three-times table and now she was happily teaching a few of the more intelligent children to chant it in one corner; Kate was at her usual task of looking after the little ones in another and Laura had the rest in a group round the blackboard, trying to encourage them to copy the letters she had written up on to their slates. In was an uphill task. Two simply sat and scratched themselves, and the three that were sitting nearest to the fire fell asleep. One boy, who hadn't been coming long, did nothing but ask when it would be soup time. But the others made some effort to make recognisable words.

Laura gazed round at the groups. She *was* succeeding, she

told herself firmly, as the irritating squeak of slate pencils grated on her ears. Most of the ragged little urchins who had come at the beginning were better dressed now, even if what they were wearing didn't fit properly. And they were obviously benefiting from getting at least one reasonable meal a day. Her eyes misted with sudden tears. She had grown really fond of some of these children, especially little Ruth, her first and by far her brightest pupil. But she worried that giving children such as Ruth the rudiments of an education was a little like opening a door on a beautiful garden and then closing it again and saying, 'But it isn't for you,' because ultimately what use would knowing the capital city of France be to Ruth, slaving in the winding room of the silk factory all day and then dragging herself home, too tired to do more than fall into bed? In her more depressed moments Laura even wondered if she might be doing more harm than good with her little school; whether these years spent learning to read and write would make the children dissatisfied with their lot in later life.

But her spirits lifted when Muriel Johnson came bustling in with Jenny, her maid, to set up the tea urn and lay out the clothing stall ready for the afternoon. She had grown to like and respect Muriel, who was not simply the patronising 'do-gooder' that Laura had first thought but had a genuine interest and desire to help those less fortunate than herself.

'They obviously like coming here,' Muriel said with a smile, nodding towards the children clustered round Kate, who was now telling them all a story.

Laura nodded. 'Yes, I told them school was over for the day when they had finished their soup but they all said they'd been told to wait here for their mothers. It probably wasn't true,' she added ruefully.

'You're too soft with them, Laura.'

'I know. But I did insist that they should sit and listen while Kate told them a story, rather than having them race round the hall like a lot of hooligans.'

'You can't blame them for not wanting to leave. It's certainly warmer in here,' Muriel said, rubbing her hands together. 'It's bitterly cold outside.' She began to rummage among the things on the clothing stall. 'Mrs Scott has given me two pelisses. I'd better put them out of the way or the girls will all be fighting over them.'

'Sadie Brockhurst's mother could do with a warm coat,' Laura said thoughtfully. 'I noticed she's been wearing that old summer dress and no coat all winter. She must be half frozen.'

'Is there a father?'

'Yes, but he's ill. Sadie says he keeps her awake at night with his coughing.'

'Oh, dear. We all know what that means.' Muriel pulled out a cash book in which she kept the accounts of the clothing club. 'Mrs Brockhurst. Yes. She pays her ha'penny regularly every week, but she always uses it to clothe the children, she never buys anything for herself.' She nodded. 'Yes, she's a deserving case. I'll see she gets one of them. And I think Lucy Green might have the other. She's pretty hard up, with five children and another on the way.'

'And a husband who spends what he earns on drink,' Laura added. She looked up as the door opened. 'Ah, here they come.'

The mothers began to arrive in twos and threes. Soon there were twenty or more and they sat round in groups, drinking the tea that had been provided for them and examining the garments that their ha'penny or penny subscription had bought. At one point a scuffle broke out in the corner as two women fought over the same pair of shoes and Muriel had to intervene.

'It was a good thing you hid those pelisses,' Laura whispered with a smile when the problem was solved.

Muriel shrugged. 'Well, what more can you expect? They have to fight for existence so you can't blame them if they expect to fight for everything else.'

At three o'clock Chris Armitage arrived. He had brought with him a large bottle of cough mixture and at a word from him all the children obediently lined up for their dose.

'I don't know how he ever finds the time to do this every single day,' Laura said, watching him, 'but he never misses.'

'He has a way with children. You can see how they love him, they're even prepared to take that vile concoction,' Muriel said with a laugh.

224

'It's not as bad as all that.' Chris Armitage had heard what she said and he came over when he had finished doing the last child. 'I mix it up myself and I assure you it's quite palatable. Try some?' He held out the spoon.

'No, thank you.' Both Laura and Muriel laughed and put their hands over their mouths.

Chris put the medicine away and gazed thoughtfully at the children clustered round the fire. 'I do the best I can but I don't know what good it does. What these people all need is decent housing. How can they keep free of colds and coughs living in those draughty hovels and tenements?' He sighed. 'But we do the best we can, between us, don't we?' He smiled at Laura. 'Have you got time for a cup of tea, Mrs Beresford? There are one or two things I'd like to discuss with you.'

'Yes, of course, Doctor.' Even as she spoke she felt her colour rise because she knew he was only finding an excuse to talk to her and that she was wrong to encourage him. But it was such a relief to be with a man who really listened to what she had to say and cared about what she was trying to do that she hadn't the power to refuse.

He took two cups of tea to a table in the corner where they could watch what was going on.

'You've really made a success of this venture, Mrs Beresford,' he said. 'The children look healthier and it provides me with a chance to give their mothers a little advice and help.'

'You're a busy man. I'm grateful that you spare the time to come here to see the children,' Laura replied carefully.

'You needn't be. I look forward to coming.' He looked at her over the rim of his cup. 'It brightens my day.'

Laura made no reply, although she could have said, 'It brightens mine, too,' because it was true. She looked forward to seeing him walk through the door and to hearing his voice and she realised just how much she depended on his help and advice. But was that all? Was Chris Armitage beginning to mean more to her than Alex? Alex, whose cold aloofness towards her was beginning to remind her of his brother Jay? The new, unapproachable Alex, who she no longer felt she even knew? She picked up her cup, her hand not quite steady,

225

trying to suppress her thoughts. She turned her attention back to what Chris was saying.

'Mrs Beresford,' he helped himself to a biscuit. 'There was something I was going to ask you. . .'

He stopped in mid-sentence with the biscuit halfway to his mouth as the door burst open and a man in a frock coat and tall hat strode up the hall.

'Oh, dear,' Laura murmured, getting up from her seat, 'it's my brother-in-law. I hope he hasn't come to make trouble.'

Jay had reached the clothing stall where Muriel Johnson was sitting. 'I have no quarrel with you, ma'am,' he said, barely polite. 'I wish to see the. . . person who is responsible for this folly.' He swept the room with his cane.

Muriel got to her feet, she was a tall woman, and said mildly, 'I really don't know what you mean by folly, Mr Beresford. We are only helping the poor, as our Dear Lord commanded.'

'Poppycock. Nowhere in the Bible does it say that the poor should be educated. Are you responsible for educating these children, ma'am?'

'No. That is my responsibility.' Laura had come up behind him and she spoke quietly.

He swung round and faced her. 'At least you've owned up! I thought you were going to hide behind this good lady's petticoats. . .' he gave a brief bow in Muriel's direction, 'begging your pardon for my plain speaking, ma'am.' He turned back to Laura. 'Do you realise what harm you are doing? Do you realise the crime you are committing? The poor are not meant to be educated. Educate them and there's no telling where it will end.'

'I'm sure that my teaching a few small children to read and write is not going to change the face of the world,' Laura said drily.

'It's a beginning, ma'am, it's the thin end of the wedge.' He rapped his cane on the table. 'It's a dangerous occupation. The poor should be kept in their place.'

'Enough, Mr Beresford!' Muriel's voice was like a whiplash. 'I have never heard such bigotry in the whole of my life. These children are human beings. They have as much right to be educated as your children or mine. The only difference is that they have no money to pay for it. And we all know the reason for *that*.' She sat down, scarlet with indignation.

'I think you had better go, Mr Beresford,' Laura said coldly, smoothing her skirt in an effort to smooth her temper.

'I'll go when I'm good and ready and not before.' He raised his voice even louder. 'And if you think I have no power to stop your antics, think about this. Any woman here today who reports for work at my factory on Monday will be turned away. Think about that, madam!'

Laura raised her eyebrows. 'I'm not altogether sure you would recognise any of your workers if you saw them outside the factory. But see for yourself.' She spread her hands.

With a snort he turned and looked round the hall. It was empty except for a few children playing in the corner.

'I scarcely think your behaviour this afternoon befits a Justice of the Peace, Mr Beresford,' Muriel Johnson remarked quietly. 'If my husband were to hear of it. . .'

Jay didn't wait to hear more. White with fury at being made to look a fool he muttered, 'Good day to you, ma'am,' turned and strode down the hall, slamming the door so hard that the windows rattled.

Chris Armitage emerged from the room at the back. 'I don't need to ask if he's gone,' he said with a grin. 'It's all right, you can all come out now,' he called over his shoulder.

Twenty women marched back into the hall, dragging their offspring with them.

''E needn't think 'e'll stop us comin' 'ere, the old skinflint,' one of the older women said as she resumed her seat by the fire.

'No, but we'll hev to be careful,' a young girl, scarcely eighteen, who had come with her sister, said, looking round furtively and biting her lip. 'We mustn't get the wrong side of the master.'

'I'd never seen 'im afore,' a small woman said with a laugh, 'an' I've worked at 'is factory for near on eighteen months. So thass a sure thing he'd never reckernise me.'

'I don't think any of you need to worry. It's highly unlikely that he'll ever come back here,' Muriel assured them. 'I know Mr Beresford well enough to know that he doesn't like being made to look silly.'

Laura sat down at one of the tables and rested her head on her hand. 'I hope you're right, Muriel,' she said with a sigh. 'I hope he won't come back.' She closed her eyes. 'Oh, and I do hope he won't complain to my husband. It would make life even more difficult. . .'

'If he does, then I'll intercede on your behalf, Mrs Beresford,' Chris Armitage said gently. 'Oh, and talk about interceding, I nearly forgot,' Chris felt in his pocket. 'My colleague, Peter Bristow, asked me to give you this note. He would have been with me this afternoon but he's helping some friends settle in to their new house, I believe.'

Laura opened the note. It confirmed what Chris had said. Peter was helping Annabel and her husband to settle into their house on East Hill, and he suggested that Laura might like to pay Annabel a surprise visit early the following week.

In the event it was Thursday before she managed to pluck up the courage to visit her old friend. During that time her mind see-sawed between longing to see Annabel and fear of opening up past wounds. Supposing Randolph was there, how would she face him? What if Annabel had discovered her secret? It was such a long time since she had seen her, perhaps over the years their friendship had become exaggerated in her own mind.

Thus she was more than a little apprehensive as, with Maudie and the children close behind her, she walked up the steps to the big blue front door and raised the heavy door knocker, praying all the time that she wasn't making a mistake in visiting Annabel. It was such a long time since she had seen her. . . She took a deep breath, preparing herself to greet a stranger.

Then the door opened and Annabel herself stood there. She had changed, gone was the vivacious, rather naive bride, full of hopeful anticipation, that Laura had known in India, and in her place was a calm, capable woman whose sweetly pretty face had matured to a quiet beauty that even the lines of suffering couldn't mar.

'Laura! Oh, Laura, my dear!' Her face broke into an amazed smile and suddenly they fell into each other's arms, both of them laughing and crying at the same time. In moments the years fell away as if they had never been.

When the first flurry of excitement and introductions were over, the children were taken off for nursery tea by Maudie and Eunice, Lolly's governess. But not before Lolly had 'seen' her new aunt by running her fingers over her face. 'You're a kind lady. Pretty, too,' she said.

Laura caught the child's fingers and kissed them one by one. 'And you're a pretty little girl, Lolly. You look just like your Mama.'

Lolly put her arms round Laura's neck. 'I'm glad Mama gave me your name.'

'I'm glad, too.' Laura hugged her. 'That means we're special to each other.'

'Run along now, darling, and play with the others in the nursery. Eunice will give you all your tea.'

They both watched as Lolly walked carefully from the room.

'It seems unnecessary to say how sad that she's blind. She seems so happy and it appears to bother her so little,' Laura said thoughtfully.

'Sight is a dimension she has never had, therefore she doesn't miss it,' Annabel said. 'We make life as easy for her as we can by making sure things are always in the same place and Eunice is an excellent teacher. Of course, it will take her a little while to get used to everything here, it's all so new and different, but she learns very quickly. And Perry will soon become a day boy at the Grammer School. I've been to see him and he's looking forward to that, because of course there's no need for him to board now that we're living so near to the school.' She turned to Laura and wriggled comfortably further into her chair. 'But that's enough about the children, now let's talk about us. Oh, Laura, I've thought about you so many times. I never thought to see you again.' She wiped away a tear and leaned forward to busy herself with the tea tray the maid had just brought in. 'But why didn't you write to me? You promised that you would.'

Laura picked up her cup and slowly sipped her tea. Then she placed the cup carefully back on its saucer, the tiny 'clink' of china sounding loud to her ears, and looked up.

'I'm sorry, Annabel,' she said. 'It wasn't that I didn't think

229

about you; I did. Oh, so very, very often. But I couldn't write to you. Not at first. Life was too difficult. And then when things got easier. . .' she shrugged, 'I guess I thought it was too late.'

Annabel raised her eyebrows in surprise. 'Why was life difficult? You said you were coming home to relatives. Your grandparents, wasn't it?'

Laura nodded. 'I found they were dead. . . I had nobody to turn to.'

'Oh, my dear. So what did you do?'

Annabel studied Laura as she told her story. She could see that life hadn't always been kind to her friend, her black hair was streaked with grey and tiny lines creased the corners of her eyes. There was also a bleakness in those deep violet-blue eyes that her ready smile didn't dispel and couldn't be altogether explained by the story, harrowing though it was, that she told.

'And that's all?' Annabel looked at her intently as she finished speaking.

Laura nodded. The only thing she had left out was the fact that she had borne Randolph's child. That was something Annabel must never know. 'Yes, that's all,' she said firmly.

Annabel let out a long breath. 'So I was wrong.' She shook her head. 'Yet it would have explained so much. . .'

'What do you mean?' Laura looked up sharply.

'Nothing, my dear.' She looked up and smiled. 'Have some more tea. Oh, it's so good to see you again, Laura. You can't begin to imagine how thrilled I was when Pete. . .' she blushed, 'Dr Bristow told me he'd met an old friend of mine. And we shall be able to see plenty of each other because Randolph is likely to stay here at the Colchester Garrison for some time.'

'Your husband is well?' Laura asked carefully, not looking up.

'Yes.' The word, spoken in a flat tone totally at variance with her earlier enthusiasm, made Laura look up.

'Annabel?'

Annabel shrugged. 'I'm no longer the besotted bride that you once knew, Laura. Perhaps you might say I've grown up. God knows, the things I saw out in India were enough to age anyone,' she added, almost to herself. Then she looked up. 'Oh, don't get me wrong, Laura, Randolph is a very brave man, none braver, and he can be quite charming when he chooses.' Her mouth twisted. 'When he chooses. The trouble is he doesn't often choose when he's at home, especially when Lolly's around.'

Laura hesitated, not quite knowing what to say. 'Most men find children a little difficult to deal with when they're young,' she ventured finally.

'Oh, it's not Lolly's age,' Annabel said bitterly. 'It's the fact that she can't see. Randolph can't bear the thought that he has fathered a child that is less than perfect and I'm afraid he takes it out on poor Lolly, leaving things for her to fall over, hiding her doll, wicked things like that. Oh, Laura, you've no idea. . .' Annabel bit her lip. Then she brightened up, smiling through tear-filled eyes, 'but he isn't here very much and when he is we try to keep Lolly well out of his way, so it isn't too bad. But it isn't poor Lolly's fault, is it, that she can't see?'

Laura shook her head. 'Lolly is a lovely child, Annabel.'

Going home in the carriage Marcus couldn't stop talking about his new friend. He was impressed by how little Lolly's lack of sight appeared to worry her and kept closing his own eyes and feeling things, trying to imagine how it must be for her.

'The thing you must remember is that you know what it's like, being able to see,' Laura reminded him. 'This is something Lolly has never known. She has no knowledge of colour, the words "green" and "blue" have no meaning for her at all, textures are what matter to her.'

'I see. So that's why her doll is dressed so strangely.' Marcus said, as if making a great discovery. 'Some of its clothes are silky and others all bobbly or rough. I suppose it's how they feel that's important to Lolly.'

'That's right,' Laura nodded.

He said no more and Laura sat gazing out of the window, busy with her own thoughts. It had been wonderful to see Annabel again and to meet her little blind namesake, but all the time she had been at the house she had been on edge, listening for Randolph's step, dreading coming face to face with him again. To her relief he hadn't put in an appearance today but she knew that now she had renewed her friendship with Annabel, sooner or later the thing she dreaded most would happen and she would have to face him.

Chapter Twenty-One

Charlotte lay in the big bed, her face nearly as white as the pillows on which she was propped. She was deathly tired and bitterly disappointed.

'I'm sorry, Jay. I was so sure it would be all right this time,' she murmured, too weak to stop the tears coursing down her cheeks. 'I tried so hard. I did everything Doctor Franklyn said.'

Jay patted her hand awkwardly. He felt stifled in the atmosphere of the sick room. It was far too hot and reeked of the rather heavy perfume Charlotte always used. He looked down at his wife's wan face and with something of a shock noticed her hair, plaited and lying across one shoulder. Once it had been thick and golden but now it looked lifeless and was liberally flecked with grey.

'Never mind, my dear,' he said a shade too heartily because he did mind; his disappointment knew no bounds that yet another son had been stillborn. Four sons and not one of them born alive meant that there must be something wrong with Charlotte. Her one success had been their firstborn, and that unfortunately had been a girl.

He bent and dutifully kissed her forehead. 'At least you will make a good recovery, my dear. Doctor Franklyn assures me that you are out of danger now.'

'And there's always next time, Jay,' she whispered, although at the moment the memory of the past few painful days was too raw even to contemplate such a thing and her whole body shied away from the thought of yet another nine months spent idly with her feet up, hardly allowed to lift a cup from its saucer, then the hours of agonising birth pains only to result in yet another disappointment. But the memory would fade, she knew this from past experience, and the urge to give Jay the son he craved would win over the dread that the next pregnancy would surely kill her.

Jay sat down beside her and took her hand. 'No, my dear. Doctor Franklyn has warned me that there must be no more.' He kept his voice level as he spoke. Disappointment over his lack of ever having an heir was tempered by the knowledge that never again would he be forced to share Charlotte's bed. Now he had a perfect excuse to move into his dressing room permanently. Nobody knew the agonies he had suffered in the marriage bed over the years, it was a secret he could never have shared with a living soul, and the relief that it was now at an end made the death of this fourth son pale into insignificance.

'Oh, Jay!' The tears spilled down her cheeks. 'I'm so sorry. I've failed you.'

He smiled at her and his smile was genuine because he was truly fond of her. 'Your health is more important, my dear. I shall abide by what Doctor Franklyn says.' The smile widened. 'My dressing room is very comfortable, you know.'

She turned her head away. She had disappointed the husband she adored.

Gently, he turned her face back to his and kissed her cheek, he could afford to be tender with her now, 'You did your best, Charlotte, my dear. I'm not blaming you.' Who else's fault could it have been? 'Now, you must concentrate on regaining your strength.'

Charlotte tried to smile through her tears. 'Yes, because we are not entirely childless. We still have Ellie.'

'Yes, we still have our daughter.' Although, of course, that was no compensation for the lack of an heir. Judging that he had stayed long enough, Jay kissed her again and got up and left the room.

Downstairs, his mother was sitting by the fire, the tea tray in front of her, waiting to see her daughter-in-law.

'Ah, good, I see Lucy has given you tea, Mama,' Jay said as he entered the room. He rubbed his hands together. 'I'm glad the maids are not entirely lacking in initiative.'

Eleanor inclined her head. 'Yes, thank you, Jay. I've been looked after very well. Can I pour you a cup?'

He sat down opposite to her, flicking his coat tails out of the way. 'Thank you, yes.' He spoke absently, gazing into the fire.

'A bitter disappointment, I know, Jay,' she said as she handed him the cup. 'I too had my disappointments. I would dearly have loved a daughter. But I was blessed with sons. The choice is not ours and we must be grateful for what the good Lord sends. Ellie is a delightful child.'

'That's as maybe, but she won't take over the running of the silk factory, when I'm no longer able, will she, Mama?' He drained his tea and stood up. 'I must get back to work. There are problems with the children in the winding room. A new boy there seems to be causing a great deal of trouble. If it goes on I shall get rid of him. I daresay he's been to the school that woman runs.' He thumped his fist into the palm of his other hand.

'Am I to take it that you are referring to Alex's wife?' Eleanor asked mildly, although she knew very well that he was.

'Of course I am. That woman has spelled trouble for this family from the day she came here.'

'Please don't keep using that expression, Jay, it's most impolite. I seem to remember that your father considered she was a person with spirit and he was always a good judge of character. Is that such a bad thing in a woman?'

'Spirit! I call it impertinence!'

'That's because she has the temerity to stand up to you, Jay. And please turn round. I object to speaking to your back.' She dabbed her mouth with her napkin. 'Personally, I find Laura quite charming. When she comes to visit me. . .'

At this he swung round. 'You don't *still* allow her to visit you, Mama? I expressly told you it was against my wishes.'

Eleanor got to her feet and picked up the large bunch of flowers she had brought with her. 'I do as *I* please in my own house, Jay, not as you tell me. Kindly remember that. And whether you like it or not, Laura is your sister-in-law and deserves to be treated with respect, even by you. Now, may I go and see Charlotte, or is she resting?'

'She's *always* resting.' Disgruntled, Jay spoke with a venom unusual when speaking of his wife.

Eleanor raised her eyebrows and said sharply, 'If Charlotte has ruined her health through bearing too many children remember it has been for your sake alone, Jay.' Sometimes she wondered if her eldest son had any feelings at all.

'I know. I apologise, Mama. Forgive me.' He held the door for his mother to pass through.

Eleanor paused and looked at him coolly. 'It is for Charlotte to do that. Not me.'

'They are beautiful flowers you've brought, Mama,' he said, trying to make amends. They were obviously hot house blooms. He hoped his mother hadn't wasted too much money on them.

Eleanor sniffed them. 'Yes, they are rather lovely, aren't they?'

She continued on through the hall and up the wide staircase, smiling to herself. She had sensed his disapproval, knowing he would only think of their cost. He would have disapproved even more if he had known that Laura had brought the flowers only that morning.

'Will you take them to Charlotte, please, Mama-in-law?' she had said, 'and give her my fond regards. I would like to visit her myself but. . .' she had shrugged, 'it would hardly be wise.'

Eleanor had nodded. 'Of course. I understand.' She had studied her daughter-in-law. There was a sadness in her face these days that had never been apparent before, and when she smiled it didn't always reach her eyes. But Eleanor was not one to pry so she contented herself with saying, 'Has Marcus fully recovered from his illness?'

'Yes, thank God. But it was a very worrying time.'

Eleanor nodded understandingly. After a moment she said, 'You have opened some kind of a school, I believe?'

Laura gave a depreciating smile. 'It hardly merits the name of school I fear, but it gives some of the poorest children a place to go to whilst their mothers are at work.'

'Rather a strange occupation for a lady, I would have thought,' Eleanor remarked.

Laura spread her hands. 'I felt I had to do something. I

couldn't bear to think of them being left to fend for themselves, or to roam the streets. So many accidents happen. It was when I heard of a child being killed through falling out of an upstairs window that I decided I must try and do something for them. Some of the children are really quite bright and eager to learn.' She became quite animated as she spoke.

'And what does Alex have to say about it all?'

Laura's expression changed. 'Alex's work keeps him very busy,' she said enigmatically. She looked at the tiny gold watch hanging at her waist. 'I should be going.'

'I understand you run some kind of clothing club as well as this school,' Eleanor went on as if she hadn't spoken.

'Yes. The mothers pay so much a week, a ha'penny or penny, whatever they can manage, then they can buy the cast-offs Mrs Johnson collects from her friends and acquaintances. It was her idea in the first place; she is a great help and very kind. It all works very well, in a small way.'

Eleanor sniffed. 'All very laudable, I'm sure.'

After Laura had gone Eleanor had remained for a long time thinking over their conversation. Alex quite clearly was not happy about the venture and she could quite see why, because there was no doubt that the fact that it was deemed necessary reflected badly on the family business. But was that all that was troubling Laura?

She reached Charlotte's bedroom, knocked and went in.

'Poor Charlotte. Another stillborn son,' Laura told Alex when he returned from work that evening.

'That's damned bad luck. Jay was counting on this one. Have you been to see her?'

'No, of course not. Your brother probably wouldn't allow me inside the house. I took some flowers to your mother for her.'

'Good.'

The conversation flagged then as it always did if there was nothing specific to discuss. Laura took up her embroidery and after a few minutes Alex got up and went into his study.

Before long he was back, a deckled card in his hand. 'This is an invitation from Dr Bristow. He's arranging a dinner party for his friends Captain and Mrs Randolph Grey to meet some of the people of Colchester on the twenty-fourth. There's no reason why we can't accept, is there?' He glanced at her. 'I seem to remember you were on very good terms with him the last time we met, at the Johnsons'.'

She took the invitation and read it. 'I would really rather not go, Alex,' she said quietly.

'Why not, for heaven's sake? Isn't this your friend Annabel from India? Don't you want to renew her acquaintance?'

'I've already been to see Annabel.' She hung her head. 'I've no wish to meet her husband again.'

'Why not?'

Her head shot up. 'Oh, Alex! Don't be so cruel and unfeeling. You know very well why I never want to see that man again. I couldn't possibly go.'

'It will look very odd if we don't go,' he remarked, watching her. 'What reason could we give? After all, his wife has no idea, has she?'

Laura shook her head. 'Of course not.'

'In that case, my dear, you will simply have to face it out.' His expression softened slightly. 'After all, if you intend to renew your friendship with his wife you can hardly avoid meeting him at some time or other so you might as well get it over with.'

She put her head in her hands. 'You don't care, do you, Alex? You simply don't care how I feel.'

'I–' he got up and came over to her, his arm hovering protectively over her. But she didn't see it, nor the pain in his eyes, because her face was covered to hide her tears. When she looked up he had left the room and gone back into his study.

The days ground on inexorably to the twenty-fourth. Laura watched the children anxiously to see if there was the slightest sign of a minor illness that could provide an excuse for not going to Peter Bristow's, but they were both disgustingly healthy and anyway she knew it would be to Maudie that they turned, not her, if they were ill.

There was no reprieve.

238

She dressed very carefully in preparation for the dinner, choosing a dress of green velvet that she knew suited her colouring and wearing the family pearls. Tonight above all nights she needed a boost to her confidence.

As Alex held her wrap for her he nodded approvingly. 'You are looking very beautiful, Laura, if a shade pale. Are you not feeling well?'

She hesitated, tempted to take the coward's way out and plead a migraine, then said, 'Thank you, Alex. I am quite well, but for obvious reasons I shall be relieved when the evening is over.' She glanced at him, wondering what his feelings were at the prospect of coming face to face with the man who had raped his wife, but his face was inscrutable.

Peter Bristow lived in a tall house not far from the hospital. Just inside the front door was a large elephant's foot which served as an umbrella stand and a tiger skin, complete with head and bared teeth, lay in front of the hearth. These together with much ebony and ivory left no doubt as to where their owner had spent a good number of years.

Some twenty guests were already there when Alex and Laura arrived but Laura immediately saw Randolph Grey and her heart gave a sickening lurch of recognition. He was standing with a group of ladies, a drink in his hand, his elbow resting on the mantelpiece, every bit as tall as she remembered, slightly thicker in build, a scar down one side of his face adding an air of rakishness to his still handsome profile. He carried his debauchery well, she thought bitterly. Or perhaps he had reformed. She managed to stay at the other end of the room, out of his way, until dinner was served, but she found to her dismay that Peter, in his ignorance, had placed her next to Randolph at the dinner table.

'My word, the frightened little kitten has come a long way since Mudkipur,' he leaned over and whispered admiringly as he held her chair for her to sit down.

'Indeed I have, Captain Grey,' she replied coolly and turned to greet the man on her left.

The meal was beautifully cooked and served but interminably long. Laura hardly ate anything, toying with the food on her plate and taking small sips of wine between the morsels she managed to force down. Sitting beside Randolph

239

Grey made her feel physically sick and every time his hand or arm brushed hers – and he appeared to take great delight in making sure this was often – her flesh crawled at his touch. But he was charmingly attentive and after his first greeting he said nothing she could possibly object to; rather he treated her like delicate porcelain and lavished his full attention on her to the exclusion of the lady on his other side. Indeed, he was so attentive that he hardly gave her any opportunity to speak to the man on her other side. Once or twice she glanced along the table to where Alex was sitting. Peter had placed him next to Annabel and they were obviously enjoying each other's company. She was glad about that; glad somebody was enjoying the evening.

She turned back as he touched her arm, offering her grapes.

'No, thank you. I won't have another,' she said suppressing a sigh.

At last Annabel stood up, the signal for the ladies to leave the men to their port. Thankfully, Laura escaped into the drawing room, where the centre of the room had been cleared for dancing. Peter had even hired musicians to provide the music and they were already playing quietly in a corner.

Annabel came over to her. 'Your husband is a charming man, Laura,' she said, taking her arm. 'We must make sure that we meet together often.'

'Yes, we must.' Laura forced herself to smile at Annabel.

Annabel leaned forward confidentially. 'Do you think it was right to hire the musicians? Peter. . . Dr Bristow was very anxious to do the right thing and he asked my advice, but it's such a long time since I was in English company that I wasn't sure. . .'

'I'm sure everybody will enjoy the dancing,' Laura said warmly. 'It was a lovely idea.' She gazed at Annabel. 'Dr Bristow is a very good friend to you, isn't he?'

Annabel coloured. 'He has helped me more that I can ever say. He's been a real friend to us and I'm– we're all very fond of him. Very fond indeed. Oh,' she turned as the door opened. 'Here come the gentlemen. They didn't linger long over their port.'

At a sign from Peter the music grew louder and Chris

240

Armitage claimed Laura for the first dance, much to her relief.

'You seem rather uneasy tonight, Mrs Beresford,' he remarked, as he whirled her round in a Viennese waltz. 'Is anything wrong?'

'I'm a little tired,' she lied. 'That's all.'

Expertly, he reversed and changed direction. 'Far be it from me to say that I don't believe you, but I fancy there is more to it than that.' He bent his head. 'I hope you would regard me as a good enough friend to confide in if you were in any trouble, Laura.' He had never used her Christian name before.

She flushed slightly at the sudden intimacy. It would be so easy to rest her head on his shoulder and tell him all the things Alex was so reluctant to listen to, but just then Alex danced by and she knew that however her husband treated her she could never love anyone else the way she loved him. 'You're very kind, Dr Armitage,' she said. Then regretted answering so stiffly because she felt him loosen his hold on her fractionally, obviously taking it as a rebuff.

She had danced with nearly every man in the room by the time the inevitable happened and Randolph claimed her for a dance. He held her so closely that she had difficulty in breathing, whispering that he had saved the best till last and that she was the most beautiful woman in the room.

'We must meet, Laura. You are older now, more mature, and eminently even more desirable than you were all those years ago. I shall arrange. . .'

She smiled brightly at him. 'You will do nothing of the kind,' she hissed through smiling lips. 'I want nothing, absolutely nothing to do with you.'

'Ah, I see you've lost none of your fire. That's good. I like a bit of fire in a woman.'

She threw her head back and laughed as if she was enjoying herself. 'If you bother me I shall tell my husband. He will deal with you,' she said gaily.

At this he got angry and whirled her round and round at such a rate that when the dance ended she lost her balance and fell against him.

'That's better,' he said, circling her tightly with his arm. 'I

241

knew you couldn't resist me, really.' He took her hand and kissed it. '*A bientôt*,' he whispered. 'I look forward to taking up where we left off all those years ago.'

She snatched her hand away. 'Oh, Captain Grey,' she replied with a toss of her head, 'I declare you're quite incorrigible.'

'What's my husband been saying to you, Laura?' Annabel had come up in time to hear Laura's reply.

'I was saying that we look forward to renewing our acquaintance with Laura. Although she was not with us for very long in Mudkipur she left a lasting gap in our lives when she left, did she not, my dear?' Randolph said smoothly, taking his wife's arm.

'Oh, indeed, that's very true.' Annabel smiled at Laura. 'We shall make sure you don't run away again, shan't we, Randy?'

Randolph's eyes met Laura's 'Indeed we shall,' he said.

Going home in the carriage Alex was tight-lipped, and he barely waited until they got inside the door before he said scathingly, 'So, madam, you lied to me.'

She was ahead of him, and had reached the bottom step of the stairs, relieved beyond words that the evening was over. She turned in surprise at his words. 'Whatever do you mean, Alex? Lied to you over what?'

'That man! Your handsome Captain Grey. You lied when you told me he had raped you. The truth of the matter was you had an affair with him and had to leave India so that your "friend" Annabel shouldn't discover you were to have her husband's child.'

She sank down on to the stair, her skirts billowing round her. 'Oh, Alex. What a dreadful thing to say. You know it isn't true.' She shuddered. 'You can't imagine how I felt when I saw that man tonight. My flesh crawled and all I wanted to do was get away.'

'I must say it looked like it. He was all over you and you gave every appearance of enjoying it.'

'You simply have no idea what it cost me to be even halfway civil to the man.' She closed her eyes. 'But what could I do? Would you have had me make a scene and refuse to speak to him? How would that have appeared? How would

Annabel have felt? She has no idea how her husband treated me when I was living with them.'

'I think she has a very good idea what went on. After all, it was under her own roof, so she could hardly fail to have seen.' He strode across to his study door and turned, with his hand on the door handle. 'She was watching you both like a cat watches a mouse, tonight. No doubt looking to see whether the attraction still held.' He opened the door.

She got up and ran after him. 'You don't understand, Alex. You've no idea what you're saying. It wasn't like that. I told you, I hated that man from the time I met him. I was dreading tonight.'

'A dread you soon overcame, if I may say so.' He went into the study and would have closed the door but she followed him in, closed the door and leaned against it.

'Why won't you believe me, Alex? I've *told* you what happened in India.'

'Your version. I suspect it was rather a case of an innocent young school girl becoming infatuated by the dashing young army officer and throwing herself at him.' He stared at her coldly for several minutes. Then he said, 'Why should I believe you, Laura? It seems to me you only tell the truth when it suits you.'

'Alex, that's monstrous! How can you say such a thing!'

'Because it's blatantly obvious.' He ticked off his fingers. 'Not only did you deceive me by not telling me of your past before we married, but your confession, when it did finally come was a pack of lies.'

Tears were running unchecked down her cheeks. 'What can I say? You are determined to believe what you wish to believe. Oh, Alex, what's happened to us?' Blindly, she turned and opened the door.

'Wait.'

She paused, saying nothing.

'You will not visit the Greys' house. You will not see Captain Grey, nor his wife. I forbid it. For her protection as well as my own.'

She swung round. 'You can't do this to me, Alex. Annabel is my friend. How can I not see her now she is living so near? What reason could I possibly give?'

'You'll find a way.' He sat down at his desk and swivelled in the chair. 'Tell her I forbid it, if you like. I'm sure she'll understand.'

'Oh, Alex.' She put her hand to her head. 'How can I make you understand what a terrible mistake you're making?'

Chapter Twenty-Two

The following weeks were agony for Laura. She received an invitation to take tea with Annabel soon after Peter Bristow's dinner party but rather than antagonise Alex even further she was forced to put her off with an excuse that sounded flimsy even to her own ears. Soon, she knew Annabel would write to her again, soon she would begin to wonder why her re-found friend was so inaccessible, and explanations would have to be given, or the friendship lost forever. But how could Laura explain Alex's unreasonable behaviour, to Annabel of all people?

She was worrying over this yet again as she walked round her garden one morning. The sun was shining but she hardly noticed the budding spring leaves and the bright splashes of colour where the daffodils and polyanthus were breaking into flowers. She recalled those blissfully happy times when she and Alex had first come to live at the house and she had planted those same flowers with her own hands to mark the birth of their son. They had been so contented with each other and with their lives, that it seemed nothing could ever come between them.

Her mouth twisted bitterly. Jack Plant had altered all that, of course, when he came to Colchester as workhouse master. He had gone now, heaven knew where, but not before he had ruined her life. And now it seemed things had gone from bad to worse. It seemed that nothing she could do would restore Alex's trust in her. She was beginning to wonder how much longer she could go on with the charade of pretending that all was well for the benefit of the outside world, of keeping up appearances, when in reality she and Alex lived more like strangers than husband and wife. As these thoughts spun round and round in her brain she was thankful that she had her little school; at times she felt that it was the only thing that was keeping her sane.

At the thought of the school she looked at the watch at her waist and then hurried across the lawn into the house. She hadn't realised it was so late. The children would be waiting.

Quickly, she changed into her 'school' clothes, made sure the bag she always took with her was packed and ready, sent Kate to the kitchen to check that Cook realised it was her day to provide the soup and then called for the dog cart to be brought round. Thank God there was a busy day ahead.

It was to be even busier than Laura had anticipated.

As Banks turned the dog cart into Maidenburgh Street a crowd of noisy children were outside the hall waiting for her. This was nothing unusual, they were always waiting, but over the winter she had managed to train them to wait in some kind of orderly fashion, warning them that if they were disruptive they would get no soup.

'Remember what I've said. You'll be sent home with no soup if you don't stop this noise,' she raised her voice as she stepped down from the dog cart. 'Now, line up in a decent, orderly fashion. . .'

The children took no notice, but clamoured round her, 'Look, Miss! Look wass 'appened!' 'Look at the winders!' 'Look inside the 'all, thass all broke up!' They all seemed to be shouting at once. Ruth and several of the other little girls were crying.

At her word the children parted to let her through. Automatically, as she went she felt for the key to unlock the door, only to find she didn't need it because the door hung open, swinging on one hinge. Carefully picking up her skirts, she stepped inside and found absolute devastation. The floor was covered in broken glass from the smashed windows, chairs and tables had been hurled against the wall and smashed, and the crockery lay in broken chards. The blackboard has been scored by what looked like the point of a screwdriver, slates had been thrown down and trampled on and all the books and paper had been torn into confetti. Laura

246

steadied herself against the one table left standing and surveyed the scene, her hand over her mouth to prevent herself from screaming.

Kate touched her arm. 'Shall I fetch Mrs Johnson, ma'am?'

Laura shook her head to clear it. 'Yes.' She changed her mind. 'No, Kate. You stay here. You can help me to begin clearing up. Send Ruth. She knows where to go. Tell her to run.'

The two of them got brooms and buckets and set to work, fury lending power to their hands.

'Do any of you know who did this?' she asked the children, as they stood around watching.

Thirty heads shook from side to side, the picture of innocence.

'Well, there'll be no school today, so you might as well go home.'

'Might as well stay 'ere. Ain't got nowhere else to go,' some of the older children said. 'We'll 'elp.' They began picking up the broken chairs and putting them in a heap. Those that could still be used they put to one side. By the time Muriel Johnson arrived the floor was clear, the wreckage in heaps round the hall.

'There's hardly anything left,' Laura said, trying to hold back the tears. 'All the things we'd collected – the books, the pencils, the soup bowls, the cups and saucers – oh, I know they were all oddments, but I'm sure they all helped to make the place seem special to the children. And the mothers, too.' She pushed a strand of hair back with her arm, leaving a dusty mark on her forehead. 'The slates, the paper, the blackboard – everything's ruined. Oh, Muriel, who would do this to us?'

'Some of the children?' Muriel asked.

They looked at the sea of dirty faces. Some of the girls were crying and the boys had all worked with a will to help with the clearing up, all the time muttering dire threats as to what they would do if they 'caught the buggers what done it.'

'No,' they both said together. 'It wasn't these children.'

Muriel pinched her lip between her thumb and forefinger. 'What about that boy – what was his name – Tompkins? He

247

was big for his age and only came for a few weeks. But while he was here he did nothing but disrupt everything. If you remember he smashed his slate over a little girl's head and cut it badly. He was a dreadful child. We were glad when he stopped coming. I suppose he might have done it out of spite?'

'No, he and his parents have left the district.' Laura gave a deep sigh and shook her head. 'Anyway, I don't think one boy could have wreaked this much havoc, Muriel. Whoever did this set out to systematically wreck the place.' She looked down at her hands, cut and bleeding from picking up glass and china. Absently, she wrapped a handkerchief round the worst cuts to stem the bleeding. 'I really don't think there's much else we can do until the door is mended and the glass put back.' She sighed. 'We'd better send the children away.' She raised her voice. 'Thank you for helping with the clearing up, children. You can go now.'

The children, standing around in groups, didn't move.

'They won't go till they've been fed,' Muriel said grimly. 'Who's doing the soup today?'

'Oh, I'd forgotten about that. It's my cook's turn.' She looked at her watch. 'I suppose Banks will be along with it before long, but we can't possibly serve it, we've got nothing to put it in,' Laura looked round the empty hall. 'There's nothing. Nothing at all. Oh, dear, I suppose I should have sent a message for him not to bring it.'

'Too late. Here he is.' Muriel nodded toward the open doorway.

Banks came in with the large can of steaming, succulent-smelling soup. This was too much for the children and the older ones began to rummage about among the broken china to find something, anything that would hold liquid. Soon every child held some kind of receptacle salvaged from the wreckage, half a bowl here, a piece of a cup, even bits of saucer.

Suddenly, Muriel began to laugh. 'You didn't imagine a small thing like the lack of soup bowls would stop them from having their dinner, did you, Laura?' she said.

Laura looked at the hopeful queue and began to laugh with her. For them both it was a laugh bordering on hysteria. 'You know, Muriel, I've grown to really love these children,' she said, finally wiping her eyes and taking the lid off the can and dipping in the ladle.

'We can come up agin, Miss, can't we?' an anxious little boy with freckles asked. 'Look, my bit o' cup don't hold much.'

'Yes, Johnny, you can come up again,' Laura told him. 'You can all come up and get more,' she said loudly. 'There's no need for anyone to go away hungry.' As she spoke she was feeding a little girl who had only a small piece of broken saucer to offer for her share straight from the ladle.

When the soup was all gone, the children sat themselves down in neat rows on the floor, marshalled by Ruth.

'What are you waiting for now?' Laura asked, wearily passing her hand over her brow. She was tired, still very angry at whoever had wrecked the hall and running short of patience. 'You've had your soup and you can see there's no school today.'

'They're waitin' for a story,' Ruth explained.

'Yeh. Tell us a story,' the children shouted. 'We ollwus hev a story arter dinner.'

Laura and Muriel exchanged amazed glances. 'Very well,' Laura said with a smile, 'if that's what you want. Which one shall it be? Red Riding Hood? Goldilocks?'

'Cinderella an' the Fairy Godmother,' they shouted.

'Just at the moment we could do with a Fairy Godmother ourselves,' Muriel muttered as she collected up the last of the makeshift soup bowls.

Laura sat down on the one chair that seemed to have been left intact. 'Once upon a time. . .' she began and thirty dirty little urchins were transported from the derelict hall in Maidenburgh Street into a world where the touch of a wand worked miracles and everyone lived happily ever after.

'What have you done to your hands?' Alex asked as he sat down to dinner that night.

Laura looked down at the bandages that swathed her hands. It wasn't until she arrived home that she had realised how deep some of the cuts were and she hadn't resisted when Maudie insisted on bathing her hands and binding them up, although it made it a little awkward to hold a knife and fork.

'I cut them trying to clear up broken glass and china after someone wrecked my school,' she said, trying to keep her voice level. 'I don't know who could have done it, but whoever it was, they left nothing whole. The place was completely wrecked. Somebody must hate me very much,' she finished quietly.

'So what do you intend to do?' He helped himself to more vegetables.

'I don't know.' She pushed her plate away untouched. 'The school was the one thing that made me feel I was doing something useful. Oh, I know you've never approved – insofar as you care about anything I do any more, Alex – but those children had learned to trust me, even to like me, and most of them were eager to learn. Their mothers, too. . .' Her voice broke. 'Oh, what's the use?' She got up from the table and left the room.

Alex half rose. 'Laura,' he said, but she closed the door as he spoke and didn't hear. He sat down again and finished his meal, went to his study and smoked a cigar, then picked up his hat and coat and left the house.

The next morning, Laura was at her desk, approving the day's menus, written out carefully by Kate because Doris, the cook could neither read nor write, when Kate came into the room.

'Ruth is here, ma'am,' she said, almost forgetting to bob, her face alight with excitement. 'She says she's run all the way to tell you that the school door's been mended and the glass put back in the winders. She says the children are all there waiting for school to open.'

'It's all mended?' Laura frowned. 'Who on earth could have done that?' She looked up. 'Ruth says the children are waiting?'

'Thass right, m'm.'

'But we've no slates. . .' Suddenly, she smiled. 'Tell Ruth to tell the children I'll be there in ten minutes, Kate.'

As she changed into her school clothes Laura pondered on what she should do. It was all very well that some kind soul had mended the hall, but there were still books and slates and blackboards, not to mention chairs and tables to be replaced.

She hurried to the kitchen. 'The menus are fine, Cook.

250

Have you any of the children's soup left from yesterday?' she asked.

'Yes, m'm. I always make enough for two days.'

'I thought so. Well, send it along at twelve. And see if you can find any old soup bowls and dishes to put it in. Even old cups and mugs would do. We must have some odd bits and pieces somewhere, surely.'

'Oh, yes, m'm. I'm sure I can find a few oddments.' She hesitated. 'I was sorry to hear about what 'appened yesterday, m'm. That was a dreadful shame. I hopes as how you won't give up, though. I gotta sister what works at the silk factory an' her little'un comes to your school. Fanny say you're learnin' her all sorts of wunnerful things. Thass a wunnerful thing, book learnin', beggin' your pardon, m'm.'

'The only thing is, Cook, at the moment I'm afraid we haven't got any books left,' Laura said with a sad smile, 'and I don't see much prospect of getting any.'

As Ruth had said, the children were all waiting more or less patiently by the newly mended door of the hall. The keys were in the new lock and Laura opened it and went inside. It was just as it had been when she started the school, nothing but clean-swept bare boards. Not even a stick of chalk had been left whole when the place was vandalised. Whoever had been responsible had been thorough. But who could it have been? Surely not her own husband! No, Alex was not a man to destroy things.

She stood aside for the children enter. One of them must know something. She watched their faces as they filed in. They were subdued, anxious about their refuge, but there was no hint of guilt about them. They filed into their respective groups and then sat down cross-legged and silent on the floor. It was as if they had been warned to be on their best behaviour or there would be no school. Laura glanced at Ruth, sitting in front of her little group and glaring at anyone who so much as shuffled a foot. It was all Ruth's doing, she thought affectionately. Ruth was determined the school should continue. And so am I, she thought fiercely.

She walked to the middle of the room. 'Now, children. . .'

Before she could say more there was a knock at the door and a heavily veiled lady came in. Puzzled, Laura went over to her.

'Charlotte!' she said in amazement as Charlotte lifted the corner of the veil. 'What are you doing here?'

'I can only stay a few minutes,' Charlotte whispered, looking over her shoulder as if she was afraid she had been followed. 'If Jay knew. . .' she didn't finish but pulled some money out of her reticule. 'I heard what happened here yesterday.' Her mouth twisted. 'Jay could talk about nothing else when he came home. He couldn't have been more pleased if someone had given him a hundred pounds.' She stopped speaking and bent over for a minute.

'Are you ill, Charlotte?' Laura caught her arm. 'Joe, fetch the lady the chair,' she called over her shoulder to the nearest boy. 'We've got one chair left,' she told Charlotte, 'the rest were smashed up.'

'No, don't bother, I'll be all right. It will pass.' Charlotte brushed aside her offer. 'It's just that I'm not used to walking this far.' She turned back to the door. 'I've seen my father this morning. He says he will help with replacing the chairs and tables. What else do you need, Laura?'

Laura looked at the money in her hand. 'This will buy slates and books,' she looked up, 'but if you have any old china – cups and saucers or soup bowls – we could do with them.'

Charlotte nodded. 'I'll see what I can do.' She looked round the room at the children, patiently waiting. 'Jay hates your school, Laura. He doesn't think the working classes should be educated, but I think you're doing a wonderful thing.' She took Laura's hands in both her own. 'You mustn't let this discourage you, Laura. I only wish I was well enough to help you.' She dropped Laura's hands and smiled wanly. 'Although of course even if I was Jay would never allow it.'

She went then, lowering her veil before she opened the door. Laura watched her go. Poor, dear innocent Charlotte, who feared yet idolised her overbearing husband and had no idea that she had just revealed his secret and provided the answer to Laura's question. That it was Jay Beresford who had ordered the desecration of the school.

Laura clamped her lips together grimly. Which was the most powerful reason of all for making sure it stayed open.

252

She squared her shoulders and marched into the middle of the room. 'Now, children, where were we?'

It was surprising how quickly things returned to normal at the school, but with even more equipment than they had had before. Sid Rankin provided proper desks with benches attached, refusing to take any payment for them; the money Charlotte had given provided a blackboard and easel as well as slates, books and pencils, and one day Laura arrived to find a globe of the world sitting on her table. Nobody had any idea where it had come from, yet at the back of her mind Laura had the feeling she had seen it somewhere before.

'You could almost say it was a blessing in disguise when the school was wrecked, couldn't you?' Muriel said one afternoon as they were preparing to leave after the last of the children had gone. 'It really looks like a proper school now.'

'Yes, and we've got nearly double the number of children we started with. We shall soon have to find more helpers. Especially as Ruth will be leaving after her birthday next month.'

'To work at the silk mill?'

Laura nodded sadly. 'I'm afraid so.' She sighed. 'If only we could afford to pay her she could stay here. She'd make a wonderful teacher, you know, Muriel. And so quick and bright.'

'She'll keep them on their toes at the silk mill, then. I hear the "education" provided there is nothing if not scrappy.'

'Yes, that worries me, too.'

'Well, I'm off.' Muriel picked up her bag. 'Is there anything else to do?'

'No, I'll just take a last look round. See you tomorrow, Muriel. And thank you.'

After Muriel had gone Laura straightened a desk that was just out of line and stood looking at the little school room. Her nightmare was that the place would again be wrecked but so far it had not been touched. Perhaps Jay was planning something more subtle, she thought grimly. She wouldn't put anything past that man.

There was a knock on the door and she went to answer it. When she saw who it was standing there her face lit up. 'Annabel! Oh, Annabel, it's so good to see you.' She took her friend's hands and leaned forward and kissed her cheek.

Annabel stepped inside. 'I must say I didn't expect a welcome like that,' she said with a little smile. 'I've been trying to pluck up the courage to come and see you but I was half afraid because I couldn't think what I might have done to displease you.'

Laura led her to a chair and made her sit down. 'You haven't done anything to displease me, dear.'

'Then why did you refuse my invitation to tea?'

'I– had another engagement.'

'Then will you come tomorrow?'

'I– no, I can't, I'm afraid.'

'Yet another engagement?' Annabel was watching her closely.

Laura looked down at her hands and shook her head. 'No, but all the same I can't accept.'

'Is it because of Randolph?' Annabel asked quietly. Then before Laura could answer, 'Laura, look at me.'

Laura looked up into Annabel's clear blue eyes.

'Laura, this is no time for beating about the bush. I value your friendship more than I can say, believe me, and for that reason I need to know the truth. Tell me, honestly, were you pregnant when you left Mudkipur in such a hurry?'

Laura bit her lip and nodded. 'Yes, I was.'

'Was the child Randolph's?'

Laura looked away. 'Oh, Annabel, why torture yourself?'

'Answer my question.' Annabel's voice was sharp.

'All right. Yes, it was. Oh, Annabel, I'm so sorry. I didn't ever want you to know.' Tears were running down Laura's face. 'I didn't want – it wasn't my fault, honestly. He. . .'

'He raped you.' Her voice was flat and emotionless.

Laura hung her head. 'I'm sorry, Annabel. I thought it best not to say anything.'

'Oh, it's me that's sorry,' Annabel said bitterly. 'Sorry I'm married to such a bastard.' Her mouth twisted. 'Don't for one moment imagine that you were the only one, my dear. There have been a whole string of them over the years, some who've gone with him willingly and some who haven't. He liked those best, I believe.' She was studying her fingernails as she spoke. She looked up. 'Oh, as you knew, I was quite

254

besotted by him when we first married and although all the evidence was there I didn't want to believe it. Even then, I saw the way he looked at you and how you tried to avoid him, but I refused to think that he could be the reason for your leaving.' She gave a hollow laugh. 'I soon learned, because he took great delight in telling me. Every last detail. But by that time it was too late. You'd left no address and you didn't write. I could understand why, of course. By the way, what happened to the child?'

'It was born dead in a London workhouse.'

'Oh, Laura, you poor thing. What you must have gone through. . .'

'I thanked God it didn't live to haunt me. I thought I could put it all behind me and forget.' She bowed her head. 'But I was wrong. They say you pay for your past and it's true. I've paid for mine, over and over again, although it wasn't of my choosing. God knows, I'm still paying for it.'

'What do you mean?'

'I told Alex everything that happened, but not until some years after we were married. It ruined our marriage because he couldn't forgive me for not telling him before. Then, when he saw your husband dancing attendance on me the other night at Peter Bristow's, he accused me of lying to him, saying that we had an affair. I couldn't convince him just how much I loathed the man.' She covered her face with her hands. 'Oh, God, what a mess. I shouldn't be saying all this to you, Annabel. After all, it's your husband we're talking about.'

Annabel ignored the last remark. 'So I suppose Alex forbade you to visit me because he thought it was only an excuse to renew this "affair" with Randolph?'

Laura nodded, not taking her hands from her face.

'How little he knows of my husband,' Annabel said with a sigh. She put out her hand. 'Laura. May I come and help you with your school? Surely, your husband can't object to that.'

She took her hands from her face and Annabel saw that it was wet with tears, but she was smiling. 'I wish you would.'

255

Chapter Twenty-Three

Annabel was an invaluable help at Laura's little school. She kept the older children enthralled by her stories of life in India and as she spun the globe to show them just how far away on the other side of the world the huge continent was their eyes grew wide with amazement. Watching the world spinning round under Annabel's hand Laura tried again to think where she had seen such a globe before, but the memory – if memory it was – was too elusive and wouldn't be caught. In the end she gave up trying to remember and concentrated on encouraging her own group to form neat letters. As she watched the little heads bent over their slates – some of the girls had tried to neaten themselves up by tying their straggly hair back with a scrappy bit of rag, and here and there the tip of a pink tongue stuck out with the effort of concentrating – she tried not to think of the grim future that most of these children faced; tried not to think of the futility of what she was doing, to convince herself that learning was never wasted.

'You're looking very pensive, Mrs Beresford.' It was Chris Armitage. He still paid his regular weekly visit to the school to check on the children's health.

She looked up with a sigh. 'I was just wondering if this is really all worth while,' she said waving her hand to indicate the groups of children in the hall.

'Oh, come now, it isn't like you to be downcast.' He smiled at her encouragingly. 'And in your heart you know the answer. Why, you've only got to look at the children's faces. They all look healthier than they did this time last year. They love coming here.'

Her mouth twisted wryly. 'It's amazing what a difference one nourishing meal a day can make. But what's the point of it all? What's the point of trying to teach them to read and write? What good will it do? Where will they all end up?'

He hesitated for a moment, then laid his hand gently on her arm. 'We can only do what we hope is right, Mrs Beresford. We don't have a magic wand to wave. Nor a crystal ball to see into the future. But at least we are making some effort to improve the daily lives of these children.' He dropped his hand, suddenly realising that he might have been over-familiar and took out his pocket watch to cover his embarrassment. 'Dr Bristow said he'd be dropping by this afternoon.'

'He'll have to be quick, then, if he's coming to see the children, because it's almost time for them to go.' She smiled. 'But I suspect they're not his prime reason for visiting these days and he'll be in time to join us for a cup of tea.' She turned away and clapped her hands. 'Put your books away and line up, children. We'll say a little prayer and then you can go.'

With some reluctance the children did as they were told. They liked it at the school and were even prepared to learn to read and write if it meant they could keep coming and having that lovely soup the ladies dished out. The older ones collected their small brothers and sisters from the corner where Kate had been minding them, little girls heaving babies that weighed nearly as much as they did themselves on to jutting hips, and stood quietly while Laura said the collect for the day. Then, with cheerful cries of 'See yer termorrer, Miss,' they left, to disappear into the squalid little streets and alleyways where they had their homes.

As soon as the last ones had gone Laura lit the kettle under the gas ring in the corner. This was really the part of the day she liked best, when the children had left and she and Annabel and sometimes Muriel, too, could sit and have a quiet cup of tea with the two doctors. All they ever talked about was the children, yet sitting next to Chris Armitage at the scrubbed deal table in an air of friendly intimacy was something that Laura valued above all else.

257

Kate made the tea and put cups and saucers on a tray and brought it over to the table, then she went off to clear up the room and sweep the floor.

Laura turned to Chris as she handed him his tea. 'I thought you said Dr Bristow would be dropping by?'

'He said he might be a little late,' Annabel cut in quickly, 'but he promised me he'd be along.'

'You met whilst you were in India, didn't you?' Chris asked. He was sitting at the end of the table, one ankle resting on his other knee, his hands locked behind his head, looking as if there was nowhere in the world he would rather be.

'Yes. I don't think I should have survived if it hadn't been for Peter. Ah, here he is.' Her face lit up with pleasure as the door opened and he walked in.

He came straight over and dropped a kiss on Annabel's forehead. This was the one place where they had no need to hide the fact that they were in love and as he sat down beside her he took her hand. 'Is all well with you, my darling?' he murmured.

She nodded. 'Oh, I can't tell you what bliss it's been whilst Randy's been away.' She gave a great sigh. 'But he'll be back this afternoon, ruining the family harmony, rampaging about the place, complaining about everything.'

'Why don't you divorce him?' Chris Armitage said suddenly. He had seen the bruises she had sometimes been at pains to hide.

Annabel blanched. 'Oh, I could never do that, Dr Armitage. Think of the scandal! Think of the effect on my children! I'm surprised you should even mention such a thing.' She was deeply shocked.

'I do apologise for upsetting you, Mrs Grey,' Chris said, 'but it's something I feel very strongly about. I consider it grossly unfair that people should be forced to go through life shackled to someone who makes their life hell. After all, we only have one life, it's up to us to make the best of it.'

'Tell that to the poor creatures who don't know where their next meal is coming from,' Peter remarked. 'Or the people who can't get a bed in the hospital because they haven't got anybody to vouch for them.'

'Nobody ever suggested that life was fair, Dr Armitage,'

Laura added gently. 'After all, it was hardly fair that the wife you loved should have died so young.'

'No. But at least I have happy memories,' Chris replied, 'and one learns to live with grief. It even fades, with time. One can even learn to love again, I've found.' His eyes were on her as he spoke.

There was a sudden charge of emotion in the room. Laura held her breath. She knew with a sudden blinding clarity that the next few moment could have a lasting effect on her life. Chris Armitage was telling her that he would welcome the chance to love and protect her. He would always be interested in her work with the children. They had so much in common. . . She closed her eyes and a picture of Alex rose before her, tight-lipped, his jaw set and hard, his eyes – she searched for the word and when it came she was surprised – vulnerable. At once she understood that she could never desert him, that underneath the steely, unyielding exterior he was still the Alex she had married, if only she could find the way back to him through the layers of protective armour with which he had surrounded himself. She picked up the teapot. 'More tea, Dr Armitage?' she asked, breaking the spell with a smile.

He pushed his cup over, taking the hint. 'Please. And another of those delicious biscuits your cook bakes. I hope you don't feed the children on these.' He bit into it with relish.

'No, these are what you might call teachers' treats,' Laura took one as she spoke.

'Little Ruth really deserves one, too. She works hard with her class,' Annabel said.

Laura got up and went over and idly spun the globe. 'Yes. She's really good with the children,' she said, 'but unfortunately she's destined for the silk mill in a few weeks' time. I know it will break her heart to leave us but what can we do?'

'How old is she?' Peter asked.

'She'll be eight when she leaves. I only wish there was some way we could keep her here, but her mother is desperate for the few coppers she will be earning there.' She closed her eyes on the spinning globe and suddenly, in a flash, it came to her where she had seen one just like it.

Eleanor Beresford had one standing in the corner of her drawing room. 'So *that's* why I thought I recognised it,' she said aloud.

'What's that?' Annabel asked.

Laura resumed her seat. 'The globe. I felt sure I'd seen one before and I've been trying to think where. I've just remembered that Eleanor Beresford has one standing in her drawing room.' She resumed her seat beside Chris and finished her tea.

'Do you think that's where this one came from?' Peter asked.

Laura burst out laughing. 'From Eleanor Beresford? Oh, I hardly think so. I imagine she would be far more likely to try and close the school down than offer help to it.' She began to gather up the cups for Kate to wash.

'Oh, we don't need to go home just yet, do we?' Annabel asked, moving closer to Peter.

'I must. I have my rounds to do at the hospital.' Chris got to his feet with a yawn and put on his coat and hat ready to leave. 'I'll be along tomorrow,' he told Laura, 'that little Susie Jones needs more cough mixture. Her cough doesn't seem to improve at all.'

He had just reached the door as he finished speaking. Suddenly, without warning, it burst open and an ashen-faced boy rushed in, nearly knocking him over.

'Mrs Grey?' he cried. 'Mrs Grey?'

Annabel rose to her feet at the mention of her name. 'I'm Mrs Grey. But what do you mean by rushing in here like this? You nearly knocked Dr Armitage over. Who are you? What's your name?'

The boy ignored her questions and carried on as if she hadn't spoken, his eyes wild with terror. 'They said I'd find you here. Oh, ma'am, there's bin a dreadful accident outside your house. I seen it 'appen. I seen the 'orse. I seen the little blind girl. . .'

Annabel heard no more of what the boy had to say. At the mention of Lolly she slid to the floor in a dead faint.

There was pandemonium for a few minutes as Laura searched in her reticule for her smelling bottle and Chris made an incongruous search for feathers to burn under

260

Annabel's nose whilst Peter cradled her in his arms. By the time they had managed to bring her round the boy had disappeared, frightened at the commotion he had caused, not even waiting for the penny he had been promised if he ran all the way.

The four of them hurried to Annabel's house on East Hill. It wasn't far; Peter went ahead on his bay and Laura supported Annabel in Chris Armitage's gig. When they arrived there was such a crowd outside the house that Chris had to use his whip to force a passage through.

Annabel was clinging to Laura and weeping, 'Oh, my baby, my poor baby. What can have happened? How did she get into the street? Somebody must have left the front door open. . .'

'Hush, my dear. We really have no idea what's happened yet,' Laura tried to console her, helping her down from the gig and into the house, where Randolph's army kit was strewn over the hall and halfway up the stairs and a trail of blood led into the drawing room to the right of the front door.

'Don't let her go in there,' Peter Bristow said sharply. He had arrived a few seconds before them and had roughly pieced together what had happened. He took Annabel's arm. 'It's all right, my darling,' he said softly, 'Lolly is safe.'

'Safe?' Annabel looked up at him, her white face stained with tears. 'But the boy said. . .'

'Come in here and sit down.' He led the way into the morning room opposite. He poured each of them a glass of brandy.

'Where's Chris?' Laura asked. She felt almost as dazed as Annabel.

'He's gone to look at Lolly.' Even as Peter spoke, Chris came down the stairs and into the room.

'Lolly's frightened and she's got a nasty graze down the side of her face. Apart from that and a few bruises she's not hurt,' he said. 'Eunice has tucked her up in bed and is staying with her so there's no cause for alarm, Mrs Grey.'

'But the blood. . . All that blood out there. . . What happened?'

Annabel was torn between going up to the child and hearing what Chris had to say. She got up and went to the

261

door, then came back and sat down as he began to speak.

'From what I can piece together, it seems that Captain Grey came home earlier than expected,' he began. 'Apparently, his batman was bringing his gear in and forgot – or probably didn't know – the cardinal rule of the house, which was never to leave the front door open in case Lolly wandered through and, being unable to see where she was going, fell down the steps. Which, in fact, is exactly what did happen.

'Not surprisingly, the little girl became confused with all the hustle and bustle, you can just imagine her stumbling about, trying to find her way among all the unfamiliar baggage lying about the place, and she lost her bearings and went out through the front door by mistake and tumbled head-first down the five steps, right into the path of a cart horse pulling a fully-laden coal cart down the hill.'

'Oh, my God,' Annabel whispered, her hand over her mouth.

'It was her father who saved her life,' Chris went on. 'Lolly's governess says it was a miracle. Apparently, he saw what was about to happen and leaped down the steps after her. He managed to grab her and literally threw her to safety. That's how she got the graze on her face. Apart from that and a few bruises from tumbling down the steps I can see no other damage. Of course, she's frightened, poor lamb, especially as she can't see what's going on.'

'My husband?' Annabel licked dry lips. 'Randolph?'

'I'm sorry, Mrs Grey, there's no easy way to tell you,' Chris said grimly.

'Eye witnesses say that he must have overbalanced as he threw her. He fell in the path of the horse, right between its legs, in fact. The horse not unnaturally panicked and kicked out. Your husband is in a bad way, Mrs Grey.'

'Will he live?' Annabel whispered.

'He's a very strong man.' It was Peter who spoke.

'I must go to him.' She stood up.

'I must warn you, Mrs Grey–' Chris began.

Annabel shook her head in a weary gesture. 'Dr Armitage. I went through the Indian Mutiny. I even helped to nurse some of the victims. I assure you I am not easily shocked.'

Nevertheless, she drew her breath in sharply when she saw her husband. He was still lying on the door which had been wrenched off its hinges in order to carry him indoors and he was covered with a blanket. His face was grey and there was a dent in the side of his head where an ugly curved wound oozed blood and something else which Annabel preferred not to identify. Under the blanket it was plain to see that his legs were lying in an unnatural position.

Peter drew her away and sat down on the stairs with her. 'This will be the end of his army career, if he lives,' he told her, holding her hand as he spoke. 'I'm afraid he will never be. . .' he hesitated, 'the man he was.'

'You mean he'll never walk again,' she said flatly.

His eyes met hers and he nodded. 'Not only that, I fear his brain will be affected.'

'Oh, God.' She buried her face in her hands. 'To think he's come to this. And he didn't even like Lolly. He's never been able to forgive her because she was born blind. He could never accept that he could have fathered a child that was less than perfect. He even tried to kill her, once.' She looked up, tears running down her face. 'Did you know that, Peter? He put a snake in her crib, but some sixth sense must have warned her and she refused to be put down. It saved her life.' She sniffed and wiped her eyes. 'It's ironic, isn't it? He tried to kill her once, yet he couldn't watch her die under that horse's hooves. And in saving her life he's ruined his own. Poor Randy.'

He got to his feet and pulled her up with him. 'I must see about moving him to hospital.'

She shook her head. 'No. We'll nurse him here.'

'But Annabel. . . There are hospitals you know for – incurables.'

She shook her head again. 'I couldn't let him go to one of those places. My mind is quite made up. He's my husband, Peter. He saved Lolly. The least I can do is to make sure the rest of his life is spent in as much comfort as I can make it. He may not have been the best husband in the world to me, but I owe him that much.'

She rested her head on his shoulder and his arm went round her protectively. 'My darling girl. You have no idea what you are taking on, but I admire your courage,' he said quietly.

She stood up. 'We must make arrangements. . .'

Before she could say more the door opened and Chris Armitage came out. She took one look at his face and drew in a quick breath, '. . . for Randolph's funeral,' she finished unsteadily.

A week later, Randolph Grey was buried with full military honours as befitted a man whose bravery was legendary. Annabel, in deepest black, followed behind the coffin, holding the hands of her two similarly-clad children. Under the veil intended to hide her grief her expression was perfectly dry-eyed and composed.

Laura and Alex attended the funeral. On their return home Laura remarked as she took the hatpins out of her wide black hat, 'I suppose I shouldn't say this, but now there is nothing to stop Annabel and Peter from marrying, in the fullness of time.'

'No, you shouldn't say it, with Captain Grey hardly cold in his grave. I'm shocked that you should be so callous, Laura. I would have expected you to have more decency than that.' Alex went into the little sitting room and poured himself a whisky.

She followed him. 'Then I'll shock you further,' she said deliberately. 'I'm glad Randolph Grey is dead. He was a dreadful man and he led poor Annabel a terrible life. If she has a chance of happiness with Peter now I hope she'll grab it with both hands.'

He paused in the act of lifting the glass to his lips and turned, a look of amazement on his face. 'But I thought. . .'

'Yes, you *thought*, Alex. But you thought wrong. I was not lying when I said how much I loathed the man although you refused to believe me. But now it's no longer important. The important thing is, there's no longer any reason why I shouldn't visit my friend Annabel, is there?'

He drained his glass and put it down. 'You may do as you please,' he replied.

She sat down and rested her head on her hand. 'Oh, Alex,' she said sadly, 'why must we always bicker like this?'

But he had left the room.

A few days later Laura paid one of her occasional visits to Eleanor.

'You are well, Mother-in-law?' she asked as she was shown into the garden, where Eleanor was sitting in a sheltered spot enjoying the early summer sunshine.

'Well enough thank you, Laura, considering my age,' Eleanor replied. She leaned forward and smiled conspiratorially. 'It's my birthday next month, you know. The years creep on – gallop on, perhaps I should say, because the older one gets the faster they seem to go.'

Laura smiled in return. 'You don't look a day older than when I first knew you.'

'Get away with you.' Eleanor waved her hand. 'I'm getting old and crotchety and my bones are full of rheumatism. But I'm not too proud to admit that I shall be sixty this year, so I suppose I shouldn't grumble.' She pulled her cashmere shawl closer. 'Oh, dear, it isn't quite as warm as I expected out here in the garden. I think we should go indoors.' She reached for her stick and got to her feet. 'How is that school of yours progressing, by the way? Yes, that's right, bring my embroidery. I may do some later.'

Laura picked up the bag of embroidery. She was surprised that Eleanor knew of the school. 'We do what we can for the children,' she said ambiguously, slightly suspicious of the question.

'I understand you had some trouble there a few weeks ago.'

Laura frowned. 'Yes, we did.'

They had reached the drawing room and Eleanor sat down and indicated that Laura should sit opposite. Then she rang for tea. When it arrived she motioned to Laura to pour. 'Of course, Jay is opposed to educating the working classes,' she said, almost to herself.

Laura said nothing. She handed Eleanor her tea, trying to think of a way to change the subject. She didn't want to antagonise her mother-in-law but if it became necessary she wouldn't hesitate to defend her school.

'I couldn't be seen to be opposing him, you understand.' Eleanor was speaking again, still, it seemed half to herself. 'It wouldn't be right. He is, after all, running the silk mill on my

265

behalf, even if I don't always agree with his policies.'

'He's a hard man,' Laura couldn't resist saying.

'He's a driven man, I fear. Driven by some demon inside him.' She shook her head. 'But what that demon is I have never discovered.' She took several sips of her tea. Then she said, 'Sometimes I think I hardly know him at all.' She put her cup down. 'I used to think he favoured his father in his shrewdness and business acumen and I was proud of him, thinking that if he followed in Javis's footsteps what a fine man he would be. But I'm beginning to see. . .' She smiled wryly at Laura. 'I suspect all mothers have a tendency to see their sons – daughters too, I suppose, although I never had one – as they would like them to be and this blinds them to what they really are. Take Charles, for instance. I spoiled him, I know I did. He was the youngest and I have to admit, my favourite. In my heart I think I must have known he was a wastrel but I suppose I cherished the hope that my confidence in him would shame him into altering his ways. It was a costly mistake on my part. I still miss my golden boy.' She picked up her cup again. 'Alex, of course, was different,' she said, looking towards the Chinese silk screen which hid the empty grate. 'I made a terrible mistake with him and I don't think he has ever forgiven me.' She shook her head. 'But I was not entirely to blame for that, we did what we thought best at the time, Javis and I, and Alex rose above it and made a successful life and a happy marriage, so in the end that's all that matters, isn't it?' She smiled across at Laura.

Laura smiled back and nodded. This was as near as Eleanor could ever get to apologising for the behaviour of the family at the time of her marriage and she accepted it for what it was. She wondered, though, what her mother-in-law would say if she knew how strained the relationship was now; what a hollow sham their life together was. She gazed round the room, searching for something to say to change the subject. As aspidistra stood on a tall, rather ugly bamboo stand in the window.

'That's a fine aspidistra,' she remarked.

Eleanor made a face. 'Charlotte gave it to me. And that awful modern stand. It's not at all to my taste but she's a sweet child so I shall keep it there for a week or two. She's not well, you know, not well at all. It seems to me that she's wasting away, but when I mention it to Jay he insists that she's perfectly healthy and merely pining because she's failed in her duty to give him the son and heir he needs to carry on the business. Those are his words – "failed in her duty".' She sniffed disapprovingly. 'Sometimes I think the man is entirely deficient in the finer feelings.' Then, with a suddenness that took Laura completely off-guard, she said, 'What kinds of things do you teach at this school of yours?'

'The three Rs mainly.'

'And are these children willing to be taught?'

'Not all of them. Some only come because they get fed and they can be quite disruptive.'

'And those you turn away, I suppose?'

'Oh, no. We never turn a hungry child away. We could never do that,' Laura said, surprised that Eleanor might think otherwise. She went on, 'But some are really keen to learn. One little girl is so enthusiastic that she can't wait to teach the others what she's learned.' She sighed. 'But she's destined for the silk mill in a few weeks, which makes me wonder if it's all worth while, or whether in effect I'm making a mistake in offering the children something which will be snatched away just as they are beginning to grasp it. I have a friend who has recently returned from India and she's been telling them about life there.' She spread her hands. 'But what good will it be to them, knowing where India is on the globe when they're incarcerated in that dreadful winding room.' She looked up. 'I'm sorry. I shouldn't have said that.'

Eleanor was smiling. 'So you're finding my globe useful, then?'

'*Your* globe?' Her eyes widened and she looked to the corner where the globe had stood. A what-not stood in its place.

'Didn't you recognise it?'

'Yes. At least, I saw the similarity, but I would never have dreamed. . .'

'You would never have dreamed that Eleanor Beresford would deign to patronise a school for children of silk mill workers,' Eleanor finished for her.

'Well, yes, I mean, no – I mean I didn't think you approved of it.' Laura blushed with embarrassment.

'I not only approve, my dear, I make sure I know what's going on there,' Eleanor said with a smile. She leaned forward. 'Charlotte keeps me informed. And between these four walls, I think you are doing excellent work. Of course, like Charlotte, I can't be seen to be supporting you, Jay would never countenance it, but if there is ever any way in which I can help you have only to let me know.'

Laura took a deep breath. Here, perhaps was the answer to her prayers. She said with a rush, 'If you really mean that, there is something you could do. Could you help me to keep little Ruth on at the school? She's the child I've been telling you about. But I'm afraid it would mean paying her what she would be earning in the winding room. Her mother couldn't afford. . .'

'And how much is that?' Eleanor cut across her words.

'I'm not sure. I'd have to make enquiries. Something like one and six a week, I should imagine.'

A look of pain crossed Eleanor's face but she made no comment. 'You hope to train this child to teach?'

'She hardly needs training. She absorbs knowledge like a sponge and she infects the other children with her excitement when she passes it on.'

'Then I agree she needs to be nurtured. I shall send half a crown a week for her wages. Will that suit?'

Laura gasped. 'It's more than generous of you, Mother-in-law.'

Eleanor shook her head. 'Oh, no, Laura. I'm not being generous,' she said bitterly. 'I'm finally making an effort to salve my conscience.'

Chapter Twenty-Four

'I visited your mother this afternoon, Alex,' Laura remarked, breaking the habitual frosty silence that accompanied their evening meal. Her husband insisted that they should eat together 'for appearances' sake' but in Laura's opinion, the two of them sitting at either end of a six foot dining table in an atmosphere that could be cut with a knife was hardly likely to fool anyone, let alone servants whose sensitivities were attuned to every nuance 'above stairs'. And she suspected, quite rightly, that the news had confidentially been spread to a good many kitchens in the town that the Beresfords' marriage was on the rocks.

He dabbed his mouth carefully with his napkin before helping himself to more potatoes. 'She's well?'

'To quote her own words, "getting old and crotchety and her bones are full of rheumatism". But she looks remarkably well considering she will be sixty next month. Did you realise that, Alex?'

For the first time he looked up. 'Sixty? Are you sure?'

'Quite sure. She told me so herself.'

'I must go and see her.'

She twisted the stem of her wine glass between her thumb and forefinger. 'Alex, I thought. . . that is, I wondered if you might think it a nice idea to have a small party for her, since it will be her sixtieth birthday.'

'A party? Where?' He was frowning.

'Well, here, of course. Where else?'

'You mean as a surprise for her?'

She nodded. 'If you like.'

269

He though about it for several minutes. 'Who would you invite?' he said at last.

'Who would *we* invite,' she corrected. 'I don't know. I haven't thought. I simply thought it might be a nice thing to do. She doesn't seem to mind people knowing she's sixty.'

'As you say, she certainly doesn't look it.'

'Perhaps that why she doesn't mind people knowing.'

The vegetables were cleared from the table and the pudding brought, and the fact that the master and missus were actually talking together was considered sufficiently newsworthy to be carried back to the kitchen with all haste.

'Obviously, we must ask Jay and Charlotte,' Alex said thoughtfully, sinking his spoon into bread and butter pudding.

'Yes, although I doubt they'll come. I can't image Jay ever deigning to cross this threshold.'

'He may stretch a point as it's his mother's birthday,' Alex said dryly. He looked up. 'And if he does, Laura, please try not to antagonise him.'

For a second she was sorely tempted to retort, 'What about asking him not to antagonise *me*', but realised that no good would be served, so she said instead, 'I'll do my best, Alex, but other than not being here I'm not sure what I can do. Your brother and I simply do not see eye to eye. On anything at all. If I as much as said it was a nice day he would look for rain.'

'He's not an easy man,' Alex conceded.

She put her spoon down with a clatter. This time she couldn't control her tongue. 'And that's an understatement if ever I heard one.'

'Maybe, but this is hardly the time to start a character assassination.' He went on smoothly, 'Now, let's see, who are Mother's friends? There's Mrs Blaxill and the Paxmans. . .'

She relaxed. 'And the Mumfords, I believe. I shall have to ask her maid about any others. Lydia will know.' She hesitated. 'Alex, may I invite Annabel? I know she will still be in mourning, but I'm sure she would like to come. And Dr Bristow. . .'

He nodded. 'I don't see why not. The Johnsons, too, if you like. We could make it quite a grand affair. With dancing afterwards.'

'No, I don't think people would want to dance after a heavy meal. How about having a ball and a buffet supper?'

'Ye-es.' He nodded. 'In fact this could be a good opportunity to combine business with pleasure. There are several people it might be useful for me to cultivate in the line of business.'

Laura laughed and he glanced up surprised, because it was a sound he hadn't heard for a long time. 'What's the matter?'

'This *is* supposed to be your mother's birthday party, Alex,' she said, still smiling.

He smiled back at her and her heart gave a funny little skip at the sight of the old Alex, even if it was gone in a flash. 'I'm sure she won't mind a few extras turning up. But is there time to organise it? To get the invitations printed and everything arranged?'

'We've got five weeks. I should think that's long enough.'

'Good. Then we'd better start making a guest list.'

When dinner was finished, instead of retiring to his study or going out as he usually did, Alex came with her to the little sitting room to continue discussing plans for the forthcoming ball. Much later, as she lay in bed after he had gone to his study for a nightcap, Laura recalled how reluctant she – and it seemed to her, Alex too – had been to end the evening. All they had done was make plans for the ball but it was so long since they had really talked to each other that it had been almost like old times. Eventually, she heard Alex's step on the stair and held her breath as he hesitated, passing her door, praying that he would turn the handle and come in. But after the briefest pause, which might even have been her imagination, he continued on to his dressing room.

It was a long time before she slept and by that time her pillow was wet with tears.

Laura did everything possible to ensure that the ball would be a success. She ordered all the furniture to be cleared from the long drawing room and the carpet rolled up ready for dancing. A little dais was erected at one end for the tiny orchestra and at the other end the large french windows were opened so that the dancing could extend to the lawn if the floor became too crowded.

271

Supper was prepared on long tables in the dining room and small tables were scattered throughout the ground floor for guests to sit at when they were not dancing. Comfortable armchairs and settees were provided for those not inclined to dance.

For days Doris, the cook, had been frantically preparing the food in the kitchen with only the help of two kitchen maids. She had been quite offended when Laura suggested getting outside help but had finally been prevailed on to secretly enlist the help of Eleanor's cook, who was, fortunately a personal friend.

The results were impressive. There was a huge ham, and a whole turbot, as well as tiny oyster and shrimp patties, numerous game pies and potted meats. With these were cold vegetables in various sauces or disguised in an assortment of flans and tarts. On another table, flanking a large birthday cake, skilfully decorated to leave no room for candles, were the sweets, jellies, trifles, petites bouchees, savoy cake and – packed in ice until the last moment – elaborately moulded iced puddings. Doris and her friend could be justly proud of their combined efforts.

To Laura's amazement, Jay and Charlotte accepted their invitation, although as Alex pointed out, they could hardly do otherwise without offending Eleanor and emphasising the family rift.

On the evening of the ball Laura dressed carefully, putting on a gown of sapphire blue trimmed with creamy lace and wearing the family pearls to which some years ago Alex had added matching drop earrings. She surveyed herself in the long cheval mirror. Yes, she'd do. The colours suited her colouring, her hair was still dark, although becoming streaked with grey, and her complexion was good. And over the years she had gained at least an outward show of poise and confidence.

She stood by Alex's side to greet the guests and direct them to where Eleanor, as guest of honour, was seated. Eleanor was wearing her customary black, but tonight it was liberally trimmed with palest lavender lace and she wore a lavender lace cap on her white hair. She was holding the posy of flowers that Victoria and Marcus had presented to her

272

before being whisked off to the nursery and was obviously excited at being the centre of attention.

The stream of guests seemed never ending and Laura's face began to feel stiff with smiling. She glanced at Alex. He didn't seem to share her worry that they might have overdone the guest list and there wouldn't be room for everyone.

Jay and Charlotte were predictably the last to arrive. He handed over his coat and hat to James, the footman, with an expression of bored superiority and Laura almost laughed at the distasteful way he touched the tips of her fingers in greeting, as if they might harbour some disease, as he nodded briefly and murmured a gruff 'Good evening, ma'am.' But Charlotte, risking his displeasure, kissed Laura's cheek delightedly and whispered, 'I'm so excited to be here, Laura. We're supposed to be leaving early, but I hope we don't.'

Laura squeezed her hand. 'I hope not, too. It's lovely to see you, Charlotte. Are you well?' She didn't look it, she was wearing an expensive dress of rose-pink shot silk and a lot of jewellery but she looked pale and seemed to have lost quite a bit of weight.

'Tolerably so,' Charlotte wrinkled her nose cheerfully and moved on.

'I think, as host and hostess, we should begin the dancing,' Alex said, as the last of the guests were divested of their wraps and the orchestra began to play. 'May I. . .?' He took her in his arms and they began to waltz.

It was the closest she had been to him for almost two years and Laura gave herself up to savouring the warmth of his arm round her waist and his hand holding hers. Every point at which their bodies touched seemed alive with an almost burning sensation, so strong that she was sure he couldn't fail to detect it. Almost involuntarily, she exerted a tiny, gentle pressure on his hand and was certain she felt him gather her a little closer in response so that her other hand slid quite naturally a little further round his shoulder. Neither of them spoke, but by the end of the dance he was holding her more closely than even the crowded dance floor warranted and she wished that it would never end.

The music finished and she thought – imagined – she felt his lips brush her hair before he released her, breaking the

273

spell by saying in such a matter-of-fact way that she wondered if her imagination had been playing tricks all the time, 'Thank you, Laura. Now, we'd better mingle and do our duty by our guests.'

Her card was quickly filled. She dutifully danced with Alex's business acquaintances, with Muriel Johnson's husband and even trundled round the floor with Joseph Mumford, the elderly husband of Eleanor's best friend.

Halfway through the evening she went upstairs to her bedroom, which had been set aside for the ladies' powder room, to repair the ravages of the warm ballroom. Charlotte was already there, sitting on a blue velvet chair and fanning herself. She looked deathly pale.

'Charlotte, let me get you my smelling bottle,' she said, full of concern.

'No, I have my own here if I need it. But a glass of water would be nice.'

Laura poured water from the carafe on the wash stand and as she straightened up the reflection in the mirror above it showed Charlotte surreptitiously slipping a little pill box back into her evening bag.

'Tell me truthfully, are you ill, Charlotte?' Laura asked as she handed her the glass.

Charlotte shrugged. 'I get this stupid pain in my side sometimes, and it gets worse if I get tired.' She fanned herself and laughed. 'Goodness me, it's no wonder I'm tired, I can't remember when I danced so much.' She made a face. 'I daresay I shall be chastised by Jay when we get home, he'll tell me I was making an exhibition of myself, but I don't care.' She caught Laura's hand. 'Oh, Laura, I'm having such a wonderful time. I don't think I've ever enjoyed myself so much.'

Laura bent and kissed her sister-in-law. 'I'm so glad, Charlotte. I was afraid you wouldn't come.'

'Wouldn't be allowed to come, you mean. Jay was reluctant, I can tell you, but he realised it would look very bad if he didn't come to his mother's birthday party.' She smiled. 'I don't think he realised it was to be quite such a grand affair. All the world and his wife seem to be here tonight.'

274

'Yes, the guest list did get a bit out of hand,' Laura admitted, 'I was beginning to think we'd need a shoe horn to get the last of them in. Have you seen Mother-in-law? She's thoroughly enjoying herself, holding court among her friends.'

'She told me last week how much she was looking forward to it,' Charlotte said, absently rubbing her side. She waved her hand. 'You should be going back to your guests, Laura, not staying up here talking to me. I shall be perfectly all right, don't worry. I'll be down in a minute or two when I've got my second wind. Anyway, I've promised Alex the supper dance and I don't want to miss that.'

Laura left her. She had promised the supper dance to Chris Armitage. Twice already she had danced with Peter Bristow whilst Annabel, in her widow's weeds was forced to sit by and watch, her foot tapping uncontrollably in time to the music. Laura knew how much she longed to join in but it would never do for a lady so recently widowed to be seen dancing; the fact that she was here at all had caused several eyebrows to be raised.

The four of them sat together at supper. 'I know it's difficult for you, Annabel,' Laura said ruefully, 'but I did so want you to come tonight.'

'I would have been furious if you'd left me out,' Annabel said with a laugh. She sighed. 'I'm trying desperately hard to play the part of the grieving widow, but it's terribly difficult because I'm not.' She looked across at Peter. 'In fact,' she said softly, 'I think I must be the happiest woman in the world.'

'And I'm the happiest man.' Peter squeezed her hand under the cover of the tablecloth. 'And in twelve months' time when I make you my wife I'll be even happier, if that's possible.'

'And everyone can see it with half an eye,' Chris warned. 'If you're not careful you'll be the talk of the town.' But he was smiling, too, happy to have held Laura in his arms at least once in his life.

Laura looked at the tiny gold watch hanging from the long chain round her neck. 'Oh, dear, I must find Alex. It's gone eleven, we should get my mother-in-law to cut her cake. She specially asked that we shouldn't keep her up too late. Please excuse me.'

She left her friends and went to find Alex, who was sitting with Charlotte and Jay. Jay, of course, never danced and so had no partner and he had studiously avoided sitting with his parents-in-law, who were enjoying themselves loudly in the far corner, to his eternal embarrassment.

A whispered word to Alex and the cake was taken to where Eleanor was sitting. Everyone clapped and cheered as she plunged the knife into the icing and someone began singing 'Happy Birthday' and the rest of the company joined in. Eleanor looked as flushed and excited as a young girl; she was obviously enjoying every minute of her party and had forgotten she had asked to go home early.

In the event it was well past midnight before the party began to break up. Even Jay and Charlotte had stayed to the end, largely because Jay had found himself an audience to which he could propound the follies of educating the working class and didn't realise the time.

Carriages were called and cloaks and wraps were brought to murmurs of 'Wonderful evening', 'Such lovely food', 'Haven't danced so much for years', as each carriage rolled away, watched by the crowd of ragged hopefuls who habitually congregated wherever there might be a penny to be earned from holding a horse's head.

Then, just as Charlotte and Jay walked down the steps to their carriage, there was a scuffling in the crowd on the pavement as a straggly-haired girl dressed in a ragged green dress and holding a grubby bundle elbowed her way through and stopped in front of Jay.

'There y'are,' she said, thrusting the bundle at him. 'You might as well take it. It's yours.' A weak, kittenish cry rose from the bundle as she spoke.

For a few seconds, it seemed as if the whole company grouped around the front door, rich and poor alike, were frozen into immobility. Nobody spoke, nobody moved. Even James, the footman, was silent, his eyes nearly popping from his head in total astonishment.

'Go on, take it!' the girl repeated, pushing it under Jay's nose as he backed away up the steps, disgusted. 'Thass your bastard, you filthy swine, an' there's plenty more of 'em runnin' about the town, too, so don't you try and deny it.' She staggered as she spoke and glanced up towards the group of people standing in the doorway in their glittering evening clothes. 'If you don't believe me you can ask any girl from the silk mill what 'is games are an' hev been for years, the dirty ole bugger. Get 'em in the fam'ly way an' then give 'em the push an' let 'em starve to death.' Her voice had grown weaker as she spoke and with the final words she collapsed in a heap at the bottom of the steps, the bundle still in her arms.

Jay made to step over her but Alex held him back.

'You two men,' he called, pointing to two of the ragged onlookers, 'take the girl and the child round the back to the kitchen. She can't be left lying there like that. Tell my staff you're acting under my orders,' he added.

Jay was trying to shrug his brother off. 'Get in the carriage, Charlotte.' He was white to the lips. 'And you, Mama. The sooner we're away from this disgusting scene the better.'

'I think not, Jay,' Alex said quietly, still holding his arm. 'I think the very least you can do is stay and help me to sort this business out.'

'What do you expect *me* to do? It's no concern of mine. You surely don't believe what the creature was saying!' Jay said angrily.

'It's not a case of believing or disbelieving. The business has to be sorted out and I can't do it without your help. Now please take Mama and Charlotte back into the house whilst Laura and I see the rest of the guests into their carriages.'

Jay had no option but to do as Alex said. Eleanor was very pale and Charlotte was crying quietly into her handkerchief. Her face had gone the colour of clay.

'Oh, for goodness sake stop snivelling, woman,' Jay said irritably. 'Crying won't make things any better.'

'It could hardly make things worse,' Eleanor said tartly.

He shrugged. 'I really don't know what all the fuss is about. The creature was obviously trying to get money. I don't know why she wasn't left where she belonged. In the gutter.' His tone was venomous.

'But she said the child was yours, Jay,' Charlotte said in a small voice. She was clutching her side and wincing with every step she took.

'These strumpets will say anything to get themselves a copper. You don't know what they're like.'

Eleanor pursed her lips. 'So are we to take it that you do, Jay?' she asked.

He flushed. 'I didn't say that. But it's common knowledge. Any man. . . Oh, this is not a fit subject for your ears, Mama. Nor yours, Charlotte. I refuse to discuss it further.'

The three of them sat in silence except for Charlotte's sobs until Alex and Laura came back into the room. They both looked weary.

'Thank goodness that's everybody gone,' Alex said with a sigh. 'Now, you and I had better go into my study and talk, Jay,' Alex said.

'About what?' Jay sounded surprised.

'You know perfectly well.' Alex stood holding the door open, his face a mask of distaste.

'Oh, very well. If you insist. But I really don't see what there is to discuss. Why don't you do as I suggest, give the creature a few coppers and send her packing.' Almost lazily Jay got to his feet and followed Alex.

When they had gone Laura left Charlotte with her smelling bottle and Eleanor watching over her and went to the kitchen. She knew that the maids wouldn't be very happy at having their privacy invaded.

She found the girl lying on the floor near the stove, covered with a blanket. It was difficult to guess her age but she couldn't have been more than about seventeen. She was as thin as a wraith and her face under the grime was colourless except for her lips, which were bluish. For the briefest of moments as she looked down at the girl Laura was shocked into a vision of herself all those years ago, when she'd been incarcerated in a London workhouse. She shook her head to clear it and knelt beside the girl.

'Have you given her broth?' she said over her shoulder to Doris.

The cook was standing by the table, her hands folded in front of her. 'She's past takin' broth, m'm,' Doris said primly, looking down her nose. 'We wetted her lips with water. Thass all she could take.'

Laura bent over the girl and her eyes fluttered open. 'Thass the God's honest truth. That is 'is kid. I wouldn't lie. Not to you, Mrs Ber'sf'd,' she said. She was so weak that her voice was barely audible. 'You bin good to my little sister. She come to your school. But she'll be workin' at the silk mill afore long an' I was afraid. . .' She wagged her head weakly. 'I 'ad to do suthin'. I don't want young Ruthie used the way that bugger used me. 'E's a animal, that man. Thass why I come. I don't want my little sister. . .' She heaved herself up on to one elbow and crossed herself. 'Thass God's truth I'm tellin' yer, Mrs Ber'sf'd. I swear it.' She fell back, exhausted.

Laura straightened up. She hoped to goodness the servants hadn't caught what the girl had said. 'Keep her warm and feed her if she can take it.' She went over to the clothes basket where the child had been laid. It was very dirty and smelled disgusting, but it stared up at her with eyes that were unmistakably, shockingly, Beresford eyes.

She drew her breath in sharply. 'Can you get the child cleaned up?' she said to nobody in particular. 'It can't be left in this state, whoever it belongs to.' She looked round at the hostile faces of Doris and the other maids. 'If none of you can bring yourselves to do it I'll do it myself,' she said sharply. 'Someone's got to show a little Christian charity.'

'I'll fetch Maudie,' Kate said. 'She's used to babies.'

Meanwhile, Jay had followed Alex into his study and he sat down in the leather armchair beside the empty fireplace, crossing one leg over the other, completely relaxed.

'Thanks,' he said, accepting the whisky his brother handed him. He drained it at a gulp and held his glass out for more. 'Bloody nerve these creatures have got. Whatever will they dream up next? I suggest you give her a sovereign and send her packing.' He watched the glass being refilled. 'That's all she's after. And you can tell her from me she's lucky we haven't set the constables on her.'

Alex carefully replaced the stopper in the decanter and stood looking down into the amber liquid in his own glass for some minutes. Suddenly, he looked up. 'Is it yours?' he asked.

'Is what mine?' Jay said irritably.

'The child.'

'Don't be ridiculous.' Jay shifted uncomfortably in his seat.

Alex said nothing, but took a draught from his own glass, watching Jay all the time.

'Oh, all right. Very likely it's mine.' Jay shrugged. 'Who can tell with these strumpets?'

Alex glance widened. 'Do you mean to tell me. . .?'

'That I consort with strumpets? Of course I do.' Jay laughed and waved his hand expansively. 'Good God, man, any chap who's a real man does.' He looked at his brother for the first time. 'Don't you?'

'No.' Alex's voice was cold. 'As a matter of fact, I don't.'

'Well,' he drained his glass and held it out, 'that's your loss.'

Without speaking, Alex refilled it yet again.

'Of course, one has to be careful,' Jay went on, holding the glass up to the light and squinting at it. 'But I have no trouble finding what I want at the silk mill. There are always young girls. . . The threat of the sack works wonders.'

'You filthy swine! Get out of my house.' Alex's voice was barely above a whisper as he tried to control his fury. 'You make me *sick*.'

Jay drained his glass and put it down carefully before getting to his feet. 'It's time we were going, anyway.' He turned. 'Oh, and by the way, I don't see there's any need to speak of all this to the ladies.' He felt in his pocket and a gold coin spun through the air, hit the desk and rolled on to the floor. 'Give her that and tell her if there's any more trouble I'll have the police on to her.'

Without a word, Alex bent and picked the sovereign up delicately between his thumb and forefinger and handed it back to his brother. Then he opened the door for Jay to pass through.

Chapter Twenty-Five

The two men returned to the dining room, where Charlotte and Eleanor were sitting quite oblivious to the dirty cups and glasses, the plates of half-eaten food and the screwed-up table napkins strewn around, detritus of the party that had ended so disastrously. At the same moment Laura re-entered the room through another door.

Nobody spoke. They had no need to. Charlotte looked first at her husband's flushed, truculent face and then at Alex, who hadn't been able to hide his feelings of sick disgust.

'Oh, God,' she covered her mouth with her hands as if to prevent herself from screaming. 'It's true, Jay, isn't it? What the girl said? It's all true!'

She turned to look at Laura, her expression begging her to deny it, but Laura turned away, unable to meet her gaze.

She dragged herself to her feet and took a step towards her husband. 'Oh, Jay, how could you?' she whispered. 'How could you do this to me?' She put out her hand but he didn't respond and she collapsed in a heap on the floor at his feet.

Immediately, Laura rang the bell and ordered Charlotte to be taken and put to bed in one of the spare rooms.

'No. Call my carriage. I shall take her home,' Jay commanded, standing over her.

'But can't you see? Look at her. She's in no fit state to be moved. She needs a doctor,' Laura motioned to James, who was hovering uncertainly and looking from one to the other, to carry her away. 'Just leave her here for tonight until her doctor has seen her. Perhaps tomorrow. . .'

'Oh, very well.' With a shrug Jay stood back and allowed

James to pick Charlotte up in his arms and carry her away.

'I'm happy for Charlotte to stay but *he's* not staying here.' Alex jabbed a finger in his brother's direction. 'I won't have him under my roof.'

'I wouldn't want to stay in a house that harbours harlots,' Jay replied smoothly.

Laura pushed her hair back and gave a weary sigh. 'For your information, the young girl you're referring to died not ten minutes ago. She died from starvation brought on because her own mother turned her out when she knew she was to have a child.' Her voice was flat and unemotional.

'And a good thing, too,' Jay said smugly. He turned to Eleanor. 'Come, Mother, I'll take you home. Naturally, I shall return to enquire after my wife tomorrow morning. You won't deny me that, I presume?' he raised his eyebrows in Alex's direction. 'See that she has the best treatment in the meantime,' he finished, speaking to nobody in particular.

Eleanor made no move. She was sitting with her hands folded over the head of her walking stick. 'Thank you, Jay, but I would prefer to remain here, if Alex and Laura have no objection. I am very tired.'

Laura went over to her and kissed her. 'Of course, Mother-in-law. I'll have a room made ready for you right away.' She turned to Alex. 'Alex, I really think Jay ought to stay, to be near to Charlotte. She is *very* ill, you understand.'

Jay was in process of snatching up his hat and coat. Now he paused and an expression of alarm crossed his face as he intercepted the look that passed from Laura to Alex.

'It's nothing. I assure you it's nothing. Charlotte has had these turns before,' he blustered. 'She'll be perfectly all right. I'll return in the morning.'

'I think it only right that you should wait and hear what the doctor has to say, Jay.' He heard the warning in his mother's voice.

'Very well. If you insist.' He sat down, bolt upright, on a small gilt chair by the door, his coat still on his arm and his hat in his hand.

'You'll get pretty cramped if you intend to sit there like that all night,' Alex remarked caustically, but Jay stared straight ahead and said nothing.

It was a different story after Dr Franklyn had been and examined Charlotte. He told Jay as kindly as he could what everybody else had suspected and Jay had pig-headedly refused to recognise, namely that Charlotte was suffering from cancer. He also warned him that it was likely to kill her within days. For some months now he had been giving her what he could to alleviate the pain and keep her comfortable. Now there was nothing more anybody could do. No, he was sorry but there was no point in calling in a second opinion, all the money in the world could not change the prognosis.

For the next three days Charlotte hovered between life and death. For most of the time Jay sat beside her, holding her hand, his face a wooden mask. He had loved Charlotte very much in his undemonstrative way but even now, when her hours were numbered, and time was running short, he still couldn't bring himself to bare his soul, to tell her just how much she meant to him and how he had never intended to hurt her. Instead, he sat in miserable, isolated silence whilst his family thought him cold and uncaring.

On the odd occasions when Jay left Charlotte's side his place was taken by The Revd. Arnold Paterson, an Anglican priest who, quite unknown to the rest of the family, had been visiting Charlotte regularly over the past six months, preparing her for the death which she alone had realised was imminent. It was Arnold Paterson and not Jay who was with her when she drew her last breath.

Jay alone arranged his wife's funeral. He did it with clinical precision and correctness, and no expense spared; with black draped carriages drawn by plumed horses and the undertaker's mute slowly leading the cortege along the road to the cemetery.

Afterwards the mourners returned to the house on North Hill where there was exactly the right amount to eat and drink; not too much so that it looked ostentatious; not too little so that he could be accused of meanness. If he shed tears nobody saw them but his shoulders seemed to have acquired a stoop that had never been there before and suddenly he seemed to have aged ten years.

Sid and Lottie Rankin, Charlotte's parents, were beside themselves with grief at the death of their only and much loved child. Nevertheless, after the funeral Jay left them to preside over the guests whilst he closeted himself in his study with Arnold Paterson. Reluctantly, Alex went with them. He could hardly bring himself to be civil to his brother since the revelations at the night of Eleanor's party, but the young priest had been insistent that he should be there.

Jay sat down behind his desk and indicated chairs for the two men. Arnold sat down on a chair near the door but Alex remained standing and looking out of the window.

'Alex, will you thank your wife for making Charlotte's last days as comfortable as she could?' Jay said, his voice expressionless.

'Is that all you've got to say?' Alex asked, without turning round.

'What else would you have me say?'

Alex swung round. 'I would expect some explanation for the scene that took place outside my house only last week.'

Jay sighed, 'Oh, that.'

'Yes, that. I've said nothing about it before, but I think it's time you gave some kind of an explanation for the disgusting double life you must have been leading for God knows how many years! My God, and to think of the way you've always despised those factory girls who slave their lives away to make money for you. How they must loathe and detest you, the way you exploit them by day and fornicate with them after dark.'

Jay shrugged but said nothing.

'This was why I wanted you to be present, Mr Beresford,' Arnold Paterson said, getting to his feet. 'I've talked to your brother and I think I may be able to shed some light. . . perhaps help you to understand. . .'

'As far as I can see it's beyond all understanding,' Alex said shortly. 'I can find no excuse for his behaviour at all.'

The young priest nodded. 'I realise how hard this is for you, Mr Beresford.' He paused for several minutes, then went on slowly, 'But perhaps I should tell you that some men have great difficulty. . .' he began again, choosing his words carefully. 'Some men, when they marry place their wives on a pedestal of purity and virtue. I think it is hardly too strong a word to say that they worship them.' He waited for that to sink in, then went on, 'That being so, how can they then defile them with their natural animal lusts without a feeling of self-disgust and shame?' He looked at the two brothers. Alex, frowning, was watching him intently. Jay had risen from his chair and was standing by the window, studying his fingernails.

Arnold continued, still speaking slowly, 'What I have discovered in some of the cases that have come my way is that these men find that recourse to women of the streets is a convenient – even, dare I say it, a more satisfactory – way to conduct that side of their lives; a side which deep down inside they feel ashamed of and should really be suppressed. Thus the shame is two-fold, which in a strange kind of way makes the experience even more exciting.'

'Only in my brother's case the excitement came not only from women of the street but from unwilling little virgins in his employment,' Alex said, his lip curling in disgust. He looked Jay up and down. 'Oh, my God, you make me sick! You fill me with absolute disgust!'

'I think your brother needs help, not castigation,' Arnold said gently. He turned to Jay. 'Tell me, Mr Beresford, have you any idea how many girls you've used in this way?'

Jay shrugged without looking up. 'I've no idea. It was all one to me. I never bothered to look at their faces.'

'You callous swine. Well, tell us this. Have you any idea how many bastards you've fathered?' Alex shouted.

Now Jay looked up at him and a suspicion of a sneer fleeted across his face. 'No, I haven't. But you've adopted one of them.'

Alex froze. 'Little Victoria? Kate Taylor's child?'

'Was her name Kate? I forget.'

'But Kate let us think the child belonged to Charles.' He let out a long breath. 'I suppose you threatened her with what you'd do to her if she told anyone it was yours. God, Jay, you are a bloody monster.' Alex turned away, completely sickened.

Arnold went over and stood by Jay. 'Might I suggest that you go away for a while, Mr Beresford? Away from Colchester, away from the temptations of the flesh?'

'And where would you suggest I go?' Jay asked, without

apparent interest.

'To a Retreat House. I know of a very good one in Norfolk where you can rest, take sensible counselling and, please God, find peace. Because whatever you may pretend or say, Mr Beresford, there is no peace within you, nor ever has been.'

Jay turned on him. 'Are you suggesting I should incarcerate myself in a bloody monastery?'

'Not a bloody monastery, Mr Beresford, just a monastery. It's quite small and you'll find the monks there – Anglican monks – very sympathetic and helpful.'

'I'm not shutting myself up in a place like that.'

'It's only for a few weeks.' Arnold paused. He had never once raised his voice, yet his words compelled attention. 'It could save you from an act that would land you in the law courts. I think you know what I mean, Mr Beresford. You haven't quite gone that far yet, I take it.'

At this Jay seemed visibly to crumple, and all his bombast disappeared. 'No,' he sighed, and as the light caught his face tears glistened on his cheeks.

When she reached home after the funeral Laura went up to her room and took off her hat and coat. She studied herself in the mirror. Unrelieved black really didn't suit her, especially now when she had dark circles under her eyes and her face was pale and drawn. The funeral had been difficult, with Lottie and Sid both ravaged with grief and Jay tight-lipped, saying hardly anything so that it was difficult to know what his feelings were. He seemed to have invited half the town to the house after the funeral yet somehow gave the impression that their presence was an intrusion. Perhaps because there was no warmth.

Laura had loved Charlotte more than she realised and she grieved at her death but she was glad Sid and Lottie Rankin had taken their little granddaughter to live with them for the time being. Much though she loved little Ellie, Laura felt she had more than enough to cope with at home for the present. For one thing there was the business of the dead girl's baby, still being looked after in the kitchen. What was to become of that?

She went down the stairs to the little sitting room. To her surprise Alex was already there. 'Sit down, Laura I have something to tell you,' he said without preamble.

She went and sat down, wearily resting her head on her hand. Her emotion felt too raw to cope with much more. But as he began to speak, to tell her what had passed in Jay's study she sat up and her eyes widened.

'Jay! Of all people!' she said, when he had finished. 'I would never have thought that of him, not in a million years. He was always so supercilious, so scathing about the girls he employed. . .'

'As Arnold explained it, he loathed the girls for the temptation they provided and loathed himself even more for succumbing to his baser instincts.'

'Then I suppose he's to be pitied rather than blamed.' She nodded. 'And in a funny sort of way I do feel sorry for him, poor man. I hope he'll find help and healing. That's what the Reverend Paterson feels he needs, isn't it?'

Alex nodded. 'Is that all you've got to say, Laura?'

She looked at him in surprise. 'What else would you have me say?'

'Have you no word of censure for the things he did?'

She gave a wry smile. 'I'm surprised you should even ask. Doesn't the Bible say, "Let him that is without sin cast the first stone"?'

He turned away, a look of pain on his face. But all he said was 'Oh, Laura.'

There was silence for several minutes. Then Laura said, 'We have to do something about the dead girl's baby, Alex. They're still looking after it in the kitchen. I would suggest we adopt it ourselves, but,' she shuddered, 'I have to confess I don't like the thought of adopting a child that belonged to – that man, even though he is your brother.'

'That's something I didn't tell you, Laura. We already have,' Alex said bluntly. 'Jay admitted today that Victoria was his child, not Charles's as we thought.'

'But Kate said. . .'

'Looking back, I don't believe Kate actually *said* Charles was the father,' Alex said thoughtfully. 'We assumed it was Charles and she let us go on thinking that way. After all, he

287

was dead and Jay would have denied it if she'd accused him.' He looked at her. 'Will it make any difference to the way you feel about her, Laura? Knowing Jay is her father?'

Laura shook her head. 'No, of course not. After all, it isn't her fault, is it? And anyway, she looks so like Charles that I'll always feel somehow that she belonged to him.'

'So could you adopt this baby? I feel we have a responsibility towards it, but if you object. . .'

She nodded slowly. 'Yes, perhaps we should, Alex. As I've just said, it's not the child's fault.'

He looked up, the thought only just striking him. 'By the way, what is it?'

Her mouth twisted. 'It's a boy. It's the son Jay so desperately wanted and Charlotte tried so hard to give him. Only born on the wrong side of the blanket.'

They were both silent for several moments, digesting the tragic irony of the situation. Then Alex said, 'What do you think we should call him?'

She didn't hesitate. 'Why, Javis, of course. What else?'

'What else, indeed.' Alex nodded. His mouth twisted wryly. 'I just hope that when he grows up he will favour his grandfather and not his real father.'

Chapter Twenty-Six

Arrangements were quickly made for Jay to go to Norfolk. The whole town sympathised with poor Mr Beresford on the loss of his wife and thought it entirely natural that he should need to go away for a long holiday to recover from it. Charlotte's parents, Sid and Lottie Rankin, were only too pleased to take their little granddaughter into their home because Lottie felt, for some reason she couldn't put into words, that young Ellie would be safer with her and Sid than with her own father. Jay had always given her a feeling of unease and she felt that somehow he hadn't done quite right by Charlotte, although she could never have said quite in what way. After all, it wasn't his fault that Charlotte couldn't bear a boy that lived. But looking after Ellie would go at least some way towards filling the gap Charlotte's death had left in their lives.

Eleanor too was ignorant of the precise reason for Jay's sudden holiday. He merely informed her he needed to get away for a while and that he was leaving the factory in charge of two of his more trusted men. This in itself surprised her because she had been unaware that he ever trusted anyone at all. The fact that he refused to leave a forwarding address added to her perplexity, especially as Alex was evasive when she asked him where his brother had gone. The whole thing was very strange, but she consoled herself that Jay was a strange man; he had always been aloof and had kept himself very much to himself ever since he was a small child. Perhaps he had been more fond of Charlotte than anybody realised.

There was no word of him for three months. Alex told her not to worry, but she couldn't help being anxious. Apart from anything else, with Jay away the factory was sure to suffer; the silk industry was not so flourishing that the master could go off and leave it for months on end, even if he could trust his men.

Then a letter came, postmarked Norfolk. Its contents had Eleanor calling for her carriage almost before Jenks, the coachman had finished his breakfast.

Laura was sitting opposite to Alex at the breakfast table making desultory conversation. For a time she had thought – had hoped – that Charlotte's death and the dreadful business with Jay might bring them together again and that they could regain at least something of the happiness they had once known. But although they were on reasonable terms now, insofar as they ate together and conversed on daily matters, he rarely so much as touched her hand and never, ever attempted to kiss her. Neither had he ever shown the slightest desire to return to her bed. Sometimes she wondered whether he, lying in his narrow bed in the dressing room next door to her bedroom, ached for her presence as she ached for him. She would often lie in the big bed in which they had once demonstrated their love for one another with such uninhibited enthusiasm weeping bitter and lonely tears for a love that seemed on his side to be as dead as yesterday's mutton, destroyed by a past she had tried to forget and over which she had had no control. She gave a long sigh and pushed her plate away, a half-eaten piece of toast still on it.

Alex looked up. 'You look tired, Laura. Is this one of your school days?' he asked. He no longer raised any objection to her little school, in fact in the end he had admitted that it was he who had paid for all the repairs after his brother had ordered it to be wrecked.

She shook her head. 'No. Annabel will be there today. And Ruth.' Since Eleanor had been paying Ruth's wages for her to learn to become a teacher she had blossomed almost out of recognition and it was difficult to realise that she was still only eight years old. She was paid nearly twice what she would have earned at the silk mill and so her mother, partly through remorse at the untimely death of her eldest daughter, allowed her to keep sixpence for herself. With this Ruth bought soap to keep herself clean and a gingham dress with a ribbon to match for her hair. She was saving hard for new boots. Ruth had been given the chance to escape a life at the silk mill and she had taken it with gratitude and enthusiasm, hardly able to believe her good fortune. One day she was determined to have a school of her own.

'Is there more coffee?' Alex asked, rousing Laura from her reverie.

She picked up the coffee pot and refilled his cup and her own.

'Thanks.' He took it and picked up the newspaper. He was in no hurry. His own business was now flourishing to the extent that he no longer had to start early and work late.

They both looked up as the door bell rang what could only be described as imperiously. Callers at the main entrance were unusual at this hour of the morning. But they hardly had time to speculate on who it might be before Eleanor swept in, not waiting to be announced. She was brandishing a letter as she came.

'Alex! What is the meaning of this?' she cried before she was hardly inside the door.

Alex got to his feet. 'Mama! Whatever's wrong? Now, come and sit down and have some coffee. Or would you prefer tea? Whatever it is I'm sure you'll do yourself no good by getting distressed.' He guided her to the table and held a chair for her to sit down. 'Agnes, another plate and a cup and saucer for Mrs Beresford, please. Oh, and bring some more toast whilst you are about it.'

'No, I couldn't eat. . . Not with this on my mind.' Eleanor waved him away with the letter still in her hand.

'But I'm sure you could manage a cup of coffee, Mama-in-law,' Laura said. 'Ah, thank you, Agnes, that will be all.' She took the cup and saucer Agnes had brought and poured coffee for Eleanor.

'Are you sure you won't have a piece of toast, Mama?' Alex said, helping himself from the replenished toast rack.

'No. Don't keep fussing. I've told you, I couldn't eat a thing. I'm much too upset. Read this.' She handed the letter to Alex and then picked up her coffee cup with hands that were trembling.

He read it and then blew his cheeks out with a sigh as he passed in on to Laura. 'Ah. So he's decided. Well, I'm glad he wrote and told you himself. I was afraid he might leave it to me,' he said, reaching for the butter.

'Oh, poor Jay,' Laura said when she had read it. 'But perhaps it's the best thing for him.'

'So you knew all about it! You both *knew* he had gone to. . . to. . . that place!' Eleanor couldn't bring herself to utter the word monastery. 'Why wasn't I told? Oh, Alex, for goodness sake, stop spreading that toast and concentrate on what I'm saying. Why wasn't I told?'

Obediently, Alex put down his knife. 'Yes, we knew about it. After all, Charlotte spent her last days here so we could hardly fail to know what was going on,' he said. 'We didn't tell you where he was going because he – well, you must understand, Mama, Jay wasn't well.'

'What was wrong with him?' Eleanor sat up in her chair, her back like a ramrod. 'I wasn't aware that he was ill. He looked perfectly healthy to me.'

'It was his mind. He was very. . .' he searched for the right word, 'troubled,' he said gently.

'He went to Norfolk to find peace within himself,' Laura added.

Eleanor frowned. 'I don't understand. I know he was fond of Charlotte in his way, but I wouldn't have thought that her death would have affected him as badly as that. Now, if the business had failed. . .' Suddenly, she put her elbow on the table and rested her head on her hand. 'I don't understand it. He was always so strong, so forceful. And now, all of a sudden he writes to tell me that he intends to stay at that place and become an Anglican monk. What on earth has brought this about? He's never been even remotely religious. Why, when I tried to persuade him to attend church after Charlotte had lost one of the babies he called it a lot of mumbo-jumbo, which upset me more than I could say.' She shook her head. 'Yet now he says he intends to become a monk!' She looked up. 'You'll have to go and see him, Alex. Ask him what all this nonsense is about. Talk to him. Bring him to his senses.'

292

'I'll certainly go and see him, Mama, but I know I won't make him change his mind. I wouldn't even try to.' Alex put out his hand and covered hers as it lay on the white table-cloth. 'He was never a very happy man, was he, Mama?'

She shook her head. 'No. I could never understand why.'

'Well, maybe he was always searching for something that eluded him. And maybe, in an atmosphere of contemplation and. . .' he hesitated, but took courage and went on, 'celibacy, he's found it at least.'

Eleanor frowned. 'Found what?' She was finding Alex's explanation quite beyond her comprehension.

He lifted his hands. 'I don't know. Some kind of fulfilment. Some kind of spiritual peace.'

Eleanor was quiet for a long time. In spite of refusing any breakfast she drank three cups of coffee in rapid succession. Neither Alex nor Laura spoke, but watched her and waited for the inevitability of Jay's letter to sink in.

At last she said in a weary voice. 'I don't begin to under-stand it, but if what you say is true then I suppose there's nothing to be done but to accept the situation.' She put her hand out to Alex. 'You're all I have left now, Alex. Both my other sons have gone.'

'A poor substitute, I fear, Mama,' Alex said with a wry smile.

'What do you mean?'

'I mean, I am a poor substitute for your sons, Jay and Charles.'

Eleanor's head shot up. 'That's an unforgivable thing to say, Alex.' Her voice trembled with fury. 'When have I ever treated you any differently to my own sons? If you thought you were slighted, it was all in your own mind and you know it. Javis and I promised your father that we would treat you as our own son and with God's help we did.' She turned to Laura. 'Laura, tell me, just because little Victoria is not of your own body do you treat her any differently to Marcus? Do you love her any less?' Then, seeing the look of aston-ishment on Laura's face her jaw dropped. 'Do you mean you don't *know*? Do you mean Alex has never told you he is not my natural-born son?'

Laura looked from Alex to Eleanor and back again,

shaking her head dumbly.

Eleanor turned on Alex. 'What sort of a marriage do you have, Alex, that you couldn't trust Laura with the circumstances of your birth? Do you think she wouldn't have understood? Do you think she would have blamed you for something over which you had no control?' She turned to Laura. 'Well, it's time you knew, Laura, and if Alex won't tell you then I will. . .'

'No, Mama. Leave it. I'll tell her. Later.' Alex said, holding up his hand. Then he passed it across his brow. 'But you're right, of course. It was unforgivable. I should have told Laura years ago.'

'I think you should tell her without delay.' Eleanor reached for her stick and got up stiffly from her chair. Suddenly, she looked an old woman. 'For my part I've had quite enough upset for one day. . .'

'Won't you stay with us, Mama-in-law?' Laura asked, getting up and going to her.

'No.' Eleanor patted her hand. 'I prefer to go back to my own house if you don't mind. I have much to think about and I need to be undisturbed. But I'll be glad if you'll both come and see me this afternoon.' She looked down at the letter again and shook her head. 'There is so much we must discuss. The silk factory of course will be yours now, Alex.' Her mouth twisted wryly, 'You may feel that in giving it to you I'm offering you a poisoned chalice, but it was a good place once and could be again. I wonder, maybe Jay hated it. Maybe. . .' She shook her head again, 'Oh, what's the use? Anyway, it will be yours to do with what you will.' She looked him up and down, the man who had turned out to be so much more to her than her natural-born sons. 'I am sure you will make it a better place.' Her voice dropped. 'I have been so ashamed at some of the things I have heard about it.' She turned to her daughter-in-law with a smile. 'At least I know that the children will get educated. Perhaps you can incorporate your school and make it a part of the factory, Laura? I should like to see that done. You know, I have great admiration for what you have done with those children.' She gave a sigh. 'Ah, well, all these things we can discuss later. But I know that with both of you the silk mill will be in good hands.'

294

Alex saw his mother to her carriage. When he came back Laura had resumed her seat and had her head in her hands. She looked up as he came into the room. 'Alex?'

He nodded and sat down. 'Yes, I know I should have told you. I should have told you right at the beginning. I'm sorry, Laura.'

She got up and went and stood by the mantelpiece. 'I'm ready to listen now.'

'I think you should sit down. It's quite a long story.'

Obediently, she resumed her seat, folding her arms on the table and watching him attentively.

He pulled the sugar basin towards him and began to make patterns in it with the spoon to avoid looking at her. 'Old Javis, as you now realise, wasn't my father. He was my uncle. I am the son of his elder brother, Alexander,' he began. 'By all accounts Alexander was a bit of a rake – a bit like young Charles, I suppose. Maybe that was why I always had a soft spot for Charles. Anyway, in the time-honoured way, Alexander fell in love with a chorus girl. Well, that was all right, until to his family's disgust he insisted on doing the honourable thing and marrying her. Fortunately, or unfortunately, according to which way you look at it, she died giving birth. My father, penniless and at his wit's end, brought the baby, me, to Colchester and begged his brother Javis to bring it up for him. Neither Javis nor Eleanor were happy about this – worried about the introduction of "bad blood" into the family, no doubt – but in the end they agreed, provided Alexander went away and made no claims on the child. He agreed.' His lip twisted. 'I guess he was only too glad to be shot of me. Anyway, he never came back and years later they heard he'd gone to the Gold Coast and died of a fever there.'

Alex hadn't once looked up while he was speaking. Now he did and Laura was shocked at the pain in his eyes. He continued, staring once again into the depths of the sugar bowl as if it was a crystal ball, 'I knew absolutely nothing of all this until my sixteenth birthday. Then my parents, as I had always regarded them, thought I was old enough to be told the truth.' He shook his head. 'I was completely devastated. I felt as if my world had collapsed round me. Everything I had built my life on turned out to be false. My parents were

295

no longer my parents, my brothers weren't my brothers. I wished they had never told me at all, yet at the same time I felt deceived because they hadn't told me sooner. Because suddenly I felt like an outcast, although to be fair to them they were treating me no differently to the way they had always done.'

He looked up again. 'Laura, How can I describe the pain, the isolation I felt? And that pain, that feeling of isolation has remained, locked up inside me. My mother, Eleanor, asked why I hadn't told you about my birth. What she could never know was that I've never been able to speak about it to anybody; I couldn't even bring myself to think about it. It was like suffering from some unspeakable disease, something lurking there, all the time, just below the surface, like a festering sore.' He made an impatient gesture. 'Oh, how can I expect you to understand?'

Laura gave a faint smile. 'I do understand, Alex. I understand exactly how you felt. I tried to bury my own past, if you remember.'

He ran his fingers through his hair. 'Oh, God, I should have known. . .' He leaned across the table and took her hand. It was the first time he had touched her voluntarily for a long time and she savoured the warm strength that seemed to flow from him. 'Oh, Laura, can you forgive me? Above all people, I should have understood what you'd been through. But selfish bastard that I am I didn't stop to think of your feelings, I just felt I'd been lied to all over again and I simply couldn't take it.' He got up from his chair and came to stand behind her, cradling her head against his breast. 'I realise now that it wasn't what had happened to you that I couldn't forgive, Laura, although perhaps I was stupid enough to think it was at the time. No, what I couldn't forgive was the fact that you hadn't trusted me enough to tell me. I couldn't take having been deceived a second time. Yet I was deceiving you in exactly the same way and I knew it. God knows, what happened to you was not your fault any more than I was to blame for my birth, so if anyone should have been understanding and forgiving it was me.'

She reached up for his hand. 'Perhaps that was your defence, Alex. While you didn't forgive me you could justify your own deception.'

He pulled her gently to her feet and put his arms round her. 'Sometimes I think you know me better than I know myself, my darling. I don't deserve you, but I love you very much.'

She rested her head against him. 'Oh, Alex, I've waited so long to hear you say that.'

They remained locked together for a long time, both reluctant to break away. Finally, Alex said, still holding her close and stroking her hair, 'It wouldn't be fair to expect you to have anything to do with the silk mill, Laura, in spite of my mother's fanciful ideas.' He smiled wryly, 'I think I'm sensitive enough to realise it would be far too painful for you to ever want to set foot in that place again. But I have no choice but to be responsible for it. Unless, of course I sell the whole damned can of worms. I don't think my mother would object to that.'

She pulled away from him a little. 'No, you can't sell it, Alex. If you sell it you'll lose all control over it. But if you keep it we can make it a better place. There is so much we can do. . .'

'We? But, my darling, as I've said I would never expect you. . .?'

She shook her head vigorously. 'But I want to, Alex. Remember, I know what it's like. I've worked there. I know what needs to be done. I have so many ideas. . .'

'You mean you'd really be prepared to go back there?'

'Yes. I would.' She smiled up at him wickedly. 'I seem to remember that the last time I was in your father's office he was sharing a partner's desk with your brother Jay.' She put her head on one side. 'The point is, how will you feel about sharing that desk with me, Alex?'

He didn't return her smile. Instead, he bent and kissed her. 'If it means that each time I look up from my work you'll be there and each time you look up I shall be there, I shall be content. What more could we ask, you and I?'

You have been reading a novel published by Piatkus Books. We hope you have enjoyed it and that you would like to read more of our titles. Please ask for them in your local library or bookshop.

If you would like to be put on our mailing list to receive details of new publications, please send a large stamped addressed envelope (UK only) to:

Piatkus Books 5 Windmill Street
London W1P 1HF

PIATKUS

The sign of a good book